The meagre lighthouse all in white, haunting the seaboard as if it were the ghost of an edifice that had once had colour and rotundity, dropped melancholy tears after its late buffeting by the waves.

— Charles Dickens, *Little Dorrit*

there is
a light
that
never
goes
out

David M. Barnett is an author and journalist based in West Yorkshire. After a career working for regional newspapers he embarked upon a freelance career writing features for most of the UK national press. He is the author of the critically-acclaimed Gideon Smith series of Victorian fantasies, published by Tor Books, and teaches journalism part-time at Leeds Trinity University. David was born in Wigan, Lancashire, in 1970 and is married to Claire, also a journalist. They have two children, Charlie and Alice.

Also By David M. Barnett

Calling Major Tom
The Lonely Hearts Cinema Club
The Growing Pains of Jennifer Ebert
Things Can Only Get Better
The Handover

DAVID M. BARNETT

there is
a light
that
never
goes
out

ORION

First published in Great Britain in 2023 by Orion Fiction,
an imprint of The Orion Publishing Group Ltd,
Carmelite House, 50 Victoria Embankment
London EC4Y 0DZ

An Hachette UK Company

1 3 5 7 9 10 8 6 4 2

A CIP catalogue record for this book
is available from the British Library.

ISBN (Mass Market Paperback) 978 1 3987 1129 7
ISBN (eBook) 978 1 3987 1130 3

Typeset by Deltatype Ltd, Birkenhead, Merseyside

Printed in Great Britain by Clays Ltd, Elcograf S.p.A.

www.orionbooks.co.uk

To Claire, whose dedication to the family has been
a shining light, especially in the darkest times

I

Gwyn

Here I go again, over the sea to Ynys Dwynwen in my little boat. Always a sad time, this, but one tempered with happiness. Because a keeper is leaving, but that means the island has worked its peculiar magic once again.

Three years almost to the day, it was, when I brought George Benson over here, him steely-eyed and impassive as we bounced through the churning waves from the mainland, his gaze fixed on the white and red hoops of the lighthouse framed against the grey, drizzly skies.

'The Walrus of Love!' I'd said, upon him introducing himself to me. 'You'll have to say hello to our colony of seals over on Bethan's Reef.'

'That was Barry White,' he'd said testily. 'George Benson was a jazz guitarist. "Nature Boy". "Nothing's Gonna Change My Love For You". That sort of thing.' He'd looked at me. 'I'm a fifty-seven-year-old white man from Birmingham. I have a very common name that just happens to be shared by someone who no one in their right mind could mistake me for.'

And that was the end of *that* conversation. To be honest, I never thought that Ynys Dwynwen's magic would work on George Benson. It doesn't every time. Some people are impervious. But the island chooses well – and if you think people decide to come to Ynys Dwynwen, you're mad as a mongoose. Ynys Dwynwen chooses the people who come to her.

And yet, almost three years later, here I am, pulling the dinghy in to the jetty on the island, George Benson waiting for me, his duffel bag on the rocky grassland beside him, the lighthouse rearing up against a blue, cloudless sky.

He's smiling, tanned, fit-looking. A world away from the pasty-faced, dour, overweight man who I first brought to the island.

'Happy birthday, George Benson!' I hail to him, as I hop out of the dinghy and tie her up on the jetty. 'All set for the return?'

As I reach George Benson and grab his bag, he gives his side a rub and looks back at the tower. I say, 'How's the hip?'

'Bloody painful,' he grunts. 'But the operation's in a month. I'm not sure I'd have got the go-ahead for it if I hadn't come here, and stayed in Birmingham, slowly eating and drinking myself into a useless blob.'

'I daresay you won't miss all the stairs in the tower.' I heft his bag on my shoulder and head down to the jetty.

'I won't miss the stairs,' he says, still looking back at the tower. 'I won't miss the storms. I won't miss those bloody kids coming once a year. I won't miss the appalling racket of those sodding birds. I won't miss trying to pronounce the name of this place.' He pauses. 'Een-Niss Doyn-Winn.'

'Close enough, George Benson,' I say, having stowed his bag in the dinghy and jogged up to help him down the slope to the jetty.

'However ...' finally he turns his back on the tower. 'At the same time, I *will* miss it. I'll miss all of it. This place ...'

I laugh. 'It's magic, George Benson.'

He leans on me as we descend to the jetty. 'I didn't believe in magic three years ago and I don't believe in magic now, Gwyn. But I've seen things in my time here I can't explain.'

I help him into the bobbing boat and he settles himself at the prow, his back to the island. 'And the island has turned my life around. I'm sixty years old today and I've never felt better. I'm getting my hip sorted. And Janice ... well, five years ago I never thought I'd see her again, when the divorce was finalised.' He shakes his head. 'Funny how things turn out. Like I had to turn my back on the world, on everything, for it all to come good.'

I pull the engine and turn the dinghy around, heading back to the Llyn Peninsula. George Benson is now facing Ynys Dwynwen, as it recedes behind us. 'Sometimes you have to take a step back to see things properly,' I say.

George Benson says nothing, just looks at the island, and the tower, and it might just be spray hitting his face, or it might be something else, but he quietly rubs his eyes.

'What'll happen? With the tower? And the light? The light never goes out,' he says, softly, echoing Ms Davies's words.

'The light never goes out,' I agree. Hywel Davies and I will keep the tower running. Heledd Davies has placed an advertisement already, I believe, for your successor.'

'For the new Keeper of Ynys Dwynwen,' says George Benson. 'I wonder who it will be? I wonder what they're running from? I wonder how the island will work its ...'

'Magic?' I say, the mainland and my stone jetty approaching rapidly.

'Yes,' says George Benson finally, with a smile of happy, gentle surrender. 'I wonder how Ynys Dwynwen will work its magic on them, just like it did on me.'

3

Year One

Year One

2

Martin

After the day I've had, it's hardly surprising that I decide to go and live in a lighthouse.

Or maybe it is surprising. I mean, it's not what normal people do after a shitty day, is it? Most people would crack open a bottle of wine or call a friend or order a takeaway or put a movie on. I'd done all of those things before I made the decision to live in a lighthouse.

After all, it had been a *very* shitty day.

It begins at 5.45 a.m., which would be bad enough had I not been due in work fifteen minutes earlier. There are three missed calls on my mobile, all from my supervisor. I slept through them because my phone is in the corner of the living room under the TV stand, which is where I'd thrown it last night when I realised I'd run out of credit. Which also means that I cannot call work to tell them that I am on my way. And if I do not call within an hour of my start time I will lose my shift and likely not be offered more. They're that spiteful.

There is only one thing for it. I have to go and see Mrs Carruthers. She will be the only resident in the block up at this time. God help me.

I press Mrs Carruthers' buzzer and wait while she scrutinises me through the spyhole. Then her door, which is directly across the hall from mine, is flung open and she hoves into view. Mrs Carruthers is vast, with a bird's nest of black hair – obviously and inexpertly dyed – piled on top of her head. She is wearing a floral smock that billows around her huge body, as though she is a medieval warship making sail. She squints at me for a second and says, 'Ah. The idiot.'

'I'm sorry to bother you, Mrs Carruthers. But I know you're always up early—'

'No milk? Run out of electricity cards? Suddenly had an epiphany about the wretched state of your life and come to beg my sage advice?'

She knows me too well, does Mrs Carruthers.

'No,' I say. 'I need to use your phone. My mobile is … broken.'

'Out of credit,' she says with a smirk. 'Again. Come in, you know where it is.'

Stepping into Mrs Carruthers' flat is like walking through the wardrobe into … well, not quite Narnia, but maybe her version of it, a bohemian enclave choked with incense, lit by dull lamps draped with multi-coloured silks. She always has the TV on with the sound off, and issuing from somewhere there is usually some hippy-dippy music. Today's sounds like a scratchy recording of a Tibetan yak herder playing finger bells in a snowstorm. She has a huge, shapeless sofa covered in throws and, on the wall above it, is a massive canvas of a naked woman draped on a chaise longue, rendered in oils. Mrs Carruthers says this was her in her *salad days*. She calls it *Rabelaisian*, and says it was painted by a very famous artist with whom she had a brief but lusty dalliance. The painting is *very* detailed, and I turn my back on it as I dial my supervisor's number on the highly impractical rotary landline. I look up

8

and see a birdcage in which sits a naked, filthy Barbie doll on a swing. I have to start again twice as I lose my place with the dial ... how on earth did people ever use these things?

The call connects almost immediately to Jordan. He is twenty-two and fresh out of university. He thinks I am an old, washed up nobody with zero prospects and no ambition. His assessment is not unfair.

'Fulfilment, Dispatch and Logistics, where dreams are given wings,' he says in his professional voice, not recognising the number. Then, when I start speaking, he sighs and says, 'Mister Burney,' in the way people do when they are using the honorific ironically, and don't think you deserve any such respect.

'I'm sorry, Jordan I ...' I pause and look at my mobile, wondering what is the best lie to tell. 'It's my phone. It ... broke.' Behind me, Mrs Carruthers harrumphs. 'The alarm didn't go off. I'm using a neighbour's phone.' *Too much information.* 'I'll be there in an hour.'

'Forty minutes, or don't bother. Do you know how many people are queuing up for your job?'

The line goes dead and I replace the receiver. I obviously place it the wrong way because Mrs Carruthers elbows past me and turns it around. 'Thank you,' I say. 'I'd better go and get dressed.'

She looks down witheringly at my grubby dressing gown and flip-flops. 'I certainly hope so. Have you broken your fast?'

'No time,' I say. 'I have a ten-minute break after four hours. I'll grab something from the vending machine.'

'Pshaw,' she says, steering me to the table by her big bay window. 'Sit. I have waffles and bacon and maple syrup already on the go. And coffee. Real coffee. Not that rubbish you get in a jar.'

9

'I really don't have time,' I say. I won't even make it there in forty minutes, unless the Gods of the Manchester Trams are looking down on me benignly.

'Nonsense,' says Mrs Carruthers, putting her hands on my shoulders and forcing me to sit. 'Ten minutes to eat, ten minutes to dress, and ten minutes in a taxi to your place of work. I shall organise your transport with Mr Ali at the radio cab office.'

Less than a minute later Mrs Carruthers serves up a plate of waffles and bacon, smothered in syrup, and I have to admit it's most welcome. What did I eat last night? The remnants of the pizza from the night before. As I tuck in she goes to the phone and loudly organises a taxi for exactly 6.30 a.m., with the warning that if I am not delivered to my place of employment precisely nine minutes later, then Mr Ali can no longer count upon her patronage.

Mrs Carruthers takes a seat at the table, watching me stuff waffles into my mouth. She puts her head to one side, early morning sunlight lancing through the windows and illuminating her wide, lined face. 'How old are you, Martin?'

'Thirty,' I say through a mouthful of breakfast. These waffles really are very good.

'Uh, how uncouth,' she says with a wink. 'No manners, your generation. I may not have been able to keep my legs closed when I was your age but I could certainly keep my mouth shut when I was eating.'

I pull a face and mumble an apology, my appetite suddenly deserting me, and take a sip of the strong black coffee.

Mrs Carruthers says thoughtfully, 'Mrs Howell on the third floor had her son come to visit yesterday. He is also thirty. He has a job with a renewable energy company. Very high up. Nice house in Chorlton. Lovely wife. Two children. I believe one is quite a prodigy on the piano.'

Mrs Carruthers knows everything about everyone, at least in these flats. In another life she could have worked for the secret police of some Eastern Bloc country, I'm sure. I squint at her. I've no real idea how old she is, but she's quite ancient. It's entirely possible she did.

I shrug and say, 'I know. I'm a failure.'

'No,' says Mrs Carruthers. 'You can't judge whether you have failed at life until you're dead. You are, though, an idiot.' She nods at my cup. 'Drink up. You have ten minutes to try to make yourself look marginally less like an itinerant pedlar who goes door to door sharpening scissors.'

As she lets me out of her flat she says, 'You are an idiot because you are wasting your life. You have a soul-crushing job which you hate. You have a girlfriend who, I should imagine, is about to dump you. You are perpetually broke, chaotic and aimless. You are drifting, Martin, but not in a good way. Take control of your life. Steer your own course. Shine your own light through the darkness.'

It's only when the car drops me off at the huge, squat warehouse near the motorway that my sleep-deprived brain finally processes Mrs Carruthers' words. *You have a girlfriend who, I should imagine, is about to dump you.* Is she really psychic, as she always claims to be? Or are the signs so obvious that only I am oblivious to them? I don't have time to call Imogen, and I don't have any credit anyway. I shove my phone back into my pocket and hurry in to my job.

The first person I see when I swipe into the warehouse is Harry, in his long brown coat and flat cap, pushing a wheeled bin full of brown packages between the shelves that reach right up to the corrugated ceiling.

'Ah, the prodigal returns,' says Harry with a crooked smile. 'His Lordship was on the warpath about you earlier.'

Harry calls Jordan 'His Lordship' because he thinks he's a cut above everyone else, and he's got a full-time position rather than a zero-hours contract.

'I phoned earlier. It's fine,' I say, grabbing my brown coat from the hook.

'Little tit, he is,' says Harry. 'Right, I'll see you at break. Better crack on, giving wings to dreams.' He snorts loudly. 'My arse.'

I take my hand-held terminal from the rack on the wall and sign in with my thumbprint. The little screen displays my first set of jobs. I work in fulfilment, which is rather ironic, as I'm pretty much the most unfulfilled person you could ever meet. People sit at home and order anything they can think of from the company website, with the promise of next day delivery. This is only kept thanks to the army of people in brown coats like Harry and me who work ten-hour shifts with three ten-minute breaks. We get paid minimum wage for the privilege, with no idea if there'll be another shift the next day. 'Where dreams are given wings' is the motto of the fulfilment centre, where we are not even allowed to talk to each other or have a wee apart from in our breaks.

I have done this job for three months and I hate it with every single fibre of my being. But it pays the rent, just about, and lets me live a minimal existence. Until something better comes along, it'll have to do.

So it could be seen as something of a mixed blessing that in precisely five hours and thirty-seven minutes I will get fired.

3

Martin

Because I'm late I have to make the time up at the end of my shift, and I'm glad of the breakfast Mrs Carruthers forced on me as it gets towards my first break of the day. Because Harry is over sixty-five, he gets four ten minute breaks per shift ... the company is good like that. Can you see me rolling my eyes? He takes his second one to coincide with mine.

In fact, Harry is over sixty-five by a good decade. He's been widowed for six years and lives in Salford. When I first started I asked him why he was still doing this godawful job at his age. He'd just shrugged and said it stopped him from sitting in the house slowly rotting. I can think of about a billion things I'd rather do to stop me slowly rotting than working here. Including slowly rotting.

It's not even as though he needs the money, I don't think. Harry was a third officer in the merchant navy for much of his life, which gives him a decent pension. I know about merchant navy pensions because my mum got some, along with a payout, after my dad died. I think that's why Harry is so nice to me, because of what happened to my dad.

I take a piss and go to the staff-room to have a quick cup of HBL from the vending machine. That's one of Harry's. HBL is Hot Brown Liquid, which he says is the only way to describe what comes out of the machine. *I'll call it coffee over my dead body.* He's sitting in one of the plastic chairs reading a magazine. I know he's going to give it to me when he finishes. He has done for the past three months. It's called the *Maritime Gazette* and is full of articles about shipping that are either incomprehensible or deathly dull, usually both. Harry thinks I'm interested in it because of my dad. He couldn't be more wrong. I couldn't give less of a shit. But I don't want to hurt the old boy's feelings so, when he pushes the magazine across the table, I nod, roll it up and stick it in my back pocket.

Harry rolls down his sleeves, covering the faded tattoos on his thick forearms, and buttons the cuffs. 'Back to the grindstone.'

'Yep.'

Harry's face is craggy and permanently wind-burned, and he has closely trimmed snow-white whiskers. He looks at me with his piercing eyes, as green as the sea. 'You ever thought of following in your dad's footsteps?'

'Go to sea?' I say, crumpling my paper cup and tossing it in the waste bin. 'Not really my scene.'

'And pushing a trolley full of other people's crap is?'

'It's not for the rest of my life,' I say. There is exactly thirty seconds of break time left.

'That's what Dan Pearson used to say. He was about your age.'

I frown. 'I don't know a Dan Pearson.'

'You wouldn't. A little bit before you started.'

'So he left?'

'Died,' says Harry, nodding towards the door. I walk out of the staff-room ahead of him. 'Just before his second break. Keeled over. Gone before he hit the deck. Turned out, it *was* for the rest of his life. Just think on. You never know what's around the corner.'

Two brothers are often on the same shift as me. I don't know their names, which sounds a bit stand-offish but it's because we're not allowed to talk while we're on the warehouse floor, and they never take their breaks at the same time as me. Harry calls them Tweedledum and Tweedledee. I just call them Dumb and Dumber. I mean, this job doesn't exactly need a PhD, but I'd be surprised if even *they* know their own names. I hear them before I see them, raucous cackling and shouting. I turn into aisle forty-nine and there they are, right at the bottom, roaring with laughter and egging each other on. I usually like to guess what's in the packages but there's no mystery to this one. It's a football, covered in bubble wrap, and Dumb and Dumber are heading it to each other in the aisle.

Obviously, this is the worst possible infraction in the fulfilment centre. We give dreams wings, but that doesn't mean the stuff should fly about like this. It's a sackable offence, no questions asked. Dumb and Dumber either don't care, or the Pavlovian draw of a football is so overwhelming they can't help themselves.

The item I need to collect is about halfway down and I'm quietly putting it in my trolley, hoping to get out of the aisle before they see me. I have no such luck.

'Oi, Burney!' shouts Dumb (or it could be Dumber) and then, to my horror, he hoofs the football straight at me.

'On your head!' shouts the other brother.

I have never been any good at football. Traumatic memories of PE sessions come flooding back and I flinch as the package flies towards me with an unerring aim. I turn slightly and it bounces off my head, continuing its trajectory with renewed force towards the far end of the aisle.

Just then Jordan rounds the corner, intently staring at a tablet in his hands.

'Cracking header, Burney!' laughs one of the brothers, just as the bubble-wrapped ball hits Jordan square in his very surprised, very angry face.

'Needless to say, you're all fired.' Jordan is sitting behind his desk and we are standing in a row like naughty schoolboys.

'Don't care,' says Dumb.

'It's a shit job anyway,' says Dumber.

'Hang on,' I say. 'How am I going to pay my rent?'

'You should have thought of that before you decided to wilfully damage customer property. I'll have Harry escort you off the premises.'

Outside, Dumb and Dumber walk off without a word.

'He's a tit, that Jordan,' says Harry, taking the opportunity to roll a cigarette. 'But you know what this place is like.' He lights up his fag and looks at me for a moment. 'Probably a blessing in disguise.'

'It doesn't feel like it.'

'Have you got the magazine?'

It's still in my back pocket, rolled up. 'Yeah. Maybe I can use it as toilet paper when things get really bad.'

Harry sticks out his hand and gives mine a firm shake. 'Good luck, lad. I'm sure something will turn up.'

He goes back inside and I watch one of the lorries departing from the loading bay, the company logo on the back. More dreams given wings. Mine are limping around in the gutter, flightless and broken, waiting for a cat to put them out of their misery.

I go and put some credit on my phone then call Imogen to see if she can meet up for lunch. Imogen doesn't have a job, but I'd never say that to her. She's an influencer. Or at least, she aspires to be. She's five years younger than me and spends her days posting pictures on social media, tagging brands in the hope of getting free stuff. So far, her haul has included a handbag, a haircut, a weekend in a three-star hotel in Coventry, and a year's supply of foot cream. We met at my last job, a pub in the Northern Quarter. I got sacked for spilling a tray of drinks over someone who turned out to be a mid-level Manchester gangster. I didn't tell Imogen I'd been fired, I told her I was leaving to pursue my dream of writing a novel. She said she was going to pursue her dreams as well, and handed in her notice. The difference was she had a nice little allowance every month from her rich daddy. And I haven't put one word down on paper.

'Such exciting times, babes,' says Imogen when we meet outside a bar next door to the pub where we used to work. 'Des wants to represent me.'

'Des?' I say, wondering when she's going to ask me about my day. Imogen is slim and quite beautiful and always well dressed and ... I squint at her. There's something different about her face. I say, 'Have you had ...?'

She pouts at me and says, 'Just a few fillers. You like? Des says it gives me a more individual look.'

Except you just look like every other twenty-five-year-old, I don't say. I *do* say, 'Des?'

'He reps a lot of the Manchester influencers,' she says, scrolling through her phone. She's had her nails done again. 'He says he can take my career to the next level.'

I bet he does. Imogen looks up at me at last, head cocked to one side, curls tumbling over her bare shoulders. 'He reckons I need to make a few changes, though.'

'Imogen—'

17

'Lifestyle changes.'

'Imogen, look, there's—'

'To streamline my brand.'

'Imogen, something happened and—'

'And I have to agree with him, babes. I have to think about my career, now. I'm sorry, but—'

'Imogen, I got fired.'

'Martin, we're going to have to split, babes.'

We stare at each other. 'You got fired?' she says, in a tone of voice that suggests she has made precisely the right decision.

'You're dumping me?' The broken-winged bird that represents my dreams looks up from the gutter to find a stray moggy licking its lips.

'Don't see it as me dumping you,' she says, looking back at her phone. 'See it as ... growth. As a conscious uncoupling.' She looks up and gives me a broad, white smile. 'Think of it as an opportunity.'

'But all the good times we've had ...' I say desperately. Mainly I'm thinking of the three-star hotel break in Coventry which, now I remember it properly, consisted of perfunctory sex punctuated by me taking photos of Imogen in the hotel room, lobby and car park as cars and lorries whizzed past on the M6.

She puts a rather patronising hand on mine. 'That's it, babes. Focus on the positives. By the way, I'm going to the Maldives in two weeks. Research trip. Des is going to introduce me to some contacts out there.'

'You're going to the Maldives with Des,' I say numbly. I think about making love with Imogen in Coventry. I had a sneaking suspicion she was looking at her phone behind my head as I whispered in her ear that I loved her.

Imogen's phone buzzes and she checks her messages.

'Babes, I really need to go. Got a forward planning meeting with Des at two.'

Planning meeting. Right. She stands up and gives me a chaste kiss on my cheek, then smiles. 'Take care, Martin. Be happy for me. And I'm sure something will turn up for you. Hey, maybe you could finally write that book, eh?' I watch her walk away into the crowds thronging the sunlit streets of the Northern Quarter. Lost my job. Lost my girl. I feel like I'm living in a crap country and western song. I wonder if I should ask Mrs Carruthers what's going to happen next.

I pay the bill and wander off, not really knowing where I'm going or what I'm going to do. I just walk, my feet leading me south through the city as I brood. I'm so lost in thought that I almost don't see the small, chanting crowd that's blocking the pavement outside the crown court on Minshull Street. They're waving placards, something about pollution in the river. I smile inwardly. Protests about the environment. I'd go on them when I was at university. And thinking about that makes me think about—

A figure appears on the periphery of my vision, and when I blink, it – she – is lost amid the chanting protesters. It looked like ... surely not ... after so long ...

Then my phone vibrates in my pocket. My heart sinks at the number on my screen.

'Hello?' I say cautiously.

'Mr Burney? This is Liz, from Pennant Gardens. We need you to get to Manchester Royal Infirmary as soon as possible. It's urgent, Mr Burney.'

4

Gayle

'Happy birthday, Gayle,' says Sam, shoving a folder into my hands as I walk up the steps into the crown court lobby.

I look down at what she's handed me, a manila file spilling out documents. 'It's usually tradition to give a card ...?' I look over my shoulder, frowning, through the doors at the chanting protesters. I could have sworn just before I came in I saw ...

'Last minute submission from Irwell Paints. The office just sent me over with the printouts.'

'Last minute is right,' I say, leafing through the documents. 'The court is never going to accept this. They're considering their judgement.'

'They've already accepted it,' says Sam, wrapping a bobble around her ponytail. 'It includes a deposition in support of the company's activities from the local councillor, who apparently is a member of the same golf club as the presiding judge.'

'Great.' I open my bag and shove the folder inside. There isn't time to read it, but I can guess what it says. Irwell Paints is a long-standing company which provides employment for a large number of local people and any infractions of environmental regulations are purely accidental, while any financial penalties imposed on the company could prove punitive, as well as lowering the company's standing in a highly competitive market. I've heard it all before. But someone has to take a stand, and that's what these people outside are doing. And why my company, EnviroMonitor, is representing them.

A bell rings and the court ushers start to allow the protesters inside to sit in the public gallery. Sam says, 'Looks like you're on. Good luck.'

The judge is exactly the sort of man you would expect to sit in the golf club bar having a brandy with the local councillor, and probably the boss of Irwell Paints as well. I've put a good case and couldn't have done it better, but I'm not hopeful.

'In the case of Irwell Paints v. EnviroMonitor, representing the action brought by the residents of the area around the company's main headquarters, a judgement has been reached.' The judge peers over his half-moon spectacles. 'Would Mr Simon Smythe, representing Irwell Paints, and Miss Gayle Reiss, for EnviroMonitor, please stand up.'

While we do, the judge considers his notes, then clears his throat again. 'We accept that Irwell Paints is a venerable company that has operated in this area for more than one hundred and fifty years, and is a major employer of local people.

'Situated on the river that bears the company name, it is true that this factory has, over the past few decades, seen a huge growth in residential properties around it. And many people who buy property in this now highly desirable area would prefer that the industrial activities associated with the factory would not take place at all.'

Here it comes.

'Irwell Paints was on this site for a long time before the area grew into the busy, thriving suburb it is today. And there is an argument that anyone buying a property here should accept that.'

I can feel Simon Smythe positively glowing beside me. I wonder if he drinks at the golf club, too.

'That said,' continues the judge, 'Miss Reiss, for Enviro-Monitor, put forward a very clear case that the company must be held accountable for the various infractions of environmental regulations that has seen the company release proscribed chemicals into the waterways.' The judge takes off his glasses and looks directly at Smythe. 'I must say, I am inclined to agree. No one wishes to stand in the way of progress and business, but that progress must be with a clear conscience, that business must be conducted in accordance with the rigorous adherence to protecting the environment.'

I risk a glance sideways at Smythe. He's tugging his collar and his smile is faltering a little. The judge says, 'For that reason, I am minded to find in favour of the complainants. There shall be a financial penalty for each of the unregulated chemical releases, with an order that Irwell Paints gives a full account of the measures it intends to take to stop this happening again in the future.' The judge puts on his glasses and stands up. 'Thank you.'

There's a heartbeat and then the public gallery erupts into cheers and whistles. Smythe gives my hand a perfunctory shake and heads straight off to lodge his appeal. I glance over at Sam, who gives me a double thumbs up. We won.

It takes me the best part of an hour to get out of court, running the gauntlet of the jubilant protestors, every single one of whom wants to shake my hand and pat me on the shoulder. I can't help feeling good. I might not be saving the world like I thought I would be back in university, but I'm doing my bit.

I'm walking back to the EnviroMonitor offices when my phone rings. It's Donna.

'Did you win?'

'Actually, I did.'

'Knew you would. What are you doing now?'

'Heading back to the office.'

'And later?'

'Later I'm going to go to my flat, get my pyjamas on, order a takeaway, drink a gallon of tea and binge-watch something on—'

'Bollocks to that,' says Donna cheerfully. 'It's Friday night. It's your thirtieth birthday. We're going *out* out. We're going to drink cocktails till we puke.'

'Donna, I've got to be at my mum and dad's for Sunday lunch tomorrow.'

There's a pause. 'Tomorrow's Saturday.'

'I know, but they're busy on Sunday. So I have to go to-morrow. And it's my birthday so Mum's doing a roast.'

'You're far too accommodating, you know.'

'Which is why I want a bit of me-time tonight.'

'Like I said,' says Donna. 'Bollocks to that. I'll see you at eight.'

5

Martin

Mum is hooked up to machines and monitors, looking all wizened and tiny like a grotesque doll.

She's had a massive stroke. She's asleep and all the left side of her face is drooping, as though she sat too close to the fire. Liz from the care home met me at the hospital and warned me that things were not good. Mum is not expected to recover. She's only sixty.

She went into Pennant Gardens three years ago, when it became apparent that her moments of forgetfulness and disorientation weren't just middle-aged brain fog. She'd barely come out of the menopause when she slid into early onset dementia. I remember sitting in the doctor's office, talking about how her condition was deteriorating rapidly and it was not going to be long before she could not live on her own. He'd looked at me and asked if I was prepared to be responsible for my mother's care.

It sounded like one of those *damned if you do, damned if you don't* questions. If I said yes, then I would have to move back into the rented house on the edge of Prestwich and ... what? Cook her meals? Get her to bed? Wipe her arse? If I said no, then did that make me the worst son on the planet? In the entire universe?

Fortunately, there was another option. Thanks to my dad

paying into his merchant navy pension there was Pennant Gardens, a care home for sailors and their families. In return for giving up her widow's pension, Mum was able to move into Pennant Gardens' dementia wing. It was a lovely place, the staff were fabulous, she had all the care and company she needed. And I was off the hook, and free to carry on living my dissolute, aimless life. If she needed her arse wiping, I didn't have to worry about that.

Now it looked like nobody would have to worry about that ever again. According to Liz, Mum had been sitting in the day room watching *Loose Women* when she'd just slid off the chair. They knew what was happening and had got her to hospital straight away. I'd spoken briefly to a doctor before they let me in to see Mum. They weren't even sure she'd regain consciousness, but advised me to talk to her anyway, because she might be able to hear me.

I have no idea what to say.

The last time I'd gone to visit Mum she had no idea who I was. She thought I'd come to fix the central heating. The time before that she thought I was her brother Albert, who'd died in the Falklands War.

'So!' I say with forced jollity. 'Got yourself in a bit of a pickle here, Mum.'

She lies there, pale and unmoving, the machines beeping and humming. There's a monitor with a line on it exactly like you see on the telly, peaking and troughing in a jagged trajectory, accompanied by a high-pitched *pip-pip-pip*. She's alive, for now.

'I suppose I was always a bit of a disappointment to you.' Her nose twitches, like a rabbit's, as though to say *A bit? A bit of a disappointment?* And she'd be right. In the nine years since I left university I've done ... well, precisely nothing. Oh, I've always worked, to some degree, always made just

25

enough to survive. And to be honest, not many lads from my school actually went to university, so I suppose that must have made her a bit proud. But I never did anything with my degree. Came away from three years at university with a scroll of paper and ... my breath catches briefly in my throat as I think of something, of someone, I haven't thought about for a long time. A scroll of paper, and a broken heart. With a start I remember walking past the court earlier, and thinking I'd seen ... but no. Surely she's not even in Manchester anymore. And then something else occurs to me. It's the seventeenth of June. Her birthday.

I try to push the memory away, concentrating on Mum. But I can't help wondering, how things could have been different, how my life might have taken a different route, if I hadn't screwed things up back then. Maybe I'd have actually made Mum proud.

I put her tiny, bony hand in mine. She feels cold and I panic, looking wildly at the monitors, which are still showing the steady, jagged line, and at her chest, rising almost imperceptibly beneath the thin sheet.

Then I feel the slightest pressure from her bony fingers. Her eyelids are flickering, but they don't open. Her dry, chapped lips start to work, and I hear the faintest whisper, like a soft breeze.

'Mum?' I say. Should I be getting a doctor or one of the nurses? 'Mum? It's me. Martin.'

'I should have ...' she slurs, the left side of her mouth drooping. I lean in closer, holding my breath to try to catch her words. 'I should have told your dad, don't go to sea. I should have known I'd lose him. But it was in his blood. It was the making of him.'

'Mum.' I stand up, leaning over her. 'Are you feeling better? Should I get someone?'

She shakes her head, a tiny movement I almost miss. 'I'm going. I'll see your dad. Just let me go in peace.'

I can't see her properly because tears are blurring my eyes. I hold her cold hand tightly. 'Don't go, Mum.'

Then her eyes do flicker open, shining brightly. Or maybe it's just my tear-clouded vision that makes it look so. She gives me a droopy smile. 'You're right. You are a bloody disappointment. But it's not too late.'

Then the light in her eyes goes out.

I can't remember whether I shout or press a button or go and get someone, but suddenly the room is full of people and I'm being gently but firmly pushed to one side and everyone is surrounding the bed so I can't see Mum anymore, I can just see the monitor with the line that is no longer jagged but flat, as flat as the horizon on a millpond-calm sea, and accompanied by a single, unbroken note, like the mournful voice of a foghorn.

'To lose either a mother, a girlfriend or a job would be considered unfortunate,' says Mrs Carruthers, pouring me a huge brandy. 'To lose all three on the same day is ... sheer idiocy.'

'None of it was really my fault,' I protest weakly, sitting in the big, moth-eaten easy chair in her flat.

Mrs Carruthers is sitting at her table in the window, expertly rolling a fat joint. She seals up her bag of weed and lights the joint with a silver lighter. Between puffs she says, 'This Zippo was given to me by an American GI in the war. For services rendered.'

That would surely make her at least ... ninety years old. Maybe she is. Who knows. After the day I've had, whether Mrs Carruthers is telling the truth or not is way down my

27

list of priorities. I swirl the brandy around in the big balloon glass, because that seems to be the done thing, then knock it back. It's my third one. I am a bit drunk.

Suddenly, Mrs Carruthers is looming in front of me, holding the joint upright. 'Take the edge off,' she says, exhaling a cloud of white smoke.

At the hospital, Liz from Pennant Gardens, as if sensing my confusion and distress – or, perhaps, having gleaned from my previous visits to the home that I am a useless sod – said that she would take charge of the red tape my mum's death would generate, and start the ball rolling with regard to the funeral, and would call me in a couple of days. She probably imagines me sitting at home, upset, numb, crying. She probably does not picture me sitting in the flat of an elderly fantasist smoking a joint with a kick like a mule. Mrs Carruthers begins, apropos of nothing, to regale me with a story about a carnal encounter with Keith Richards in the back of a bread van in Bolton.

At some point, Mrs Carruthers packs me back across the hall to my own flat, pressing on me a brace of one-litre Coke bottles filled with wine she has made herself from, she says, motherwort and hawthorn. 'Good for heartbreak,' she says. She ruffles my hair fondly. 'Things will look better in the morning.'

'Will they?' I say, standing on the threadbare carpet between our apartments, the strip-light buzzing and flickering.

She considers the question. 'Actually, no, not if you drink all that vino. But you'll feel so awful you'll probably not care about your troubles. Be well, dear heart. You're an idiot, but I'm very fond of you.'

Back at the flat I realise I haven't eaten since Mrs Carruthers cooked me breakfast, so I order in a massive doner and side of chips. When the food comes I try to watch a movie but I can't seem to concentrate. My thoughts feel like a parade of unconnected images that morph into scenes involving Mum, Imogen, and work. I don't know if that is the wine, the strong marijuana or the various levels of grief and pissed-off-ness the day has generated. I probably should try to get some sleep, I think, as I open the second Coke bottle. I really need to speak to someone.

I scroll through my phone, squinting with one eye. I don't really know anyone. Anyone who would care. Everyone I know from university, every friend I picked up in my twenties, has moved forward. They have careers and families and houses in the suburbs or the countryside. Everyone has the sort of life that someone just turned thirty should have. Everyone except me. For almost ten years I've stood still, as though waiting for something to happen. And now everything has happened, on the same day, and none of it is any good.

I really want to talk to Imogen.

I try her number three times and it goes to her answerphone every time. I open her Instagram and see she's posted a series of pictures in the last ten minutes. She's at the opening of a new city centre bar. She's wearing a small, tight white dress, her arms and legs shining with fake tan. She's laughing, drinking cocktails. She looks disgustingly happy. There's a figure beside or behind her in many of the shots. In one picture she's laughing as he whispers something into her ear. He looks to be in his forties, with a chiselled jaw and short, dark hair, dressed in an expensive-looking blue suit. This must be Des, then. After each picture there's a string of hashtags ending #LivingMyBestLife. My thumb hovers over her number again, then I switch off my phone. What's the point? She's living her best life.

I'm drunk, and stoned, and sad, and annoyed. I should just go to bed. As I clumsily brush my teeth I think about Dad, which I don't do very often. Mainly because he died when I was four, and I don't really remember him other than as a big, vague, blurry, irregular presence. My memories of him are inherited, stories from Mum, photos, yellowing cuttings Mum kept in a scrapbook, about the incident and the inquiry and the court case.

Finally, I feel some kind of connection to him, some proper kinship. We have something in common, at last, other than blood and borrowed memories.

We're both lost at sea.

I lie in bed, staring into the darkness, then switch on the bedside lamp. The *Maritime Gazette* is on the floor in the tangle of my jeans. Guaranteed to bore me to sleep. I lie back and flick through its pages, reading about GPS buoy systems and shipping lanes and European regulations. My eyes start to droop as I turn the last pages, to the situations vacant ads.

There's one with a big red ink ring around it, evidently scrawled by Harry. I blink, and sit up in bed, folding the magazine over to study the page. It's a short, unremarkable ad in the bottom left corner. Barely any details. Just an address, a closing date, and the heading.

WANTED: LIGHTHOUSE KEEPER

6

Gayle

The problem with turning thirty is that everyone sees this as some kind of green light to marry you off.

'I was twenty-two when I had you,' says my mother. 'Just think on.'

'Which meant you spent your twenties knee-deep in nappies, doing the school run, and trying to forget you could have had a career,' I say back, pulling faces at the phone.

'And how did *you* spend your twenties?' says my mother. She doesn't wait for me to reply, which is a good job, because there are things about my twenties I really wouldn't want her to know. She goes on, 'Working, partying and having relationships with unsuitable men.'

I want to retort, *You say that like it's a bad thing*, but I bite my tongue. She doesn't draw breath anyway, ploughing on, 'Say you met someone today. And say you decided to settle down and give it a go. So it'll still be a couple of years before you get pregnant. And let's not even talk about the biological clock.'

No, let's not, I think, looking at the actual clock on the wall of my flat, wondering how long she's going to bang on.

A bit longer, it seems. 'So you'll be, what, thirty-three, thirty-four before you have a baby? And when your little baby is thirty, like mine is, you'll be sixty-four.'

'Gosh,' I say. 'Sixty-four. Stop all the clocks.'

My mother sighs loudly. 'Your grandma was only sixty-five when she died. Just think on.'

'Is there anything else you'd like to talk about?'

'No,' says my mother. 'I just called to wish you a happy birthday. Are you still coming round for lunch tomorrow?'

'I'll be there at one,' I say. 'Love you.'

'Love you, too,' says my mother. 'Oh, I forgot to tell you. Your dad has booked a test-drive for a sports car. And he's bought some new trainers. Do you think he might be having an affair?'

'Do you?'

We both pause, then laugh together, cackling like a pair of witches. 'See you tomorrow, Mum.'

'Your mum is right,' says Donna, putting another – my third? – porn star martini in front of me. She picks up the little shot glass of Prosecco. 'Did we decide whether we do these before or after?'

'Right about what? That I should get married and start popping babies out?' I say, necking the Prosecco. 'Before. I think.'

Donna is my best friend. Well, going off the fact that there are just two of us celebrating my momentous thirtieth birthday, my *only* friend. Which is a bit unfair. I do have plenty of friends, it's just that some of them are indeed married with children, and some of them live a long way from Manchester, and to be honest I didn't really want a fuss. I mean, is it that big a deal, really?

'No,' says Donna, slamming her shot glass upside down on the table. 'Well, not unless you want to. I was more referring to her rather astute observation about your string of unsuitable men.'

'You think *all* men are unsuitable.'

Donna considers her drink. 'This is true. I did try to sleep with a man once. It was awful. But you, for some reason, seem set upon continuing this course of action. There is a world of predominantly straight men out there, and yet you have failed to find one who isn't an utter twat.'

'That's a bit strong,' I say, without much conviction.

'Look around,' she says. We are in a bar in the Northern Quarter on a Friday night. It's packed. More than half of the clientele are men. Some of them very nice looking. As if reading my mind, Donna says, 'If you threw that empty shot glass into the crowd you'd be guaranteed to hit the biggest twat in the room. And then embark on a six-month relationship with him while he treated you like crap.'

'That's ... a little unfair,' I say, though I know I'm on a hiding to nothing.

Donna waves at the waiter for more drinks, a look of glee on her face. 'Shall we examine the evidence?'

'I'm the lawyer,' I say, but I know there's no stopping Donna now. She brushes her blue-dyed hair off her face and starts to count off on her fingers.

'Zac. He of the chiselled jaw and broad shoulders. And wife and two young daughters in York which it, rather incredibly, took you three months to find out about.'

'He told me he had to go back there during the week to look after his sick gran. And it wasn't my fault he was a pathological liar, and a good one at that.' Donna taps her second finger. 'Trevor. Aside from the fact you decided to go out with a bloke called Trevor ... you chose one who was embezzling from his employer and ended up in jail.'

I've stopped protesting. Donna is right. They were twats. All of them. But she's not finished yet.

'Chris. Who only got with you so he could get close to She-Who-Must-Not-Be-Named.'

Otherwise known as Sara, once one of my closest friends. Now Chris's wife somewhere in the Pennine countryside, where they have a small-holding which, from what I've seen on Instagram, he stalks around wearing a flat cap and braces. I hope they both get swine flu.

'Jamie,' says Donna, and waggles her little pinky at me.

'That wasn't why we broke up,' I say.

She shrugs. 'Rupert. Who had three other girls on the go at the same time.'

'Twat,' I agree.

'Timothy. Who liked to wear your knickers and bra while you were out and had a rather large online following under the name of Little Mister Panty-Boy.'

'He's working through his issues,' I say, holding up my hands in surrender. 'Enough, Donna. Please. I get the picture.'

She sits back in her chair. 'In fact, the only guy who was ever any good for you was—'

The waiter interrupts her with a clearing of his throat, and places another porn star martini in front of each of us. He also puts a bottle of what looks like eye-wateringly expensive champagne, with two flutes, on the table.

'I didn't order that,' says Donna, squinting at the label. 'And I'm definitely not paying for it.'

The waiter leans in conspiratorially. 'It's been sent over by a gentleman. Behind me, to my left. About four tables back. White shirt. Jeans. Dark hair, nice bit of grey at his temples. Verrrry hot.'

Donna is craning her neck to look at him. 'Mmmm, you're right. I wonder if he has a sister.'

The waiter straightens up. 'This is all a bit eighties

romcom for my tastes, but it must work for him. And that is a very expensive bottle of fizz. Would you like me to open it for you?'

'Hell, yes,' says Donna. She looks pointedly at me.

'What?' I say.

'Well, he's not sent it over for me, has he?'

I risk a glance towards the table. The waiter is right. He is very hot. He sees me looking and lifts a glass filled with amber liquid. He raises an eyebrow.

Oh, my.

I'm awakened at some ungodly hour by my mother calling my mobile. I don't even need to open my eyes to know it's her. In fact, opening my eyes would be a definite disadvantage, the way I'm feeling. I feel around on my bedside table. The table feels higher than it should. Has my bed sunk? Have the legs fallen off? My fingers brush a glass before closing around the phone.

'Morning,' I croak.

'Not for long,' says my mother breezily. 'It's nearly midday.'

Oh, God. I have to be there in an hour. I need twice that to come round and shower, never mind the half-hour drive. I say with as much brightness as I can muster, 'I'll be setting off in a bit.'

'Could you do me a favour, darling? Your father forgot to buy horseradish. Could you pick a jar up on the way? Nothing own brand.'

'Sure,' I say, and end the call. I really am going to have to get up now. Well, soon. Maybe opening my eyes would be a good start. I reach out to put my phone on the bedside table and it clatters to the floor. What is wrong with that table? I open one eye.

It's not my bedside table. It is in a room that is not my room. It is a bedside table that is beside a bed that is not my bed. I am enveloped in a flawless white Egyptian cotton duvet cover that stretches on like the Arctic tundra. The walls are white and displaying monochrome art. Sunlight is streaming in through a floor-to-ceiling window.

And I am not alone in the bed.

I turn and train my one eye on the figure lying there. No longer wearing a white shirt and jeans, in fact, not wearing anything. Tanned, toned, and, just like the waiter said, ver-rrry hot.

'Good morning, Gayle,' he says in a voice so rich and deep that I think all my mother's Christmases might have come at once.

It all comes flooding back in an info-dump of blurry images. Champagne. More champagne. Another bar. A club. Putting Donna into a taxi. Well, pouring Donna into a taxi. Getting into a cab. Coming back here. And then … Oof. No wonder I'm half-dead. The last time I remember looking at my phone's clock it said five in the morning.

'Um,' I say, trying to think what comes next. 'Where are we, exactly?'

'Alderley Edge,' he says with a lopsided grin.

'Nice,' I say, lying back in the huge marshmallow-soft pillow, then immediately sitting bolt upright, my head banging like a kettle-drum on a rollercoaster.

'Alderley Edge? Shit. I need to be at my parents' in an hour. I need to get home and get showered and changed and buy some horseradish and—'

He puts a finger on my lips and I think I might die. 'Shush. Why don't you shower here? Then I'll run you home, you can quickly get changed, and I'll zoom you over to your parents'. What's the address?'

36

'You don't need to do that. You can call me a cab, though.'

'I insist,' he says, getting out of bed. He's completely naked. And utterly gorgeous. Every single inch of him.

'You mentioned horseradish? I make my own,' he gives that crooked smile again. 'Just a hobby, really. You can take a jar.'

I open my mouth and then close it again. 'Um,' I say eventually. 'That would be ... very kind of you. All of it. Thank you.'

'Do you want to jump in the shower first?' he says. 'Or ... to save time ... we could shower together.'

There's that raised eyebrow again. I mean, what's a girl to do?

7

Gayle

The plan is that I will be dropped at the gate of my parents'
semi and, having exchanged numbers, we'll arrange to meet
up soon. My mother has other ideas.

I'm not sure what the car is but it's silver and sleek and
seats two people and is very, very fast and growly. As soon
as we pull up at the kerb my mother is practically running
down the drive, wiping her hands on a tea towel. 'Gayle!'
she says, her reprimanding tone accompanied by a twinkle
in her eye as I climb out of the car. 'You didn't tell me you
were bringing a guest!'

'Oh, I'm not,' I say, glancing at him.

'Nonsense!' says my mother. 'There's plenty! Aren't you
going to introduce us, then?'

'I'd love to,' I say through gritted teeth as he comes round
the car to the pavement. I don't add that I've been trying to
remember his name for the last hour.

'Mrs Reiss, I'm Tom Cassidy. Delighted to meet you.'

Tom Cassidy. Good, strong name. Reliable name.

My mother has gone all girly and giggly. I glare at her.
Tom says, 'And I certainly don't want to impose.'

'Not in the slightest!' says my mother. 'In fact, we insist.'

38

She turns around as my father wanders up. 'Don't we, Paul?'

Dad is wearing chinos and a polo shirt and white trainers. I furrow my brow at Mum, who shrugs.

'Yes, no problem,' says Dad, though I know he wasn't even listening. 'By heck, is that what I think it is?'

'Alfa Romeo Spider, 115 series,' says Tom, grinning.

Dad runs a hand reverently over the bonnet, as though he's in the presence of the Ark of the Covenant. 'What a beauty.'

'This is Tom,' says Mum. 'He's joining us for lunch.'

Tom looks at me, 'Well, only if it's all right by Gayle ...'

Mum frowns as though what I think absolutely has no bearing. She links arms with him and guides him up the drive, saying, 'So, what do you do, then, Tom?'

I look quizzically at Dad. 'Have you dyed your hair?'

He touches the sides a little self-consciously. 'A bit. Come on, your mother has a new toy to play with. We'd best not keep her waiting.'

'Property developer,' says Mum admiringly as she puts the roast beef on the table, as though Tom has just told her he's an astronaut or a brain surgeon. I can't remember when I last ate something, and the smell of the beef has me salivating.

'Here, let me,' says Tom, taking the carving knife and fork from Mum's hands and starting to expertly slice the beef. I swear, she looks like she might be having a hot flush as she sits down. She might even be in the throes of a quiet orgasm.

'Must be a pretty penny in that,' says Dad, pouring the wine. 'Property development.'

'I don't make a bad living,' says Tom disarmingly, using the fork and knife to pile beef on everyone's plates. 'It's all about having an eye for it; when I see something and know it's right, I go for it.'

And he looks straight at me with his piercing blue eyes.

We start to eat as Dad presses Tom about his business, and Mum suddenly throws her head back, her eyes closed, as though she's one of those Victorian mediums channelling the dead.

'Oh! My word! This horseradish is the best I've ever tasted! Where did you get it?'

'Tom made it himself,' I say, and Mum looks like she's about to tell Dad to move out.

'How old are you?' says Dad.

'Paul,' says Mum warningly. 'He's not here for an interview.'

And yet, that's precisely what this feels like. An interview as a prospective suitor for their daughter. And so far he's passing with flying colours. I half expect my mother to offer him a dowry before the bread and butter pudding comes out. 'Forty,' says Tom. 'I must say, Mrs Reiss, I've never had beef done so immaculately in all my life. And I've eaten at Michelin-starred restaurants.'

Mum giggles like a schoolgirl. 'Oh, please. Call me Heather.'

After lunch, Tom insists on loading the dishwasher, while Dad goes into the back garden for a crafty fag. I follow him out and say, 'I thought you'd given up.'

'I'm trying,' he says. 'But, you know, living with your mother ...'

I look his outfit up and down. 'New clothes?'

He nods, then looks sheepish. 'Do you think they're too young for me?'

'Dad,' I say. 'You're fifty-three. That *is* young.' I pause. 'Mum says they're too young for you, doesn't she?'

He sighs, and exhales a cloud of smoke. 'I think she can't wait to be a grandmother,' he says. 'She's always going on about you having kids.' He looks off into the middle distance. 'I sometimes feel like life's passing me by, Gayle.'

I take the cigarette out of his hand and take a drag on it. I've not smoked for a couple of years now. It tastes good. 'She joked to me yesterday that you might be having an affair.' I look sidelong at him. 'Are you?'

He shakes his head and gives a little laugh. 'Of course not. Where would I find the time?'

I hand the cigarette back. 'You do realise that's what every man who has an affair says, don't you?'

He grinds the butt under his shoe and pops an Extra Strong Mint into his mouth, offering the packet to me. 'I'm not having an affair. I love your mother. I just don't want to get old, Gayle. Not yet.'

When we go back into the kitchen Tom is writing down his horseradish recipe for Mum, who's got her hands clasped together and is gazing at him with adoration. He looks up and says, 'Ah, Mr Reiss—'

'Paul. Please.'

'Paul. I wondered if you fancied taking the Spider for a spin round the block ...?'

As soon as they've pulled away from the kerb, the engine growling, Mum grabs my arm in the front garden and hisses, 'Why didn't you tell me about Tom yesterday when I phoned you?'

I don't say it was because I hadn't actually met him.

'How long have you known him?'

In the Biblical sense? About twelve hours. I don't say that either. I don't need to say anything, in fact, because nothing's going to stop her talking. 'Well, he's a catch, Gayle.

A real catch. You don't need me to tell you that. I just hope …'

'You just hope what?' I say, suddenly annoyed.

'Well,' she says, turning and walking back to the house with me. 'You don't exactly have a good track record, do you?'

'And that's my fault, of course.' I remember what Donna said about all of my failed relationships last night. 'They were all twats. The only mistake I made was choosing badly.'

'Don't swear,' says Mum mildly. 'I'm sure Tom wouldn't like it. Such a refined man.'

I think of the utter filth he was growling in my ear in the early hours of this morning with my legs wrapped around him and my fingernails digging into his back.

'Yes, you're quite correct, dear Mama,' I say. 'I shall be in the drawing room with my needlework if Tom comes to call. Please have the footman show him in.'

Dad has a fire in his eyes that I've never seen before as he and Tom tumble back into the house.

'Handles like a dream!' declares Dad admiringly. 'And the power! Never felt anything like it!' He looks at Mum. 'Imagine us in one of those, Heather? Driving down to Cornwall? You'd love it.'

'And how much do they cost?' says Mum.

Tom tells her and her eyes widen. 'Well,' she says tightly. 'I think the Mondeo will do for us, for now. Who's for coffee?'

As Mum is pouring it the doorbell rings. Dad says, 'I'll get it.'

'You must let me bring you some of the special blend a chap in London makes me,' says Tom. 'Liberica beans. Very sweet and smoky.'

42

'Like you!' says Mum, slapping his arm. Her face is flushed. She's had too much wine. Thankfully, Dad walks in, scratching his head.

'Delivery. For Gayle.'

I frown. 'Who knew I'd be here?' Dad hands me a slim package wrapped in brown paper.

Tom pulls a face like that of a naughty schoolboy. 'I'm afraid that might be me. When you gave me your parents' address ...' He shrugs. 'Happy birthday.'

I tear off the paper and open the box. Inside is the most beautiful white gold bracelet studded with diamonds that I have ever seen.

I think my mum is going to cry.

'Whoa, back up,' says Donna on the phone later. 'Too much information. Let's start again. That guy from the bar last night ...'

'Tom.'

'Tom. You shagged him?'

'Yes.'

'And you stayed at his place? In Alderley Edge?'

'Yes.'

'Was it posh?'

'Very.'

'And you shagged him again in the shower this morning?'

'Yes.'

'And you took him to meet your fucking parents?'

'Well, it wasn't quite planned like that. He dropped me off, and well ... you know my mother.'

'And he had a bloody diamond bracelet delivered to your parents' house while you were there? On a Saturday afternoon?'

'That's about the size of it.'

'Then what happened?'

What happened then was Tom drove me to my flat and dropped me off, and we exchanged numbers, and arranged to meet on Tuesday evening for a drink in Manchester. I look at the bracelet glinting on my wrist. And suddenly it seems I have a boyfriend.

'Well,' says Donna. 'By anyone's standards, that is very fast work. The question is, how is Tom going to turn out to be a twat?'

'I'm not actually sure he is,' I say in a small voice.

'Bloody hell,' says Donna.

'I know,' I say. 'Bloody hell.'

We both sit in silence for a while, then she says, 'Did I do anything to disgrace myself? I can't remember getting home. I can't remember much, to be honest.'

'You took a piss behind a skip on St Peter's Square,' I say, struggling to remember myself. 'You might have thrown up on a pigeon.'

'Standard,' says Donna. She pauses, then says, 'Gayle?'

'Donna?'

'If he does turn out to be a twat, I'm always here for you. You know that.'

I feel like crying suddenly. I say, 'I do know that. But somehow ... I don't think he will be. I think ... I think Tom might be the one who isn't.'

I can almost feel her shrug at the other end of the line. 'OK, kiddo. Well. I hope you're right. But if not ... it's your funeral. Love you, you knob.'

'Love you too, you knob,' I say, and kill the call. I close my eyes and wonder what it would be like to hear Tom say *I love you* in his silky, seductive voice.

8

Martin

As funerals go, it is as good as can be expected. In that there is drunkenness, a fight, and public sex.

The drunkenness starts at the church, the moment the priest walks in — rather unsteadily, it has to be said. Mum wasn't even Catholic, wasn't a practising Christian of any stripe, as far as I knew. But Liz from Pennant Gardens told me that in her final weeks she'd embraced a newfound spirituality, and had received visits from a Methodist minister, a rabbi, the somewhat perplexed imam of the local mosque, and a burly man in an orange sheet who had spent some time in Tibet and offered spiritual guidance when he wasn't being a mechanic. And Father Murphy.

'Hedging her bets,' I told Liz. Evidently, after what the holy men didn't realise was a series of interviews, Mum went with Father Murphy. I'm not sure whether he was a big drinker before he met Mum, but as he weaves his way towards the altar on the day of the funeral it's obvious he's put away a considerable amount of the communion wine. And it's only ten in the morning.

Mum's coffin sits before the altar. I carried it in with two cousins I haven't seen for twenty years, and Harry from work. From my former work, I should say. The coffin felt so light as to be empty. I am sitting on the front row of pews, and glance around at the smattering of mourners. Myself, Harry, Mrs Carruthers, a few aunties and uncles and cousins. I messaged Imogen to tell her about the funeral. She didn't reply.

Father Murphy opens proceedings with a eulogy in a rich, Irish brogue that echoes around the almost-empty, cavernous church.

'Nathan O'Toole was a big man in so many ways,' he booms. 'Six foot four and built like a brick shithouse. A cocksman of some renown in his youth. They say he impregnated half of Cork as a young swain. And when he moved to Manchester, to work on the building sites, he could carry two hods full of bricks without breaking a sweat.' Father Cassidy ploughs on, regardless of the rising muttering among his meagre congregation. 'But a man with a heart as big as his head, Nathan O'Toole. A man whose largesse knew no ...' Father Murphy stops and squints at the sheet of paper in front of him, then at the tiny coffin.

Then he turns and roars towards the vestry, 'Marjorie! This is the wrong bloody eulogy! Nathan O'Toole is my twelve o'clock! Who's in the box?'

'That went well,' says Mrs Carruthers in the lounge of St Columba's Working Men's Club, sipping a large brandy. She pokes a painted nail at the curling crust of a meat paste sandwich, sweating in the warm sunshine that valiantly pushes through the dust-caked windows.

'You think so?' I say, contemplating a pie filled with grey meat.

She gives me a withering look. 'No, darling, I'm being sarcastic. I've never seen such an abortion of a funeral in

46

all my days. Still, at least your mother is with the saints in heaven now.'

Harry wanders over with a pint for each of us, and nods at Mrs Carruthers, who looks him up and down like a lion sizing up her next meal.

'Lovely service,' says Harry hesitantly, handing me my drink.

'Oh, we've already done that,' says Mrs Carruthers. 'We all know it was an absolute travesty.' She holds out her hand. 'Beryl.'

Harry takes it, uncertain what to do, then leans forward and kisses it as though she's the Queen of Sheba. Mrs Carruthers giggles coquettishly. 'Harry,' says Harry.

He looks at me. 'So. You got the job, then.'

I was called the very next day and invited for interview in London, at a place called Triune House. It's a grand building near Euston, with huge mahogany double doors and marble floors. Everything smells of beeswax and quiet authority.

I am shown into a wood-panelled room with thick carpets and a long table at which sit two men and two women in suits, and off to one side is a stern-faced woman of around sixty, leaning on a cane, staring at me intently.

The panel introduce themselves and I immediately forget their names, except for the woman off to the right, Heledd Davies.

'Mr Burney,' says one of the men. 'A little background for you. Triune House is the body that owns, maintains and operates all of the lighthouses—' Heledd Davies coughs and the man corrects himself, '*Most* of the lighthouses around the British Isles. Ynys Dwynwen, as Ms Davies has so rightly pointed out, is a special case. Triune House has a necessary interest in the lighthouse there, but it is owned and run by the Davies family who built it in 1876. Our role here is to aid Ms Davies in finding a suitable candidate to act as lighthouse keeper on Ynys Dwynwen and—'

'Give him the job,' says Ms Davies in a lyrical Welsh accent.

The man looks at her. 'Excuse me?'

She stands up, leaning on her stick. 'No one else has applied, have they? We've all read his application.' She fixes me with her glare again. 'He's lonely, aimless and without prospects.'

'I didn't write that on my application.'

'You didn't have to, Mr Burney,' says Ms Davies, walking towards me. 'We all read between the lines.'

She turns back to the panel. 'He's got the job. I'll take my leave.' She pauses and taps my chest with the head of her stick. 'Ynys Dwynwen is a special place, Mr Burney. Respect it and look after it and we'll get on just fine.'

I watch the woman let herself out of the room and turn helplessly back to the panel. The man shrugs and says, 'Congratulations, Mr Burney. It appears you're now a lighthouse keeper.'

'How thrilling,' says Mrs Carruthers. 'To live by the tide of the oceans, polishing your lamp every night. A beacon of hope for those in peril on the seas!' She sighs happily. 'How romantic, and yet so terribly tragic.'

I excuse myself and go to talk to the uncles and aunts and cousins, circulating for half an hour until the doors to the lounge burst open and in marches a troop of tall, broad, blocky men in black suits, and women with faces as though carved from limestone, wearing a variety of hats. 'Oi, fuckwad!' bellows the first man, a scar running from his forehead to his chin, pointing at one of the uncles who is putting a pork pie to his mouth. 'That's my daddy's fucking buffet!'

I approach him with my hands held out in supplication. 'I'm sorry, I think there's been some mistake. This is the wake for my mother and—'

'Get the fuck out of it, you eejit! Your fucking wake is in the snug! My mammy was up all night making these fucking sandwiches you bastards are shoving into your Brit gobs!'

A little old woman steps out from behind him, shaking her fist at me. 'Belt the fucker, Patrick! It's what your daddy would have wanted!'

Patrick, being a good boy, does what his mammy tells him, and swings a fist as big as a ham. I duck just in time, and he connects with one of my cousins from the Moss Side branch of the family, sending him sprawling. Then all hell breaks loose.

I stay low as the cousins and uncles start trading punches with Nathan O'Toole's family. As a chair flies over my head I crawl under a table. As if things couldn't get any worse. There's shouting and screaming and a crashing of crockery. No doubt the police are on their way, and what I really don't need right now is to be arrested the day before I head off to my new job. Spying a gap in the melee, I crawl on my hands and knees towards the men's toilets. I can hide in there until it's all calmed down.

I escape into the loos and stand up, my back against the door. It sounds like chaos out there. I bet this wouldn't have happened if Mum had gone with the imam.

Slowly I become aware of voices underneath the noise of the ruck from the lounge. Here in the toilets, which are cold and smelly, the grout grey and mouldy, the cisterns dripping with clockwork timing, I hear someone in the end cubicle. They sound like they might be in trouble.

I pad along the tiled floor which is wet from a leaking urinal, and cautiously push open the door, just as Mrs

49

Carruthers, her dress around her waist and her voluminous legs clamped around Harry's naked thighs, begins to issue a series of moans and yelps in a rising crescendo that culminate in what even a philistine like me recognises as an ecstatic rendition of 'Nessun Dorma'.

I can never unsee this. Please, God, get me to Wales.

It is raining when the bus drops me on the road by a squat building that sits on a tiny harbour with nothing else around it for miles save the rolling hills and fields of Anglesey.

Apart from one thing. Ynys Dwynwen, five miles out on the choppy, slate-grey sea, the red and white hooped light-house, standing proud against the bruised sky.

I pull up my hood and drag my case along the uneven stone path to the boathouse, pushing open the door to a tinkle of a bell. I'm in a grocery shop, it seems, one carved from a lost age. Tins and packets gather dust on the shelves, there is a spinner rack of comics and magazines, months out of date. A chest freezer clanks noisily beside a row of wooden shelves bursting with vegetables and fruit. I wonder who shops here. I haven't seen a house for miles.

'With you in two shakes of a lamb's tail!' comes a voice from the back of the shop.

Presently a man emerges. He's short, with a shock of black hair, and darkly piercing eyes. He's in shirt-sleeves and shapeless trousers, wiping oil from his hands with a dirty rag.

'Bloody generator clapped out this morning, didn't it?' he says, giving me a toothy smile. He nods towards the freezer. 'Nearly lost the Viennettas, touch and go, it was.'

'I'm Martin Burney,' I say. 'I was told to report here ...?'

The man frowns. 'Are you here for Blodwyn's prescription? I told her it wasn't ready.'

He walks over to the far end of the counter and heaves

up a grey sack. 'Though I think there might be a letter in here for her. Not had a bloody chance to go through it since Evans dropped it off yesterday. Let me look and you can take it for her.'

'I'm not here for Blodwyn's prescription,' I say. 'I was told to meet a Mr Jones here ...?'

The man scratches his head. 'Gareth Jones, the sheep farmer? Or Eddie Jones, the bus driver? Though you just got off his bus, so no. Surely not Wyn Jones? Heap of trouble, that man. Can't see as you'd be wanting him.'

'It's to take me to the island. The lighthouse,' I say.

The man beams a huge smile again. 'Ahhhhh! You're the new keeper! Why didn't you say so! That'd be me you're wanting! Gwyn Jones!' He reaches across the counter to shake my hand. 'Pleased to meet you, Martin Burney!'

'You're the boatman?'

'Boatman, pharmacist, postmaster, shopkeeper, everything!' says Gwyn happily. 'Meet me round the back in ten minutes while I lock up.'

It's still raining and I wait behind the shop, by the tiny stone harbour, until Gwyn emerges wearing a yellow oilskin coat and a Greek fisherman's hat. He points to a tiny blue and white wooden boat fitted with an outboard motor bobbing in the water at the bottom of a flight of stone steps. I look out at the grey sea, waves rolling and crashing. 'We're going out there in that?' I say doubtfully.

'Safe as houses! And you're in good hands with Gwyn! Come on then, Keeper! Time's a-wasting! Let's get you to Ynys Dwynwen.'

9

Martin

It takes the best part of an hour for the little boat to cleave through the choppy grey seas towards the island, bouncing on the waves. I cling to the wooden seat as I'm sloshed with cold, salty water. Gwyn's in his element, singing anatomically detailed verses about two sisters of dubious morals entertaining an entire rugby team. Every time I squeal when the boat shoots up and slaps down he breaks off for uproarious laughter.

'Look! Martin Burney! To the port side!'

I shake my head from side to side, trying to remember which is port. I should really get to know these things. Finally I spot what he's pointing at, half a dozen black dots in the sea.

'Sharks?' I say tremulously. Gwyn roars again and slaps his knee. 'Seals! There's a colony of Atlantic Greys on the reef on the far side of the island. They've come to say hello to the new keeper, haven't they?'

As Ynys Dwynwen gets closer the rain stops and the sun eases through the clouds. Not for the first time in the last week, I wonder what the hell I'm doing. Cutting myself off from the world, an hour's boat ride from the mainland, with nobody for company. Not that I really had much company in Manchester. Not even with Imogen. I was lonely but didn't even realise it. Besides, it seems I'll have *some* company; a colony of seals. And then there's the lighthouse, this tall stone tower painted in white and red. My new home.

It's quite breathtaking to see as we approach. I wasn't really prepared for how ... majestic it looks. How in keeping with the nature of the island, and yet apart from it. The glass enclosing the lamp at the top of the tower glints in the emerging sun. I imagine the beam striking out through the darkness, lighting the way for those at sea. And I think of my father, and my impending loneliness feels suddenly a little weightier.

'Beauty, isn't she?' says Gwyn. 'Stood tall and proud for nearly a hundred and fifty years, a beacon of light and hope. And now she's under your care, Keeper.'

Gwyn steers the boat against the waves, heading for a wooden jetty built on a shallow inlet on the mainland-facing side of the island. As we approach I see a figure shaking the rain from an umbrella.

'The duchess,' says Gwyn, steering the boat in. 'Not a real duchess. Just what we call her.'

It's Heledd Davies, the woman who gave me the job, and she does indeed look quite regal as she stands on the jetty, wrapped in an oilskin coat and boots, watching us bump against the wooden platform.

'Mr Burney,' she says as I struggle awkwardly out of the boat, dragging my case behind me. 'Welcome to Ynys Dwynwen.'

We stand at the foot of the tower, looking up with hands shading our eyes as the clouds drift apart to let the sun blaze through. Ms Davies says, 'One hundred and fifty feet tall, Mr Burney.' She points with her umbrella at the doorway, then moves the tip to aim at the small square windows. 'The

53

entrance room. The store. Two floors of oil storage. The kitchen. Bedroom. Living room. Service room. And finally ... the lamp.'

I feel dwarfed by the lighthouse and the sudden enormous responsibility of the job. 'Oil storage?'

'Do not fear, Mr Burney. The light is almost fully automated these days. Not like when my great-grandfather built it in 1876.'

'Fully automated,' I say. I feel a slight disappointment. 'Is there actually anything for me to do, then?'

'There is a great deal for you to do, Mr Burney.' She turns away from the lighthouse and surveys the small island. 'Maintenance. Cleaning. Overriding the automated systems in the event of unexpected weather conditions. And making sure that the light of Ynys Dwynwen that has shone every single night since it was built continues to shine under your stewardship. It is a great responsibility, Mr Burney.'

A little way to the left of the tower there are two dilapidated, tumbledown cottages, one with no roof at all. Grasses grow up to the glassless windows and piles of stone and slate are heaped by the doorways. 'My great-grandfather, Edward Davies, lived on Ynys Dwynwen. He had a soulful affinity with this island. Said it was a place of magic, where the walls between this world and the next were worn thin.' She looks at me with her icy cold eyes. 'He said the light of the tower acted not just as a warning to guide ships to safety, but as a beacon to those who wished to cross over from the other side.'

I imagine being here alone at night. I really wish she hadn't told me that.

'Poppycock, of course,' says Ms Davies, marching on through the tall grasses, using her furled umbrella as a walking stick. 'Come. Let me show you the island.'

The land rises as we walk, and Ms Davies leads me along a rough path to the far side of the island, to a cove that slashes inland, and where the waves crash on jagged rocks a hundred feet down. She says, 'If you could see the island from the air, you would note that it is shaped roughly like the traditional drawing of a heart, precisely one mile in circumference.' She points with her umbrella at the two headlands of the cove. 'This would be the point where the two arcs fold inwards.' She turns and points back to the jetty. 'That would be the point at the bottom of the heart. Hence the island's name, Ynys Dwynwen.'

'Which means what?' Ms Davies raises an eyebrow. 'I thought you would at least have googled it. Dwynwen is the Welsh patron saint of lovers. A tragic tale indeed. She falls in love with a man, Maelon, but her father has promised her to someone else. She beseeches God to make her heart cold towards Maelon, and an angel appears, and taking her request quite literally, turns her lover to ice.'

'Be careful what you wish for,' I say.

'Quite. One of those stories,' says Ms Davies. 'God grants Dwynwen three wishes; that Maelon be turned back to human form; that Dwynwen, if she cannot have Maelon, remains unmarried for the rest of her life; and that God looks kindly upon all true lovers, in memory of her sacrifice.'

Ms Davies begins to stalk off to the left. 'This island has been known as Ynys Dwynwen since around the fifth century, so quite how anyone could have known it was shaped like a love heart back then is a little beyond me. But, still.'

I watch the glittering sea on the far side of the island as I hurry after Ms Davies. 'An interesting fact, Mr Burney. You cannot see Ireland from Wales, even on the clearest day. Yet you can see Wales from Ireland.'

She has stopped by what I think is a rock, close to the edge of the cliff as it starts to slope steeply towards sea level, but when I catch her up I see it is a weathered flat stone, carved with a name. Edward Davies.

'Your great-grandfather is buried here?'

'He is. And looking out to sea.' A faraway look comes into Ms Davies's eyes. 'You have not asked me why he built the lighthouse, Mr Burney. You are not a very curious sort, are you?'

I shrug. 'Why did he?'

'My family back then owned a shipping company, which mainly operated out of Belfast. There was much traffic between Northern Ireland and the ports in England and Wales. Edward's young wife, Bethan, was intelligent and eager and insisted on working with the company.' Ms Davies points out to sea with her umbrella. 'See that ridge of rocks just sticking up through the water?'

I squint and nod. She says, 'If it had a name before 1876, nobody knows what it is. Now it is called Bethan's Reef. Named by my great-grandfather after the ship his beloved wife was returning home in was lost after those jagged teeth ripped out its hull.'

She turns to survey the tower, now framed against a brilliant blue sky. 'Edward built the lighthouse so that no such maritime tragedy could happen again. He built the cottages to live in. He became a recluse, a hermit, burning the light every night.'

'But not just to warn ships,' I say slowly.

'No. Very good, Mr Burney. Because as I have said, on Ynys Dwynwen, on this heart-shaped island of love, Edward Davies believed the border between this life and the next was whisper-thin. And he built the lamp to help Bethan find her way back to him. And when she did not, he was buried here, looking out to the seas on which she was lost, and maintained in his will that the light should shine every night. For the ships, and for his errant love.'

We are both silent for a while, then Ms Davies begins to march back towards the lighthouse. 'Come. Gwyn Jones is waiting patiently to take me back to the mainland, and there is still much to show you.'

An hour later, I am helping Ms Davies into Gwyn's boat. She seats herself at the prow and looks up at me as Gwyn fires up the outboard. 'I appreciate there is a lot to take in, Mr Burney, but you have all the books and instruction manuals. Acquaint yourself with them. There's nothing else for you to do, after all.'

I nod, feeling simultaneously excited and anxious as the boat pulls away, leaving me utterly alone. 'Just remember, Mr Burney!' calls Ms Davies as Gwyn steers the boat into the waves. 'The light never goes out!'

I watch the boat shrink to a dot in the grey seas, then head along the path to the lighthouse.

A wrought-iron spiral staircase winds up through from the bare stone entrance room. The first floor, the store, is lined with cupboards filled with dried and tinned foods. The next floor houses the old oil store, a big metal tank, now rusting and unused. The third floor was also an oil store, but that has somehow been removed and replaced with two chest freezers and a curtained-off primitive bathroom. At the back of the lighthouse, on the outside, is a generator housed in a wooden shack, and its care and maintenance is detailed in a thick lever-arch file among the many books piled on the table on the next storey, which is the kitchen. There is an electric oven, a microwave, a fridge, and a sink. On a little table to one side is an ancient Underwood typewriter, with a stack of yellowing sheets of blank paper beside it. 'What keepers of yore used to type out their reports,' Ms Davies said. On a whim I scroll a sheet of paper into it and give one of the dusty keys an experimental tap. The ribbon is evidently in good condition because it leaves a clear, distinct mark. I type out, 'the quick brown fox jumps over the lazy dog'. Then I move on.

Above that is my bedroom, a single bed by a window that looks out towards the mainland. The circular room is painted white, spartan but somehow cosy, hidden away within the thick stone walls. Then there is the living room, with a battered couch, an easy chair, a television and a desk. The final floor houses a battery of machines which operate the lamp above, and which come with a pile of books and manuals half as tall as me. And then, above, the light itself.

The lamp is huge and has four faces, as big as lorry wheels, shining out to all points of the compass through thick glass walls that must be kept clean and clear at all times, according to my instructions. A hatch leads out to a steel balcony that runs around the outside of the lamp room and, after making a simple meal of beans on toast, this is where I find myself as the sun begins to dip towards the sea far to the west.

From here I can survey my kingdom, my domain. Ynys Dwynwen. Where I am the lighthouse keeper, having withdrawn from the world and forsaken all others, in order to keep the seas safe for mariners, and maintain a promise made by a long-dead man to his long-lost love.

I look out to the west, watching as the sun sizzles into the sea on the far horizon, drawing the veil of night down, the stars winking into life in a sky so black and as I have never seen.

I feel a thrumming below my feet, the whirring and

clanking of machinery waking from its slumber. Darkness has fallen, and the lighthouse is rousing itself. I hold my breath, gripping on to the cold metal balustrade.

And then, like a supernova, like an atomic bomb, like night being suddenly, impossibly, made day, the lamp explodes into life behind me. It casts my long, lonely shadow out over Ynys Dwynwen and the endless, rolling ocean.

Year Two

Year Two

10

Gayle

17 June

It's my thirty-first birthday party and I am not remotely drunk. Not even tipsy. Not so much as merry. Instead, I am grinning like a lunatic and most decidedly not enjoying myself.

I feel like a spectre at my own feast, drifting around Tom's house, smiling wanly at people I don't know. Well, Tom's and my house, I suppose, after he asked me to move in at Christmas. No, that doesn't feel right. It's Tom's house. I just live here.

In the Arctic white expanse of the kitchen Tom is talking to three other property developers, all wearing open-necked shirts and suits. He catches my eye and beckons me over.

'Bill, I'd like you to meet Gayle.' Bill, who has a shining bald head and a paunch, doesn't break off from talking about investment opportunities in Salford. Without even looking at me he presses his empty glass into the hand I have outstretched to shake his.

The other two men, intently listening to the exchange between Tom and Bill, also hand me their glasses. Tom murmurs out of the corner of his mouth, 'Sorry, darling. But if you could be so kind ...?'

At the wide American fridge-freezer I place the glasses on the marble work surface and pour four more glasses of expensive champagne. I could really do with one myself, but Tom had taken me in his arms an hour before the party, after telling me how ravishing I looked in the ethereal Alice Temperley trouser suit he bought me, and asked me to 'keep my wits about me'. There were going to be a lot of important contacts at the party.

As I take the drinks back to Tom and his friends there's a buzz at the front door. Tom raises an eyebrow at me and smiles, turning his focus back to Bill.

'Fine,' I mutter. 'I'll just have time to answer the door before I take the nibbles round.'

I'm expecting another clutch of Tom's friends, sharp property developer types and their haughty wives who look down on me as though I'm something they've stepped in. What I get when I open the door is a cloud of cigarette smoke and a long belch.

'Donna,' I say, my heart soaring just as my stomach flips.

'Happy birthday, knob,' she says, pushing a bottle of Jack Daniels into my hands. She looks me up and down. 'Or is it your wedding day? Either way, my invite got lost in the post.'

I look over my shoulder, through the entrance hall door and into the kitchen. 'Erm, yeah, sorry I ...'

'You're loved up with Tom and you forgot your best friend. In fact, you haven't spoken to me for three months.'

Donna throws her fag on the step and grinds it under her Doc Marten, making me wince, then pushes past me into the house, looking around and whistling. 'Very nice. Fallen on your feet here, Gayle.'

'Look, Donna, I'm sorry. It's not that kind of party, really. I was going to give you a call to go for a drink, me and you ...'

She takes off her jacket and throws it over the glass and steel bannister. 'I didn't even know your address. I had to use my journalistic wiles to find it.'

'How's work?' I say, taking her jacket and hanging it on the coat stand by the door.

'I left,' she says. 'I sent you a message. Weeks ago. I'm at the *Manchester Evening News* now.'

'Oh, Donna, that's brilliant!' I say. She's always wanted to move up from the little paper she was working on, and the *Manchester Evening News* was always her big ambition.

'Yup. Now, what does a girl have to do to get a drink round here?'

Before I can stop her, Donna marches into the kitchen, and everyone pauses in their conversation to look at her. Her hair is pink now, and she's got one or two more piercings than I remember. 'Hello!' she bellows. 'I'm Donna. Best friend of Gayle.'

After a beat the conversation resumes, just as I catch up to Donna. She glances at me. 'Jesus, Gayle. Do you know *anyone* here?'

'I've met a few of them before,' I say miserably.

'This isn't a birthday party,' she says, grabbing two glasses from the worktop. 'It's a fucking networking event. I presume you've got a garden?'

Of course we have a garden. Of course *Tom* has a garden. A lavishly-landscaped affair with a big swing seat, which Donna and I sit on as she pours two big measures of Jack Daniels.

'I meant to invite you over, but things kept getting in the way,' I say.

'Yeah, life's like that.'

'You're sulking, knob,' I say, nudging her with my shoulder.

'Of course I fucking am! You ditched me for a bloke, Gayle. Whatever happened to sisters before misters?'

I put my hand on her shoulder and she turns to me. 'Donna. I didn't ditch you. You're my best friend. You always will be. It's just ... things have moved pretty quickly the last couple of months. I did mean to get you over.'

'Apart from the fact Tom hates me,' she says mildly.

'He does not!' I say, knowing deep down that while *hate* might be a bit of a strong word, Tom hasn't exactly taken a shine to Donna on the three or four occasions they met after we first got together.

'Anyway,' she says, changing the subject. 'I saw that amazing court case you did. Suing that company that was pumping shit into the river. Brilliant work. I was thinking, it might be cool to do a big feature on your lot. Everyone's getting more aware of environmental issues.'

I've worked on the legal team for EnviroMonitor for five years now. It's a brilliant, scrappy, hard-nosed little charity that was set up in Manchester in the nineties. It keeps a close eye on companies infringing environmental rules and regulations. It was a really good use of my law degree, after I'd been through the hell of working the magistrates' courts as a duty solicitor for a couple of years after university. Satisfying work. Noble. Making a difference.

'I quit,' I say. 'I put my notice in last week.'

Donna stares at me. 'But you loved that job! Did you get head-hunted? Where's the new job? Are you still working in environmental?'

'There is no other job,' I say, and feel suddenly wretched and stupid. 'Tom's work isn't nine-to-five, he's away at weekends a lot and in the evenings, and with me working so hard it felt like we weren't seeing each other much and, well, we don't really need the money and—'

66

'You just *quit*?' says Donna, aghast. Then she stands up and grabs my head, and starts rifling through my hair.

'Ow! Get off!' I yell. 'I just had my hair done this morning! What are you doing?'

'Looking for a … a switch or something,' says Donna. 'You've gone full Stepford Wife, Gayle. You've been replaced by a robot.' She holds me by my shoulders and stares intently into my eyes, scowling. 'Who are you and what have you done with my best friend?'

I take a deep breath. 'Look. It's not quite as simple as all that. I loved my job but I always felt … you know, sometimes, that I wasn't good enough. Looked down on a bit. Working class girl, on a fast-track on-the-job training course straight out of her degree. Felt I was a bit of a diversity hire, sometimes.'

'Bollocks,' says Donna. 'You were good at the job and nobody gave a toss if your dad hadn't been to Eton.'

'Gayle …?'

Donna lets go of me and turns as Tom walks towards us along the gravel path. He smiles thinly. 'Donna. I didn't know you were coming.'

'Thought it might be nice for Gayle to have someone she actually knows at her birthday party,' says Donna, smiling sweetly.

Tom makes a harrumphing noise, then smiles. 'Anyway, you're just in time for the cake. Gayle? Want to come in and do the honours …?'

'I'm afraid I have to leave anyway,' says Donna.

I look at her. 'What? You've only just got here!'

Donna taps the side of her nose. 'Big story I'm working on. Can't say anything. Project Stepford. Very top secret.'

I make a face at her and stand up, fixing my hair. Tom moves to my side and puts his arm around me. I'd always

67

thought it sweet and protective. Under Donna's glare it suddenly feels ... proprietorial. I say, 'Let's fix up a drink. What about this weekend?'

'We've got dinner at the Bryce-Perezes' on Saturday,' Tom reminds me.

'Well, the weekend after, then?'

Donna drains her glass and hands it to me. 'Sure. Let me know what Tom's got planned and we'll fit something in.' She smiles at him, then kisses me, and walks back to the house.

We watch her go and Tom shakes his head.

'What?' I say, annoyed.

He shrugs. 'Nothing. Come on, cake time!'

We walk back to the house, where the lights are off in the kitchen, and as we pass through the bifold doors a chorus of 'Happy birthday' strikes up, sung by complete strangers.

I awake early the next morning, on account of having had almost nothing to drink, save for a couple of glasses of fizz after the excruciating episode where I cut the cake in front of a sea of unfamiliar, mostly uncaring faces. Who, it turned out, couldn't wait to get back to what Donna had been correct about: the main business of the evening, which was networking and cutting deals. I suppose I can't blame Tom really; he does have to work pretty hard in what's a cutthroat business. He seemed pretty pleased with the business he'd done during the evening, and I didn't have a wholly terrible night, despite how it might sound. Plus, he gave me an absolutely stunning Tiffany necklace, which I finger at my throat as I make myself a coffee from his eye-wateringly expensive Fracino Classico machine. I'd probably prefer a Nescafé to be honest, but I haven't had instant since moving in with Tom.

Tom was up before me and away at the gym. He got me a membership there but I don't like it. So exclusive and every woman seems effortlessly toned and trim and perfect. I felt like a fish out of water, huffing and sweating and red-faced in my sloppy joggers and vest top.

I've got my own dressing room in the house and I look at the gym gear he bought me, the tags still on it. Maybe I should make more of an effort. All the wives and girlfriends of his friends who came last night look like they don't skimp on the gym.

I put it back and turn to a pile of boxes I still haven't un-packed yet, just trinkets and personal stuff. On the top is a shoebox full of old photos. A lot of them are from my uni-versity days, where I first met Donna. She was doing Media Studies, me Law. We were on the same floor in the halls of residence in the first year, and then got rooms in a truly dis-gusting shared house together.

I start to flick through the photos and then sit down on the carpeted floor, taking more time to pore over them. We both look so young, so carefree, so full of life and the expec-tation that whatever was thrown at us in the following years, we would handle it.

So many people I've lost touch with. So many friends. I have no idea where they are, what became of them. Lisa and Therese and Vicky and … the next photo brings me up short. Me and a boy, smiling broadly, drunk and happy, our arms round each other, cheeks pressed up tight. I feel a sudden hitch in my breath, a faint yet noticeable thrum of blood in my ears. Gosh. I haven't thought about him for years.

I wonder what he's doing now.

I I

Martin

June

Every morning I do three circuits of Ynys Dwynwen, whatever the weather. I started off walking, then alternating
between walking a hundred yards and breathlessly jogging a
hundred yards, and now, almost one year since I arrived on
the island, I can run the three miles almost without breaking
a sweat.

I stop to stretch at the foot of the lighthouse, wondering
what to have for breakfast. Supplies are running low and
I'm expecting a visit from Gwyn Jones this afternoon, his
first for almost a month. It's been a long time since I spoke
to anyone face-to-face. I don't mind it. The one thing that
I thought I'd hate about this job, the thing that I feared
would make me give up, especially in the first couple of
the months, I now treasure. The solitude. The sense that,
apart from the ships that pass by, sometimes on the horizon,
sometimes closer, I am utterly alone in the world.

I've got a bit of cramp seizing up my right calf, and I
decide to do another circuit, just walking this time. It's a
bright, clear morning and there's a little puffin colony on
the south-west of the island. I'd like to see how their eggs
are doing.

As I walk past the tumbledown cottages, a rapid movement on a broken windowsill catches my eye. A brown
shape darts inside. The Dwynwen Vole, a species apparently
unique to the island. First time I saw them sporting in the
dusk I nearly lost my mind. I thought the place was infested
with rats. Fortunately, among the piles of books left for me in
the lighthouse was a handwritten volume detailing the wildlife of the island, with beautiful watercolour illustrations. It
was written by Edward Davies, Heledd's great-grandfather.
It should be in a museum really, it's such a gorgeous artefact.
But it has proved fascinating. From Edward's book I know
that the Dwynwen Vole was probably introduced accident-
ally by humans to the island some time after the last Ice
Age. Since then they've evolved into their own subspecies,
and live for about eighteen months. Fortunately, they are
very prolific breeders, which is doubly good because owls
often make the non-stop five-mile flight from the mainland
to Ynys Dwynwen to feast on them in the dead of night. I
guess the voles have evolved to be exceptionally tasty. This
place must be like a Michelin-starred restaurant for those
owls, otherwise why would they undertake such a perilous
journey?

Out on Bethan's Reef I can see the Atlantic Greys sporting in the surf crashing on the jagged rocks. Sometimes they
swim over to a little inlet just to the west of the big crevasse, and sun themselves on a little shingle beach. I stand and
wave at the seals, though they never wave back.

Above the reef, riding the thermals from the warming sea,
are a dozen birds, Manx Shearwaters, their wings straight
and stiff. They're silent now, but when night falls they cry
out in a way that had me clutching my bedcovers in terror
the first time I heard them. According to Edward's book,
the undulating shrieks might have given rise to tales of sirens

luring sailors on to rocks. Even the Vikings would not approach an island on which they nested because they thought their cries was the screeching of trolls.

I walk on, to where the puffins have made their nests on a little outcrop. Ten breeding pairs arrived on Ynys Dwynwen towards the end of March. They like this bit of the island because there are lots of rocks with overhanging spaces to secrete their eggs, and a few burrows made by Manx Shearwaters. Each breeding pair lays just one egg, which the puffins fiercely defend, raucously seeing off incursions by razorbills or gannets. I drop to a crouch as I approach, the puffins turning their orange bills and querulous eyes to me. Each pair laid its egg towards the end of April, just over a month ago. They could hatch anytime now, or over the next thirty days.

Not for the first time, I feel a quiet frisson of pleasure that I, Martin Burney, whose previous knowledge of wildlife was limited to seeing the odd urban fox foraging for fried chicken, knows so much about the natural world.

Living alone on a deserted island will do that to a man. As Ms Davies said to me what feels like an aeon ago, there isn't much else to do. I watch the puffins for a while, hoping to see an egg hatch, but as my legs get stiff from crouching I stand and skirt around the colony, walking back to the lighthouse. I'll use up the last of my bacon then polish the lamp, and wait for Gwyn Jones.

I stand on the jetty, watching Gwyn's boat slicing through waves glittering with the afternoon sun. He waves when he sees me, steering the boat expertly in and throwing me his mooring line to secure to the jetty. Behind him there is a huge refrigerated box with my supplies, and a waterproof bag by his side.

'Terrible news, Martin Burney!' says Gwyn as he heaves the bag towards me, which I catch and place on the jetty. 'Awful news!'

'What's happened?' It could be anything. Someone might have died. Ms Davies? For all I know, there could be a nuclear war. I learned very quickly on the island that there is no internet connection whatsoever, nor mobile phone signal. My only contact with the mainland is via a short-wave radio that is touch-and-go at best, and the only person on the other end of it is Gwyn, who often forgets to turn his on.

'The school visit!' says Gwyn, heaving the edge of the refrigerated box out of the swaying boat. 'Here, get on the front of this while I get round the back. It's only off, isn't it?'

Gwyn has lost me as we carry the box along the jetty. 'School visit?'

'Happens every summer. You just missed it last year. Little kiddies from the city.' He frowns at me. 'Did the duchess not tell you? I'm sure it must be in one of the files.'

'Gwyn, I have no idea what you're talking about.'

'Oh! I have something for you!' he says, and scuttles back to the boat. He comes back with a fishing rod and a square wicker basket. 'I found this in the back of the shop when I was cleaning some old rubbish out. Used to go fishing off the rocks. Thought it might be a nice little pastime for you.'

I take the rod and look at it. I've never been fishing in my life. Gwyn is pointing enthusiastically across the island. 'Get over that side, between the island and the reef. It'll be boiling with fish over there, where the seal colony feeds. Bass, mullet, flounder. You'll be able to stock up that freezer. Bloody good for you, fish, isn't it? Brain food, they say. Stop you going bonkers. Although ...' Gwyn pauses and looks at me quizzically. 'Good God, Martin Burney! The state of you! Wild Man of Ynys Dwynwen, is it? When did you last cut your hair? Or shave?'

I rub my chin and tug at what I can't deny has become a mullet. It's been a while. Three months or so, I'd imagine. 'Never mind that, Gwyn. What about this school visit?'

Gwyn scurries back to the boat and brings up a little leather bag. 'Good job for you I was on my way to do Huw Evans. I've got all my kit. Sit on that box and I'll do you now.'

As well as postmaster, shopkeeper, boatman and pharmacist, Gwyn Jones is, I learned in my first year, also a mobile hairdresser, gardener, home brewer and God knows what else. He sits me down on the box and tilts my chin up to him. 'This beard coming all off?'

'No, I quite like it. Just tidy it up. So, school visit ...?'

As Gwyn gets clipping at my beard he says, 'So the Davies family has a link with this school. Back your way, I think. Manchester. I don't know why, but every year they bring the little kiddies across to Ynys Dwynwen. Look at the lighthouse, see all the wildlife. It's the keeper's job to show them round.'

I don't know how I feel about this. The invasion of my island by a bunch of schoolchildren. I'm suddenly feeling quite protective. I don't want a load of snotty kids tramping over the grass, upsetting the nesting puffins. Frightening the voles. I say, 'But it's not happening?'

'I had word from Ms Davies today. Apparently they haven't got enough staff at the school. Rules and regulations, see? Got to have so many teachers per so many pupils, or they can't go on visits and suchlike. Such a terrible shame. They do love coming here, those kiddies.'

I can't say I'm particularly upset by the news. Gwyn

brushes at my beard with a towel then sets about trimming my hair. 'Poor kids. Inner city sorts. Don't get out in the countryside much. Broken homes. Not much hope for them in life. That kind of thing.'

'Ah, well, can't be helped,' I say, suddenly feeling quite jolly. I can't actually think of anything worse than a school visit to Ynys Dwynwen. Gwyn steps back and eyes my hair critically, then looks at me with narrowed eyes. 'Martin Burney, when did you last take leave? I don't believe you have done, have you?'

I shake my head. I'm supposed to get three weeks' holiday from the job, during which time Ms Davies will arrange for a relief keeper. But in my first year I haven't taken any leave at all. I say, 'Where would I go? I'm fine. I don't need a break.'

'Not good for a young man like you to be cooped up all alone on this island,' says Gwyn with a frown. 'You must have friends and family out there somewhere?'

Gwyn's words suddenly bring those feelings of isolation and loneliness from the first weeks on the island crashing back to me, like the waves on Bethan's Reef. I kept switching on my useless phone, vainly trying to connect my laptop to a non-existent Wi-Fi. When I was wondering what Imogen was doing, aching to log on to her socials to find out. When the sudden absence of the meaningless stream of updates from people I didn't know felt like a missing limb. When the lack of pointless stories about celebrities made me feel as though I had gone to Mars, not to Wales. My only link to my old life is the letter that Mrs Carruthers sends me about every three months. Her last one was all about signing Harry up to a gym so he could build up his strength to cope with her strenuous sexual demands, and telling me about a young gay couple who have moved into my old flat.

Then there were three pages of an eye-wateringly detailed account of a liaison Mrs Carruthers had with Gerry and the Pacemakers. All four of them. Then, one day, I woke up and didn't think about my old life at all, and instead went to look at the seals, and the puffins, and watch the porpoises leaping in the sunrise far out to sea, and then spent the night lying on my back in the cool grass, watching the light sweep across the island and the sea. The light from *my* lighthouse.

I shake away the feelings, and they are gone as quickly as they arrived. Gwyn is holding up a square, cracked mirror, and I nod and approve his handiwork.

'Let's get this food in your fridge,' he says. 'And think about taking a break, Martin Burney. It might be paradise on Ynys Dwynwen, but unlike this place' – he stamps his foot on the earth – 'You are not an island.'

'I appreciate your concern, Gwyn, but I'm fine,' I say as we carry the box to the lighthouse. I cast a glance towards the mainland. 'There's nothing for me back there.'

12

Gayle

July

It is Tom's idea to cook a birthday meal for my mother, which is a lovely gesture. He really is so thoughtful. I suggest a barbecue, as it's July and quite nice weather, but he insists on a full Sunday roast. We can, he says, have drinks in the garden afterwards if the weather holds. He also surprises me by suggesting I should invite Donna, who I haven't seen since my birthday, despite our best efforts.

'I thought you didn't like Donna,' I say as I make us coffee.

'Have I ever said that?' says Tom, the Sunday papers spread out on the kitchen island. He's poring over the business pages, hemming and hawing at this and that.

'I suppose not,' I say, putting his drink in front of him and sliding on to a stool, grabbing one of the magazines.

'She's your best friend,' he says absently, running his finger down a column of figures on the shares page. He pauses and looks at me with those eyes that still make me melt inside. 'I don't think she likes me much, though.'

'She's just . . .' I trail off. Just what? I feel as though I should make some sort of excuse for Donna, but I don't really know what I'm making excuses for. It's true. She *doesn't* like Tom.

77

And I know why. I'm not stupid. She thinks I've given up my career for him, my financial independence, any sort of control I have over my life. I look around the kitchen, with its clean white lines and expensive, classy appliances. I think about Tom, expertly and lovingly bringing me to a bone-shuddering orgasm in bed this morning. I glance through the window at the convertible Mini Cooper parked on the drive, registered in my name. I have everything I want. I don't really understand why Donna can't just be happy for me. She knows my family didn't have much money when I was growing up. I suspect she thinks I'm seduced by all this because of that. Thinks of me as some kind of class traitor.

'Why don't you come to the gym with me tomorrow morning?' says Tom. 'You've never properly been since I signed you up.'

And then Tom leans over, pokes my stomach, and says, 'I'm going for a shower,' leaving me looking down in horror at the slight bulge of my tummy over the waistband of my PJ bottoms.

'He did what?' says Donna a couple of days later, holding up a top against herself in Selfridges. 'What do you think of this?' She looks at the price tag. 'Jesus fucking Christ.'

'He was only joking,' I say self-consciously. 'But I have got a bit chubby. All that eating out. I have started going to the gym.' I nod to the top. 'How much is it?'

Donna shows me the price tag and sticks the top back on the rails. 'You look fine. How was the gym? Fucking awful, I bet?'

I pick up the top she's put back. 'It was actually all right. I'm starting a legs, bums and tums class tomorrow. There's a pool and a steam room and everything. I could sign you in as a guest if you want to come.'

'Is there a bar?'

'There is, actually.'

'Sign me into that and I'll wait for you while you get in shape for Tom.' She picks up a pair of jeans. 'Fucking hell. Price of these. Remember when we used to buy everything from Affleck's Palace?'

I do. Wandering the aisles buying vintage clothes and CDs, and incense burners and wind chimes and posters. I have a sudden flash of a memory, an afterburn that I thought had long since faded, having an argument in Affleck's and walking away. For the last time. Not from Donna, though. From—

'These are gorgeous,' Donna says, holding up a pair of cork wedges and sniffing the leather. When she puts them back I pick up a pair of size fives and put them in my basket with the top and jeans. While she wanders off to inspect the underwear I pay for the clothes, and then present them to her.

She looks into the bag at the top, jeans and shoes. 'Gayle. Seriously. You shouldn't have. Jesus.'

'It's not my money. It's Tom's.'

A cloud passes over her face. She doesn't approve. I say, 'Just come on Sunday. Please. Keep me company.'

She considers it, then says, 'Only if you come and get pissed with me now. Like the good old days.'

I pull a face. 'Tom's cooking dinner tonight and—'

Donna pushes the Selfridges bag back into my chest and raises an eyebrow expectantly.

'OK,' I sigh. 'Let's get pissed.'

'This lamb is absolutely divine, Tom,' says my mother. 'And the mint sauce …'

'I make it myself.'

Dad and I exchange a brief glance, not about Tom's

79

prowess in the kitchen, but because my mother is doing her usual thing and speaking to Tom in the sort of voice you might reserve for a garden party at Buckingham Palace.

'How's the wine?' says Donna. 'I didn't make it myself, but I did pick it up at the Co-op.'

'It's lovely,' says my dad. He's always liked Donna, whereas Mum thinks she's a bad influence. I think he considers her unruly and wild and he likes that.

'I've got a lovely Meursault chilling for the pudding,' says Tom. He frowns into the glass of red. 'Might take the edge off this, a little.'

'Tom is an absolute marvel in the kitchen,' I say. And it's true. I've never met a man who could cook as well as he does. He could open his own restaurant, if he wanted to.

When we finish the lunch I tidy the plates away. He says, 'Why don't we do presents before dessert?'

Mum claps her hands delightedly. 'I must say, this is the best birthday ever.'

Dad looks over at her. 'Better than that weekend in Morecambe?'

We all laugh, and Donna says, 'I'll go first,' thrusting a bottle wrapped in newspaper at my mother. 'Don't bother to unwrap it; it's the same plonk we just had. Happy birthday, Heather.'

'Dad?' I say.

'Oh, I gave your mother her present this morning.'

Her face turns sour. 'A new iron. And they say romance is dead.'

Dad looks crestfallen. 'You did say you wanted one.'

Heading off a potential argument, I go to get the gift bag from the worktop, handing it to Mum. It's a lovely gold charm bracelet. She gasps and says, 'Gayle! This must have cost a fortune! It's absolutely beautiful.'

As Dad helps fasten it to her wrist Tom coughs and hands over a long envelope to her. I catch his eye and frown. What's this? I didn't know about another present.

'Just a little something else from Gayle and I,' he says, winking at me. For some reason it infuriates me. Why is he buying presents from both of us that I know nothing about?

Mum opens the envelope and slides out the printed sheets inside, and gasps, looking at Dad. 'Oh, Paul! It's two plane tickets to Paris!'

'And two nights in the Hôtel Plaza Athénée,' smiles Tom, somehow managing to pronounce all the accents in the name. 'Our treat. Happy birthday, Heather.'

Tom has made a brioche bread and butter pudding and his own custard from scratch. It's utterly mouthwatering. Dad says, 'How's business, Tom?'

'Good,' says Tom. 'Great, in fact. Business is booming. We're snapping up some properties really cheap and we've got plans to turn them into really high-end residences.' When Tom says 'we' he means the network of like-minded individuals he chops and changes with, pooling their resources to buy low and sell high. I have to confess, I don't like many of his colleagues. Any of them, really.

'Is that what Manchester needs?' says Donna. I can sense an edge in her voice that means she's just about to tip over into having had too much to drink. 'High-end residences? People are struggling to get on the property ladder as it is.'

Tom shrugs. 'There's a demand out there. I'm just meeting it.'

'Tom's also been developing a new school,' I say, trying to mollify Donna a little, show her it's not all millionaire boltholes.

'State school?' she says, glaring at him.

'Well, no. Private.' He gives a little smile. 'Obviously.'

'Obviously,' says Donna, the word dripping with ice. 'And that'll be another drain on the state education system.'

'How can that possibly be, Donna?' says my mother. 'Surely a new school is good news for everyone, whether it's private or not? I mean, I keep hearing about class sizes and the fact schools are struggling to recruit—'

'And this makes it worse,' says Donna. 'Any decent teachers'll get lured in by the wages. Which leaves a big skills hole in state schools that, as you rightly point out, Heather, they're struggling to fill anyway.'

'I suppose that's just the way things work,' says Dad, quickly trying to change the subject by addressing Tom. 'Did you see the new two-seater Tesla they announced?'

But Donna is having none of it. 'I did a story a couple of months ago on an inner-city school in Manchester. They're struggling for staff so much they've had to combine classes. Sometimes as many as sixty kids in one lesson. They can't even get classroom assistants. This school, it's got this long-standing arrangement with a family who owns an island off the coast of Wales. Every year they take the kids to visit the island. There's a lighthouse on it. Loads of wildlife. Seals. Puffins. These kids, it's often the first time they've been beyond the end of their own street.'

'Sounds lovely,' says Mum.

Donna points her spoon at her. 'Except, Heather, they couldn't go this year. Didn't have enough staff, or classroom assistants. Couldn't engage enough parents to go along. So there wasn't enough of an adult-to-child ratio to make the visit viable.' Donna sits back. 'One bloody day-trip to Wales, once a year. For kids who don't have two pennies to rub together and have never had a holiday. And they couldn't do it because they can't retain enough staff.'

'That's awful,' I say. I think about those little kids on their estate. Looking forward to their trip to the lighthouse. And then being told there's not enough staff. I get a lump in my throat.

'And yet, I bet the parents all have flat-screen TVs and mobile phones,' says Mum, nodding sagely.

I put my head in my hands and even Dad reads the room better than Mum. He puts a hand on her arm and murmurs, 'Heather.'

Donna stands unsteadily. 'I'm going. It was a lovely meal, Tom. Thank you for inviting me. And I hope you have a lovely rest of the day, Heather. Happy birthday.'

'Already?' I say. 'Stay a bit.'

Donna shakes her head. 'Early shift tomorrow.' She takes out her phone and taps at it.

'Want me to run you home, love?' says Dad. 'I've only had a couple.'

'You will not!' says Mum. 'It's bad enough you spent all that money on that stupid sports car without going and getting banned for drink-driving!'

'S'fine,' says Donna. 'I've got an Uber.'

I stand up and Donna embraces me. 'I'll see myself out. Give us a kiss, Gayle. See you soon.'

When she's gone my mother raises her eyebrows and sips her wine, looking over the rim of the glass at Tom. 'Always was a bit highly-strung, that one.' Then, as if by way of explanation, she mouths at him, 'Lesbian.'

'Who's for coffee?' says Tom brightly.

As they all start to chat and bustle around, I take out my phone and quietly text Donna.

What's the name of that school?

83

13

Martin

I am four years old. The sun is slanting through the half-drawn curtains in the living room, and I am sitting on the Chinese rug in front of the gas fire that has not been on for some time because it is summer. Around me, snaking along the perimeter of the rug, is a circular railway track. On it is an engine, which runs off batteries and which is circling the track endlessly. If you put a spot of cooking oil in the chimney it heats up and emits puffs of sour-smelling smoke. I sit on my knees and watch the engine going round and round and round, while my mum talks to two men in the dining room.

They have been in there for what seems like hours. I am hungry and want my dinner. My auntie is with my mum, and the door has been closed, and as you have to go that way to get to the kitchen I daren't interrupt them so I can get a bag of crisps or a KitKat. Instead, I just watch the engine going round and round, not realising that I feel incredibly anxious, and do not know why.

Eventually, the door opens and through the doorway I watch my auntie escort the two men along the hall to the front door. They are speaking in very hushed tones, and it is only when my auntie closes the door on them I realise there is a noise coming from the kitchen. It is someone crying. It is Mum.

My auntie pauses at the door of the living room. I can see she has been crying, too. She beckons for me to follow her and when I walk into the dining room my mum is hunched over on a chair, her face streaked with black tears from where her make-up has run down her cheeks. When she sees me it is as though a sob is ripped from her, and she opens her arms. I run to her, feeling sad and upset myself, though I don't know why.

Until she tells me.

'Martin,' she whispers in a cracked voice into my hair. 'Daddy isn't coming home.'

'Not ever?' I say.

'Not ever,' she says back, taking a deep, ragged breath. 'Your daddy has been lost at sea.'

The next day Dad's face is in the newspapers, along with photos of five other men and a picture of a ship called the MV *Cygnet*. They read out his name on the TV news. I am sure Mum is mistaken and Dad will come back. He doesn't. I am kept off school for a week and when I go back a group of older children push me into a corner in the playground and sing 'What Shall We Do With The Drunken Sailor?'. I don't know what I'm supposed to do but when they sing 'Way hay and up she rises' over and over I put my face in my hands and cry until a teacher comes to see what the fuss is all about.

It takes four years for an official report to be published into the sinking of the MV *Cygnet*. I am still too young to fully understand it, but life has got a little easier. There has been what Mum calls an interim compensation payout, and after the report comes out there is a court case which takes a further two years, and then there is another compensation payout, all of which means we can still live in our house and buy things even though Dad is not here.

By this time I am about to start big school and I have read the report into the sinking of the MV *Cygnet* so many times that I could recite it off by heart. In fact, I think it helped me at school. Nobody else in my class could spell 'exacerbated', or 'structural flaws', or 'longitudinal strength'.

My dad, Terry Burney, was a crewman on the MV *Cygnet*, which was a bulk carrier built in the Netherlands in 1967. She was owned by a company based in Grimsby and registered under a flag of convenience in the Cook Islands. Terry Burney had signed on for one trip only, taking limestone from Colwyn Bay in North Wales down to Cowes on the Isle of Wight.

Not far into her journey, the MV *Cygnet* ran into trouble ten miles off the Llyn Peninsula. A storm blew in unexpectedly on the back of a force eight gale. The ship sank, and a search and rescue mission involving the Holyhead coastguard, lifeboats from Pwllheli, Abersoch and Portdinllaen, RAF Sea King helicopters, and an Irish Naval patrol ship was put out in terrible conditions. Half of the twelve-strong crew survived. Of the six that did not, Terry Burney was among their number. The rescued crew told how, during the storm, a huge wave crashed down on the MV *Cygnet* and effectively broke the back of the ship. The enquiry and subsequent report concluded that this had occurred because the huge quantities of limestone that formed the cargo had been stacked in the centre of the ship, putting tremendous stress on the structure of the vessel.

This, coupled with a poor record of maintenance, and the ferocity of the storm, sunk the MV *Cygnet* and put the ship, upside down, some eighty metres off the coast of Wales.

And there she lies now. Not five miles out, not forty-four fathoms deep, from where I stand, on the balcony of my lighthouse, taking my morning coffee.

Way hay and up she rises, Way hay and up she rises, Way hay and up she rises, Early in the morning!

The sun rises every morning. The MV *Cygnet* stays firmly where she is. And my dad with her. I drain my coffee cup and turn to go back into the lighthouse, and begin my morning chores.

Gwyn Jones spent an afternoon in summer showing me how to assemble the rod, how to attach the lead weight to the line, how to use the big reel. He showed me how to dig under the little shingle beach to the wet sand and catch lug-worms to fasten to the hook, and how to cast the line out in a long, *zzzzzzzzzz*-ing arc until it plopped into the water out towards Bethan's Reef.

Today, the colony of seals is on the reef, watching me with interest as they laze in the September sun and I poach in their feeding grounds. I already have half a freezer full of bass, snapper and mullet, but I find angling is as good for the soul as it is for the belly. The next time Gwyn comes I'll send him back with a freezer box for his shop. I have started giving him Mrs Carruthers's letters when I have finished with them as well – I think he finds them most entertaining, especially the latest missive in which she details a summer she spent with a guru in India in the early seventies, which resulted in her becoming one of his eighteen wives, until she fled in a stolen light aircraft with the guru's ruby necklace, allegedly the source of his mystic power.

'It's all tosh, of course, but entertaining tosh,' Gwyn had said to me. 'You sure she won't mind me reading them?'

'She does love an audience, Mrs Carruthers,' I said.

When I went for the interview at Triune House they outlined where Ynys Dwynwen was, and asked me if I had any knowledge of the area, or affinity with that part of Wales. I did not tell them that I had spent my early teenage years poring over charts of the Irish Sea off the Llyn Peninsula, pinpointing the exact area where the MV *Cygnet* had gone down, extrapolating the distance between the wreck site and the shore, trying to work out if it was possible to swim that distance in a force eight gale.

Until I was sixteen I was firmly of the belief that my dad could have survived. He might have been washed up on Anglesey or the Llyn, possibly suffering from amnesia. Maybe he had spent years eking out a living, working on farms, maybe even following instinct and going back on the ships, with no knowledge of who he really was or the fact he had a wife and son at home in Manchester. One day, I thought, perhaps a loose boom would swing by and catch him on the head, and his memories would come flooding back. We would receive a phone call, or more likely, I would be playing in the street outside our terraced house and he would come walking down it, bearded and windburned and lean, his duffel bag over his shoulder. When he saw me he would stop, and drop the bag, and we would run towards each other. And no matter how old and big I was he would pick me up in his strong arms and spin me around, then we would go into the house together and give my mum the surprise of her life.

I reel in the line, check the lugworms, and cast out again, the sun high above me now. I have been here an hour and not had a bite, yet. The seals are sitting up in a row, and I hear their distant barks on the wind, as though they are laughing at me. One of them belly flops into the water and I see it swimming towards where my line pierces the water, as if to say, *hey, you want to see how it's really done?*

The seal circles my line a couple of times, then dives under the waves. He surfaces just half a dozen metres from the beach and paddles there, watching me. I recognise him. He's a big male with an oval of scars on his left side. Gwyn told me it's likely he had a tussle with a blue shark. I'd gaped at him. 'There are *sharks*? In Wales?'

Gwyn had laughed. 'Blue sharks, basking sharks. Bluefin tuna. Minke whales, too, sometimes.'

The seal rolls in the surf, letting the tide bring him further in. He's never been so close, before. I call this one Bruce, after the nickname the crew gave the mechanical shark on the set of *Jaws*. Bruce pokes his dog-like face out of the water, his wiry whiskers glistening in the sun, his deep, black eyes watching me as I suddenly feel a tug on the line.

Bruce seems to back off to one side, to watch me with interest as I turn the reel, bringing in my catch, a glittering sea bass of reasonable weight.

I'm not quite sure why I didn't tell the Triune House panel that my dad was lost at sea not far from Ynys Dwynwen. To be honest, they probably knew, if they'd done their research. It's in all the newspaper archives, and it of course mentions the tragic loss of life and the families left behind.

I think that after they gave me lots of warning about how lonely life on the island could be, and that it didn't do for everyone, I didn't want to give them any reason to think that I might be mentally unfit for the job. '*Mr Burney, are you quite sure you aren't taking this job in the hope of getting some kind of closure about the death of your father?*' That's what they would have said, or something like it.

And the truth is, after a death like that, after any kind of death, no matter whether it's in a force eight gale or if it's in a small hospital room, attached to a machine, there is no such thing as closure. There is only denial, and grief, and eventual grudging acceptance. And perhaps the odd, nagging feeling that if the miracle of life can be snatched away in a heartbeat, perhaps it can also be gifted back, perhaps death can be reversed, perhaps that hard, stony truth can be made into a lie.

I don't believe my dad is ever coming back, in the same way I know my mum is gone. But the niggling doubt is always there, whenever I look out at sea. *We never found him. What if ...? What if ...? What if ...?*

I slide my net under the wriggling sea bass and lift him out of the water. A fine specimen. I reach into my basket for the slim, metal cosh that Gwyn gave me – the priest, it's called, for administering the last rites to your catch – and bash out its brains. But then I see Bruce, swimming closer, propping himself up in the shallows. He's big. Almost as long as me. I wonder for a wild moment whether he might attack me. Seals can be pretty vicious, I'm sure I read. But his round black eyes are on the fish, not me.

'You hungry, Bruce?' I unhook the fish and I toss it at the seal. He takes it out of the air with an expert bite, throws back his head, and gulps it down whole.

'Hope you enjoyed that,' I say, reaching into my bucket for more lugworms.

'I did, thank you,' says Bruce in a rasping, barking voice. 'It was lovely.'

It's fair to say I am rather surprised.

14

Gayle

January

The first day back at school after the holidays, I know better than to ask the children what they got for Christmas. Britannia Brook is not that sort of school where you ask the kids to write essays on what they did on their holidays, or their favourite present, or what mum and dad do for a job. Today I'm helping out with the Year Fives, and my presence as a classroom assistant has enabled the head of year, Mrs Gaskell, to split the sixty-five pupils into two classes since September, when I started, at least for the two mornings and one full day that I work.

Being a classroom assistant at Britannia Brook is part teacher, part social worker and part zookeeper. I worry about these kids. And I worry about some of the other teachers' attitudes. It's like they've been written off already. Like all there is in their future is jail, alcoholism, teenage pregnancy, drug addiction. It sounds bleak and judgemental, and it is. But that's what people think of these kids. My mum, for one. However, nothing is set in stone, no future is tied to train tracks. Some of these kids are really bright, and even the ones who aren't would have a guaranteed, comfortable life if their families had money to throw at private schooling.

All they need is that one push in the right direction, that one glimmer of hope, that one signpost that points to a route that takes them off the road their lives have set them on. Oh, I don't think it's going to be as easy as that. These kids have been written off by everyone before they've properly started. Even their own parents, half the time.

But I have to try.

A lot of the kids look actually relieved to be back at school after the Christmas break. I can only imagine what it must be like in those houses on the Shakespeare estate where most of the pupils live, the constant bombardment of adverts demanding they spend, spend, spend money they don't have. Loan sharks prowl from early November. And now, in the opening weeks of the new year, they'll be knocking on doors again to collect their first payments.

To that end, I'm not focusing on the recent past, or even the present. I'm asking these kids about the future. Specifically, what they want to be when they grow up.

Kaden wants to be an astronaut. Lyra wants to be an astronaut, too. But I suspect that is because she is infatuated with Kaden. Jamie wants to be a train driver. Kara, Beth and Sorya want to be influencers. Jack wants to be a YouTuber. George, who is a pale, unblinking, slightly disturbed child who mutters to himself constantly, wants to be a Labrador. The class howls with laughter until I calm them down. Taylor wants to be a burglar, like his dad. The class erupts again. Eventually, Maya puts her hand up and says, 'What did you want to be when you grew up Miss Reiss?'

'I always wanted to be a lawyer,' I say. There's a chorus of booing. Lawyers, like the police, like any authority figure, are regarded with suspicion and mistrust on the Shakespeare estate.

'Why didn't you, miss?'

I pause, then say slowly, 'I did. For many years.'

'So why did you stop?' says Maya.

I don't really know the answer to that. Instead I pick up the book I'm reading to them today. *Oh, the Places You'll Go!* by Dr Seuss. Well, one can but try.

This being my full day this week, at lunchtime I sit in the staff-room with the teachers and other classroom assistants, eating an avocado and boiled egg wrap that Tom has pre-pared for me, along with a flask of real coffee. The lunch makes me feel self-conscious among the ham sandwiches and leftover pizza slices everyone else is having, washed down with tea and instant coffee. I know they think I'm slumming it a bit at Britannia Brook. My clothes and my hair and my nails mark me out. But, as they say, beggars can't be choosers, and they're glad of the extra help.

I wonder when I became that person. I never was before. It's just a year since I moved in with Tom and ... well, I suppose I have changed. Not deliberately, but through the gentle osmosis of living in Tom's house, in Tom's world. I bit the bullet and now go to the gym three times a week. I'm a member of a book club run by a property developer's wife. I hardly drink these days. I have no idea who I am.

Mrs Gaskell, the head of Year Five, is a large woman who wears smocks and stripy tights. Bohemian. Had ambitions to be an art teacher, I suspect, though ended up at Britannia Brook twenty years ago and never left. She bustles in and places a sheaf of printed papers on the table in front of me.

'Gayle, can you give these to your Year Fives this after-noon? We need them back signed by whoever's nominally in charge of them by the end of the week. I've printed out double what you need because at least half of them won't make it home, and half of what's left will be thrown away. That's why we have to send them out so early.'

I pick up the top sheet. It's a letter asking for the parent or guardian to give permission for their child to go on a day trip. 'Ynys Dwynwen,' I read. That's the place Donna mentioned back at Mum's birthday lunch. 'This is the trip that was cancelled last year?'

Mrs Gaskell nods. 'We always do it for the Year Fives. Last year was the first year we missed. So we're going to take the Year Sixes as well. We should just be able to scrape together enough staff, so long as nobody leaves or goes off sick between now and June.'

'It sounds lovely,' I say, reading the letter. 'A lighthouse! The kids must love that. How is it that the school goes there?'

'They do love it,' says Mrs Gaskell, watching her green teabag stew in her mug. 'It's a very long-standing arrangement. The island is owned by the Davies family. They're Welsh, but they once owned a large shipping company and had offices in Manchester and Liverpool. Old Edward Davies who ran the company at the time was something of a philanthropist; he had Britannia Brook built for the children of the men who worked for his company unloading ships on the Manchester Ship Canal. Before they built the Shakespeare estate in the sixties all this area was slum housing where most of the dock workers lived. Davies was something of an environmentalist, very ahead of his time, and thought it important that the children get out to experience the natural world.'

'I can't wait,' I say.

Tom had been somewhat nonplussed by my suggestion that I apply to Britannia Brook for a classroom assistant post.

94

'But you don't *need* to work,' he'd said, crinkling his brow as though I'd just told him I was going to Mars.

What he meant was I didn't need to earn money. But that wasn't the same thing as needing to work. I'd never not worked since leaving university a decade before. 'I just want to feel useful,' I'd said.

'You *are* useful.' He'd taken me in his arms and kissed my neck, pressing himself against me. 'Very, very useful indeed.'

Now he is accepting of it, even if he still does not fully understand. I get home to find him in the kitchen, drinking a smoothie, still in his shorts and T-shirt and with a sheen of sweat on his forehead.

'Good squash session?' I say, tossing my bag in the corner.

He wipes his mouth, puts the glass down, then picks up my bag and hangs it off the back of a chair. 'Yep. Good day at work?'

'The kids were a bit of a handful this afternoon,' I say, opening the fridge. I hesitate for a moment and then take out a bottle of wine and pour myself a glass.

'Evidently,' says Tom, eyeing the glass. He's very much what you'd call a social drinker, and even then, what he counts as social occasions are usually always work-related. I'm not sure we've ever been out with other people where some kind of business wasn't discussed. Even that first night, on my thirtieth birthday, he was in the bar to meet someone he was working with. And even when he is out, he never drinks to excess, never loses control.

His disapproval riles me suddenly, and I lift up the glass and say, 'Cheers!' before knocking half of it back.

Tom shrugs and loads his smoothie glass into the dishwasher. 'I'm going to grab a shower. Fancy a bite out tonight?'

I don't, really. The day has worn me out. But it will be nice to get Tom out somewhere and relax, just the two of

95

us, where I don't have to be a passive observer to shop talk and can talk to him as an equal.

'That'd be lovely,' I say. 'Where are you thinking?'

'Roberto's, in town.'

I frown. I've been past that place but we've never been in. Very old fashioned Italian restaurant, by the looks of it. Not Tom's sort of place at all.

He takes off his shirt, flexing his abs and pecs and glancing at himself in the polished silver surface of the fridge-freezer. 'Had word today that the old boy that runs it is on his last legs, and the family are thinking of selling up.'

I sigh. So it *is* work, then. Tom takes another look at himself then heads up to shower. I pour myself another glass of wine and fire up my laptop.

'Ynys' means island in Welsh, I learn, and Dwynwen was a mythical figure who is the inspiration for St Dwynwen's Day, on 25 January, which is basically the Welsh Valentine's Day. Her story is terribly romantic and tragic.

There are some photos of Ynys Dwynwen, including an aerial one that shows it to be a tiny, roughly heart-shaped island in the Irish Sea, off the coast of North Wales. It's dominated by a lighthouse, painted in white and red stripes, and two derelict cottages. There are seals, and puffins, and voles, and all kinds of flowers and grasses. It looks idyllic, with the lighthouse framed by a brilliant blue sky. I suppose it's all very well in summer, but I can imagine it isn't much fun there in winter. The website of Triune House, which apparently is the organisation that runs British lighthouses, says the island employs a lighthouse keeper to live there all the year round. I look out of the window as freezing rain lashes the panes.

Imagine that. Five miles from the mainland, utterly alone on a tiny rock, no one to talk to. Complete isolation. What

sort of person would take a job like that, I wonder, taking a
sip of wine and looking around at my perfect life.

15

Martin

25 January: St Dwynwen's Day

On the flat patch of land in front of the derelict cottages I finish assembling the pyramid of wood and rubbish, taking a step back to admire my handiwork. It is the morning of 25 January, and this will be my second St Dwynwen's Day on the island.

When I first arrived, I asked Gwyn what I should do with the garbage. The food, he said, if there's any leftovers, should go to the wildlife. The paper and cardboard packaging, and anything else I accumulated, should be kept for the bonfire. He would also bring over pallets and bits of wood, and I was told to forage for fallen branches from the small clutch of trees on the south-east end of the island, but I wasn't to break limbs.

The bonfire is a little taller than me, but that is all that is required. I will light the fire at around four o'clock, as the daylight begins to fail, and it will burn until sunset, when the lamps will blaze into life.

I take off my gloves and blow into my cupped hands. It is bitterly cold, and oppressive cloud has hung low over Ynys Dwynwen for two weeks. The salty air precludes snow on my small island, but the temperatures are surely low enough.

So long as it keeps off rain, the St Dwynwen's Day bonfire will be lit.

I take one more look at it, then head back to the lighthouse to prepare for my visitors.

'I think I might have found your dad,' says Bruce. He's flopped up on to the shingle beach, out of the cold January sea. The colony swims over at high tide during winter, when Bethan's Reef is almost covered, sheltering from the biting wind. I learned to stay away from them during these times, even after Bruce started talking to me. Only Bruce talks, and though he assured me that the other Atlantic Greys meant me no harm, I still thought it judicious to give them a wide berth.

The rest of the colony is still on the reef, huddled against each other for warmth. Bruce peers back at them, then catches the fish I toss at him. It's a snapper, one from the freezer that I left out overnight. 'If you've any more I'll take a couple back for the others,' he says.

When Bruce first spoke I leaped to my feet and ran all the way back to the lighthouse. I hailed Gwyn on the short-wave radio and shrilly cried, 'Gwyn! Can seals talk?'

There was a long, static silence then Gwyn said, 'Hmm. You really do need a holiday. Do you want me to come over? I have a third-class degree in psychology from the Open University, haven't I? Got it after Eddie Jones's wife had that episode in eighty-three. Terrible business, that was. Had to talk her down from the roof of Woolworths in Pwllheli. Naked as the day she was born, apart from the top hat and feather boa. Quite a knack for dealing with the mentally unsound, I have. That's why I got the qualification.'

'I'm not mentally unsound, Gwyn,' I'd insisted. 'It was just a dream. Sorry to have bothered you.'

Then I cautiously went back to the shingle beach, where Bruce was patiently waiting. I perched on a rock some way from him and called, 'Are you really a talking seal or am I mentally unsound?'

'Does it matter?' said Bruce. 'Now, are you going to catch me another fish?'

After I'd accepted that the options were acknowledging an Atlantic Grey seal was talking to me, or being psycho-analysed by Gwyn, I came to the conclusion that, as Bruce had said, it didn't really matter. We quite hit it off. And it wasn't long before I was telling him about my mother dying, losing Imogen, and my life in Manchester. And, inevitably, what happened to my dad.

'Oh, he's probably down there,' said Bruce. 'I see loads of them.'

'What?' I'd said. 'Down where? Loads of what?'

'Down on the Bottom. Men. Who've been sunk with their ships.'

'Their skeletons? Their bodies?'

'Sometimes, Keeper. Skeletons and bodies that talk, though.'

'You mean *ghosts*?'

Bruce had shrugged, and it surprised me that seals could shrug, though to be honest once you accept that one can talk, anything goes, pretty much. 'I don't know what a ghost is. They're just men who went down with the ships. I can ask around, if you like.'

In the four months that I've known Bruce, he's come to me three times with potential news about my father. And this is the fourth.

★

It was late October (says Bruce) and it had been a long journey from Australia for the *Royal Charter*, bound for Liverpool. But it was a trip worth making for this chap, because he'd struck it rich at the gold diggings and was coming home a rich man. Rich enough to buy all the fish he needed, I imagine.

They were coming around Anglesey when the weather worsened. This fellow reckons he and a number of other passengers begged the skipper to put in at Holyhead, but he was determined to press on.

Big winds came in. Very big winds. What you'd call force ten. Huge waves. Big as your lighthouse, Martin. The winds got worse. Force twelve, they say, though they'd rarely seen such things.

Late at night, well into the dark, they tried to anchor off the coast but the waves broke the chain, tossing that ship about like a bit of seaweed. Threw the thing on a sandbank, which might have been all right for them, but more winds had come and more waves had come and tossed it right on the rocks.

One man, he says, swum all the way to shore with a rope, so that others could follow. A few did. Most of them were dashed on the rocks, though, their heads breaking open like gull eggs. This chap, he drowned. Couldn't swim ashore, his belt so full of gold. He wouldn't leave it behind, see? Four hundred and fifty souls lost, all told.

Bruce rolls over and licks at the scars pocking his left side. 'Sound like your dad?' I smile. 'I don't think it's my dad, Bruce. But thank you for trying.'

'I'll keep my eyes open,' says Bruce. 'You mentioned fish ...?'

I unwrap the other two defrosted snappers and hold them out for Bruce, who takes them gently in his teeth. 'Mmmff huehu, Mfarifffit,' he says, and rolls unwieldily off the rock and into the water, and swims back to his colony.

At around three-thirty, as the thin, pale light grows cottony, I stand on the jetty and watch Gwyn's boat approach. He isn't alone. He pulls alongside the platform and throws me the mooring rope, and when the boat is secured I help Heledd Davies out.

It is the first time she has been to the island since last St Dwynwen's Day, only the third time I have seen her since I arrived. Ms Davies is wearing oilskins and a woolly hat pulled over her ears, and still manages to have an almost royal bearing as she takes my hand and steps on to the jetty.

She looks me up and down. 'Mr Burney. You are looking well. Life on Ynys Dwynwen suits you, I think.'

'It does, Ms Davies,' I say, finding myself inclining my head. 'It was a tough winter, and I had one day when the generator completely clapped out, but thanks to Gwyn I was able to get it up and running again. The light has never gone out.'

'I know,' says Ms Davies with a thin smile. 'I see it every night from my home on the Llyn Peninsula. It is as much a comfort to me as it is to the sailors who mark their positions and steer a true course around the treacherous reef.' I've spent many a balmy evening over the past two years standing on the observation balcony, watching the winking lights of the ships out in the black ocean, taking pride in my job, knowing that on those vessels they see my light, and pilot their ships safely, and send up silent thanks to me, the Keeper of Ynys Dwynwen.

Ms Davies, Gwyn and I walk towards the bonfire, which I have already doused in oil. We wait while Ms Davies gathers her thoughts.

She begins. 'My great-grandfather, Edward Davies, lit a fire here on every St Dwynwen's Day from the death of his beloved wife Bethan on the cruel rocks of the reef that bears her name. Though he believed the lighthouse would help guide her home, if she was ever of a mind to cross over from that world to this, he also was convinced that the veil was lifted yet higher on St Dwynwen's Day, the day of lovers, of true love lost. If there was ever a day that Edward and Bethan would be reunited, it would be this day, the twenty-fifth of January.'

She pauses and Gwyn nods at me, and I flick my lighter into life, touching it to a clutch of thin twigs bound by twine and dipped in oil. It catches immediately, and I put the flame to the balled-up paper and kindling at the foot of the bonfire.

As the flames crackle and rise, engulfing the dry wood, Ms Davies continues, 'Edward's soul has gone on to its reward, just as Bethan's must have. And yet, we cannot be certain if they ever found each other in the world beyond. So we light the bonfire on St Dwynwen's Day, the day of lovers, and we hope that even for one day each year, in the eternity of endless death, their hearts might come together, here on this precious, sacred isle, their spirits might entwine with the rising smoke, their souls might dance together, found at last.'

Ms Davies lowers her head, as though in prayer. 'And we light the bonfire for all lovers, wherever they are, parted or together, known or unknown, and hope that our flame might bring them together, even for a brief moment in time.' She looks at Gwyn. 'A drink, I think, to toast the lovers.'

Gwyn nods and brings out a flask, which he offers to Ms Davies first. She takes a swig and wipes her gloved hand over the neck, then passes it to me. 'Keeper?'

I take it and the hot Welsh whisky burns my throat, warming my chest. I pass it to Gwyn and he glugs down twice as much as we had.

The lighthouse bursts into life behind us, its four lamps sending cold white beams spearing out into the night, like pale bridges between the worlds. Ms Davies looks up for a moment, her face painted silver by the light, a look of satisfaction on her face.

Then she turns to me and shakes my hand. 'Happy St Dwynwen's Day, Mr Burney. I hope that if you have a love, out there somewhere, the light brings them to you.'

'Ms Davies ...' I say, haltingly. 'This place, this island ...' I know what I want to say, but I don't have the words. Or rather, I do have the words, but my life up to now has pushed those words away, locked them out of my vocabulary. Because there has been no need for them, no requirement to even think of the things they suggest. Not in my humdrum, boring life in Manchester. But now, with the stories of Bethan and Edward, the everyday miracle of nature, and the extraordinary impossibility of Bruce, those words are feeling their way back to me. Or, to be specific, one word.

'Magic,' I whisper. I don't even know how to put it in a sentence. So I just say it again. 'Magic.'

Ms Davies glances at Gwyn, and the look that passes between them feels supercharged with something like the electricity which powers the lighthouse, yet as intangible as the light that issues from the lamps.

'Magic, Mr Burney?' says Ms Davies, a smile playing on her lips. Then she turns and walks back to the boat with Gwyn, and I follow and stand on the jetty. I watch them disappear into the night, wondering if there really is a love for me beyond the shores of this heart-shaped isle, and whether they can see my light, wherever they might be.

Year Three

Year Three

16

Gayle

July

'Three men went to mow! Went to mow a meadow! Three men, two men, one man, and his supersonic sausage dog with rubber wellies on its feet and a Hitler moustache on its face, went to mow a meadow!'

We have only just passed Chester and the children have been singing this relentlessly since we left school at the crack of dawn this morning. With a few variations, it's a version of a song we used to sing on school trips. The novelty, it has to be said, has somewhat worn off.

'I suppose we should be gratified they even know who Hitler is,' says Mrs Gaskell, sitting up at the front of the coach with the teachers, classroom assistants, and the few parents who have been coerced into coming along. We have filled two coaches, the other one following behind and no doubt equally raucous. Mr Jensen, who teaches the Year Sixes, gives Mrs Gaskell a withering look. 'What they don't learn from us they'll learn at home.'

'Ken,' murmurs Mrs Gaskell. 'Don't be horrible. That's such lazy stereotyping.'

'Well,' says Mr Jensen, looking out of the window as we cross into North Wales. 'Bloody Shakespeare estate. Most of them on there wouldn't know the Bard if he came up and snapped their vapes in two.'

Mr Jensen has been at Britannia Brook even longer than Mrs Gaskell. He's probably not even fifty, but he's pale and hunched, his face etched with lines. *Must have had a tough paper round*, Donna would say, and I suppress a smirk.

We sit in silence for a bit until the children start chanting, 'It's all gone quiet at the front! It's all gone quiet at the front!' Then a scrunched-up supermarket own-brand crisp packet flies over and bounces off Mr Jensen's grey hair.

'Right!' he bellows, standing up and facing down the coach. 'Who threw that? Kaden Miller-Price, was that you?'

Maya tugs on his beige jacket and he glares at her. 'What?'

'I ate all me Jaffa Cakes sir and I feel sick,' she says, then splurges a brown and orange vomit on his slip-on shoes. The coach erupts in wild cheering.

A little under three hours after setting off we arrive at the Llyn Peninsula, sticking out into the Irish Sea like a finger below Anglesey, curling in around Cardigan Bay. Our two coaches pull up on a country road by what looks like some kind of general store with nothing else around it. We get the kids off the two coaches and assemble them in lines so we can take a head count. 'See,' mutters Mr Jensen. 'Like the bloody Nuremberg Rallies, isn't it?'

'Look, miss!' shouts Taylor, pointing out to the sea glittering in the June sun. 'I can see the lighthouse!'

He's right. Out on the small island, Ynys Dwynwen, shimmering in the summer haze, is the lighthouse.

'Do we get to go up it, miss?'

Mr Jensen groans and shudders beside me.

'I'm not sure, Taylor. We'll find out when we get there.'

A small, dark-haired man with a beaming smile emerges

from the shop. 'Britannia Brook, is it? Welcome back! I'm Gwyn Jones!'

'Mr Jones,' says Mrs Gaskell, walking over to shake his hand. 'Oh, we missed our visit last year.'

'And Ynys Dwynwen missed you, Britannia Brook,' says Gwyn. 'We have a new keeper, by the way. Old Benson had to call it quits. His hip wasn't up to the stairs.'

'Nothing lost there,' murmurs Mr Jensen to me. 'Right crusty old bugger, he was. Hated the kids.'

'More than you do?' I say.

Mr Jensen pulls a face. 'If I hated those kids, Gayle, I wouldn't have been at Britannia Brook for nearly twenty-five years.' Then his head snaps round, as if through some sixth sense, and he yells, 'Put it away, Brooklyn Simms! Nobody wants to see that!'

Gwyn Jones claps his hands. 'Right, Britannia Brook! The boat's all shipshape and Bristol fashion and there's a lovely packed lunch on board for everyone. Who wants to go to the island?'

Mrs Gaskell quiets the cheering children and says, 'Right! Everyone get into pairs! Hold your partner's hand and we're walking like a crocodile around the headland to the boat!'

Everyone pairs up except for pale, thin George, who looks around anxiously. I hold out my hand to him. 'Come on, George, you can be my partner.'

He puts his tiny hand in mine and we walk in a long column along the grassy verge until we come to a stone jetty on which a battered pleasure cruiser is moored.

'Ain't she a beauty?' beams Gwyn. 'The *Angharad*. Have you all got your sea legs, Britannia Brook?'

The kids shout, 'Yes!' and Gwyn says, 'Well, follow me, then!'

It takes half an hour to get the kids on board, then Gwyn

puts on a Greek fisherman's hat and takes the helm, beckoning me and George over as he pilots the boat out of the little cove and towards the island. George says, 'How far is it, Mr Gwyn?'

'Five nautical miles!' announces Gwyn, wrestling with the wheel. 'You know what a nautical mile is, George? One point one-five-oh-eight land miles!'

As the boat chugs on, Gwyn points out to sea. 'See those? Seals! Come to say hello!'

George stares at them, wide-eyed, the wind whipping his thin, blond hair. He tugs at my sleeve. 'Miss, I don't want to be a Labrador any more when I grow up. I want to be a seal.'

'Good choice!' roars Gwyn, laughing. 'No better life than that of an Atlantic Grey! The new keeper'll tell you that! They live on the reef on the far end of the island. You'll be able to see them later.'

'He lives there all alone?' I say. 'In the lighthouse? What's he like?'

Gwyn leans in to me and taps his forehead with a weathered finger, the nail bitten to the quick. 'Mad as a box of frogs, if you ask me. But I've said too much. Lovely bloke, really. And I know he's looking forward to seeing you all.'

It takes about an hour to get across, and we have only five bouts of throwing up, which is pretty good for so many children. Gwyn steers the *Angharad* in to a sheltered little cove with a long wooden jetty, then leaps off to secure the boat.

'Come on, ye landlubbers! Welcome to Ynys Dwynwen! I'll go find the keeper, tell him you're here.'

It takes another half an hour to disembark the children, then get them standing in rows again so we can do another head count. 'Good job there's not a gift shop on here or we'd have to empty their pockets before we left,' says Mr Jensen under his breath.

'Ken, will you *stop* that?' says Mrs Gaskell. 'If you were really a good socialist you wouldn't be branding them with stupid labels.'

'Sorry,' says Mr Jensen, looking genuinely contrite. Suddenly, he frowns. 'Carol, did you do a count? How many have you got? I'm one down.'

The children are fidgeting, looking up at the lighthouse framed by the brilliant blue sky. It is an impressive structure. I wonder what it's like to live here? A fairly spartan life, not much in the way of home comforts. I look around the island. Tiny little place, though beautiful. And those two tumbledown cottages must have been lovely in their prime. I wonder who lived in them?

'You're right,' says Mrs Gaskell. 'We've lost one.'

'Bloody hell,' moans Mr Jensen. 'We've barely got off the boat. Who is it? Do we need to do a register?'

I look around wildly. I suddenly know who's missing. 'It's George. He was right here a minute ago.'

'Oh God,' says Mr Jensen. 'He could be anywhere. He's always doing this. Wandering off. Are we sure he got off the boat?'

I run over to Gwyn. 'Have you seen the little boy who was with me? George?'

Gwyn frowns and rubs his chin. 'I haven't, love. I'll go and get the keeper, see if the little 'un's gone into the lighthouse.'

Mrs Gaskell is organising a search party of the adults, while Mr Jensen is trying to keep the children in their rows. Damn. George was with me. I should have kept a closer eye on him. I feel myself pale in the June sunshine. What if something happens to him? You hear about that all the time on school trips, don't you? Teachers not taking enough notice of the kids.

I moan and start to stalk towards the lighthouse after Gwyn, praying that George has just gone there for a look. He's so easy to miss, such an invisible little boy. Hardly anyone takes any notice of him. Such a simple thing for him to slip away unnoticed. My heart is already breaking for him even as terror is churning in my gut.

Then I happen to look across the island and I see a tiny figure picking his way through the tall grasses. George. I set off at a run after him.

'George ...' I say carefully and slowly. 'George, come away from the edge, sweetheart.'

He's standing right on the brink of what must be a thirty metre drop. The island has risen up from where we docked, to a cove that plunges down to some vicious-looking rocks, the waves crashing on them. George is pointing out to sea, to the narrow ridge of what must be the reef Gwyn was talking about.

'Seals, miss!' says George happily.

'Yes, George, seals.' I hold out my hand to him. 'Why don't we take a look at the lighthouse first and then the nice man Gwyn will give us a better look at the seals?'

George gazes out at the ocean, reflecting the shimmering sun. 'I want to be a seal, miss.' Without taking his eyes off the shapes on the reef, he says in a small voice, 'Do you think daddy seals hit the boy seals when they haven't done anything wrong?'

Oh my god. My heart is cleaved in two. I shake my hand at him. 'George. Please just come here, baby.'

'I bet they don't,' he says. 'I bet daddy seals are the best daddies in the world.' He takes a step forward, and I hear a sprinkling of stones falling into the chasm. Should I make a grab for him? What if I panic him and he falls? I look frantically behind me. Thank God, the rest of them are coming. Gwyn and Mrs Gaskell and Mr Jensen and another man, stalking ahead at the front. The lighthouse keeper. But they're still half the island away, and George is edging closer to the brink.

'I bet they'd let me be a seal,' says George. 'I bet there's a daddy seal who would look after me and make me the happiest boy seal in the world.'

'George,' I say. 'Come with me and I promise I won't let anyone hurt you again. I'll make sure of it. Just take my hand.'

George half turns and smiles at me. Then the ground crumbles under his feet and he cries out, and disappears from view. I scream and fly forward, hands grasping for where he stood, and then I feel the edge of the cliff give way and there's suddenly nothing under my feet.

17

Martin

I lean on the balustrade that runs around the lamp room and watch the school visit disembarking from the *Angharad*. I already feel as though I have been invaded. The prospect of dozens of snotty kids trampling over the island fills me with anxiety. In fact, the thought of so many people around me at all makes me shiver. In two years the most company I've had is Gwyn and Ms Davies on two St Dwynwen's Day bonfires. Heledd writes to me occasionally to remind me I am due three weeks' leave every year, but I have no desire to depart Ynys Dwynwen, even for a week. I mentioned that to Bruce this morning.

'What exactly would you do if you left the island?' says Bruce, sunning his belly and chewing thoughtfully on a mullet he's caught himself.

I shrug. 'I could go back to Manchester, I suppose.'

'Is that a ship?' I forget he only knows the sea, and the island, and ships. For a crazy moment I imagine taking him with me, pushing him along Deansgate in a trolley, him expressing amazement at the buildings and shops.

'No, it's a city,' I say. It's too much effort to try to explain what that is. 'Or I could go on holiday. Abroad.'

'Is *that* a ship?'

'No. It's ...' I wave my arms vaguely at the ocean. 'Everything else that isn't here.'

Bruce rolls himself on to his stomach with a great deal of effort. 'And what do they have in this *abroad*?'

'Beaches. Sunshine.'

'So, like here, then.' Bruce nods to himself, as if trying to understand why somebody would swap one thing for another if it was exactly the same.

'Except there are more people.'

Bruce waggles his whiskers and looks at me. 'Is that what you want? More people?'

'Not really. Not at all. I don't have much choice today, though. It's the school visit.'

'The Little People!' says Bruce happily. 'They didn't come last year. Are they here today? I'd better go and tell everyone.'

'How many of these visits have you seen, Bruce?'

The seal frowns. 'Ten? I don't know. Something like that.' He starts to flop towards the sea then pauses. 'Oh, yes, I think I might have found your dad.'

Did you know (says Bruce), that they make ships that go underwater? On purpose? Not sinking ships, but ships that swim like whales and can go right down to The Bottom, and come back up again?

That's what this fellow was in. Called the *Thetis*. They built it in a place called Liverpool, which I suppose now is one of your cities, like your Manchester.

They had one hundred and three men on board, one of them being this chap. Sailor. But an underwater sailor. Submariner, he calls himself. Only a young chap, at least when he got sunk to The Bottom.

Apparently they were testing out this boat. To see if it

could sink, and not drown everyone, and come back up, like a whale breaching the surface.

It didn't go very well.

Way this fellow tells it, the underwater boat wouldn't go underwater properly. So the men, they all scratched their heads and tried to open all these tubes where water was supposed to come in and out. So, says the chappie I spoke to, somebody had the bright idea of opening one of these tubes inside the boat. Nobody knew why. And what happens if you open a door in a boat? The sea comes in.

The boat sunk good and proper then. One hundred and fifty feet down to The Bottom ... as deep as your lighthouse is tall.

They had this plan, though, see. Get a man in an escape chamber, fill it with water from the outside, and let him swim up. They did this four times but the last time the man panicked. Didn't shut the door properly. Nobody else could use this hatch then. So the rest all died. Ninety-nine of them. Including this fellow I was talking to. Slow death. Poisoned by the gases that came out of their own mouths.

'Horrible,' I say, thinking of almost a hundred men cramped together in a submarine. 'But not my dad, Bruce. Thank you anyway.'

'No problem,' says Bruce, rolling himself into the sea. 'Have fun with the Little People. Bring them over here to wave at us.'

'I will,' I say. 'Best not speak to me, though, when they're here.'

Bruce shrugs. 'If you say so.' Then he dives into the depths, surfacing near Bethan's Reef.

There's probably about ninety-nine of these kids milling about down there, I think as I finish my coffee on the platform. Imagine being stuck in a stricken submarine with that lot. I shudder. The teachers are organising them into rows, and I see Gwyn wave at me. I groan. Well, the sooner this begins, the sooner it'll be over. I decide to head down and take the bull by the horns.

I've barely got down to the entrance when Gwyn comes rushing in, all of a panic. 'Keeper! They've only gone and lost one of the kids! Little lad, isn't it.'

'Already?' I say. 'They've barely got off the boat! Where's he gone?'

Gwyn grabs my arm. 'If they knew that, he wouldn't be lost, would he? Come on, we need to help.' I take off my jacket and roll up my shirtsleeves as we exit the lighthouse.

'Mrs Gaskell,' says Gwyn to a large woman in a flowing smock. 'This is our keeper, Martin Burney. Knows the island like the back of his hand.'

'Tell me about the boy,' I say.

'George, nine years old, about this high,' she says, holding up her hand. 'Pale, quiet boy. Blond hair. He—'

'Look!' says a grey-haired man, pointing across the island.

I follow his outstretched arm to where there are two figures, standing right on the edge of the crevasse on the far edge of the island. I turn to Gwyn. 'Ropes. Just in case.'

Gwyn nods and heads to the lighthouse as I begin to stalk through the grasses towards the figures, the teachers falling in beside me.

'Who's that with him?' I say.

'That's one of our teaching assistants,' says Mrs Gaskell. 'Her name is—' But then she's cut off as there's a distant scream and both figures disappear from sight.

Shit. They've gone over.

Gwyn has caught us up and I grab the coiled rope from him and set off at a sprint for the edge of Ynys Dwynwen.

'Stay back!' I order the others, and edge forward to the crumbling earth at the lip of the crevasse. I lean forward as far as I dare and peer over, and heave a sigh of relief. There are two of them, on a narrow ledge about ten feet down, hidden in the shadow of the cliff.

'Are you both all right?' I call. 'Any injuries?'

'I've got a slight cut on my head but George is fine.'

'Stay still! I'm coming down.'

I tie the end of the rope securely to a rock buried in the earth, then loop it under my leather belt. I hand the other end to Gwyn. 'I'm going to abseil down. Feed this rope out as I go. Then I'll tie it to the kid and the teacher and you can pull them up one at a time.'

Gwyn nods and takes up the slack. I lean backwards over the edge, pulling on the rope, and look down to the ledge. 'I'm coming down! Don't move.'

The other teachers take hold of the rope with Gwyn, as though in a tug-of-war, and I start to step backwards, leaning out and putting one foot over the other as I descend into the craggy depths. I look down at the teacher – teaching assistant, whatever the woman said – who's hugging the boy. The ledge is narrow, only three or four feet, but just enough for me to stand on. As my boots hit the ledge I tug on the rope to let Gwyn know to not let any more out.

'OK,' I say. 'I'm going to tie this rope around the lad and we'll have him pulled up then you can go next, Miss ...?'

She looks up at me, and her brown eyes widen. My breath catches in my throat.

'Martin,' she says.

I stare at her.

'Gayle.'

The kid, George, is absolutely fine. In fact, he seems to have become a bit of a celebrity by the time we all get back up. 'I just wanted to be a seal boy,' he says happily as the others crowd round him. 'Then I fell over. Then Miss Reiss fell over.'

Miss Reiss. Then she's not married. Or she could just not be using her married name at work. Or might not have taken her husband's name at all. My mind is whirling and my stomach is flipping. Everything seems speeded up and slowed down, as though I'm drunk or high. I need to anchor myself to the here and now, and then, thank God, someone speaks and gives me something to focus on.

'Ooh, that looks like a nasty gash,' says the teacher, Mrs Gaskell.

I inspect the cut on Gayle's forehead, trying not to look into her eyes. 'It's not too bad. I've got a first aid kit in the lighthouse.' I turn to Gwyn. 'Would you mind taking them round while I take Ga— Miss Reiss to the lighthouse? Show them the puffin chicks, but don't let them get too close. And Bruce sa— Erm, then show them the seals on the reef.'

Gwyn salutes and leads them off along the shoreline, and I walk back to the lighthouse with Gayle.

Gayle. I mean. *Gayle.*

I try not to look at her but at the same time feel the weight of her stare as we near the lighthouse. Eventually she says, 'So. Lighthouse keeper. Wow.'

I turn to look at her at last, and it's like I've been punched in the gut. 'So,' I say. 'Teacher.'

'Teaching assistant. Big difference.'

'Not a solicitor, then?'

She shakes her head tightly, her dark hair swishing over her shoulders. Good God, she's beautiful.

'Not for a while,' she says. 'I was but I …' She trails off.

'Lighthouse keeper. Wow, though.' She looks me up and down. 'You're looking well, Martin. *Really* well. So tanned and fit.' She pauses, suddenly embarrassed.

I shrug, suddenly awkward, like a teenager. 'It's been a while.'

'Ten years,' she says.

'Nine years, nine months, two weeks and four days,' I mutter and she laughs.

'Sorry, did I say that out loud? I'm not used to people. Not anymore. I forget myself, sometimes.'

She looks at me quizzically but says nothing else until I lead her into the lighthouse and up to the kitchen. I sit her at the table and hesitantly clean her wound. She closes her eyes as I rub an alcohol wipe over it. Then I apply a couple of butterfly bandages to close up the cut. It feels ... odd, touching her again. My fingers spark with something like static electricity as they brush her skin. Something like it. She opens her eyes and they meet mine.

I forget to breathe for a long, long moment.

It's as though the air has stilled. The seabirds have been frozen in the blue sky. The wind has ceased its whispering through the grasses; the voles have paused their scratchings.

There is nothing but her eyes and mine.

Nine years, nine months, two weeks and four days. Since my heart was shattered into more pieces than there are stars in the sky.

Then there is a brittle scream and laughter outside. Whatever spell was wrought for that elongated moment here is broken.

'They're back,' I say. 'We'd better continue the tour.'

18

Gayle

'Martin?'

'Yes.'

'*Martin Burney*, Martin?' says Donna.

'Yes.'

'Martin. The "feckless, hopeless, unambitious, jealous twat" that you never want to see again Martin?' says Donna.

'Yes! Martin!'

Donna takes a drink of her wine and says, 'Fucking hell.'

'Fucking hell,' I agree. I could not wait to tell her what had happened as soon as I got back from Wales.

'And he's a lighthouse keeper?'

'Yes.'

'And he's tanned and lean and has a beard?'

'Mm-hmm.'

'And he saved your life and a kid's after you fell off a cliff?'

'Pretty much.'

'Fucking hell. Even *my* ovaries are exploding.' She pauses and considers her drink. 'And you're definitely sure it's the same Martin?'

I'd met him in the first term of uni. He was on the floor above me in halls, and I found him in the basement, where the washing machines were, staring at the open door of the appliance as though it were a gate to hell.

As I loaded my knickers and leggings into an empty machine, I watched him with a sideways glance. He was rubbing his chin and shaking his head. He was thin and wiry and his hair was a mess. He had a nice face, though.

'You need a washing tab,' I said to him. 'And some fabric conditioner.'

He looked at me blankly. I said, 'Have you never used a washing machine before?'

He raised one eyebrow. I nodded. 'Mummy's boy.'

He didn't argue, nor did he stop me throwing one of my tabs in with his clothes and pouring some of my conditioner into the drawer. I set it to the general programme and pressed the button. Martin's face broke into a wide, infectious grin as the machine whirred into operation.

'Martin,' he said, holding out his hand. 'Martin Burney.'

I laughed and shook his hand. 'Gayle. Gayle Reiss.'

'Thank you,' he said, scratching his head. 'I should ...' he trailed off. 'Do you want to go for a drink?'

'Now? It's only half-ten.'

'No, no, later. Tonight.' His face suddenly looked stricken. 'Or tomorrow. Or not at all. Have you got a boyfriend? I didn't mean ... I meant a drink. To say thank you.'

'You already said thank you.' I didn't like teasing him but it was like shooting fish in a barrel. His contorted expressions of awkwardness and confusion were ... well, quite cute.

I decided to put him out of his misery. 'Meet you in The Pipers at eight?'

His features rearranged themselves into a grin. 'Brilliant. See you there, Gayle.'

★

It took us until the following April to sleep together, and that was more by accident than design. We'd flirted with each other for months, but I certainly wasn't looking for a boyfriend, and definitely not in my first year. I had a number of liaisons with highly unsuitable boys, none of which led to anything more. We were in the student union bar one night, me with my friends – including Donna – and Martin with his, and some mutuals who drew our circles together like a Venn diagram.

Also there that night was a guy whose name I can't remember, a boorish, rather thick medical student who cared more for rugby and beer than learning how to heal people. I'd slept with him the month before, and not returned his calls or messages after that. He was a dull, mechanical shag who put his own short-lived pleasure before mine. However, with his rugby mates and full of booze, he'd decided a return fixture was on the cards.

It wasn't, but that didn't stop him constantly harassing me and trying to feel me up among the crush of people. I told him loudly and clearly to fuck off, and suddenly Martin was at my side, dwarfed by the other guy, asking if I was all right.

'Piss off,' said the rugger bugger.

I remember Martin's face cycling through a number of the expressions before he settled on one he must have imagined was quite menacing. 'No, you piss off. She's not interested. She just told you.'

Half an hour later Martin was sitting on my bed in halls, his head tipped back while I dabbed the blood pouring from his nose. 'I don't think it's broken,' I said. 'That was a very stupid thing to do. But also quite sweet.'

I kissed him. He didn't go back upstairs until the following morning.

After we returned from the summer break for second year – me doing Law, Donna Media Studies, Martin English – I did something I hadn't done in first year. I slept with the same boy twice. Which made Martin and I, somehow, something of an item. Then we became a couple. And it seemed I had a boyfriend. And Martin was sweet and thoughtful and funny and sexy and it was all rather heady and fabulous.

'You're mad,' Donna had said in the kitchen of the frankly disgusting student house we'd moved into with two other girls.

'You don't like Martin?'

'I think he's lovely. But you're nineteen. And you've tied yourself down.'

'I haven't,' I said, peering at what looked like a sprinkling of mouse droppings just under the fridge. 'It's not like we're getting married or anything.'

Donna filled the kettle. 'Have you seen the way he looks at you, Gayle? He's utterly in love with you. He's like a puppy. He thinks this is it, he thinks you're the one. You're going to break his heart, you know.'

After we graduated, Donna got a job on a little weekly newspaper in Cheshire. I started my solicitor's training and temped at a firm in Manchester. Martin moved back into his mother's house and declared he was writing a novel.

My job involved making tea and coffee and accompanying the solicitors to the magistrates court, where they would be handed files and asked to defend what was quite often the indefensible. One morning I asked Aiden, one of the senior solicitors, how he could with a clear conscience defend a man who had spent a night in the police cells after being arrested on a charge of beating up his wife.

'Because the fundamental right to be treated as innocent until proven guilty is enshrined in British law, as well as under Article 11 of the United Nations' Universal Declaration of Human Rights,' said Aiden with a sigh. 'Even for ...' He checked his notes. 'Even for Barry Tomlinson, who has, almost without a shadow of a doubt, been using his poor wife as a punchbag for several years now, looking at his antecedents.'

Aiden looked at me. He was about thirty-five, dressed well, was nicely groomed, smelled nice. Handsome, charming and witty, if a little world-weary. 'Come for a drink with me after and I'll explain how we as solicitors reconcile this with our own principles.'

I was thrilled he'd said *we as solicitors*. I was still in training but he'd counted me in his number. So of course I said yes.

I'd been in the job for six or seven months when it all kicked off. Donna, Martin and I were in town on a bright April Saturday afternoon, traipsing around Affleck's Palace so Donna could spend her meagre wages on vintage clothes, incense and tarot cards. Martin trailed after us, evidently sulking.

'What is it?' I demanded eventually. Electronic music was pumping out from a CD stall. It was giving me a headache, but I had been out until nearly two that morning, drinks after work.

'Yeah, Martin, what's up? Your face looks like it just discovered it's related to your arse,' said Donna.

'It was our anniversary last night,' said Martin sulkily.

'Which one?' I said carelessly. Martin was big on anniversaries. The date we'd officially become a couple. The date we'd been on holiday together for the first time, to Greece. The date we did a Lidl shop together. I thought it was sweet at first. Now I found it cloying and childish.

'You know. The night I got in that fight. And we ...'

'Jesus Christ,' I muttered.

'Was *he* there last night? I suppose he was.'

By *he*, Martin of course meant Aiden. I'd taken Martin on a couple of work nights out, and he immediately took a dislike to Aiden. And nobody really liked Martin. They were all hard-working, professional go-getters. Martin was increasingly dressing like a tramp, and the much-vaunted novel amounted to a few pages of quite frankly up-its-own-arse postmodern crap.

'Of course Aiden was there. He's a colleague.'

Martin snorted. Donna decided to take matters in hand. She stood between us, a hand on each of our chests. She looked at me. 'Gayle. Have you shagged Aiden?'

'No!' I said.

Donna turned to Martin. 'Then pull your big boy pants up and chill your boots.'

But I was hungover, annoyed, and this felt like the last straw. I narrowed my eyes and said, 'You know what, Martin, I've had enough.'

He stuck out his bottom lip. 'I'll go then, shall I? Call me later.'

'No,' I said, taking a deep breath. 'Martin, you're a feck-less, hopeless, unambitious, jealous twat and I never want to see you again.'

Then I stalked off, out of Affleck's, and into the April sunshine, feeling simultaneously gutted but also lighter than air.

'It was definitely the same Martin,' I say to Donna as she waved for more drinks. 'Except totally not the same Martin at all.'

'Wow,' she says. 'Did you tell him about Tom?'

I start on my next glass of wine. 'No. Why would I? We really didn't get much chance to talk, to be honest. Other than to ask each other how we were. And he fixed up the cut on my face.'

Donna's eyes widen. 'You mean, like you fixed up his busted nose the night you first shagged him?'

I shrug non-committally.

'And there was nothing between you? No spark? Nothing?'

I think about how our eyes met in the lighthouse, how everything seemed to suddenly melt away, how time seemed to stop. How I remembered all the things I'd liked about him. No, all the things I'd *loved* about Martin, and suddenly couldn't recall the things that made me dislike him at all.

'Donna,' I say. 'It's been nearly ten years.' *Nine years, nine months, two weeks and four days.* 'Of course there was no spark. It was just nice to see him again, know he's doing all right.'

Donna nods and takes a drink, not taking her eyes off me. 'Liar.'

19

Martin

August

Once a month I take my fishing nets and load them up into the dinghy and head a little way into the Irish Sea, doing a full, leisurely circuit of Ynys Dwynwen. But I'm not after sea bass, snapper or mullet.

I'm catching plastic.

I'd noticed it in my first year on the island, washing up on the shingle beach opposite Bethan's Reef, gathering in the swirling eddies near the jetty. Carrier bags, bottles, burger boxes, beer can rings. Sometimes things like petrol cans, Tupperware boxes, even a couple of kayak oars. When I've gathered enough I burn it, not on St Dwynwen's Day but in a dark, bleak ceremony that's almost the antithesis of the Welsh day of love. A pile of plastic doused in oil that sends black, acrid fumes up into the clear sky, a dour reminder not of love, but of hate. Because, we must hate the planet to choke its seas with this shit, right?

I suppose I've become quite evangelical about this sort of thing. Never used to give it a second thought before I became the keeper of Ynys Dwynwen. I was as wasteful and careless as everybody else, stuffing plastic and cardboard into the bin and then not thinking about it any further.

But here, on the island ... I fire up the outboard motor and steer the dinghy out a hundred yards or so, to where a carrier bag floats just under the surface like an obscene parody of a jellyfish. I scoop it up in my net and put it into a bin liner. I suppose I've become a lot closer to nature. A lot more conscious of how fragile everything is, how finely balanced. Left to its own devices, nature maintains a course, keeps its equilibrium. Everything has a role, a place. The Dwynwen Voles scamper around the derelict cottages; the owls fly over from the peninsula to feed on them, keeping their numbers manageable. Fish swarm around the reef, the seals feed on them. Sometimes, blue sharks feed on the seals, or try to. Nature corrects what it can, tips the scales so everything is in harmony.

But what nature can't correct is our influence. It can't legislate for plastic filling the seas. So until we stop, I do what I can. I steer the dinghy into the late summer sun, aiming for a clutch of water bottles bobbing like buoys.

And, like I have done for the past couple of months, ever since the school visit, I think about Gayle.

The thing I realised in Affleck's Palace, as Gayle glared at me, was that I would never be good enough for her.

And I don't mean that in a passive aggressive way. I don't mean to suggest that she really thought I was never going to be good enough for her. I mean she was a better person than me, and I could never live up to the standards she'd set herself.

I felt like a failure moving back in with my mother after university. Gayle had got herself a flat, she was working as she put herself through solicitor school. But I couldn't even broach the subject of us moving in together. I couldn't afford to pay my way. I was on benefits. I couldn't even go out and get a job, even something casual or manual. Not with Mum how she was.

It would be another seven years or so until the dementia began to bite hard and she'd move into Pennant Gardens, but looking back the signs were already there. Just little things, forgetfulness and blank moments. But that wasn't the only reason I had to stay. Mum had increasingly bad episodes of anxiety, that crippled her and kept her confined to her bed for days. She begged me not to tell anyone, and for some reason I didn't. Not even Gayle. I suppose she was embarrassed or ashamed, I don't really know, looking back. For her generation, mental health wasn't something you shouted about. People talk about it more now, people wear the badges of their diagnoses with pride. Which is as it should be. For Mum ... I think after so long keeping everything together after Dad died, she thought people wouldn't understand why she was having problems now. So she begged me not to say anything, and I kept my promise.

Which meant for those long stretches where she took to her bed I was stuck in the house, worrying about her. I told Gayle, told everyone, that I was working hard on my novel, but in truth I'd only written a few pages of utter crap. And while all this long, drawn out nothingness was happening for me, Gayle was hitting her stride.

I was so proud of her job at the law firm, they were going to take her on as a solicitor proper when she qualified. I could see she loved working there. There was a lot of drinking after work, that was the culture.

OK, I suppose I did get a bit jealous. Especially when I met that Aiden. I could see the sort of bloke he was straight off. And he obviously fancied Gayle. I mean, who wouldn't?

'What do you do?' he asked when Gayle took me on a night out.

I didn't really know what to say. A writer? But I hadn't written anything. I didn't have a job. I was caring for a depressed mother who had sworn me to silence. I just stared at him, with his expensive suit, chiselled face and piercing, mocking eyes. I said nothing. I saw him glance over at Gayle, and then at me, and he practically had a thought bubble over his head, like in comics. *What on earth is she doing with this loser? If this is all I have to compete with, she's going to be no problem at all.* I always think that was the moment Aiden decided he would seriously try to sleep with Gayle. I stared at the wedding ring on his finger, desperately trying to think of something to say. Eventually Gayle came to rescue me, but with a slight frown, a crinkling of her brow, the seed planted that I was different from these people.

When the day came, when we had that row in Affleck's, it was almost a relief. The pressure had been building up and it was inevitable there would be a storm. And I didn't have to pretend any more, didn't have to pretend I was writing a novel, that I had a normal life, that I wasn't caring for my mother in secret. I could just go home, abandon any pretence, and begin my slow, inexorable slide to becoming nothing at all. At least that was one thing I managed to accomplish with style.

By the time I've done a complete circumnavigation of Ynys Dwynwen I have a full bag of plastic plucked from the sea. It's only a fraction of what's out there, a fraction of a fraction, but I have to do it. Have to try.

I spent my whole life making no difference to anyone or anything. I'm playing catch-up.

As I approach the jetty I see the speedboat. Small, sleek, modern, expensive. Definitely not Gwyn's, unless he's won the lottery. But I have visitors. Heledd Davies? She doesn't usually turn up unannounced. Triune House, come to inspect the lighthouse?

I'm mooring the dinghy and hauling up the bag of rubbish when I hear the distant sound of a dog. Shielding my eyes against the sun I scour the island, seeing a clutch of figures by the shingle beach. Who the hell is that? I dump the bag and stalk off towards them.

There are four human figures, and a small brown dog that's barking at the distant seals on Bethan's Reef. Smoke is rising, and I can smell the food cooking on their two large disposable barbecues.

'Hey!' I call as I approach.

There are two men, in pastel shirts and dark shorts, and two women, one in a sundress and one in a bikini. They glance over at me and wave.

'What are you doing here?'

One of the men is hunched over the barbecues, flipping burgers. He ignores me. The other is lying on his back on the grass, shirt open to display his flat stomach and toned abs.

'Fabulous island,' says the woman in the sundress. The one in the bikini is standing on one leg with her eyes closed, doing some kind of yoga.

'You're not supposed to be here.' A greasy wrapper skitters off across the island, caught by a breeze. Nobody moves to catch it.

The man on the grass cracks open a beer and offers it up to me. 'Are you the lighthouse keeper? Can we go up to the top?'

'That would look great on Insta,' says the woman in the sundress.

'Ynys Dwynwen is a private island,' I say. 'It's not open to visitors.'

'Yah, we've seen it loads. We always come to the Llyn for summer,' says the yoga woman, standing on two feet and opening her eyes. 'Always said we'd come over here.'

The dog can't stop barking at the seals. 'Can you shut that thing up? The seals had pups in summer. Your dog is going to distress them.'

'Pups!' says the woman in the sundress. 'Oh, Pete, can we take the boat over? I want to see the seal pups.' She turns to me. 'It's OK to pick them up?'

'No!' I say. The man at the barbecue swears and holds up a burned sausage, tossing it into the grass. 'You can't go over to the reef. Not when the seals have young. And you certainly can't touch them! And can you stop littering the island?'

'Jesus, man, cool it,' says barbecue guy.

'You want this beer or not?' says the other, who introduces himself as Pete.

I pinch my nose between my fingers. 'Can you please leave the island now? And take your crap with you? And stop your dog barking?'

Pete pushes himself up on his elbows. 'Fuck's sake, man, stop being so intense. Where's the sign that says it's a private island?'

'It just is,' I say, trying to keep my voice steady. 'I'm asking – no – I'm *telling* you, now, to please leave.'

'Do you even know who we are?' says yoga woman.

'Should I?'

'Go and ask around Abersoch, they'll tell you. Pete and Jama, and Ryan and Lois. We've been spending summers here since we were like, yay-high. We're practically locals.'

The sort of locals who spend a month of the year on the Llyn and price out the people who grew up here. Yeah, I know who they are. I don't have to go to Abersoch to ask around.

Pete stands up. 'Come on, then. I'm bored already. Let's go back and have dinner on the harbour.'

Barbecue man stands up, and kisses yoga woman hard on the lips. 'You ready, baby?' He looks at me. 'Shit island anyway, mate. Those old cottages are infested with mice or something. Benji here did you a favour and killed a couple.'

They let their fucking dog loose on the Dwynwen Voles. I shudder with fury. They start to walk back towards the jetty, the dog running ahead of them, barking at the gannets swooping high overhead. I stare at the barbecues, the food still sizzling on it, and the empty cans and wine bottles, the rubbish blowing over the shingle beach.

'Hey!' I shout after them. 'What about all this stuff?'

Pete glances over his shoulder. 'Oh, yeah. Sorry. Help yourself. You can get rid of the crap for us, right? See you later, man.'

I watch them go, too impotent with rage to follow. Nature corrects itself, rebalances. But what can it do in the face of us?

No, not *us*, I think, as I see them climb into their boat, their tinkling laughter carried on the breeze. Battle lines have been drawn. Not us. Never us.

Them.

20

Gayle

October

I have never laughed with another person as much as I laughed with Martin. Not with any of the men that came after, not Tom, not even Donna.

It wasn't just that he was funny, which he was, but that he found me funny. There's something intoxicating about that. It's like a chemical reaction, one as strong as physical attraction, as heady as the heart-thumping, stomach-churning flutters of early love. Being funny is one thing that you cannot do alone. If you tell a joke in an empty forest, does anyone giggle? But to have someone howl with laughter, clutching their stomach; to throw back your head and roar with abandoned delight so hard you think you might wee, because of some stream of consciousness nonsense that you've conjured up together, that only you and this other person could ever have come up with? That was like plucking magic from the air or sculpting a block of marble into a unique, abstract shape ... I sometimes think *that*, after lust has cooled and love settles into a steady rhythm, is the basis for long-lasting romance.

I wake with a smile on my face, having dreamed of nothing specific, but some amorphous, fractured, jump-cut edit of my memories. A taverna on a tiny Greek island. A festival, pouring with rain, my welly coming off in the sucking mud. A dour seaside hotel in Blackpool, a bed collapsing under our frantic lovemaking. A beer garden in the blazing sunshine. And every moment was soundtracked by laughter; kind, inclusive, warm laughter.

It's as though my subconsciousness ... or maybe my heart ... is trying to compensate for those memories that I summoned of Martin after meeting him again after all this time. When the only thing I could think about was how it all went wrong, as though that was a wall I had thrown up around all the good memories, which were buried inside.

My stupid brain has decided, since then, to chip a hole in that wall, to let those good times trickle out.

'What's so funny?'

I stretch and yawn, tangled in the huge duvet as Tom opens the curtains. Rain is battering the window and the skies are steel-grey. He's placed a little tray with coffee and cream on my bedside table.

'Just a funny dream.' I look at my phone. 'God, look at the time!' He sits beside me on the bed and strokes my bare arm. 'You obviously needed your sleep. I've been for a run already. Maybe you should join me one morning? Better than lazing in bed. Sets you up for the day.'

'Coffee and funny dreams set me up for the day.'

Tom scowls. 'Well, today you were probably better off lazing in bed.' *There's that word again. He thinks I'm lazy?* 'Bloody foul out there. I think we'll be confined to the house for the party tonight.'

The party is my idea, and I don't think Tom is that enamoured with the prospect. It's Halloween and I've always loved it, ever since I was a little kid. I love a fancy dress party.

A memory rises unbidden, Martin and I at a Halloween party in our last year at university. We went as Morticia and Gomez Addams. Martin kept kissing my arm and talking to me in French. When I woke up in the morning I was all itchy between my legs. I spent an hour in bed with Martin gently snoring, while I was silently furious with him. I was completely faithful to him, so if I did have something, he must have been sleeping around. I scratched furiously at my groin and finally found the source of my discomfort; his Gomez moustache stuck to my muff.

I push the memory away. 'Well, it's not as if we don't have room for a big party here. I'm looking forward to it.'

'And another lie in tomorrow,' says Tom. He pauses, then looks at me. 'You know, if you weren't at the school, you could get more sleep.'

It's October half-term, so I've not been in all week, and I have to admit that I have enjoyed being lazy. 'But it's only three mornings a week I have to get up!' I protest. 'I'm not exactly a delicate little flower, Tom.'

He shrugs. 'I know. But for what they pay you ...'

'It's not about the money. I like working there. I feel useful.'

'You could work with me!' he says brightly, as though the idea has just occurred to him. 'I've been thinking I need a PA. Someone to deal with emails and take calls, organise the diary, that sort of thing.'

I sit up in bed and sip my coffee. *And have me under your watchful eye*, I think. Tom has offices in Manchester, which he goes in to a couple of times a week, mainly doing his business on the hoof, taking calls and answering emails on his phone. It's a shared workspace where other people in the property development world also have a base. I suppose it might be nice to work right in the city centre a couple of days a week. Near Harvey Nicks and Selfridges.

'I couldn't leave the school halfway through the academic year,' I say. *And not before the next visit to Ynys Dwynwen*, my subconscious mind offers. I silently reprimand it.

Tom shrugs and stands up. 'Well, let's think about it closer to next summer. I might have to get a temp in between now and then. I'm going for a shower.'

I am dressed as Slave Girl Leia from *Return of the Jedi*, which involves me wearing a bikini and a rather pointless skirt which hangs at the front and back and at least covers my arse. Tom is Han Solo, which involves him wearing a pair of black trousers, a white shirt and a waistcoat.

I am furious.

Tom had said he wanted to surprise me with the costumes for the Halloween party, and presents my outfit to me in the afternoon. 'Are you kidding me?' I say. 'I'm not dressing in that.'

'But babe, you have a gorgeous figure,' he says, his face crinkling like a little boy who's done wrong. 'I just want to show you off.'

I do not have a gorgeous figure. My arse is too big and my tits are too droopy and my belly is too bulgy and my thighs are dimpled like oranges and and and ...

He wants to show me off?

I am ten years' Tom's junior. Most of his peers in the property development world are ten years older than him. I am to be paraded around my own house (*Tom's house*) for the benefit of a bunch of pervy old men looking like ... *a space whore.*

And that is not the worst of it. Not by a long shot.

★

'Trick or treat,' says Donna on the doorstep, holding out a plastic bucket shaped like a pumpkin, in which she has put two bottles of wine. She looks me up and down. 'What the actual fuck have you come as?'

'Slave Girl Leia,' I say, tugging self-consciously at my plait. Donna is wearing a bin bag with holes for her head and arms, stripy tights, and has painted her face green. 'What have *you* come as?'

'A witch, obviously,' says Donna, pushing her way into the house. 'I had a little hat but it blew off when I got into the taxi and I couldn't be arsed to chase it. It's Halloween, you're supposed to dress as something scary, not a Miss World contestant. Here, put this cheap shite in the fridge and get me something expensive to drink.' She casts an eye over my costume again. 'Your idea?'

'No, Tom's,' I say tightly.

Donna follows me into the kitchen, which is filled with knots of people talking shop, an incongruous scene of devils and superheroes and film characters. Everyone looks classy. The women look toned and tanned and their costumes are subtle. I look like a cheap slut.

I feel everyone's eyes on me as we push through to the fridge. Donna says, 'I could hang this bucket on any one of a dozen Viagra stiffies in this room.' She looks at me. 'Interesting that you're going all out to piss Tom off, if you don't mind me psychoanalysing you.'

'It's sort of backfired anyway,' I say, pouring Donna a huge vodka. 'Look over there.'

Over there is where a young woman stands, I presume with her mother and father. Her dad is one of Tom's closest business partners. The girl is in her early twenties and she is dressed as … Slave Girl Leia. Except she looks like she's just walked off a film set.

'Fuck,' says Donna. 'That's bad form, isn't it? Coming in the same costume as the host? Like wearing a wedding dress to someone else's wedding.'

'I haven't breathed out all night,' I squeak. 'My tummy muscles are killing me.'

Donna frowns and looks around. 'What the fuck is this music, Gayle? Middle of the road shite. You're supposed to have "Monster Mash" and "Time Warp", not Ed Sheeran.'

Tom waves me over and I hiss at Donna, 'Don't upset anyone, Grotbags.' Then I pull my stomach in even tighter and walk over to Tom with as much dignity as I can muster with my boobs banging together like two tennis balls in a hanky.

'I'm seeing double!' says the other Slave Girl Leia's dad, Trevor, jovially, looking from his daughter to me. Trevor and Catherine have come as Humphrey Bogart and Katharine Hepburn from *The African Queen*. None of the costumes in this house – apart from Donna's – are home-made. I smile wanly and the girl raises an immaculately plucked eyebrow in response to her father's comment. It screams, *As if.*

'Gayle,' says Tom. 'This is Trevor and Catherine's daughter, Rachael. She's just finished a degree in business management and is at a loose end before she does a gap year in East Asia.'

'Lovely,' I say, not quite knowing how I'm meant to respond.

'So you know this morning I was saying I need a PA? Rachael's going to do the job for a couple of months. Isn't that fabulous?'

'Fabulous,' I say, staring daggers at Tom. Is this his revenge, then, because I won't give up my job at Britannia Brook? Get some gorgeous twenty-one-year-old without an ounce of fat on her and a face that would break Instagram?

'I think it will be great experience,' says Rachael, looking at Tom with puppy dog eyes.

Tom winks at her and says in an American accent, 'Watch your mouth, kid, or you'll find yourself floating home.' Everyone laughs except me. I don't get it. Tom says, 'It's from *Star Wars*.'

Suddenly there's a murmur rising from the partygoers as the music changes into a jolly, scratchy old tune with a mad female vocal. I turn around to see Donna grinning at me from across the room, holding my phone. She's hacked into my Spotify and changed the playlist.

A jaunty, folky song comes on which, from the repeated refrain, is obviously called 'I Want to Marry a Lighthouse Keeper'. Donna is practically wetting herself, leaning on the worktop and clutching her stomach.

'What on earth is she doing . . .?' murmurs Tom.

Donna begins to sing along as best she can, repeating '*I want to marry a lighthouse keeper*,' over and over.

She catches my eye and collapses in fits of giggles again. I shake my head and mouth at her, 'Bitch.'

21

Martin

January

'Storm coming in,' says Gwyn.

I frown at him. I've had no alerts from Triune House about bad weather, and their monitoring is usually bang on. It's a cold January morning, the sky cloudless and Alice blue. You get to know the names of every shade of blue out here, the sky a canvas constantly reinventing itself. The same with greys, for the ever-shifting Irish Sea.

He points at the far horizon, and I squint to see what he's indicating; a thin, almost invisible line just above the sea level, so indistinct as to be practically not there. 'You get a feel for these things, living by the tides. That thing out there, it doesn't even know it's a storm yet. Give it six hours. It'll know what it is, and so will you.'

'Tea?' I say, turning back to the lighthouse. The exterior paint is chipping a little; I'll have to give it a new coat before summer, I think.

Before the school visit.

Shut up, I tell my head.

As if reading my mind, Gwyn says, 'I'll bring you some paint for that. She's about due a fresh coat.'

'How do I do it?'

'Rigs and pulleys. Basically, abseil down,' says Gwyn, following me up the spiral staircase to the kitchen. 'Old Benson hated the job. Always looks quite fun, to me.'

I brew a pot of tea and offer Gwyn a biscuit from the tin he's just brought over. 'Left over from Christmas,' he'd said. 'We had boxes and boxes of the things. There's only so many Bourbon creams a man can handle.'

I haven't seen Gwyn for a couple of weeks, so I'm hungry for news, even if it's people I don't know. He reels off the gossip as I pour the tea. 'Eddie Jones had a puncture up on the headland, hit a patch of ice, and was almost off the bloody edge. Like *The Italian Job* it was, at the end. You know? Michael Caine, *hang on lads, I've got an idea*.

'Wyn Jones, that bloody idiot, got done for being drunk and disorderly on New Year's Eve, didn't he? Only painted "Fuck the English", excuse my French, on the side of Gareth Jones's flock up in his top field. One letter per sheep, he did. Took a photo of himself stood in front of them and put it on that Facebook. Bloody idiot. Daffyd Jones the constable was right on him.' Gwyn takes a sip of tea. 'Except the bloody sheep wouldn't stand still, would they? Wouldn't stay in order. So by the time the drunk bugger had taken the picture the bloody message on the sheep was "The Sulking Chef". Nigel Evans who runs the kitchen at The Three Leeks thought it was aimed at him – he's got history with Wyn Jones, hasn't he? – and went to kick his arse. Good job the constable got to Wyn before Nigel did, if you ask me.'

I'm not even sure if Gwyn's stories are true, but I find his outlandish tales of the locals quietly comforting. I wonder what they make of me. The taciturn Englishman who has never left the island in almost three years. The thought of even setting foot on the peninsula fills me with anxiety. All that ... solid ground. Filled with people. I think of

143

Manchester, hordes crowding its tarmac streets, the fumes of the cars, the street lights bleeding orange haze, obscuring the stars. I feel almost breathless at the thought of it. And no sea for miles and miles and miles.

'Blodwyn came round on Boxing Day, as usual,' says Gwyn, inspecting a custard cream. 'Read the tea leaves, as per. I got her to do a reading for you.'

'Oh? And what does my future hold?' I take a Bourbon cream. I like Bourbons. Chocolatey, but not chocolate. Biscuits from the chocolate dimension, where everything is varying grades of chocolatiness. I miss chocolate, suddenly. I'll ask Gwyn to bring me some next time.

'Oh, it's all a load of nonsense, if you ask me,' says Gwyn. 'Lots of old guff about true love and the past coming back to haunt you, and righting wrongs. Usual bag of dung. Still, it keeps her happy, old Blodwyn.'

Gwyn finishes his tea. 'Right, I'll be off. Can I use your loo? That tea's gone right through me, what with this cold snap. Don't want to get caught short.'

I stand on the jetty and wave at Gwyn until he's midway across the channel, then turn back to look at the sea. Gwyn's right; that line has thickened slightly out on the horizon. Looks like we are in for a storm, after all.

The winds are whipping up when I walk over to the shingle beach, where Bruce swims up to greet me.

'Storm coming in, Keeper.' I toss him the sea bass I've been defrosting all day. 'Think I might have found your dad.'

She was called the *Diamond* (says Bruce), and she'd sailed from New York with a cargo of cotton, potash, and apples, and a passenger manifest of thirty. I don't know where New York is, one of your cities I suppose. They set off two

144

weeks before Christmas, and it was January second when they rounded into Cardigan Bay, bound for Liverpool.

See those big ships that go past? The huge ones? Full of people? Well, seems to me that the *Diamond* was the forerunner of them. Wooden, it was, but its hull had been covered with copper. Captained by a man called Henry Macy. This chap I've been speaking with, he was a passenger. Businessman coming to England to deal in cotton. Ran a place where they grow the stuff. Cotton grows, Keeper, did you know that?

Didn't like this fellow much, to be honest. Had a bearing about him. Said something I didn't quite understand, about this cotton. Picked by other humans that he owned. I mean, how can a person own another person? I know I'm only a seal, but that makes no sense to me.

Anyway, this ship, copper hull or not, went down on what they call Sarn Badrig, big reef out in the bay. Apples washing up on the beaches for days. This fellow went straight to the bottom. Can't say I'm sorry, Keeper, and you have my sympathies if it's your father.

'It's not my father, Bruce,' I say. 'But thank you for looking.'

'Quite pleased about that,' says Bruce. He rolls himself noisily into the water. 'Not a nice man. I'm going to bring the colony over here for when the storm hits. I can smell it on the wind. It's not far off now. Stay safe, Keeper.'

As the January darkness falls early, the winds rise, and freezing rain starts to spatter the windows. Even high up in the tower, I feel safe and secure, stoking the wood burner in the kitchen and making a pot of coffee. I search through the boxes of food that Gwyn has brought over, and fix myself a tea of pie and chips.

By the time I've finished, the storm has settled over Ynys Dwynwen, rattling the windows and howling through the gaps in the frames, as though banshees are circling my lighthouse, shrieking to foretell a death.

In my room I have a crate of personal effects. Trinkets, letters, ticket stubs, silly little things. Among them is a small, square box, and after I eat I rummage through it.

I take out a ring, white gold, with a diamond set in it. It was my mum's engagement ring. I remember her sliding it off her finger when she was ill with her nerves, not long after I'd moved back in with her.

'You're serious about this girl? This Gayle?'

I'd nodded. Mum had met her very briefly once or twice, but then she'd got ill and taken to her bed. She held up the ring to the light. 'I remember your dad saying he was serious about me. That's how he put it. "I'm serious about you, Julia. So I got you this". It cost him two week's wages.'

Mum paused, then handed me the ring. I said, 'What do you want me to do with this.'

'Maybe give it to your girl. Gayle. If you're serious about her.'

I'd stared at the ring, then at her. 'You mean, get engaged? Ask her to marry me?'

'If you want to. If you think she wants to.' Mum had looked out of the window at the terraced houses opposite. 'Maybe that would give me something to get out of bed for. I don't know.'

'I can't. It's your ring. It's your *engagement* ring. That Dad gave you.'

Mum had shrugged. 'Your dad's gone. Long gone. Shame for such a lovely ring to be cooped up in this house with me.'

'OK ...' I'd said. 'I'll ... I'll think about it.'

'Don't think about it too long,' Mum had said. 'If she's as wonderful as you say she is, she might not wait around for ever.' Then Mum had frowned and said, 'Have I had my tea, yet?'

I carried the ring around in the little box that Mum gave me for it for nearly a month, trying to build up the courage to ask Gayle to marry me, trying to work out if it was the right thing to do. For her. For me. For both of us.

Eventually, I decided it was. And I had it in my pocket that day at Affleck's Palace. The day I was going to do it. The day Gayle told me that she never wanted to see me again.

I hold the ring up against the electric light, flickering as the storm begins a fresh assault. Then I put it back in its little box, and put that in the big box, and I am just about to slide it back under the bed when a brown A4 envelope catches my eye. I open the flap, and slide out a few sheets of musty paper.

My novel. Or at least, what amounted to it ten years ago. Which wasn't much, as Gayle had caustically pointed out.

Against my better judgement, I start to read the first page. It's rough and flowery and self-conscious and probably truly awful. But I don't hate it as much as I should. And the story I was haltingly telling myself in these first, uncertain pages comes flooding back to me. And it's a good story, or at least, a good idea of a good story. And the more I think about the story, the better it seems, as though ten years has given the story a patina of age and, to some extent, wisdom; as if living and growing for a while has allowed the story to do the same, breathing dustily in this manila envelope.

The story has been quietly burning at the back of my head, I realise. Percolating like coffee on the stove. After Gayle had ended things, after I'd admitted that I was as hopeless and feckless as she thought, after I'd accepted that writing a novel – or at least pretending to – was actually what I was most decidedly *not* doing, it came as something of a relief. I could just abandon the idea and get on with doing nothing much at all.

But the story hadn't abandoned me, it seems. It was a flame that kept itself lit, patiently waiting for me to blow on it, fan it, let it ignite again in my imagination. It was a light that hadn't gone out, despite me shutting it away in a dark box.

As the wind howls and my window panes shudder and rattle, I go back down to the kitchen and, on a whim, get the Underwood. Scrolling a piece of paper into it, I sit with the storm at my back, and stare for a long, long time at the blank sheet, wondering if I have the courage to fill it.

Year Four

22

Gayle

July

I think Tom is fucking Rachael.

I don't have any evidence. No texts, emails, direct messages. No lipstick on his collar or strange perfume on his chest. No subtle chilling of his attitude towards me. But when you know, you know. He's definitely fucking Rachael. Tom's too clever to slip up. Too methodical in everything he does. But when he sets his sights on something, he gets it. And he definitely set his sights on Rachael at that Halloween party last year. I wonder if that's why he made me dress in the same costume – to assess us side by side. I could positively smell the musk seeping from his pores every time he cast a hungry glance in her direction.

Tom is definitely fucking Rachael.

'Are you all right, miss?' says Willie, a little boy with glasses that are always fixed with Sellotape or Blu Tack. He's an odd one, Willie, one of those lonely kids. My heart goes out to him as he kicks around the playground on his own, or sits in a corner doodling in the margins of his exercise book. He doesn't seem to have any friends, but he doesn't seem to mind, either. Happy in his own company. He never misses anything. Always watching, always taking mental notes.

He reminds me a bit of George. I thought I was going to get sacked over George. When we came back from Ynys Dwynwen I called an old police contact from my solicitor days about his dad hitting him. Turns out there are protocols about that sort of thing, I should have discussed it with the staff; social services should have been informed. You'd think as a trained lawyer I would have known all that. And I probably did, or could have guessed. But I was so heartbroken about what he said about wanting to be a seal, and wondering if daddy seals hit their little boys, I just saw red.

Turned out George's dad wasn't his dad at all, wasn't even his stepdad. Just the latest in a long line of no-marks his mum had hooked up with. And, the police confided in me later, he was pretty handy with his fists around her as well. He was charged with assault under the auspices of the Domestic Violence, Crime and Victims Act 2004, given a short custodial sentence, and a restraining order preventing him going anywhere near George and his mum for two years.

After the prosecution, any complaints about me not following procedure were quietly dropped. I call that a win.

But here is Willie, looking up at me with red-rimmed eyes, and I wonder what's going on at home. There are endless Georges and Willies coming into Year Five, bound for who knows where or what.

He says again, 'Are you all right, miss? I thought you were going to be sick.'

I do feel a bit queasy. The water is choppy, and Gwyn's boat is bouncing up and down. I've never been seasick before, but there's a first time for everything, I suppose. Early start, no breakfast, too much coffee, and the one-hour sea crossing to Ynys Dwynwen. It's all contributed to me feeling, quite frankly, as sick as a dog.

There may well be another reason. As we near the jetty, there he is. Standing in his thick trousers and white shirt and blue jacket, tanned and lean and bearded. I feel a slight twitch, and that shocks me.

'Ho, Keeper!' calls Gwyn, waving as he pulls the *Angharad* alongside the jetty. 'Britannia Brook here, all present and correct!'

'I hope so, Gwyn,' Martin shouts back, catching the mooring rope and securing the boat. 'We don't want any more excitement on the cliffs.'

Oh yes we do, says a stupid, unreconstructed voice inside my head. *We* liked *getting rescued*.

'Traitor,' I mutter.

Willie looks up at me. 'What did you say, miss?'

'Nothing!' I say brightly. 'Right, come on, let's get on the island.'

After nodding in my direction when we disembarked, Martin studiously ignores me. I know this because I am studiously ignoring him too, apart from the odd sly glance to see if he is looking at me. He never is. Unless he's doing the same thing as I am. Which is entirely possible, because we used to say we were so alike that we were worried we might actually be related. We joked about never doing those family tree DNA tests, because we'd probably find out we were long-lost siblings.

It's a lovely day, despite the winds that have whipped up the sea. Mrs Gaskell and Mr Jensen make everyone sit in front of the lighthouse for the packed lunch provided by Gwyn.

'Meat paste or ...' Mrs Gaskell inspects the sandwich in her hand. 'Vegan meat paste?'

'Not for me,' I say. 'I'm feeling a bit nauseous, actually. That sea crossing.'

I sense him at the side of me suddenly. I smell him first, an earthy mix of briny sea air and the faint tang of engine oil. Then something familiar that makes my head spin.

Issey Miyake. He always used to wear Issey Miyake. Ever since I bought it for his birthday when we were first together.

'Would you like a little tour of the island. You were otherwise occupied last year,' he says. He might be twelve years older, he might have somehow developed a toned, tanned physique (*Stop it!* I chide my chattering, clenching groin) and a beard, and the bearing of, y'know, an actual *adult*, but there's still the ghost of the hopeful, unsure, eager-to-please little man-child.

'That would be lovely,' I say, catching his eye. An electric current flows between us.

'Is that seal waving at us?' I laugh, pointing to the colony on what Martin tells me is Bethan's Reef. I missed the whole tour last year due to the cliff business, so this is all new to me. Martin looks oddly shifty. 'Uh, no he's just ... airing his flipper.'

How curious. He's lying. And I know instinctively that he is. Not in the way that I suspect Tom is lying about Rachael – though to be fair I haven't asked him if he's fucking her, so it's more a sin of omission than actual lying – but in the way that I know Martin is lying because I know him so well.

Knew him so well, I remind myself, even as the years we've been apart seem to shrink and contract and fold into hardly any time at all, like some weird origami. Besides, I'm probably wrong. A seal waving is an odd thing to lie about. I change the subject and say, 'So why's it called Bethan's Reef, then?'

154

When Martin has finished the story about the man who built the lighthouse to illuminate the way home for his heart's love lost at sea, I'm almost exploding. It's the most romantic thing I've ever heard. Perhaps it's listening to it here, on the island, the reef where the boat was lost right in front of us, the lighthouse built over a hundred and fifty years ago strong and proud behind us. Martin, telling me the tale, here beside me. It's all those things, all together, all mixed up, and making my heart pound.

'You look really well, Gayle,' he says suddenly.

I look down at my tanned arms. 'We went to Mauritius. Late birthday present.'

'We?' says Martin, hesitantly, as though he's scared to cross a line.

'Tom and me.' I risk a glance at him. He meets my eyes.

'Your husband?'

'No. We're not married ...' I let it hang. The word *yet* feels as though it's foundering at the end of the sentence, trying to find purchase. Are we going to get married? We've never discussed it. There doesn't seem to be any actual need. Do I *want* to get married? Do I want to get married to *Tom*? What a ridiculous question to ask myself.

I say, 'So, we never got the chance to talk properly after all the excitement last year ... Why this?' I wave my hand around. 'Why a remote island off Wales? A lighthouse? You're the last person I'd have put here.'

Martin looks out to sea, narrowing his eyes. If you took a photograph of that and put it on Instagram you'd laugh at it and say it looks pretentious and wanky. Here in real life, with the warm wind blowing off the ocean, and the cry of seabirds in the blue sky above, it's the sort of image to make your heart leap to your throat. I wish I could take a photo. Though quite how I'd explain that at home I have no idea.

Instead I just blink rapidly, as though my eyes are lenses, committing the picture to memory.

'A few things happened,' he says. 'All on one day. I lost my job. I lost my girlfriend.' He looks at me. 'And I lost my mother.'

'Oh, Martin. I'm so sorry.'

I knew of course that he'd lost his dad at such an early age in that horrible accident. And I knew he was close to his mum. He moved back in with her after university. Just before we—

'She'd been ill,' he says quickly. 'She'd been ill for a long time. Dementia. It started quite some time ago.' He looks at me. 'It started, really, before I'd moved back home. You had that job at the solicitors.'

'That must have been horrible for you.'

'It wasn't much fun. I don't suppose I was much fun to be around either.'

'You were writing a novel,' I say airily, too cheery. But my mind is whirling. Pieces are dropping into place. 'Did you ever finish it?'

'I wasn't writing a novel.' He winces. 'I was trying to, I wanted to, but ...' He turns and takes hold of my forearm, gently but firmly, and turns me to face him. 'She was ill then. But she wouldn't let me tell anyone. It was awful. I was pretty much caring for her all that time. When we ... When we ...'

Oh my god. When we broke up. When I thought he was just a hopeless, unambitious waster, who never applied for anything, never pushed himself. While me, little miss professional lawyer, was driving forward her career. And I was too good for him. I needed someone with as much drive and ambition as me.

All that time, he was looking after his mum.

'It's all right,' he shrugs.

'No, it's not,' I say. But I don't know what to follow that with.

'It was a long time ago.' He lets go of my arm. I want him to hold it again. He starts to walk along the beach. 'Come on, let's get round the island. The children will have finished their lunch soon, and they'll be wanting to go up to the observation balcony.'

'Martin,' I say.

He looks back at me. 'What, Gayle?'

My mind goes blank. My heart pounds. 'Issey Miyake,' I say, helplessly.

'I found a bottle in my things,' he says with affected nonchalance.

'You wore it for me.'

He doesn't deny it. He looks at the lighthouse, vibrant against the blue sky. 'I painted the lighthouse.'

I grin crookedly. 'For me? The aftershave would have been enough.'

And then he's grinning too, and a little surprised yelp escapes my mouth, and he chortles like that dog off the cartoon, who was given the medals and had them ripped off. I start to giggle.

'Dipshit,' we both say simultaneously. Just like we used to do.

The laughter drains away, like water down a plughole. Martin coughs, then glances away. 'I think they're ready. We should go back to the lighthouse.'

'Of course,' I say, falling in behind him as he strides through the long grass, not quite knowing what to think.

23

Martin

I haven't laughed like that for years. Literally for years. In fact, I haven't laughed like that, I'm pretty sure, since Gayle and I broke up.

The laughter we used to share is embedded in me at a cellular level. Like a vaccine that only we were administered, to stave off infection by the mundane world. Except once we parted ... well, it's no big deal shutting out the world when you were already so alone. Which is the real answer to Gayle's question of *Why this? Why a remote island off Wales? A lighthouse?*

Except I never realised that properly before this moment. I thought I was just running away from the world. What I was really doing was stopping the world from running to me. All this time, all these long years, I never really understood ... I didn't really want a world that didn't have Gayle in it.

And now she's back and I don't really know what to do. So I stutter some excuse about the children finishing their packed lunches and stalk off back towards the lighthouse.

Dipshit. We used to say that to each other all the time. It was our magic word, guaranteed to defuse any situation, make us smile, release tension, cheer us up.

That day outside Affleck's Palace, as Gayle walked away

from me without a backwards glance, I whispered, 'Dipshit.' Except, I wasn't talking to her, I was talking to myself. And it was suddenly just a word, all magic washed from it like a photograph left out in the sun. It didn't mean anything. Until five minutes ago, when we said it together, laying down cards we'd been keeping up our sleeves for over a decade, then saying, 'Snap.'

Suddenly it was a magic word again. The last thing I need right now is magic. Well, that sort of magic. Gayle and Martin magic. The last thing either of us needs.

I wonder what Tom is like.

'So!' I say as I approach the children and their teachers. I sense Gayle behind me, feel the weight of her stare on my back, smell her scent on the breeze. Chanel No. 5. I used to buy that for her every birthday. 'So, who wants to go right to the very top of the lighthouse?'

'Kyra! Can you please stop leaning over the balcony!' says Mr Jensen in a tremulous voice, waving frantically at a girl with her socks ruched around her ankles at the same time he's dragging a boy back from the balustrade.

'Get off me, Doctor Octopus!' the boy yells. 'I'm Spider-Man!'

Jesus Christ. How anybody copes with having kids is beyond me. I point out landmarks to the children who are not actively trying to kill themselves. Bethan's Reef, the shores of the Llyn Peninsula, the distant, hazy shape of Snowdon. Out to the north I can see a pod of dolphins sporting in the diamond-glitter of the sea. The children all go 'ooooh'.

We're taking them up in groups of ten, which means it takes quite a while to get through the whole class. As they wind up the staircase they point at my kitchen and bedroom.

'Do you sleep here on your own?' says a pale little boy.

'Willie, don't be rude,' says Gayle. But I feel her eyes on me, as though she's interested in the answer as well.

Willie looks up at Gayle. 'I only wondered if there's a Mrs Lighthouse Keeper.'

It is more than three years since I last had sex, when Imogen broke up with me. I don't say that to Willie though. Obviously. I'm not sure that's the level of detail nine-year-olds require about the life of a lighthouse keeper. Instead I say, 'No, no Mrs Lighthouse Keeper. I'm too busy to get married.'

'Too busy polishing your lamp?' says Willie.

Gayle snorts then pretends she just coughed. I feel laughter rising inside of me, too. We were always like that. Sometimes it would just take a look and we'd be off. I cough as well and lead the party up into the bright sunshine dappling the island.

And then, it's time to go. As the children file on to the *Angharad* under Gwyn's watchful eye, I stand with Gayle on the jetty.

'A bit less eventful than last year,' I say.

She looks at me. 'You think?'

And I don't know what to say to that. Because it does feel as though something has happened today. As though something has been rekindled. I feel it in the pit of my stomach and the soles of my feet. There's a lightness to me that I'd thought long gone. Like a hot air balloon rising into the blue sky. But as soon as I think that, I feel the weight of it all, feel the pull of gravity. The balloon is punctured and I come crashing down to earth.

'I'll see you in a year, then, I suppose,' says Gayle.

'Yes, I suppose you will.'

We stand and stare at each other for a moment, then Gwyn calls for the stragglers to get on board. I lean in to Gayle, my arms wide, then pull back, just as she moves towards me as well, missing her footing and stumbling. That must have been the worst aborted hug in history. Instead we just shake hands, and she gets on to the *Angharad*, and stands at the prow, watching me as Gwyn reverses the boat away from the jetty.

'She seems nice,' says Bruce, sunning himself on the rocks at low tide off the shingle beach. I throw one of the leftover sandwiches at him and he plucks it from the air. 'What is this again?'

'Meat paste.' I pause. 'I'm not even sure it's a good idea to feed seals sandwiches.'

'Meat paste,' says Bruce, licking his lips. 'Is that a fish?'

'No,' I say. 'It's out of a jar.'

'I said, she seems nice.'

'I heard you.'

'What's her name?'

'Gayle.'

'Gayle.' Bruce nods. 'Force nine?'

I raise an eyebrow at him.

'That was a joke, Keeper.'

'If I were you I'd stick to sealing rather than joking.'

'So, you going to tell me about Gayle, then?'

'I'd rather not talk about her, if you don't mind. I don't ask you about your love life,' I say, a little testily. I toss him another sandwich, a little harder this time so it bounces off his wide, flat nose.

Bruce glares at me. 'I know you did that on purpose. But ask away; I've nothing to hide.'

'OK, then, Bruce, do you have a wife?'

Bruce looks at me then does an actual smile. He barks out a harsh laugh, and even rolls over on to his back, slapping his flippers together.

'A wife. Oh, Keeper, that's a good one. A wife.'

'So seals don't get married?'

Recovering his composure, Bruce, rolls back on to his belly. 'Martin, we're *polygynous*. Do you know what that means?'

'No.' I have a taste of one of the meat paste sandwiches myself. It's not bad. 'It's a good word, that. I met a scientist in one of the boats on The Bottom once that used it. It means, come mating time in the autumn, I'll probably have liaisons with about seven young ladies of the Atlantic Grey persuasion.'

I have never before seen a seal with what can only be described as a smug expression. I say, 'Lucky you.'

'It's not a bad life, if you keep your strength up.' Bruce flops into the shallows. 'Thanks for the human food. Think I'll stick to fish, though. Right, I'll be off, see if I can find your dad.'

'Bruce,' I say, as he starts to swim away. 'The other seals ... are you sure they can't talk, too?'

He circles back and gives me a look. 'Don't be ridiculous, Keeper. I'll report back if I find anything.'

It's a shade after midsummer, and the sun doesn't properly set until nearly ten o'clock. I stand on the balcony, looking out towards the mainland. I like seeing the lights come on in Gwyn's shop, and in the houses dotted along the coast. I find it reassuring that the world's still there. Suddenly, I miss it. The warmth, the people, the activity. It's like everything else, everything out there, is safe and cushioned in some kind of ... I don't know. *Womb*. I'm on the outside. Separate. Perhaps there is something in what old Edward Davies believed, about Ynys Dwynwen being at the junction of worlds, on the borderland between life and death. It feels as though time has stopped here, like the island exists in a bubble. And with it, me too.

But now Gayle has come along again to poke a hole in that bubble, and to let the world in.

Right on cue, as night settles over the land and water, I feel whirring beneath my feet as the machinery shakes off its slumber, its nocturnal gears clashing, the twilight engines grinding into life. I close my eyes and wait. The lamps fizz and then sunbursts into cold, white light.

I raise my hand, letting the silvery light play over it, as dense as nectar. No. I do not need the light of the world on Ynys Dwynwen. I have my own light, guiding ships in the dark, steering them away from peril, providing comfort and succour to those who live their lives by the tides, and those on land who wait for their loved ones.

Gayle Reiss is out there, somewhere, far beyond the reach of my light. Landlocked and cosseted, with her job and her partner and her holidays in Mauritius. Her life is not mine, and my life can never be hers. Paths have been chosen. They do not run parallel.

She has only been gone from the island for a matter of hours but the feelings that had broken the surface of my isolation, like the rocks of Bethan's Reef, begin to subside, ebbing away like the tide. The laughter I rediscovered in her presence seems like an alien, hollow thing.

I am the Keeper of Ynys Dwynwen. I have no use for that world anymore. Nor for the things I felt today. I wish with all my heart that Gayle had never come here.

That selfsame heart shivers and cracks at the prospect of a whole year passing before I see her again.

24

Gayle

July

A week after the visit to Ynys Dwynwen I meet Donna for a coffee in Alderley Edge. She has news; she is being promoted to the newsdesk of the *Manchester Evening News*, which means she will sort of be a boss.

'I'm really happy for you,' I say. 'You've worked so hard. You really deserve this.'

'Bollocks to that. Tell me about the lighthouse.'

I sip my coffee and wince as it goes down. 'There's not a lot to tell. No drama like last year. Managed to not lose a kid or fall off a cliff.'

Donna frowns at me. 'Are you all right?'

'Fine,' I say. 'I've got a bit of a stomach cramp; had it on and off for a few weeks now.'

'Probably some undercooked shit you ate in Mauritius,' she says. 'It looked terrible on Insta.'

Mauritius was wonderful, as it happens. Tom surprised me a month before my birthday. Azure seas, endless sunshine and unbroken blue skies, a beach hut over the ocean on stilts, but with a TV and Wi-Fi.

'Quite literally, a guilt trip,' says Donna, looking over the rim of her coffee cup at me.

I wish I'd never told her that I feared Tom was having an affair. 'It wasn't like that,' I say. 'He was completely attentive. Didn't do a minute of work while we were there. I might have been wrong about him and Rachael ...'

Donna makes a sound that suggests she is far from convinced. 'You're not the jealous type, Gayle. If your gut told you Tom is screwing around, I'd listen.'

I look into my cup. 'Well, it doesn't really—'

Donna holds up both hands. 'Whoa. Whoa. Were you going to say *it doesn't really matter*?'

'No!' I protest, though that's exactly what I was going to say.

'It doesn't really matter because he takes you on five-star holidays? It doesn't really matter because you go to Paris for the weekend? It doesn't really matter because you've got a kitchen island?'

I stare at the people passing on the pavement. Donna reaches across the table to put her hand over mine. 'OK, I'm sorry. None of my business.'

Except she's my best friend and it *is* her business, and she's exactly right. I have a charmed life. I have everything I could possibly want. And while I'm absolutely, one hundred per cent convinced that Tom is, or at least has been, shagging Rachael, I've not done anything about it. I've not delved too deeply. I've not asked searching questions, or kicked up a fuss when he's worked late, or had to go away for a couple of days to look at an investment opportunity.

I hate myself.

'I mean,' Donna is saying. 'You could always get your revenge in other ways ... if you haven't already.'

I frown. 'What do you mean?'

'You haven't told me how your school trip went.'

'Donna!' I say, scandalised. 'Even if I wanted to, I'm

hardly going to nip off for a shag with the lighthouse keeper on a school trip!'

I don't tell her about how I felt. Mainly because, since coming back, it all feels rather silly and ridiculous. There's something heady and wild about being on that island, like it's separate and apart from everything else in the world. Emotions get heightened. It's like having a holiday romance. It's mad and exciting but, once you get back, reality settles around you like a weighted blanket.

'Look, it was nice to see him again. We had a little chat, and it was all fine.' I frown again, my stomach flipping. It feels like I'm going to be sick.

'Gayle, are you OK?'

'Just going to go to the toilet,' I say through a grimace. 'My stomach ... I've been feeling sick a lot lately. A *lot*. I don't know what it is.'

When I come back from the loo Donna puts a long white box on the table in front of me. I pick it up and laugh. 'Where did you get this?'

She shrugs. 'In my bag. There's all sorts in there. For emergencies.'

'Did you just nip to the shop?'

'A lady never tells. Now go and pee on that and I'll get us more coffees.'

Ten minutes later Donna is holding the test under the table while I drum my fingernails on my cup. She eyes me and says, 'What those nails probably cost, I wouldn't do that. You don't want to break one.'

'Is it ready yet?'

'Not yet.' The coffees arrive and, when the waiter has gone, she says, 'Are you sure you didn't bang Martin?'

'Positive!'

166

'And despite the fact we think Tom's dipping his wick in that little slapper, are you still banging him?'

I think of Tom in Mauritius. He was absolutely ravenous. Every morning, every night. It was like when we first met. Which, partly, is why I've started to think that even if there was something going on with Rachael, it must be over now.

'Well, it's a good job Tom's good at property,' says Donna.

'Why?'

She holds up the stick, displaying its two blue lines. 'Because you need a nursery conversion.'

I'm in a private hospital, of course, because Tom would never countenance putting his baby in the hands of the NHS.

I have a private room in a discreet little hospital in the Cheshire countryside. It overlooks a lovely landscaped garden. The food here is practically Michelin-starred.

Tom comes bursting into the room, his face a picture of panic. 'Oh my god! Gayle! I'm so sorry! I was in a meeting and I didn't get the texts and—'

'It's OK.' I feel weirdly disconnected from everything. I know I look an absolute state, pale and drained. I'm sore between my legs.

My face crinkles. I feel tears fall down my face, but I feel strangely numb. 'I'm sorry, Tom. I lost our baby.'

I am – was – exactly thirteen weeks gone. Unlucky for some. When I told Tom, he was over the moon. He immediately started rushing around, measuring up one of the spare rooms to turn it into a nursery.

'I love you, Gayle Reiss,' he'd said, taking me in his arms. 'I'm going to look after you and our little son for ever.'

'Wouldn't be happy with a daughter?'

'I don't care!' grinned Tom. 'This is the happiest day of my life.'

I didn't get as far as the first scan, and everything wasn't all right, because within a few days my stomach was cramping up, leaving me in agony, and I was bleeding.

The gynaecologist is sitting by my bed, Tom standing beside him. I have been sleeping and they have given me some kind of medication. I don't know what it is but I don't care because I'm as high as a kite. The doctor is talking but I'm not taking it in.

I have had an ectopic pregnancy. The fertilised egg had implanted itself in my fallopian tube rather than my womb.

'Why?' I keep asking.

'We think you have something called Pelvic Inflammatory Disease, but we're going to do more tests. That can be a common factor in ectopic pregnancies.'

'But why?'

'Again,' says the doctor, glancing at Tom, 'We're not really sure yet. PID is often caused by naturally occurring bacteria in the vagina. Sometimes by sexually transmitted diseases.'

'I've never cheated on Tom,' I slur. 'I can't have the clap.'

'No, well, like I said ...' I catch the doctor looking at Tom again. 'The root cause isn't quite clear right now. But we're going to give you a course of medication to treat all possible options, just to be on the safe side.'

'When can I have another baby?' I say, trying to focus on Tom but just seeing the window beyond, the sun shining in like the beam from a lighthouse.

'Get some rest,' says the doctor. 'We can talk about that later.'

★

I am in hospital for a week, even though within a couple of days I feel fine. Physically, at least. Mentally, not so much.

The likelihood is that this will keep happening if I try to have more babies. The doctor is still not quite sure what has caused the PID that has led to the ectopic pregnancy. As a precautionary measure I am given a course of tablets called doxycycline. When I get home I look them up on the internet. They are used to treat chlamydia.

'Are you really disappointed?' I ask Tom, knowing that there's no real answer to that question. I feel vaguely, amorphously angry, and I want something to be angry at. I want him to say the wrong thing.

'I'm just glad you're OK,' he says, holding me tight in his strong arms, and I melt into him, sobbing into his chest, and cry and cry and cry until I can't cry any longer, and then cry some more.

'At least I've got the children at school,' I say, bursting into yet more tears.

Tom holds me at arm's length, and frowns. 'Are you sure you should go back in September? Maybe the stress of all that …'

'It isn't stress, Tom,' I say. 'And yes, I'm going back in September.'

'We'll talk about it nearer the time,' he says.

Tom takes two weeks off work, but that money won't make itself, and gradually he goes back, and the meetings start again, and the trips to look at investment opportunities.

One weekend, while he's away, I find a box of pills at the back of the bathroom cabinet. Doxycycline. What I had, but the box has his name on it.

Either I gave chlamydia to him, or he gave it to me.

'You absolute bastard,' I say, closing the cabinet and glaring at my reflection in the mirrored door.

25

Martin

25 January: St Dwynwen's Day

'This coming summer shall mark the commencement of your fifth year on the island,' says Heledd Davies, the embers of the dying St Dwynwen's Day bonfire painting her face red. 'How are you finding life here, Mr Burney?'

Now there's a question. I watch Gwyn using a stick to drag the baking potatoes from the edge of the fire, and getting the butter out of his little cool box. 'To be quite honest,' I say slowly, 'I can't really remember my life before Ynys Dwynwen. It all feels like ...' I search for the right analogy. 'Like a movie I once saw.'

Ms Davies gazes into the glowing coals. 'Have you given any thought to how long you might stay?'

I open my mouth and close it again. It has never really crossed my mind that one day I might leave. How curious. I am taking each day as it comes, the past receding, the future a shore that is never in sight. I am living in the moment. Eventually, I say, 'I'm not quite sure what I'd do out there any more, Ms Davies.'

She turns her piercing gaze on me. 'You'd *live*, Mr Burney. But perhaps you aren't quite ready for that, just yet.

After all, one needs something to live *for*. Otherwise, one is merely existing.'

'Plenty of butter, is it, Ms Davies?' says Gwyn, holding out a small plastic bowl.

'One of my increasingly shrinking number of vices,' sighs Heledd, taking the steaming dish and proffered fork.

'And here's another,' says Gwyn, popping the cork on a bottle of Prosecco. Our St Dwynwen's Day ritual. Baked potatoes and fizz.

'A word of warning, Mr Burney,' says Ms Davies. 'You might think yourself not quite ready for life, but life might have other ideas.' She raises her paper cup. 'Cheers.'

The novel I am writing is about a man who withdraws from the world, after having his heart broken. But slowly he begins to realise that the world is not the harsh, unfeeling, cold place he believes it to be, and after being reunited with his lost love, he gradually returns to society. They say write what you know. Which is why, although I have the first bit of the book down pat, I have now completely stalled.

I sit in the darkening afternoon staring at the words on my typewriter copy paper.

Withdrawing from the world because of heartbreak I know all about. I can write that from experience. The feelings and sensations flow from my fingers.

It's the being reunited with his lost love and embracing life bits that I'm utterly stumped by.

Obviously, I cannot write this book without thinking about Gayle. But when I try to navigate my feelings about seeing her again it feels like piloting a boat through thick fog. I have only the charts of imagination and the instruments of hope to try to plot a course.

None of them are up to the job. Every time I try to write,

it is merely wish fulfilment vomited on the page. It is not compelling, it is not readable, it is not truthful. Inhabiting my fictional avatar, I have imagined a hundred different ways we could get back together. None contain the remotest seed of likelihood. A hundred possible futures, a hundred forks in the road ahead, and all of them impassable.

They say truth is stranger than fiction. The truth in this case, my truth, mine and Gayle's, is not just stranger than fiction, it is far more impossible. The words I write, the scenarios I invent, are as implausible as the most outrageous science fiction. I look out of the window, at the dulling sky, and the moon rising big and yellow. There is more likelihood of me flying there than the things I write happening.

In a fury, I tear up the last two thousand words and decide to go for a walk.

The Dwynwen Voles are active in the dusk. *Crepuscular*, as Edward Davies was fond of calling them. His notebooks show their twilight activities as watercolours.

I crouch and watch the voles scampering around the tumbledown cottages. They don't hibernate, as I learned from Edward's journals, but instead grow a thick coat of winter fur, giving them the appearance of round little fluffballs. They'll moult that coat in spring. They're entirely herbivorous, feeding off the grasses that grow in abundance around and inside the roofless stone structures.

It is February tomorrow, the long final furlong towards spring. March will bring the northward equinox, and lighter nights. April brings balmier weather, and for the last couple of years May has been hot and dry. Then June, and summer proper, then July and the visit from Britannia Brook ...

There's a sudden movement in the darkening sky and I look up to see the shape of an owl, ghosting on outspread wings, like a magnificent, terrible envoy from another world.

It is hunting, its keen eyes zeroed in on the vole it has selected, its claws outstretched as it begins to swoop.

I could do something. I could jump up from where I'm crouching in the grass, shout and wave my arms. The owl would flap away, the voles would scatter. But who am I to make that decision? Save a vole's life, deprive an owl of its meal. It's not my place to interfere. So I just watch.

But the island has other ideas. The lamps in the tower blaze into life, and the owl issues a startled shriek and ascends into the black sky. The vole is safe for now; the owl will be back. Though the lighthouse was built by a man, by Edward Davies, it feels a part of the island now. More like a natural stone growth than an intrusion of modern life. Ynys Dwynwen would not be Ynys Dwynwen without the lighthouse. It is as much a part of the natural order as the voles and owls. Nothing living on this earth remembers a time before the tower. Generation upon generation of seal, dolphin, cormorant, razorbill, vole, squirrel, has lived with the beacon's light shining out into the darkness. Minke whales must surface far out to sea, marking their course by the lamps. Blue sharks must hunt below the surface in the dappled illumination cast by the tower. The lighthouse is part of the fabric of this tiny, enclosed world I live in. Whether it is a comfort to those creatures, or a mystery, I don't know for sure. Maybe I'll ask Bruce.

You'd live, Mr Burney. But perhaps you aren't quite ready for that, just yet. After all, one needs something to live for. Otherwise, one is merely existing.

That's what Heledd Davies said, when I asked her what I would do if I left the island. I do have something to live for. My life here on Ynys Dwynwen. Anything else, I think, as I gaze up at the reassuring light cast by the lighthouse, by my lighthouse, is unthinkable, a highly unlikely fiction that will never, as far as I am concerned, be written.

The next morning is clear and bright and I decide that after my run – I can do five circuits of the island now without pausing – I will give the generator a quick overhaul and re-fuel it with the red diesel Gwyn brought over last week.

On my final lap Bruce hails me. 'Good fishing today, Keeper! Lots of mullet around!' I wave and tell him I'll be over later.

Servicing the generator is something I do a couple of times a year. The first time it almost made me weep with its complexity. Now I barely even need the manual. I dismantle the crankshaft and clean up the components, wipe down the polarised magnet array, and replace any of the tightly wound wires that have stretched or thinned, especially during the long winter months where they've been getting a lot of use. There's one perpetual fault that I can't seem to fix, which an-noys me. Nothing to do with the running of the generator, but a spring-loaded access door which, every time I close it, pops out violently, causing me to jump back to avoid being smacked in the face. I've taken apart all the catches and the spring and even had Gwyn bring me a couple of replace-ment components, and still the bloody thing does it. I think that generator has it in for me, in some way, though I'm not sure what I've done to deserve it.

My overhaul has the generator humming quietly and ef-ficiently, and I celebrate with a shower that heats up almost instantly thanks to my endeavours. Then I get my fishing tackle and head down to the beach.

Bruce is right; the mullet are swarming between the island and the reef, and I pull a dozen out in the first half hour. Bruce swims in the shallows, watching me, and even declines a couple of fish. 'Been scoffing mullet all morning, Keeper. Couldn't look another in its little fishy face.'

I fill my net and set about dispatching the mullet so I can gut them and store them in the freezer. Bruce says, 'Oh, I think I might have found your dad.'

I straighten up, wiping my hands on a cloth. 'Do tell, Bruce.'

'Big fella. Long red hair and beard. Angry-looking, to be fair. Went down with a big, long, wooden ship, all those round shields on the side. Had a big axe. Didn't get too close.'

'I don't think so, Bruce.'

'No, me neither. Bit pillage-y and plunder-y to be your dad, I thought. Which is why I didn't really stick around to find out what brought that boat of theirs to the bottom.'

'Probably wise.'

Bruce ruminates. 'They do these big fancy funerals, that lot, don't they? Burning boats.'

'Vikings? Yeah, I think they did.' I frown. 'How do you know that?' Bruce shrugs. 'I pick up all sorts, Keeper. Quite fancy that myself, when I go. Burning boat.' He pauses. 'I'll keep my eye out, anyway. Your dad's bound to turn up.'

'Bound to,' I agree. 'Thanks for looking, Bruce.'

Back at the lighthouse I clean and freeze all but one of the mullet, and take another shower to wash away the smell of fish. Then I bake the mullet I'd saved with butter, garlic and a few herbs, and boil up potatoes for a bit of mash.

As I sit at the table, eating my meal just after the light has come on, I reflect that it's a kind thing Bruce is doing, looking for the ghost of my dad. But I don't really expect him to find my father. And, to be honest, what would I say if he did?

I take my coffee up on the balcony, wrapped up in my fleece and thick jacket to ward off the cold. It's enough, I think, my hands cupping the steaming mug as I look over the dark ocean, and see the lights of a distant ship. It's enough to know that ship, and hundreds like them, are kept safe by my tower. I don't need Bruce, or Edward Davies's light, to bring my father to me.

I don't need anyone brought to me.

Except maybe …

No, I think firmly, there's no good to be had in thinking like that.

But then I recall Heledd Davies's words. *You might think yourself not quite ready for life, but life might have other ideas.*

Year Five

26

Gayle

March

'And you believed him.' It's not a question. It's a statement of Donna's utter certainty that I am a complete idiot.

'Doxycycline is used to treat a variety of infections,' I parrot hollowly. 'Tom picked up a bit of a chest infection. He's prone to it and he spends a lot of time in dusty old properties ... you know ...' I tail off, hating how I sound.

It's already March and it's taken me so long to pluck up the courage to tell Donna about the tablets in Tom's cabinet. Mainly because I've already decided he's telling the truth, even if I don't really believe it. But Rachael has gone, off to work in London, and ... well. Let sleeping dogs lie, and all that. Sleeping, lying, shagging dogs.

Donna says, 'Where is he, anyway?'

I go to get us another coffee from the pot on the stove. 'He's looking at some old farmhouses in Derbyshire. He'll be back today.'

As I put the mugs in front of us, Donna grabs my hand. 'And you're OK? You're sure you're OK?'

I am OK. Though I wasn't for a while. For a long time, after losing the baby. I wasn't what I'd call sad. Or angry. Or upset, even. I was just ... numb. And didn't want to go anywhere, or see anyone. Especially not Tom's friends. More than anything, I felt like a failure. It's meant to be the most natural thing in the world, right? To grow a baby inside you. And I couldn't even manage it. It's doubtful I'll manage it ever. Even when Tom had thrown himself on my mercy and begged me not to believe he was having an affair (though I wouldn't dignify what I think he was doing by calling it an affair ... it was sex) and I'd eventually capitulated and told him I accepted what he'd said, more from exhaustion than anything, I wasn't really upset at losing the baby.

In a weird, shameful, secret way, I was almost relieved.

As ever, Donna puts my whirling, spiky, knotted ball of wire wool thoughts into one succinct sentence, as if reading my mind.

'To be honest, I never thought you were bothered about babies. I never heard you talking about them.'

I burst into tears, not because of what happened last year, but because I've got Donna, who understands me so well, and I feel awful that I've barely seen her since it all happened.

'Stop blubbing,' says Donna mildly. 'It's not all about you. Ask me if I've got any news.'

I laugh through my tears and dry them on the piece of kitchen towel she thoughtfully gets for me. 'Have you got any news?'

'Actually, yes,' says Donna. 'I've got a new job. At the BBC.'

'What? This is huge! Are you going to be on the TV?'

'Don't be an idiot,' says Donna. 'They don't put women with pink hair, a proclivity to spots, and pierced labia on the teatime news. They don't want to frighten the horses. I'll be working as an editor. At MediaCity at Salford Quays.'

'Wait. You've pierced your labia?'

180

'Yeah,' says Donna, looking at me over the rim of her mug. 'Katya likes it.'

'Katya?'

'That's my other bit of news. We've been seeing each other a couple of months. Think I might be in love, Gayle.' She looks around the kitchen. 'Got something a bit stronger than coffee? I feel this calls for a celebration.'

I open an expensive bottle of wine. 'To be fair, though,' I say, as we clink glasses. 'I don't think they'd see your piercing on the evening news.'

An hour later we're drunk and we don't hear Tom come in. I have my laptop open on the kitchen island and Donna is cackling at my photos of Ynys Dwynwen, specifically the shots of Martin standing in front of the lighthouse with the kids around him.

'Oh my god!' she says. 'He's actually quite … handsome?'

'He always was!' I say, then frown. 'Wasn't he?'

Donna belches. 'Good for you.'

'What's good for Gayle?' says Tom behind us, making us jump. I automatically go to close the laptop but stop myself, deciding that will look too guilty. I hold my breath as Tom leans over us.

'Ah, Gayle's little island. You're right, Donna, it is good for her. Though she's not short of trips away, I can tell you. We're doing Madrid in a couple of weeks.'

Tom is peering at the laptop, the full screen photograph showing Martin in his little black hat and roll-neck sweater, standing in front of the two tumbledown cottages, framed against the blue sky. He looks particularly handsome and a teeny bit rugged in this one. I took it when he wasn't looking last year, and he's glancing off camera, towards the distant horizon. It always gives me a little bit of a hitch in my breath, this photo.

'Hang on a minute,' says Tom, frowning and leaning closer.

Donna glances at me and pulls an *eek* face, taking a big swig of her wine. Tom points at the picture with his forefinger. 'That ...'

'That's ...' I begin, not knowing where to take this.

'That cottage ... wait, is it two cottages?' Tom absent-mindedly brushes my hand away from the trackpad and blows the picture up, the image of Martin disappearing off the margins. 'Hmm. Need a bit of work, but the potential in those ... I mean, really, you'd have to knock them down and start again. Listed? Maybe not. But the location. What did you say the name of this island is again?'

'Sees an investment opportunity in everything,' I laugh to Donna. She raises an eyebrow, looking me up and down, my hair, my nails, my subtle little fillers, my Dior jeans, my Bella Freud sweater, my Louboutin mules.

'Yeah, he's got a good eye for a fixer-upper, I'll give Tom that,' says Donna, sticking her tongue out at me.

I mouth *'fuck off.'* 'I doubt they'll be for sale, Tom,' I say. 'It's a private island. It's all about the lighthouse.'

Tom straightens, and grabs his bag. 'Everything's for sale. You just have to know the price.' He smiles tightly at Donna and says, 'I'm going to shower. Don't forget we're off to dinner soon.'

On the May Bank Holiday we have a barbecue. Tom even lets me invite Donna, and of course Mum and Dad are coming. Except, when they arrive, it's just Mum.

'Is he all right?' I say, worriedly, as she walks in quite regally, her head held unnaturally high.

'Not my circus, not my monkeys,' says Mum.

I frown. 'What are you talking about?'

She looks at me, her eyes prickling with tears, even

though I can tell she's furious. 'Your father has left me, Gayle. He's got a flat. He packed up all his new clothes, those stupid young clothes, and his vinyl collection, and his ... his fucking *yoga mat,* put them all in his stupid little sports car, and told me that our lives are no longer intersecting and he thinks it's for the best if we consciously uncouple.'

I stare at her wordlessly. I've never heard Mum say the F-word. Eventually I squeak, 'What? When?'

'A week ago.'

'And you didn't think to tell me?'

Tom, wearing a striped apron and brandishing a pair of tongs, has come into the hall and is listening from the doorway. Mum, half out of her jacket, slumps against the wall. 'Because you've been through enough recently.' She looks at me tearfully, all pretence of strength crumbling. 'What am I going to do, Gayle?'

Tom is already taking off his apron. 'What's the address, Heather? His flat?'

'Tom,' I say, as he hands me the tongs. 'What about the barbecue?'

'Oh, this lot can take care of themselves. You take your mum into the kitchen and stay with her. I'm going to go and have a talk with Paul.'

Tom is right. His friends barely notice his disappearance, so long as there is plentiful alcohol flowing. The alpha males fight over barbecue duties, and I take a couple of bottles of wine into the living room with Donna and Mum.

'Is he off shagging?' says Donna.

'Donna!' I say.

Mum puts a hand on my arm. 'Well, she's right, isn't she? Classic mid-life crisis. How he pours himself into those skinny jeans I have no idea. And that stupid car. You can barely fit two Waitrose bags in the boot.'

'You shop at Waitrose now?' I say, raising an eyebrow. 'What's wrong with Sainsbury's?'

'Your dad decided we should,' sighs Mum. She looks straight at me. 'It's Tom, you realise that? Your dad is in awe of Tom. He wants to be just like him.'

'Hence the shagging question,' mutters Donna, but I silence her with a look. The last thing I want to do is have that conversation with Mum right now.

'All men are shits,' says Donna, refilling our glasses. 'You should all join the Lesbians Club. I can recommend you for membership, if you like. We meet every second Thursday.'

Mum looks at her curiously. 'Is there really a club?'

I put my head in my hands. 'Jesus. Donna, can you shut up?'

Just then we hear the front door and all look up. Tom comes into the living room, and behind him, looking suitably shamefaced, is Dad.

Mum fixes him with an icy stare. 'Barbecue with all the movers and shakers of Cheshire too good an opportunity to pass up, Paul? Thought you might get tips for your ISA? Or have you come to try to pick up a twenty-year-old?'

Dad has had his hair cut very fashionably. He is wearing a polo shirt and pastel slacks. He stares at the rug and says, 'I'm sorry, Heather. I've been an idiot.'

'You have been an idiot.' She looks at Tom. 'What did you say to this one?' Tom shrugs. 'Nothing. I called round and he was sitting on a packing crate eating a ready meal with a cheese fork.'

'I wondered where that had gone,' says Mum mildly.

'Hadn't got round to buying cutlery,' mutters Dad. 'Or furniture. Or much of anything.'

There's a long silence punctuated by Donna. 'Not exactly the last of the famous international playboys, Paul?'

Dad shakes his head sadly. 'No, it's not, Donna love. Sorry to hear about you and that girl.'

'Oh, you know. These things happen.'

Dad blinks and looks at me, and then at Mum. In a strangled voice he says, 'I'm sorry, Heather. Can I come home?'

'I thought you'd taken out a lease on the flat.'

'Well, it wasn't so much a lease. It's owned by a chap from the squash club. He's between tenants. I said ... well, I said I'd house sit for a couple of weeks. I thought, until I find my feet ...'

'Come here,' says Mum softly. Dad bounds over like a puppy and they embrace.

'Can I please come home, Heather?'

'Are you going to stop being an idiot?'

Dad nods. 'I promise.' He turns to Tom. 'Thank you. For talking some sense into me. I could murder a burger.'

'Then come with me,' says Tom with a flourish. Mum looks at me, her eyes filled with tears. Happy tears.

'That man of yours, he's a marvel. I don't know what he said to Dad but ...' She shakes her head. 'A keeper, Tom is.'

She follows them out into the garden. Donna is looking at me. I give her a glare she knows means she should say precisely nothing.

27

Martin

July

It's a bright, clear, sunny day when Britannia Brook comes to visit.

I stand on the jetty, twice-bathed, beard trimmed, clothes pressed. I even had Gwyn come over last week and give me a haircut. I am drenched in Issey Miyake. I am trying to show Gayle that I am not the Martin Burney she walked away from that day in Manchester so many years ago. I am new. I am better. I am ...

What am I? What am I trying to prove? What do I want to happen?

I feel foolish and silly as the *Angharad* slides into dock and I search the faces on board.

Then I see her, and my eyes lock with hers, and I don't feel silly any more. I feel like anything could happen. Even if I don't quite know what that could be.

'Keeper!' calls Gwyn. 'Wake up!'

I realise he has tossed the mooring rope to me and it's lying on the jetty, snaking into the water. I shake my head, reach for it, and secure the *Angharad*.

'Good work, Keeper!' says Gwyn. 'Now, who wants to go and see the lighthouse?'

Well, this is going all rather horribly and awkwardly. Not the visit; that is all going according to the plan. Tour of the island, wave at the seals, crouch down quietly to watch the Dwynwen Voles skittering around the cottages, see the puffins and their young, marvel at the trees that arch towards the mainland, grown bent by decades of winds blowing off the Irish Sea. The children are relatively well-behaved. Nobody tries to throw themselves off the observation balcony.

No, it's with Gayle that things seem ... off. She greets me warmly enough, and she looks absolutely beautiful in a green and yellow print summer dress. So much so that I wonder if she's made as much of an effort as I have. But when we finally get some time alone, when the children are eating their packed lunches on the grass, everything feels a little strained.

We're pleasant enough, asking how things are, what we've been up to (Gayle: holidays in Madrid and Christmas parties in barns in the Lake District, skiing in Val-d'Isère, West End shows and a new car; me: living in a lighthouse). But we seem to be talking over each other, always apologising for interrupting, then having long silences we don't know how to fill. We walk around the island, but the ease with which we chatted last year has evaporated, and I start to feel uncomfortable in my skin, pulling at my collar, the smell of my aftershave overpowering and sour. I cast sidelong glances at her, but she doesn't look at me, or at least if she does, not at the same time.

I feel like a castaway on my island, trying to gently blow a spark into a flame in a howling gale. I think back to getting up in the pale dawn light, and the growing excitement I felt. Stupid, stupid, stupid.

I'd dreamed of Gayle. Woke up flustered and hot, tangled

in my sheets, as the cries of cormorants welcomed the day. It was early, the sunrise diffuse and preternaturally hazy, as though the weight of my sudden expectation had drawn a veil over the dawn.

'You still love her,' I'd said to myself, sodden with sweat, my mind stained with the patina of the dream.

We were in Greece, sheltering from the blazing sunshine in the cool bowels of a harbour taverna, racing each other to pick the last cubes of feta from the salad we shared.

'Why do they call it a Greek salad?' Gayle had said. 'Surely it's just a salad here.'

I'd shrugged, our fingers wrestling over a chunk of sweating white cheese. 'Why do we ask for a full English? Surely that's just a breakfast.'

She'd half-stood, leaning over the table, and grabbed the front of my T-shirt, dragging me towards her and planting her hot mouth on mine, her tongue sliding over my teeth. She pulled back and sat down, face flushed, her eyes holding mine. 'Do they call it a French kiss in Paris?'

'I love you, Gayle Reiss.'

'I love you, Martin Burney.'

'I love you, Gayle Reiss,' I'd said, waking up with a start. Later, staring at myself in the mirror, scissors poised to trim my beard, I said to my reflection, 'You still love her.'

I'd decided to take two baths.

When I said that to myself it felt like puncturing a bubble that a child had blown, iridescent in the sunlight as it floats above a summer fete. It is like pointing out that a magician has the ace of hearts hidden up his sleeve. It is like opening your eyes before you are supposed to, and spoiling your own surprise party.

I should not have said that. I should not have dreamed

of Gayle. I should not have made those feelings real. It was better when we danced around our feelings, delicious expectation that could go either way, rather than setting out my stall in the dawn light, making it concrete and solid.

It is Schrödinger's cat. When the box is unopened, it can go either way. But by starting awake and yelling *I love you*, I opened the box. And forced her hand, even though she did not know it.

On the far side of the island, looking back to the lighthouse, Gayle picks up a dandelion and blows on it. A breeze picks up out of nowhere, taking the dandelion clocks and drifting them on the warm air. She blows.

She loves me.

She blows.

She loves me not.

She blows.

She loves me.

She blows.

I take the green stalk from her fingers and throw it on the grass. She frowns at me. I could not tell whether there were one or two blows left in it. I cannot take the chance. I say, 'The children have finished their lunch. We should go back.'

After the tour of the tower, when the children are sitting on the grass drawing the lighthouse in crayon, Gwyn sidles up to me. 'Martin Burney, we've got a problem, haven't we?'

I frown at him. 'Have we?'

He sniffs the air. 'Can't you smell it?'

I can't smell anything but the grass and the warmth, and the peculiar odour of thirty nine-year-olds.

'Storm coming.'

I look up at the clear blue sky, and laugh. Gwyn shakes his head. 'Storm coming.'

I look out to the horizon. There's no tell-tale, almost invisible grey line. There's nothing but unbroken blue.

'Gwyn, you're wrong, I—'

Then a sudden wind takes my hat off, and a spot of rain spatters against my forehead. Clouds seem to materialise out of nowhere, crashing together in the sky, and there's a distant rumble of thunder.

'Squall,' says Gwyn. 'Big one. Bad one. Better get the children in the tower.'

I'm still about to protest when there's a clap of thunder right above us, and the heavens open. Gayle looks at me, stricken.

'Everyone in the lighthouse!' I order.

Half an hour later we're all in the kitchen, the children cramped on blankets on the floor. It's only late afternoon but the sky outside is blacker than night, fizzing with electricity. The children gasp and grab each other as winds howl around the tower like wailing banshees. Gwyn comes up to me, having tried to reach the coastguard on the radio for some kind of forecast.

'Can't get through to anyone. Static. The squall's set in, Keeper. I can't take the *Angharad* back in this. Not with the kiddies.'

'For how long?'

Gwyn shrugs and nods towards the little window, the pane rattling in its frame. 'My experience, this is on us for the night.'

I hold a whispered conference with the teachers on the bedroom floor. It's so dark I've had to manually override the timer and switch the lighthouse beams on, which at least distracts and thrills the children.

'Stay overnight?' says Mr Jensen, appalled. 'How are we going to do that?'

'We've got blankets. I've got more in the *Angharad*, if I can board her in this,' says Gwyn. 'The keeper has plenty of food.'

'But we can't get in touch with the children's parents if the radio isn't working,' says Mrs Gaskell. 'And what will we do about plates?'

Gwyn shrugs. 'I'm not sure what I can say. We're not going anywhere in this, and my feeling is it's not going to let up until morning.'

The teachers have a quick confab. Gayle looks at me and I smile. She smiles back, but tightly, anxiously. I share her misgivings, but I have to go with Gwyn's instinct. He's lived all his life by the tides. He knows better than me.

'All right,' says Mrs Gaskell. 'It appears we have no choice. I imagine the children will actually be thrilled.'

'I'll go and get some food on,' says Gwyn.

'Martin?' says Gayle. 'Maybe you could tell them a story?'

I stare at her. 'What?'

'Tell them a story,' she says. 'After they've had their tea.'

'A story?'

'You were always good at telling stories.'

So, after getting through my entire freezer, the children are all huddled in blankets in the kitchen. I stand by the window, gathering my thoughts. The storm is assaulting the tower, but it has stood proud since 1876, and suffered far worse than this. Rain pelts against the windows and winds howl in the gaps. Lightning illuminates the sky, skittering across the black clouds like sidewinders.

I call for quiet, and when every child is silent, I start

to speak. 'Once upon a time, there was a woman named Dwynwen ...'

And at that moment, the lights go out.

28

Gayle

The children scream, and everything seems to happen at once. The teachers and I switch on the torches on our phones, illuminating the terrified but also slightly thrilled faces of the Year Fives. Mrs Gaskell calls, 'Everybody stay calm. It's just a temporary power cut.' She looks at Martin. 'It is, isn't it?'

'Bloody generator gone,' he mutters. 'There are candles under the sink.'

'Keeper,' says Gwyn, and there's a sudden volley of shrieks as a crack of thunder sounds right above the tower. 'Keeper, the light ...'

'I know,' spits Martin. 'The light never goes out.'

I peer through the rain-lashed window. The beam is still there, but weak and diffuse.

'It's on emergency back-up, but it won't last,' says Martin through gritted teeth. 'I need to get the generator up and running again. Gwyn, there's a hand-crank on the back-up generator ... it'll buy us a bit of time with the main beams.'

'You can count on me, Keeper,' says Gwyn, heading for the staircase to the back-up generator housed on the floor below.

'Now, now, quieten down everyone!' calls Mrs Gaskell. 'Who can I trust to hold a candle?'

As the children all raise their hands Martin follows Gwyn to the spiral staircase. I say, 'Can you fix it?'

He smiles at me. 'I'll find out when I get there. Look after the kiddies. Tell them I won't be long.'

As he disappears down the steps I look at Mrs Gaskell and Mr Jensen, who are marshalling the children and calming them down somewhat. I decide they have things in hand, and set off after Martin.

I pass Gwyn, sleeves rolled up and sweating as he turns a handle on the back-up generator. I pause uncertainly and say, 'Can I help? Take over?'

'No,' he grunts. 'In my rhythm now, aren't I? Go see if the keeper needs any assistance.'

On the bottom storey I push through the door and gasp. The storm is right above us, biblical in its fury, apocalyptic in its force. Gods of storm are battling it out right over us, thunderheads clashing and lightning strikes clanging like a blacksmith's forge. The sky rumbles and grumbles and lets loose curiously warm rain, driving down so hard it stings the flesh on my arms.

I have barely stepped outside into the flashing, clashing darkness and I am soaked to the skin, the wind whipping my hair across my face, my dress clinging to me. Feet squelch-ing in my shoes I run around the lighthouse to where I find Martin, as drenched as me, hauling up the cover on the boxy generator at the side of the tower. He has a big toolbox open on the ground beside him and is shining a powerful flashlight into it.

'Can I help?' I shout, but the wind whips my words away.

I run over to him, slipping on the sodden grass, and take hold of the generator cover. He looks at me in surprise, then nods. 'Gayle. Thank you. If you can hold that up for me ...'

He balances the torch on the side of the generator and

grabs an adjustable spanner, leaning so far inside the silent, motionless engine I think he might fall in.

There's clanking and banging then he straightens up, digging in his toolbox for a screwdriver. Back in he goes, cursing and grunting as he works, the rain pounding us both. I look up. The tower beam is fading, despite Gwyn's ministrations on the back-up. Martin follows my gaze and our eyes meet.

'The light never goes out, Gayle.'

'No,' I whisper. 'I don't think it does.'

We stare at each other, the rain sluicing our faces, until there's a sudden flash and a boom of thunder right above us. Martin shakes his head, as though emerging from a day-dream, and leans back into the generator. He reaches out his hand and says, 'Flywheel cracked. There's a spare in the box. Can you pass it?'

I hold up what I think it is. He glances over and shakes his head. 'Bigger.'

'This?'

He nods. I don't know if it's the static generated by the storm, or the generator's residue of charge but, as I pass it to him, there's a crackling shock.

Martin leans in, working feverishly. Above us, the beam is dimming almost to the point of being snuffed out. I wonder how Mrs Gaskell and Mr Jensen are doing with the children. Then Martin yells, 'Got it!'

He pulls on a starting cord, the sort you see on motor-boats. Once, twice, three times, then the generator judders into life with a whine of protesting gears. He stands back, and we look up. The beam from the tower, almost faded into nothingness, surges forward, casting its light over the storm-tossed seas. I hear an indistinct cheer from above.

'You did it,' I say.

'We did it. Thank you.'

He puts down the cover and secures it, then opens a smaller hatch set within it, and proceeds to fill what I presume is the fuel tank. Martin presses down on the little hatch and turns to me, about to say something.

Then the hatch springs up, smacking him straight in the face.

'Ow!' he says, holding his nose. 'Ow! Fucking thing! Always doing this!'

I move closer, taking his hands away. Blood is pouring from his nose, mingling with the rain on his face. The lights are on but the storm is not abating.

The fury of it, the intensity of it.

The passion of it.

I gently brush my thumb over his mouth, wiping away the blood. Our eyes are locked together. We are thinking the same thing.

That it's just like the first night. In my room in halls. When Martin had taken a punch to defend my honour.

'Gayle,' he says, eyes still on mine.

I must look a fright. My hair is drenched and the rain runs off my face, no doubt taking my mascara with it. My thin summer dress is plastered to my body. Martin's white shirt is drenched to the point of near transparency, his chinos stained dark. His chest heaves with shallow breaths. So does mine.

'Martin,' I say.

And then he's on me, or I'm on him. Like two starving, lost travellers who have been traversing a desert for more than a decade, finally chancing upon a verdant oasis. The rain intensifies, the wind howls, the thunder bangs and crashes. Our bodies are moulded together, our mouths finding each other's. I drag him backwards, or he pushes me, I don't know. But then I'm up against the wet stone of the lighthouse, and Martin is kissing my neck, and I'm wrapping my arms and legs around him, my body remembering his even if our minds have done their best to forget. Something inside us, some essence of us, singing as we entwine.

Lightning flashes, thunder rumbles, the beam of the lighthouse pierces the stormy night, an everlasting beacon to guide home the souls of those abroad on this foulest of nights.

Except the two souls moving together at the base of the tower, crying out with abandon, the wind whipping away their formless shouts.

Those two souls, they are already lost.

I wake at dawn, stretching, and realise I'm in Martin's bed. I leap up in horror, then note I'm fully dressed. And Martin isn't here. Quietly, I descend the staircase to the kitchen, where the children are still sleeping, huddled together like puppies. Mr Jensen and Mrs Gaskell are sitting against the wall, his head on her shoulder, both snoring gently. I'm hoping they won't have noticed I didn't sleep down here, or will at least have the good grace not to mention it. Martin is sitting on the staircase.

He turns as he hears me, and gives me a dazzling smile. I'm not sure what to do back, but fortunately Gwyn pops his head up from the staircase below and bellows, 'Good morning, Britannia Brook! Well, seems like we've caused quite the stir, haven't we?'

As soon as the storm had abated, the local police on the mainland had been in touch via the radio. Parents back in Manchester had been beside themselves when the coach didn't return, and they were unable to contact any of the staff. The police put their minds at rest, saying nobody was foolhardy enough to attempt the crossing in what had turned out to be the biggest storm in living memory.

Some of the parents, the few with their own cars, are making their way over to Wales to pick up their kids. The coach is ready for the rest of us. The children slowly rouse, being given orange juice and toast by Mrs Gaskell and Martin, and once Gwyn has given the *Angharad* the once over and declared her fit to sail, we all troop out of the lighthouse into a day as bright, warm and clear as it was when we arrived yesterday morning.

'Never seen anything like that,' says Gwyn, shaking his head. 'Seen storms, seen squalls, but never one come on so fast and last so long.'

Martin and I have steadfastly said nothing to each other all morning. As the children file on to the boat, then the teachers, we are the only ones on the jetty.

'Gayle,' says Martin.

I don't say anything, looking back across the island, at the lighthouse. What am I supposed to say? That I am happy in my relationship with Tom? That what happened last night was a mistake? That we should forget it and never speak of it and really try to pretend that it didn't happen.

I think about him, pressing against me, pulling the shoulders of my summer dress down, feeling the roughness of the lighthouse wall against my back.

That is exactly what I should say. There is nothing else to say. Nothing at all.

I must not think about his lips on my neck.

I must not think about my leg wrapped around his.

I must not think about ...

No. I must not think about any of these things. Last night ... like the storm, was a freak occurrence. A one-off. A thing that should not have happened, and must never be repeated.

'Gayle,' says Martin, and I know exactly what is coming next. I remember the exact inflection of his voice, the tone he used, almost hesitant, a little breathy, whenever he said those words. Those three words.

'I have to go,' I say tightly, finally meeting his piercing stare, then hurrying down the jetty and climbing on to the *Angharad*.

As we head back to the mainland, the sun drying my still-damp dress, I sit at the stern, watching him watching me, until we are too far apart.

29

Gayle

By the time I get home, I am feeling wretched. The further I got from Ynys Dwynwen, the heavier the weight of what I had done pressed upon me. I have been unfaithful to Tom. And though I suspect Tom has probably also been unfaithful, while this is of course about him, it is also about me. This is not what I do. I do not have tawdry little affairs or seedy one night stands. I am crushed.

As I drive home from the school, a tiny voice in my mind tries desperately to rationalise it. *You are letting Tom remake you in his own image. Is it any wonder you take on his worst characteristics?*

'Shut up,' I say decisively, parking on Tom's drive. I take a deep breath and let myself into the house. I stop dead.

In the hall there are two cases, on top of them an envelope addressed to me. My stomach somersaults and my mind goes into freefall. He knows. Tom knows. Somehow he has found out what happened on the island and he's taken the opportunity to pack my cases and write me a note, telling me to get the hell out of his house and life.

I look around wildly but there's no sign of him, no sound of a TV or a shower, or any suggestion he's in the house. His car is outside, but he must have known I'd be home

200

round about now. Maybe he's just gone for a furious walk to calm down, waiting for me to leave before he returns.

How did he know? How did anyone know? Who told him? Crazy thoughts of him spying on me, hiding tiny cameras in my clothes, hacking my phone, tumble through my head. Is that possible? Is Tom capable of that?

With shaking hands I pick up the envelope and raggedly open it with my thumb. I take a deep breath and slide out the letter.

No. Not the letter. Tickets. Plane tickets. To Paris.

'Surprise!' bellows Tom from behind me.

Tom, of course, has booked a top hotel, knows all the best restaurants, and liveliest bars.

I only wish my guilt wasn't ruining the whole thing for me.

As we lie in the tangle of white sheets in our hotel suite on our first night, Tom stroking my hair, I say, 'If you'd told me in advance you wanted to go to Paris for the weekend an hour after me getting back from the school trip, I'd have said no.'

'I know you would,' says Tom, twisting my hair around his finger. 'Which is why I didn't tell you, and just packed your bags and made it a *fait accompli*.'

I giggle and turn to kiss him. 'Mmmm, I love it when you talk French. Do it again.'

'*Seulement cinq personnes autorisées dans l'ascenseur à la fois*,' Tom breathes into my ear, his hand sliding beneath the tangled sheets.

'What does that mean?' I say, and plant a kiss on his lips. 'It's very sexy.'

'It was a sign in the lobby,' he says. 'I think it means, no more than five people in the lift.' He wrestles me on to my back, holding my wrists. I kiss him on the nose and wriggle out from under him. 'I need the bathroom,' I say.

He tries to keep the disgruntled look from his face as I delve into my bag on the table for a tampon and wave it at him, but he considers himself far too much of a modern man to even voice his disappointment that I'm on my period while we're on a surprise romantic Paris getaway.

Which I'm not. I close the bathroom door and stare at myself in the backlit mirror. Every time Tom touches me I feel Martin's hand on my skin, and I feel sick. Not with disgust at what we did, with self-loathing at what I've done. Whatever Tom has done in the past, or whatever I've suspected him of, I love him and he loves me. And I don't want to think about that storm, about Martin pushing me against the wall of the lighthouse, about …

I really don't want to think about that. I'm not on Ynys Dwynwen. I'm in Paris. With Tom. And so ridden with guilt that I can't even let him touch me, even though I want nothing more than him to make love to me and push away the memory of what I've done. I just thank God that Tom hasn't even realised that I was only on my period two weeks ago.

Martin would have known. I think, as I stare at myself in the mirror.

Later that evening Tom suggests a bar in the Latin Quarter but it's a lovely, warm night and I just want to walk by the Seine. Tom holds my hand and keeps bending forward to kiss me. He asks questions about school, and the trip to Ynys Dwynwen, which makes me feel dreadful. How could I have done that with Martin? How could I have risked throwing everything with Tom away like that?

And yet … even as I feel safe and loved and wanted in Tom's presence, gazing out at the river, it feels like there's a dangerous undercurrent, one I can't quite escape. In a tiny corner of my mind I wonder what it would be like to be walking hand-in-hand with Martin, wonder what he'd say, how he'd make me laugh.

I quiet the voice, push the thoughts into the furthest, darkest corners of my mind, slam the door on them, and lock it tight. What happened with Martin was passionate and beautiful and unexpected, but it was a mistake. It was a terrible mistake. And it can't be allowed to happen again.

'Un *centime* for your thoughts,' says Tom, and I realise I've been lost in my own head, and he's gazing at me.

'They're worth more than that.'

He raises one eyebrow. 'Really? Premium content, are they? Very dirty stuff?'

I can't help but laugh. 'Maybe.'

He enfolds me in his arms and whispers in my ear, 'Then maybe we should go back to the hotel and you can tell me all about them. As that's all we can do this weekend.'

I'm sure he doesn't mean it to sound as petulant as it does.

When I tell the children about my weekend in Paris, it's the highly sanitised version, of course, but I still immediately regret it. It might only be an hour and a half from Manchester, but I might as well have been telling them about a trip to Mars. I show them some pictures, and when I get to the ones at the Eiffel Tower, little Jamie shoots his hand up and says, 'I've been there, miss! I love Blackpool!'

'You're dead lucky, going on a plane,' says another boy. 'I'd love to go on a plane.' He puts his arms out like wings and makes a whining noise with his mouth. 'I'd shoot down the Germans.'

'We're not at war with the Germans!' says one of the girls indignantly.

'Well who are we at war with then?'

I have to loudly call for quiet before a war breaks out in the classroom about who we're at war with, which ranges from Russia, to most of Europe, to, rather disconcertingly, the Isle of Man, for reasons that aren't quite clear but may be to do with it being the home of someone's cousin who once broke their Xbox.

'Anyway, my mum says you're not supposed to go on planes,' says Summer, a small girl who always wears charity shop clothes. 'Because it's killing the planet.'

'My mum says your mum's a hippy,' says a boy, and I have to once again cut them all off before it descends into bullying.

'Summer,' I say. 'That's an interesting point. You're right. Air travel is very bad for the environment. Who knows what the environment is?'

A forest of hands shoots up. I pick one. 'It's the world, miss. And the animals. And the trees.'

'And why is that important? Anyone? Joe?'

'Because if we hurt the planet, miss, we all die. My dad says the job's buggered anyway.'

Everyone laughs, and I don't reprimand Joe for his language, instead guiding the conversation to a discussion about what we're doing to the planet, and what the children think about it. Half an hour later I walk out of the classroom to get a coffee at break time feeling ... well, more optimistic about the future.

The next day I meet Donna for coffee, which turns into meeting Donna for cocktails. Her job is going well and she seems to be enjoying life. She asks me what I did in Paris, and I tell her about the touristy stuff. When I mention Tom she holds up her hand and says, 'Nope.'

I frown at her. 'What?'

'I want to know what *you* did in Paris.'

'I'm telling you. But I went with Tom and—'

She presses an imaginary buzzer on the bar table and makes a *nrrrrrrrrrr* sound.

'What?' I say again, more crossly this time.

Donna waves at the barman for more drinks and puts her hands on mine. 'Gayle. It occurred to me that every single time we meet, we fail the Bechdel test. All we do is talk about men. And I'm not exactly at fault here.'

'Oh,' I say, mildly affronted. 'You make me sound like some kind of ... I don't know, shallow reality TV star or something.'

'We used to talk about all kinds of things. Remember, you wanted to save the world?'

'Oh!' I say, suddenly excited, and tell her all about the session in school. 'These kids, you know, they're really switched on. They know the score, even though they're young. It's not just middle class kids who are interested in the environment.'

'Well, maybe they're realising they're the ones with most to lose when everything goes tits up,' says Donna, as the drinks arrive. She looks at me for a long time. 'You were good, you know. At the lawyer thing. I was proud of you.'

I feel suddenly teary. I was good at it. And I was getting better. I feel something in the pit of my stomach, a yawning gap, a sense of loss. I blink rapidly and say, 'Well, nothing is forever. I can go back to it any time.'

Donna nods, not convinced, and we have our drinks and talk about anything other than men. It feels good. We swap critiques of books we've read, we arrange to go to the cinema next week. Then Donna says, 'Oh, it was your school trip last week, wasn't it? How did it go? Bearing in mind the

Bechdel test ...' She waves at the waiter. 'Two more over here please.'

I take a deep breath. 'It went fine. There was a massive storm and I had sex with Martin against his lighthouse.'

Donna stares at me open-mouthed and wide-eyed for a full thirty seconds. Then she says, 'Fuck the Bechdel test. Tell me everything.'

Year Six

30

Martin

What follows is quite possibly the longest year of my life.

Seasons crawl into one another, like sluggish runners in the world's slowest relay race. When summer hands over the baton to autumn, the taste of Gayle is still sweet upon my lips. As autumn staggers over the line to waiting winter, the storms and rains remind me, in every rumble of thunder, in every flash of lightning, in every single drop of water, of that night. As winter finally cedes the race to spring, the awakening wildlife, the blooming flowers, the burgeoning grasses, mirror my own growing anticipation. And as spring lazily loops round to give summer its lead, my dreams are still full of Gayle, my waking moments punctuated by her, my final seconds before sleep conjuring images of her.

And then it's time for the school visit once again.

I don't sleep the night before. I don't even know if she will be on the *Angharad*. That is the problem – as well as the attraction – of living in splendid isolation. No internet, no newspapers, no communication. Anything could have happened to her. She might have left the school, moved to another country. Got married and had twins. I stare at my reflection in the bathroom mirror, my clippers paused.

There's a lot more grey in my beard than I remember. The start of my sixth year on Ynys Dwynwen. Five years older than when I arrived here, though time has in many senses stood still for me. But out there ... anything could have happened.

There could have been a terrible accident. She might have died. My eyes widen in the reflection. *She might have died*. I imagine myself, upon hearing the news, travelling to the mainland, back to Manchester, standing on the periphery of her funeral in some rain-swept cemetery, unknown, unnoticed, until everyone has left the open graveside and I walk over and drop a single red rose on her coffin lid.

'You're a romantic idiot,' says Bruce later that morning when I tell him all this. He's sounding suspiciously like Mrs Carruthers. 'Can't you find out all this stuff before she comes over with the Little People? Instead of waiting for her to come here once a year, why don't you go to visit her reef?'

'She doesn't live on a reef.' I have thought about it, to be honest, over the past year. Thought about going over to the mainland, perhaps finding an internet cafe, if they still have those things. Just looking at her Instagram, catching up.

'Her lighthouse, then,' says Bruce.

I blink and stare at him. 'What?'

'Well, if she doesn't live on a reef like me, and doesn't live in a lighthouse like you, what *does* she live in?'

'A house,' I say. 'A big one, by all accounts. With her boyfriend.'

'One female with two males,' says Bruce, shaking his head. 'You are funny, you humans. Why come the mating season—'

'Yes, I know,' I say. 'You'll have six or seven females. You don't have to go on about it.'

Bruce raises an eyebrow. 'Feeling inadequate, Keeper? I told you. Seals are polygynous. You should try it some time. Keeps things exciting.' Bruce flops from the rock where he's been warming his belly. 'Anyway, I think I might have found your dad.'

It was winter when six small merchant ships set off from Liverpool (says Bruce), though the conditions were 'fair at south west', the man I spoke to remembers well.

Was your dad a military man? These men were. Some five hundred and fifty of them, with two hundred and twenty crew split among the half-dozen barques. They were bound for Carrickfergus, which is in Ireland, and where they were to be put to war to fight other men. I was told why but I can't remember; in truth, I don't understand. You humans are always having wars. Unless it's over fish or females, I can't imagine why anybody would want to scrap. Even the shark that did this to me only hurt me because it wanted a meal. You lot ... anyway, I digress. 'Bruce, that's not my dad.'

'I'll keep my eye out, then.' He looks mildly offended as he pushes himself into deeper water. 'I'll gather the colony and we'll go swim round to the other side to welcome the Little People.' He winks at me. 'Good luck with the female. And think about what I said. No need for seven or eight, if you're not up to that. But two or three ... well, always handy in case of, you know. Sharks.'

Then he dives under the water and I watch his dark shape swimming out. He surfaces near Bethan's Reef with a snort of seawater.

'Any storms on the horizon, Gwyn?' says Gayle when Britannia Brook disembarks the *Angharad*.

'What say you, Keeper?' says Gwyn. 'Your storm sense got any better in the past year?'

I sniff the air. There's no telltale scent of ozone, no faint ripple of something on the warm breeze. 'I don't think so,' I say. 'Fair weather, I reckon.'

'Pity,' says Gayle, so quietly only I hear, and as her eyes meet mine a spark passes between us, stronger than any electrical flash the thunderheads could summon. My heart feels fit to burst.

The school has brought me a copy of the *Manchester Evening News* from last year. The storm that kept the previous trip here made the front page. When I reiterate to the children that there's no chance of them being stranded I get a volley of boos. I'm pretty glad this lot aren't going to be staying the night; they're what you might call a feisty cohort. I can see the trip up the tower is going to be fun.

Later, Gayle and I finally get some time alone, walking around the island, as has become our little ritual. When we get to the farthest point from the lighthouse she stops and turns to me, cutting off our inconsequential chatter, as laced as it is with something heavy, brooding and unspoken. 'Martin,' she says, looking me dead in the eye. 'What happened last year ... it can't happen again.'

'No, of course not,' I say quickly. 'Of course not. It was the storm. It was the situation. It should never have happened. It was a terrible mistake. You must be feeling awful. You must have hated it. Don't worry. I haven't thought about it once. Completely forgot about it. From the moment you all left. God! Of course not! I never expected it would happ—'

Gayle puts a finger on my lips to shut me up, a half-smile playing on her lips. 'You never change, do you? You didn't let me finish. What happened last year, it can't happen again ... like that. Not on a children's trip. Not while I'm working for the school. Or it'd be on the front pages for a very different reason.'

She takes her finger away, and raises an eyebrow. 'But, anyway. As you haven't given it a second thought, as you forgot about it completely as soon as I was off the island ...'

'I didn't mean that!' I say quickly.

'So why did you say it?'

I don't know why I said it. Because I knew what was coming, or at least, I thought I knew what was coming. Regret and contrition and Gayle imploring me to forget it had ever happened. What I wasn't expecting was *this*, though I'm not exactly sure what this is.

'What do you mean?' I say. 'When you say, it can't happen like *that*?'

Now it's Gayle's turn to look a little perplexed and conflicted. 'I don't know what I mean.'

She sits down on the grass, gazing out to Bethan's Reef. Bruce is doing belly flops off the distant rocks, trying to impress her. Then she tells me, haltingly at first, everything. Everyone she's ever been with since we broke up, right up to meeting Tom while she was out with Donna for her thirtieth. About the same time I moved to Ynys Dwynwen.

'He sounds lovely,' I say at the end, though obviously I don't mean it. But what else am I supposed to say? *He sounds hatefully good-looking and rich and dynamic and successful and generous and everything I am not, you live in a wonderful house in Alderley Edge and he buys you a brand new car every couple of years and you have four holidays a year. And I absolutely detest him.* So, I just say again, 'Yes, he sounds lovely.'

'He is,' says Gayle, gazing out to sea. 'Very much so.'

'So why ...' I begin.

She looks at me. 'Why did I sleep with you last year?'

I shrug. 'That and ... and why ...'

'And why have I just sort of intimated that I didn't regret it at all and that, under the right circumstances, it could happen again? Just not here on this island while I'm partly in charge of thirty school kids?'

I nod. 'Yes.'

'I don't know,' says Gayle. 'And that's as truthful and as helpful as I can be. Because as much as I love Tom, and as much as he looks after me and says and does all the right things ... there's something missing. Something I could never put my finger on, not exactly. Something I didn't even know wasn't there, until I saw what it could be.'

'And what could it be?' I whisper. She looks me dead in the eye and holds my gaze. 'It's ... I don't know what to call it, I don't know if it even has a name.'

'I think it does,' I say softly. 'I think I know what to call it.'

'No,' she says firmly. 'Do not say that.'

Then she puts her hand on mine, and it's like fireworks going off. I blink and stare. 'Now what?'

'I don't know. Honestly. I have no idea.' She bites her lip and glances at me. 'Do you ever ... ever come back?'

I shake my head. 'I've never left Ynys Dwynwen.' And then I say, 'And now, I'm almost scared to. What if ... what if this is magic, Gayle? What if this is the magic of Ynys Dwynwen? What if you only feel like this here, on this rock in the sea, where the veil is thin and—'

I shut up because she's looking at me and smiling and crying at the same time. 'And this is why,' she says through her tears. 'This is why ... that thing that we can never say, that has no name.'

As the afternoon draws to a close, and the children file

back on to the *Angharad*, and Gwyn steers the boat away from Ynys Dwynwen, I wave and know exactly what that thing is.

'I love you,' I whisper to the boat.

31

Gayle

August

'Too early for a drink?' says Donna.

I don't open my eyes. 'What time is it?'

'After breakfast but before lunch.'

'What were you thinking?'

'Cocktails?'

I open my eyes, the bright sun bouncing off the white sand, momentarily blinding me. There's a sheen of sweat covering my body, amplifying the hot sun, toasting me on the Ibiza beach.

'Cocktails,' I agree, and Donna waves for the waiter to come over to our loungers on the stretch of private beach in front of our hotel.

Donna pulls on a kaftan and sits on my lounger. She smells of coconut and sweat and cigarettes. She whispers conspiratorially, 'That guy's here again.'

I keep my face impassive and swivel my eyes behind my sunglasses. Donna's right. We've been here three days and since we arrived he's never been very far from us in the hotel. We even saw him in the restaurant down on the harbour last night, three tables away. Now he's sitting up reading a tablet, buff and tanned and toned in his close-fitting shorts. He doesn't look up but I can tell he's looking at us from behind his shades. At me.

'You should fuck him,' says Donna. 'You fancy him, don't you?'

I look at him again. He's about forty, good-looking, probably quite well off if he's staying in the hotel that Tom has paid for Donna and I to come to. It's Tom's treat for the last week of the summer holidays. He appears to be single; at least, he's not with anyone and he's not wearing a ring.

'I suppose I fancy him,' I murmur. 'On the face of it. In principle.'

'So, are you going to sleep with him?'

The waiter comes with our cocktails. He glances at Donna in her shorts and bikini top, and me in my white swimsuit. When he's gone I sip my mojito and say, 'No. I'm not going to sleep with him. Don't be ridiculous, Donna.'

'And is that because of Tom or Martin?' She tosses me the sunscreen and turns her back to me, sliding her straps off her shoulders. 'Because you slept with Martin when you were with Tom, so that means you have no loyalty to Tom, so if you're not going to sleep with that guy over there it must mean you have loyalty to Martin.'

I finish rubbing the cream on her shoulders and slap the red bits slightly harder than banter allows for.

'Ow,' says Donna, getting back on her lounger and picking up her drink.

'Your logic is terrible. It's a lot more complicated than that.' I rub sunscreen into my arms. 'And I can't believe you're even suggesting I sleep with someone just to prove a stupid hypothesis of yours.'

Donna sucks on her straw and looks at me for a long moment. 'You heteros are so confusing.'

When I came back from the island, Donna was bursting

to find out what had happened, and was positively crest-fallen when I told her. 'What? No passionate love-making as the surf crashed over your sun-kissed bodies? No running to each other across the clifftop, hungry for each other's flesh? Not even a knee-trembler up against the lighthouse?'

'Donna, I'm a school-worker,' I'd said with a sigh. 'Look at this with your journalist's head on. *Classroom assistant uses school trip for annual shag-fest with lighthouse keeper.* Can you imagine?'

Donna had pulled an impressed face. 'That's not a bad headline, really.'

Even now, in Ibiza, as we get ready to go out for the evening, she still won't let it lie. 'So what you're saying is, it was a one off?'

I massage aftersun into my tummy, pondering how just a few days of drink and food has made its mark. I'll have to get back to the gym when I get home. I can almost see Tom glancing at me and raising an eyebrow. 'You mean having sex with Martin?'

'Well,' she says, fastening her bra. 'You've done it once since you met up with him again four years ago. So I'd call that a one-night stand.' She suddenly grins. 'Or a one *light* stand, maybe. Get it? Lighthouse? One light—'

'I get it. Have you seen the straighteners?'

'The thing is, Gayle,' says Donna, taking two dresses out of the wardrobe and holding them up against her in turn. 'I get the feeling it's *not* a one-off. Which is why I was making the point about that guy at the beach. Are you being faithful to Martin, or to Tom?'

'It's not about being faithful to anyone,' I say, annoyed. 'It's about not wanting to sleep with some random guy on holiday. Why are you obsessed by this?'

'I'm not obsessed,' says Donna, choosing the red dress and sticking the blue one back in the wardrobe. 'I'm just … I'm worried about you, Gayle. I just want to know that *you* know what you're doing.'

I stare at her. 'You *hate* Tom.'

'No I don't.' She frowns. 'I hate what he seems to have turned *you* into sometimes, but I don't hate him.' She pauses. 'Actually, yeah, I do hate him. But you love him. And I love you. So, once again, I just want to be sure you know what you're doing.'

'You're right. I love him.'

Donna turns to face me. 'All I'm saying Gayle is … I know you. I know you can be a dreamer. A romantic. I know this whole idea of Martin, lonely and tortured and isolated on his island, appeals to that side of you. All I'll say is, don't play with Martin's emotions. He never got over you, that's blindingly obvious. And now he thinks you're back in his life.' She finishes buttoning up her dress. 'You have to weigh whatever fantasy about Martin you've got in your head with the reality of your life with Tom. At some point, you're going to have to give one of them up. I think you need to think very, very carefully about which one, and whether you're going to let your heart rule your head or vice versa.'

'What do you think I should do?' I say in a small voice.

She smiles at me. 'Get dressed, get out, and get pissed. And let's worry about all that stuff another time.'

The thing is, Donna's right. Tom is good for me. He does look after me. He's everything a girl could want … he's everything I could want. On paper, at least. And all that stuff with Rachael, and God knows who else … well, I'm hardly one to talk, am I? More than once I've wondered if what I

219

did with Martin was some kind of revenge against Tom, an evening of the scales.

But it wasn't. I know that in my heart. I didn't do that with Martin to get at Tom. I wasn't even thinking of Tom.

And when I say Tom is perfect on paper ... I mean he ticks all the boxes. All except one. And I don't even know what that solitary, unchecked box is. I love him, I know I do. And yet ... and yet and yet and yet. There's something undefinable, something I can't nail down. Most of the time I don't even notice it, its absence isn't glaring. But it's there, when I think about it in the dark moments in the middle of the night, when Tom is sleeping beside me. It's there when I think about Martin, and what happened on the island. It's there when I remember Martin at university, the looks we've exchanged on his island, the electricity that sparks when our fingers brush. I imagine a set of scales; all the things Tom does and says and offers on one side. Then there's this tiny ball of light, no bigger than a pinhead. It is all that Martin offers, and I have no name for it. And still, here I am, on our last day of the holiday. Standing in the reception of our hotel, looking through a rack of complimentary postcards. I select one, showing the wide, white beach I have spent the last week on, and scribble something on the back of it. Then I ask the concierge to post it for me, and do my very best to forget about it.

'You ready?' says Donna, meeting me in the cool lobby.

'Yes,' I say. 'I think I am.'

She looks at me curiously. 'What are you up to?'

'Nothing.'

'OK,' she says. 'But you're a crap liar, Gayle Reiss. Anyway, come on, let's go out and get absolutely trollied. Our last night in Ibiza!'

We decide to have one drink in the hotel bar before

heading out for a meal and as debauched a night as we dare. I scroll through my emails as the bartender mixes our cocktails, then take a deep breath.

'What's up?' says Donna.

'It's the school,' I say.

I show her the email.

Dear Gayle,

Further to the informal chat we had before school broke up for the summer, we've had a number of long talks at this end and we've come to a decision. We'd like to offer you a position as permanent, full-time Year 5 teacher at Britannia Brook. Obviously, this offer depends on your successful completion of the PGCE, but with your experience as a teaching assistant, your aptitude for the job and your high standing with both the rest of the staff and the pupils, we feel this will be nothing more than a formality and something that can be done while you continue to work. Let us know your thoughts before the start of the new term. And we'll all be delighted if you say yes. In anticipation of that, welcome aboard!

Jean Gaskell

'Wow,' says Donna. She gives me a huge hug. 'Congratulations! Full time teacher!' She pauses. 'You've told Tom, right? About applying for this?'

'Not yet,' I say tightly. 'There's time for that when we get home. Now, it's our last night. Shall we get absolutely pissed?'

32

Martin

March

I have to leave Ynys Dwynwen.

At the St Dwynwen's Day celebrations, Heledd Davies
took me to one side. 'Mr Burney. I am informed by my
management team that we must insist on you taking leave.
It's a legal requirement that we have hitherto let slide, but
we are in contravention of employment laws apparently.'
She sighed. 'So I'm afraid we must insist.'

I warmed my hands on the bonfire, looking up at the
lighthouse in the January dusk, about to let loose its beam.
'Can't I just ... take a holiday here? Not work for a week?'
Something occurs to me. 'Who'll be the keeper if I'm not
here?'

'My brother, Hywel, can step in,' said Ms Davies. 'And
no, you must leave the island. It only has to be for a few
days. Regulations.'

'When?'

Ms Davies seemed to consider this. 'March, perhaps. I
need to nail down Hywel's movements. Yes, March. I'll be
in touch when I have some dates.'

'But where will I go?' I said, mainly to myself as I watch
the light issue forth from the tower.

'It's a big world, Mr Burney.'

March arrives, and Gwyn takes me across the water in his little boat, the first time since he brought me here. The mainland looms as we approach, impossibly massive. The thought of all that land rolling out in every direction, the hills and mountains and valleys and rushing rivers ... the choked roads and packed streets, the tarmac and stone and brick and steel and glass ... I feel my throat constrict at the thought of it. All those *people*.

When Gwyn moors the little boat at the stone jetty and leads me up the steps, carrying my waterproof bag, the Royal Mail driver is waiting for him with a sack of post. 'How about you, Gwyn? And Keeper. Good to see you. I think there's a letter for you in this lot.'

Gwyn makes us a cup of tea in the shop while I consider the brown envelope. As Gwyn hands me my brew he says, 'From the literary world, is it?'

It is. My own handwriting on the front of the buff A4 envelope. For the return of the first three chapters of my novel and the short synopsis that I sent off to a London literary agency just after Christmas. This is the fourth such envelope I've had returned. I know by now that the weight of the package means all my material, bashed out on the old Underwood typewriter, has come back. If they had wanted to read more of the book, they'd have just sent a letter.

Gwyn waits expectantly as I slide out the note with my returned manuscript.

Dear Mr Burney,

Thank you for allowing us to read your work. While there is much to commend your writing, I am very much afraid that this novel is not quite right for us, so we will not be proceeding to a full manuscript request. Please do not be down-hearted though, as publishing can be a very subjective business and another literary agent might well feel differently. We wish you all the best placing this elsewhere.

'Ah, bad luck,' says Gwyn.

Except luck has nothing to do with it. My book – or the few thousand words I've written so far – is rubbish. I hand the envelope to Gwyn. 'Stick this in the recycling for me, will you?'

'Don't want to keep it to send it out again?'

I shake my head. 'I'm done with it. It's no good.'

There's a beep from outside. Eddie Jones's coach, come to take me to Bangor, where I'll get a train to Manchester. Home, though it feels odd to think that. Manchester is just a place I used to know.

'Have a good break, Martin Burney!' calls Gwyn as Eddie Jones's coach pulls away and trundles off along the coast road.

'My darling!' says Mrs Carruthers, throwing open the door to her apartment. 'How was the journey?'

'Awful,' I say. 'All those bloody people crammed into that train ... I thought I was going to suffocate. How do you cope?'

'How do you cope, living on that little island with no-body to talk to but the birds?'

'And the seals.'

Mrs Carruthers laughs uproariously. 'Come in. I've made up the sofa for you.' She pops her head to one side, plum coloured curls falling over her shoulders. 'Look at you! That beard! That tan!' She squeezes my arm. 'Those muscles! What have they done with the idiot I used to know and love?'

'Made a man of him,' says a familiar voice. I look past Mrs Carruthers to where Harry is lounging in an easy chair, reading the *Racing Post*.

I dump my bag on the floor and give Mrs Carruthers and Harry a big hug in turn.

'Surprised I'm still alive,' confides Harry in a stage whisper. 'She wears me out, that woman.'

Mrs Carruthers slaps him playfully. 'Come in, dear boy. Take off your coat. Tea? Or something stronger. You must tell us *everything* about what it's like to be a lighthouse keeper.'

'How thrilling!' says Mrs Carruthers, clapping her hands as I tell her about the rescue of the schoolboy from the edge of the cliff. Then I recount the storm.

'We read about it in the *Evening News*,' says Harry. 'Proud of you, lad.'

'It's not all like that,' I say. 'In fact, those are the only exciting things that have happened in ...' I tot it all up in my head. 'Bloody hell, I'm about to start my seventh year on Ynys Dwynwen.' I stare at the TV on a wooden cabinet in Mrs Carruthers' flat. It seems such an odd, alien thing now, to spend your evenings locked in your little box, staring at the screen, face painted by the pale light. I'm not sure I would have the attention span to sit there and do that anymore.

'So what do you do of an evening?' says Harry, pouring us all another big gin and tonic.

'Stand on the balcony and watch the light shining out over the sea. Look at the moon. Watch the voles. Walk around the island. Think. Write. On a big, old manual typewriter.'

I don't say that I talk to Bruce. That feels an odd and foolish thing now.

'Fancy a pint?' says Harry. 'I bet it's forever since you've been in a pub.'

'Yes!' says Mrs Carruthers. 'You boys go for a drink while I get our dinner on. Tarka daal all right for you, Martin? It's one of Harry's favourites. He's vegetarian now.'

At The Fleece, around the corner from the apartment block, Harry orders us both a pint of lager and two pork pies, which he shoves into his mouth, his eyelids fluttering almost orgasmically and his mouth making involuntary, 'Mmmmmmm' noises as he chews on them.

'Not quite fully vegetarian then,' I say, perched on a bar stool and looking around the pub.

'I fall off the wagon occasionally,' says Harry through a mouthful of meat. 'But it's a small price to pay. She's a bloody wonderful woman, is Beryl. I wasn't kidding about her wearing me out, though. How she expects me to keep my strength up with lentils ... the demands she puts on me I don't—'

I hold up my hand. 'Enough, Harry. I really don't need to know about your sex life.'

He takes a sip of his pint. 'I don't suppose you'll be getting any, over there. You missing it?'

Of course, I don't tell him about Gayle, and what happened almost two years ago, during the storm. Only a few weeks until Britannia Brook comes to Ynys Dwynwen again. I can feel the excitement mounting inside me.

'I said, are you missing it? Rumpy pumpy?' says Harry, nudging me out of my reverie.

'Leave it out, Harry.'

I sense him looking at me, and say, 'What?'

'I knew it would be the making of you, this job,' he says, his voice trembling a little. 'I knew it was exactly what you needed. Your dad would be proud of you, Martin. You've honoured his memory, you know. Taking this job.'

I have to admit, I do feel a lot of pride. Standing watching the beam sweeping across the sea, the distant lights of the ships on the horizon, taking their readings by the tower, steering a safe course through treacherous seas. Harry is right. My dad would be proud, I think. I can't save him, but I can do my best to keep others from his fate.

Harry clinks his glass against mine. 'To the keeper of Ynys Dwynwen.' Then he drains his glass and says, 'Two more pints and a pork pie for the road.'

We eat Mrs Carruthers' vast and luscious Indian banquet on the dining table, and drink wine and then more gin, until I'm quite drunk, unused as I am to alcohol these days. We talk into the late night, and then the TV goes on for the news, which I find both fascinating and horrifying. I want to run back to Ynys Dwynwen, shut away all this death and war and pontificating about people who are of no consequence at all.

Then Mrs Carruthers gets out her old vinyls and turns on her Dansette. She and Harry dance close to the velvet voice of Nina Simone.

My eyes are drooping and I settle back on the couch. Mrs Carruthers puts a blanket over me while she and Harry retire to their bedroom, where I hear the springs squeak. Eventually I fall asleep.

I awake well before dawn, as I have conditioned myself to do. I feel stifled in the flat, and I open the window to let the cold March morning in. I hear the sounds of the city waking up, the rumbling engines and distant shouts, the car horns and the thrum of trams, doors slamming and music drifting on the thin air. I hate it. I miss it. I wish for the sounds of my island, the cries of the birds, the crash of the waves, the barking of the seals. But there's some undercurrent of longing here, as Manchester comes alive, some vague and distant memory of life, and the hurly-burly of living, and the simple joy that I had long forgotten of merely being in the presence of other people.

I go back to the sofa and dig into my bag for my notebook, bound by elastic. It's where I jot down ideas and observations, sketches of things I've seen on the island; birds and seals and sunsets rendered in coloured pencils.

There's something else in there as well, poking up from between the pages. A postcard, faded from where it's been pinned up in my kitchen, the edges frayed and roughed.

On the front is a photograph of a wide, white, sandy beach. I feel a sudden pull towards the sea, as if the very blood flowing through my veins is now in tune with the tides. It's an island on the picture, but not my island. It's Ibiza. The card arrived on Ynys Dwynwen, from one island to another, six months ago.

I flip it over. On one side of the reverse is my address, such as it is. *Martin Burney, The Lighthouse, Ynys Dwynwen, North Wales.* I remember the day Gwyn boated it over with my supplies, back at the beginning of September.

On the other side of the card there is no message. Just a phone number. And the scrawled signature. *Gayle.*

I still have my mobile, though it's useless on the island. I put some credit on it when I arrived back in Manchester yesterday. Just for emergencies. I look at the number on the card. I punch it into my phone.

33

Gayle

'You have to come over,' I say firmly.

'When?' says Donna. 'And why? Has something happened?'

'Tonight.'

'I can't. I'm working late.'

'Shit, Donna,' I say, staring at the phone. 'You have to.'

'Gayle, calm down. What's happened?'

'Martin's in Manchester.'

'Oh, shit,' says Donna. I can hear her take a drag of her cigarette. 'Has he been in touch?'

'Yes. He phoned me this morning. Which is why you have to come over. I've invited him here.'

'What? To your house? And Tom?'

'Tom's not here,' I say with a moan. 'He's away for a few days looking at an investment opportunity. Which is why you have to come over.'

'I can't,' sighs Donna. 'Why did you invite him over? Why didn't you arrange to meet him in a bar?'

'Because I can't go out in Alderley Edge because someone will see us, and I can't go into Manchester because Tom knows literally everyone in Manchester, and I panicked a bit and just told him to come over. I thought it would be the safest thing to do?'

There's a long silence then Donna says, 'Gayle, you realise you're acting as guilty as sin already? What would it matter if someone saw you? Aren't you allowed to meet an old friend for a drink?'

'I just panicked!' I say. 'Shit. Maybe I should just cancel.'

'Gayle,' says Donna. 'Are you going to shag him?'

'No!' I say, horrified. 'OK. Deep breaths. Big girl pants on. It's fine.'

'Well, call me when he's gone,' says Donna. 'I want to know everything. Got to dash now. Love you.'

I have four hours before Martin arrives. I should tidy up, and have a bath, and find something to wear. But first, I need a stiff drink.

I watch him walk up the drive, his trainers crunching on the gravel. It seems odd, seeing him here. In my world. He looks different. He's wearing normal clothes, jeans and a shirt, not his lighthouse keeper outfit of jacket and faded blue chinos, black boots. His closely-trimmed beard – even more grey in it than the last time I saw him – makes him look like any other mid-thirties man on the streets of Manchester or Cheshire. He seems … less imposing? Not quite as rugged? As though taking him away from Ynys Dwynwen has lessened him, somehow. As though he's left a piece of himself behind.

I suddenly have a very bad feeling about this. This does not feel like when I visit Martin on his island. This feels like a man I have slept with behind my partner's back knocking on my door. It does not feel magical or romantic or wild. It feels … seedy.

I smooth down my little black dress. I wish I'd worn something else. I feel overdressed. Trying too hard. I wonder if I have time to quickly change. The doorbell chimes

again. Or, I could pretend I'm not in … hide in the down-
stairs bathroom and text Martin to say I've been called away.

Don't be stupid, Gayle. I wish Donna were here. I take a
deep breath and open the door.

He stands on the step, looking awkward, like a Jehovah's
Witness on his first day. We smile at each other, forced,
polite. He's feeling as weird about this as me, I can tell,
which makes me feel a tiny bit better.

'Hi.'

'Hi.'

Martin gestures into the house. 'Should I …?'

'Oh, god, yes.' I stand to one side so he can step in
through the door, looking around the entrance hall like a
prospective buyer.

'Lovely house,' he says.

'Yes. Thank you.' I don't know why I'm thanking him.
It's nothing to do with me. In all the years I've been here, I
haven't contributed more than the odd picture on the wall
or ornament on the table. Tom is very particular about his
interiors.

'So much space,' says Martin. 'I'm not used to it, any
more.'

'Tea? Coffee?'

'That would be lovely.'

I lead him into the kitchen, feeling strangely embarrassed
by the opulence of it. Martin breathes a *wow* as he takes in
the space and the appliances, and looks through the French
doors to the huge garden. He says, 'You've definitely landed
on your feet here.'

'Oh, this is nothing,' I say airily. 'You should see the houses
of some of Tom's friends.' Then I realise how that makes
me sound, and how I should have said *our friends*, not *Tom's
friends*. 'I mean, it's nice, don't get me wrong. I like it …'

Shut up, Gayle, I think furiously. What's wrong with me? What's wrong with us? It's like we don't know each other at all.

I start to get the coffee beans out to grind. Martin says, 'You know, instant's fine ...'

'Thank god,' I say, smiling properly for the first time since he arrived. 'I've got a jar of Nescafé hidden at the back of the cupboard.'

This little act of defiance, as I spoon the instant coffee into the mugs, seems to bring us together a little, to thaw the chill. Martin says, 'Wow,' as I fill the mugs from the boiling water tap. He says, 'Wow,' as I open the huge American fridge-freezer to get the milk.

'Will you stop it?' I say. 'You make me feel like a millionaire showing a Victorian urchin around the home of the future.'

'Aren't you a millionaire?' says Martin.

I suppose Tom is. On paper, at least. That makes me frown. *On paper.*

My breath catches in my throat.

Martin puts down the coffee and stands up.

'Gayle.'

'Martin. I ...'

I don't know how it happens, but I'm kissing him, and he's holding me, and our bodies are pressing together. Not pressing, moulding.

'I'm sorry,' I say, pulling away. 'I can't. Not here.'

'I know,' he says. 'I'm sorry. I ... I should go.'

'Wait,' I say, putting my hand on his arm. 'Where are you staying tonight?'

It turns out Martin is staying with his former neighbour, a vivacious woman called Beryl Carruthers who he has remained in touch with. I immediately love her to bits. And Harry, who Martin used to work with. And who got together with Beryl at Martin's mother's funeral. I almost wee myself laughing as he tells me the story while I drive.

Martin has called ahead to see if we can spend the rest of the evening there and when we arrive in the flat – which is full of lamps and throws and cushions and pictures haphazardly arranged on the wall and is just the loveliest, cosiest place in the world, so far away from what seems the suddenly sterile environment of Tom's house – Beryl is dishing us up the most delicious vegetable curry on a little bistro table in the bay window.

While we eat she regales us with stories about Manchester in the sixties which leave me open-mouthed. Then she says, 'Harry and I are adjourning to The Fleece. There is a pub quiz on and then no doubt the host will have a lock-in until the small hours of the morning.' She looks at me, not Martin and says, 'Harry and I shall take the sofa bed. I have put fresh sheets on my bed.'

'Oh, god, no, Mrs Carruthers,' I say. 'You've got quite the wrong idea—'

She smiles indulgently. 'That's what Ray and Dave Davies of the Kinks said when I turned up at their hotel room at the Britannia in seventy-one. I left thirty-six hours later walking like John Wayne. Beryl Carruthers never gets the wrong idea, darling.' She looks at Martin and says, 'I like her. Perhaps you're not such an idiot after all.'

When they've gone, Martin and I look at each other over the table. He pours me another glass of wine, then says sheepishly, 'I'm so sorry. She's like that. Just ignore her.'

'Martin,' I say. 'Shut up and kiss me again.'

★

233

Later we lie silently in Beryl's bed. The sheets are tangled around us. Creased. Wet. We were loud and energetic and careless about anything and everything save for each other. Nothing existed except for us, and the bed. As if it was an extension of Martin's island, as if whatever magic swirled around Ynys Dwynwen like midges in the dusk or dandelion seeds in the morning breeze, had been brought here by him, and had taken root in the equally magical domain of Mrs Carruthers.

Neither of us says anything, just lying back, staring at the ceiling, the sweat cooling on our bodies, our breathing slowing and becoming more regulated. I close my eyes and wait for the guilt to rush in. It doesn't. I don't feel anything but a deep and overawing *something* for Martin.

I don't want to say what it is. I don't even want to think about it. My hand snakes towards his and our fingers entwine.

'So,' he says.

'So,' I agree.

I hope he isn't going to ask me anything like *was that good for you?* or *did you like that?*, because it should have been patently obvious. But I know he isn't. I know he's going to ask something which is much more difficult to answer.

'So,' he says. 'What happens next?'

'It's a fair question,' says Dad, sipping a mug of coffee in the kitchen the following afternoon. 'What *does* happen next? I mean, bloody hell, Gayle. You're like a couple of teenagers. Up against the lighthouse. In some old hippy's bed. I'm surprised you didn't pull over into a lay-by on the A538 for a bonk in the back of the Mini.'

'Dad,' I say. 'Nobody says *bonk* anymore.' I look at him, my head tilted to the side. 'Did you bonk when you left Mum?'

He shrugs and looks into his coffee. 'I can't deny I thought that might be a ... possibility. Somewhere down the line. I didn't actually have anyone in mind for bonking.' He looks up at me. 'It wasn't an affair, you know. The ... episode.'

That's what we call it. *The episode.* Since Dad went off to live the life of a single man for the best part of a couple of days, we seem to have got closer, somehow. Close enough for me to sit down and splurge everything out about Martin when he called round to drop off some post that was still arriving at their house – mainly statements for a student loan that I'd never really earned enough to have to start paying off. I didn't know whether he'd be angry or judgemental or disappointed or what. Turns out he was just ... my dad.

What happened next in the short term was that Martin and I got out of bed, ate some more vegetable curry, drank some more wine, and told each other everything that had happened to us over the preceding year. Any awkwardness had dissipated; we were warm and close and it felt like ... like the most natural, best thing ever. Then we went back to bed, and stayed there until morning, not hearing Beryl and Harry come in. Dawn's light brought something else into the bedroom, a growing realisation of what we'd done, what I'd done. And the knowledge that Tom was due home this evening. And he'd be bringing with him a hefty dose of stark reality. We made slow, quiet love one more time, then I got into my car.

I sip at my own coffee and look out of the French doors, where the cleaner has hung out the bedding, as if to taunt me somehow. It's flapping in the warm winds on the washing line, like white flags of guilt, stained by proxy.

'Martin's going back to Ynys Dwynwen tomorrow,' I say, which doesn't answer the question.

'And you'll be going there as well in a few weeks,' says Dad. He puts his hand on mine. 'Does this mean you're having an affair, Gayle?'

I pull my face at the word. But how else to describe it? If I'd kept this on the island, if it had been a one-off two years ago, then maybe it could have been just laid to rest. But now ... the wind flaps the bedsheets angrily on the line.

'Do you love him?'

I blink at Dad. 'You mean Martin?'

'Yes.'

I look him square in the eye. 'I don't think I ever stopped loving him, Dad. I just ... forgot that I did.'

Dad thinks about it for a moment. 'When I had the episode, I thought that the grass might be greener on the other side. I thought there might be something else to life than what I had. And it turned out, the grass wasn't greener over there at all. In fact, there was no grass, there was just a flowery orange carpet from the seventies. And a box to sit on. And a cheese fork.' He looks at me. 'I hadn't really thought things through. I didn't know what was going to happen. How it was going to work. Have you thought things through? What is going to happen? Are you going to leave Tom?'

He looks around the kitchen, and I do too. He says, 'And if you do leave Tom, where are you going to go? Back home with me and Mum, because you know you'd be welcome. Live with Martin on the island? And do what?'

I screw up my face. 'I don't know, Dad! I've not thought that far ahead!'

'Gayle,' he says kindly. 'I love you. You're my little girl. But you know what I mean. I want you to be *happy*. What's going to make you happy? *Who* is going to make you happy?'

'I am happy,' I say. 'Happy with Tom.'

Dad looks at me for a long time. 'Do you remember when you had the guinea pig from primary school to look after for the weekend and you were told not to let it out of the cage? But you did and Tigger got it?'

'Yes,' I mutter. 'I remember killing the school guinea pig by giving it to the cat. What's that got to do with anything?'

'Because when we asked you if you'd let the guinea pig out you swore blind that you hadn't. And you had the exact same look on your face then as you did just now when you told me you were happy with Tom.'

I don't say anything. Dad puts his hand on mine. 'All I want you to do is the right thing. For everyone. If you truly love Tom, and this is just *an episode* of your own, then don't string Martin along. But if you do love Martin, do the right thing by Tom.'

I feel tears suddenly prick my eyes. I take hold of his hand properly. 'When did you become the big relationship guru all of a sudden?'

He shrugs. 'I go to this group on Wednesdays. Mum wanted me to get out of the house more. It's a man's club thing. She thinks we talk about football and golf and cars. But we sit in a circle and talk about our feelings. It's very cathartic.'

I can't help but laugh. 'That's brilliant!' I pause. 'Are you going to tell Mum what I told you? About Martin?'

He shakes his head. 'Not unless you want me to. You know how smitten she is with Tom. Better if you just make your decisions on your own, I think. Though you've always got Donna. And me.'

'Thank you,' I say. 'And I will make the right decision. I promise.'

He nods. 'Just one thing, Gayle. Sometimes ... well,

sometimes, the grass is actually greener on the other side.'

I open my mouth to answer, then the front door suddenly flies open. 'Hello!' comes a shout. 'I'm home!'

'Tom,' I call. 'You're back! Dad's here!'

I glance at Dad but he's looking down into his coffee. The sheets flap noisily on the line, but I ignore them, and go to hug Tom.

Year Seven

34

Martin

July

It was October, the mid-part of the month (says Bruce), when the *Cyprian* ran into trouble off the Llyn in a terrible storm that ravaged the land, tearing roofs off houses and uprooting trees.

Out to sea, the waves were mountainous, and spelled the doom of the *Cyprian*, built at Seacombe in 1874 and operated by F. Leyland and Co. of Liverpool, a 1,400 ton steamer powered by two engines, with a crew of twenty-seven.

She was bound for Genoa, and had rounded Holyhead when the storm hit. Still, her captain was confident she would weather the gale. Perhaps too confident, Martin; this is the chap I've been speaking to. Name of Strachan. Maybe he was right, but there were a series of incidents that meant the *Cyprian* was not up to the job. Her starboard boiler burst, and left the ship with one engine. She started to take on water, which hampered the repair of the broken engine, and that put paid to the working one.

Strachan ordered them to hoist the sail, and to get them into the calmer waters of Caernarfon Bay but the weather was too severe. The coastguard was unable to put out to

241

help, and the steamer struck the jagged rocks at Rhosgor, west of Porthdinllaen.

Captain Strachan ordered his men to abandon ship, and gave the call *Every man for himself.* As he was about to leap into the sea himself, a boy emerged from below decks. A stowaway, who had picked a very ill-starred voyage to hide out on. There was no lifejacket for the lad, so Strachan took off his own and gave it to him, and ordered him to jump.

The boy made it to shore, along with eight of the crew, and Captain Strachan went down with the *Cyprian.*

I'm silent for a while, pondering the bravery of Captain Strachan, giving up his lifejacket for a boy who had no right to be on the *Cyprian* anyway. I'd like that to have been my dad. But it's not.

'Sorry, Bruce. But thanks for looking.'

'I'll keep my eye out,' says Bruce, swimming into the shallows. 'Look lively, Martin; the Little People will be here soon. And *her.*'

There are a couple of hours before Britannia Brook arrives, so I take the dinghy out and do a quick sweep of the waters around the island. The plastic seems to be getting worse; I mean, it always does at the start of summer, as people begin to drift towards the coast, but I'm certain there's more than this time last year. By the time I've done a full circuit my little boat is piled up with bottles, bags, cans, toys ... Back on the jetty I bag it up and hide it in the bowels of one of the tumbledown cottages. I haven't burned it since that first year, when Gwyn gave me a ticking off and told me I was doing as much damage pumping that black smoke into the sky as the plastic did floating around the sea. Now he takes it away every couple of months and sorts it into what can be recycled, and what has to go and lurk in landfill for centuries.

I look at a little plastic boat, its blue hull covered in scum. Lost by some child on the beach. Maybe even last summer, bobbing around the sea all this time. It'll outlive us all, buried somewhere. Me, Gayle, Bruce, Gwyn, Ms Davies. Tom. Everyone. We'll all be dead and gone and this little boat, made in China, will be there, its form and purpose long forgotten, probably, as the sun shrinks to nothing and the world ends.

'Cheer up, you miserable bastard,' I mutter, and go to shower before Gayle arrives.

We stand at Edward Davies's grave, which could do with a bit of a tidy up. The grasses are long and almost obscuring the weathered etching of his name. Gayle says, 'Do you think she ever found her way back? Bethan? Did she ever follow the light from the tower? Were they ever reunited?'

I look out to Bethan's Reef, where the seals are sporting. Back at the tower, the brittle shrieks of the children rise on the warm wind. I say, 'I'd like to think so.'

Gayle nudges me. 'Say something more poetic than that, Martin. I thought you were a writer.'

I smile thinly; I haven't been doing much writing recently. None, in fact, since my last rejection. But I gather my thoughts and say, 'Sometimes, in winter, when the nights fall early and hard, and the winds blow around the lighthouse, I stand on the balcony and watch for Bethan's ghost. And sometimes, as the beam plays over the reef, I'm sure I can see something ... a shadow, perhaps nothing more than that, detaching itself from the water, and travelling along the cold, white light as though it's a bridge, connecting this world with the next. For the veil is thin here on Ynys Dwynwen, especially on midwinter nights. You can feel a difference in the air, like a piece of fabric almost worn through. And sometimes that shadow, for that's all it can be, meets another shadow, rising from the land right here where we stand now, and they entwine like smoke for a brief moment, and then dissipate before you're even sure you've seen it.'

Gayle sighs happily. Emboldened, I go on, 'And maybe, this being the island of Dwynwen, the tragic saint of love, it is not just Edward and Bethan who find each other. Maybe their love is so strong it is like a magnet, for others, bringing souls together who should never be parted.'

She says nothing, just tucks a strand of hair behind her ear and gazes out to sea. I've gone too far. But then she looks at me, fixes her brown eyes on mine. And the glow from them is like the bridge of light my lighthouse casts to help Bethan find Edward again. The hairs on the back of my neck stand up and my head fizzes like spacedust on a child's tongue. I want to cry and laugh at the same time, and my chest feels simultaneously full and empty.

'Gayle, I—'

She puts a finger on my lips. To silence me, I think. To not say that thing. But then, she says it. 'Martin. I love you. I've always loved you. But we're not teenagers anymore. I'm with Tom. And what we've done is wrong. But I can't escape the fact that—'

'Keeper!'

We both look round as Gwyn runs across the grass towards us. 'Keeper! Martin! Martin Burney! Come quick!'

'Oh God,' says Gayle. 'The children . . .'

But it's not the children. No child has thrown itself off the tower or fallen down the cliffs. It's far worse than that.

★

The police station on the peninsula has called on the radio, which Gwyn took while in the tower preparing the children's lunches. Gayle's father has had a massive heart attack and is in hospital. After a hushed conversation with Mrs Gaskell and Mr Jensen it is agreed that the rest of the school trip will continue uninterrupted. I will take Gayle back to the mainland in the dinghy; it will be quicker and less complicated than taking her back in the *Angharad*. Someone will collect her there and take her back to Manchester.

Gayle is silent, lost in her own thoughts, as we set off from the jetty. It will take us an hour to reach the peninsula. Gayle sits at the prow, staring blankly ahead, while I steer us from the outboard at the aft. After just ten minutes I feel the need to break the silence that weighs down over the hum of the motor, the splashing of the waves and the cries of the Manx Shearwaters in the blue sky above us.

'I'm sure it will be all right ...'

'Are you?' says Gayle without looking around.

I don't answer. Of course I'm not sure. I have no idea how bad the heart attack is, what sort of condition her father is in.

She says, 'What was it like when your mum died?'

What is there to say to that? It was awful, of course. But not hugely unexpected. And I always felt as though I should have been ... sadder. But the truth was, I'd lost my mum a long time before she died.

I say, 'It hit me so hard I went to live in a lighthouse.' It's an attempt at levity that is inappropriate and, rightly, goes down like a lead balloon.

'Well, I'm not about to do that,' says Gayle flatly, still staring ahead, the spray washing over her.

'No,' I say. 'No, you're not, are you.' And then I can't stop myself, even though my brain is telling me to *shut up*, *shut up, shut up.* 'Gayle, what you were saying, back on the island—'

Finally, she turns a little, to stare at me, her eyes no longer glowing like liquid gold, but dead and dark like parched earth. 'Martin. Please.'

I mentally kick myself. Her words still hang there in my memory, like seabirds riding the thermals.

Martin. I love you. I've always loved you. But we're not teenagers anymore. I'm with Tom. And what we've done is wrong. But I can't escape the fact that—

The fact of ... what? What fact can she not escape?

I stare at her back, at her hair flying out behind her, as the coast ahead grows bigger. She is hurting. She is grieving. This is not the time for me to think about what she said, or what she almost said. And yet, living here on Ynys Dwynwen, spending your days and nights in isolation, makes you selfish. It makes you think about yourself, because there's nothing else to think about. And even as Gayle's tears mingle with the salt spray on her face, even as I see her brow crinkle and her bottom lip tremble, I still want to know. I still want her to finish that sentence.

I can't escape the fact ...

I can't escape the fact that I will possibly never know. Because Ynys Dwynwen might be my world, but it is not *the* world. The world beyond my island is big and messy and busy and noisy and those that live there have their own lives and troubles. Ynys Dwynwen is not Gayle's world. And right now, her world is crashing down around her. I want to take her in my arms and promise her it will be all right, even as I have a doom-laden sense that it is not going to be.

'Do you believe in karma?' she says abruptly, as the stone

jetty behind Gwyn's store looms. She turns to stare at me, fixing me with her flinty gaze.

I know what she's getting at. There's no use pretending otherwise. 'Karma is when your actions are carried over to the next life ...'

'Well,' she says, a flash of annoyance flitting across her face. 'Do you believe that things you do *in this life* can come back to haunt you *in this life*? Like, if you do something terrible, do you think you pay for it in other ways?'

'Gayle,' I say as kindly as I can. 'You haven't done anything terrible ...'

'Yes I have,' she says, and we both know what she's talking about.

'What's happened to your dad isn't ...' I start, but then I have to steer the dinghy in to the jetty, and now we're back on land, now we've left the liminal state of the open sea, where such things might be discussed. Now it's down to the very real business of getting Gayle to her father's side as quickly as possible.

I help her out of the dinghy and we climb the stone steps. 'Look,' I say. 'I'm sure he'll be fine. They said there'll be someone here—'

I look around then stop. There, by the side of the road is a sleek sports car, an Alfa Romeo. And leaning against it is a tall, tanned, toned, good-looking man in a white shirt and jeans.

This must be Tom, then.

Gayle looks at him, then at me. She says, 'Martin. Do you still love me?'

I open my mouth and then close it again. I'm not sure what to say. Of course I love her. I realise now that I never stopped loving her. But this is not the time to talk about that. I look over at Tom, glancing at his watch. It is never

247

the time to talk about that. Because while Gayle might be wrong that what we have done has resulted in something terrible happening to her father, it is still wrong. Gayle is with Tom. On Ynys Dwynwen you might feel like you're shut away, that normal rules don't apply ... but that's just an illusion. Like all magic, I think bitterly. Just smoke and mirrors.

'Go to Tom,' I say numbly.

Gayle looks at me, her expression unreadable, then sets off at a run. He steps forward to meet her, enclosing her in his arms. Protectively. Lovingly. She buries her head in his chest and I see her sobbing and shaking. He walks her round to the passenger seat and helps her in, then comes back round to the driver's side.

Tom stands there for a long moment, scrutinising me. I wonder what he's thinking. I wonder if he knows about me – not about what's happened recently, but about the fact that Gayle and I used to be together. Then he's looking away, towards the island. He takes out his phone and holds it up. He's taking photographs of Ynys Dwynwen. I wonder why. Then he climbs into the car, gives me one more glance, and roars away.

I watch the car until it disappears around the bend, feeling shabby and small, and of no consequence at all. I hope Gayle's dad is going to be all right. But, if he's not ... well. She's in good hands.

35

Gayle

Tom has been an absolute rock.

Dad hung on until we got to the hospital, where Mum was by his bedside, holding his hand, and Donna was waiting in the corridor. Tom waited outside with Donna while I sat with Mum, and we held hands over Dad, while each taking hold of one of his, creating a circle, trying to inject life into him, making an electrical circuit that meant he could not die.

He died.

Dad had suffered a heart attack while driving, what Mum will never think of as anything other than, 'that stupid car'. Fortunately he wasn't going too fast, and it wasn't in a built-up area, so no one else was hurt. He ran into a lamp post, and suffered a head injury that, combined with his heart attack, proved fatal.

Donna drives me and Mum back to the family home. Tom has to tie up a couple of bits of business so he can take time to be with me. I tell him it isn't necessary but he insists. He says he will bring me clothes and toiletries, and I am to stay with Mum for a few days, for as long as she needs me.

'I won't ask how the school trip was,' says Donna over a glass of wine in Mum's kitchen later that night. Mum has gone to bed, but I can hear her tossing and turning, the occasional sob ripped from her. I just feel numb, as though time stopped along with Dad's vital signs, and I'm still waiting for them to restart.

I stare blankly at her. 'What?'

'It doesn't matter,' says Donna. 'I just asked about the trip.'

The trip. The school trip. It all feels like a blur now, a procession of jagged images. The island. The boat trip. Martin. Tom waiting for me.

Donna looks at me. 'Did you see him?'

I nod, and look away. I don't want to think about him. About all that. It doesn't matter now. My heart is frozen and I neither know nor care whether it will ever thaw again.

I stay at Mum's until the funeral. Tom is brilliant. He brings me practically all my wardrobe, and make-up and toiletries, without being asked. He's got an instinct for this sort of thing. Knows exactly what a woman wants and needs. It feels weird, sleeping in a cramped little box room after the house in Alderley Edge. I'd grown so used to it. The space. The appliances. The luxury. But, by degrees, I grow used to the smallness of Mum and Dad's ... *Mum's house,* I correct myself, and it comforts me. Like a nest, or a·womb. Safe and small and cosy. Higgledy piggledy and haphazard. Not clean and white and regimented, like Tom's house. *Your house, too*. I am always correcting myself.

Turns out that Mum and Dad aren't quite as comfortably off as I'd thought. Which was mainly to do with Dad cashing in his pension and blowing a good chunk of it on his car and *the episode*. There is life insurance, but not a huge amount, and that will be swallowed up by the funeral.

'Nonsense,' says Tom over dinner one night, around my mum's little dining table. 'We'll pay for the funeral.'

By *we* he means *he*, but I'm grateful to him for including me. Mum bursts into tears and can't thank him enough.
'And no skimping,' warns Tom. 'I want Paul to have the
send-off he deserves.'

Later that evening, after Mum has gone to bed, I sit with
Tom on her sofa. I need to be held. I need someone to
listen to me. To let me talk.

'I miss you,' he breathes into my ear. His hands range
over my body.

'No,' I say. 'Don't. I nee—'

'Gayle,' he murmurs. 'I know what you need.'

Then his phone pings repeatedly and he sighs and pushes
himself off me. 'Bloody New York,' he mutters, scrolling
through the messages.

'Can't you tell them to go away?' I say, trying to pull
him back to me. 'Please just hold me. It's eleven o'clock at
night.'

'Not in New York,' he says. He shoves his phone in his
pocket. 'Look, I'm going to have to go and email them
some documents from the laptop at home. I've got these
people hovering over investing in a big project and I can't
afford to let them cool on me.'

'OK,' I say, trying not to sulk. Tom leaves and I sit there
on the sofa, crossing and uncrossing my legs, and wondering why he can't let New York cool on him, but he's quite
happy to leave me sitting here burning up with grief.

Tom does Dad proud with the funeral. God knows how
much it cost. I don't ask. There's a carriage and black horses
and a Scottish piper. Tom books the clubhouse at his golf
club. The chapel is awash with flowers and somehow Tom
has got a personal recorded message from the manager of
Manchester United which is played at the service.

After the coffin goes into the ground I feel a dam burst inside me. The numbness and coldness and nothingness of the past two weeks are washed away by floods of tears, and once they're done I feel almost reborn. As though I can finally take my finger off the pause button and start to tentatively live again.

At the wake, Mum is all over Tom, heaping praise on him for organising and financing the funeral. All the relatives, some of whom I've not seen since I was little, are fawning over him.

'Tom is absolutely marvellous,' I hear Mum saying to an auntie. 'So successful. He looks after Gayle so well. And you should see his house, Brenda.'

I'm finding it all a bit overwhelming, and I feel awful for thinking uncharitable thoughts. I sneak out into the sunshine on the terrace, which overlooks the golf course. There I find Donna, smoking and leaning on the balustrade.

'Golf's fucking weird,' she says, not turning to look at me.

I lean on the balcony alongside her, and take the cigarette from her fingers, having a long drag. I haven't smoked since that last one with my Dad, I realise, and it hits me like a punch. No more crafty fags with Dad. It simultaneously makes me feel sick and tastes like nectar. 'Why?' I say, coughing, and handing the cigarette back.

'It just is. I mean, look at them. Swinging their big sticks, trying to get a little white blob into a tiny hole. They couldn't have invented a game that screams sexual frustration more if they'd called it Big Stick Spunky Hole.'

'Eww,' I say. 'Give me a fag, Donna.'

She hands over her packet and her lighter. 'And they call the sticks woods as well, don't they?'

'Not all of them.' I light myself a cigarette. 'Some are called drivers.'

She looks at me and we both chuckle. She says, 'Tom likes his golf, doesn't he?'

'He does a lot of business on the course,' I say with a nod. 'And the clubhouse. He does a lot of business everywhere.'

Donna turns, leaning back on the balcony, looking to the wake inside. 'Well, he's got to keep you in the manner to which you've become accustomed. And he's done your dad proud today, got to give him that.'

'Yeah. So everyone keeps saying.'

Donna watches me for a bit. 'Is it inappropriate to bring up Martin at this point in the proceedings?'

'It's my dad's funeral, Donna.'

She reaches inside her pocket and pulls out a hand-rolled cigarette. 'In that case, I suppose it's inappropriate to smoke a joint at this point in the proceedings?'

I stare at her. 'You brought weed to my dad's wake.'

'I work in the media, Gayle. Think yourself lucky I didn't chop out a line on the coffin lid.'

She doesn't wait for my approval and lights up the joint, inhaling deeply and handing it to me. 'So,' she says, trying to keep the smoke in her lungs. 'Martin.'

I sigh. What to say? The excitement I felt just a couple of months ago, the sense of delicious danger, the romance of the lighthouse, the warm feeling I had whenever I thought of him … it all seems to have receded. I miss my dad. I want him back. I don't have room for anything else in my head or my heart. Especially not Martin, so far away and so easy to be the thing that I push out of my life.

And yet … even just thinking about him now seems to ignite something, a spark from two clashing flints glowing with dull hope in a nest of dry grass. It's as though now he's back in my life, I can't imagine him not there, even if we meet so infrequently.

'Earth to Gayle.'

I blink and look at Donna, who gives me the joint back. 'Thought I'd lost you for a minute then. Look, it's fine, you don't want to talk about it. I shouldn't have brought him up.'

'It's fine,' I say, sucking on the joint and feeling a little giddy. 'The short answer is, I don't know how to answer that question. It's all very confusing.'

The door opens from the clubhouse and I throw the joint over the side of the balcony in to the grass below. Mum's had a couple of glasses of wine and is looking more than a little tipsy.

'There you are!' she declares. 'What are you doing out here?'

'Just watching the men play Big Stick Spunky Hole, Heather,' says Donna. 'Want to join us for a bit?'

Mum frowns as she approaches, looking me up and down and sniffing. 'Gayle, have you been smoking?'

'Oh, that's me, Heather, you know what I'm like,' says Donna airily. 'How's it going inside?'

'That's what I came out to find you for,' says Mum. 'I was going to say a few words ...'

Back in the clubhouse, the buffet decimated – including the whole salmon laid out on the long tables – Mum stands up, a little unsteadily to my eyes, and taps a fork on her glass.

'Thank you all for coming,' she says when the crowd that's gathered around her has quietened down. 'It's been a very sad day, but it's also been lovely to see so many people come and pay their respects to Paul. He'd have been so grateful to know how much he was loved.' There's a chorus of *hear, hears*, and Mum goes on with a sigh, 'If the silly bugger had realised how well thought of he was, he might never have gone and bought that stupid car and tried to get into those skinny jeans.' She shakes her head. Does she glance at Tom when she says that? Does she blame him for Dad's death? Because he encouraged him with that sports car? If she does blame Tom, she's not quite got over her infatuation with my boyfriend, if what follows is any measure of it. She says, 'Anyway. I just wanted to say thank you to everybody, but especially to one person who I could not have got through this without.'

Donna nudges me and I smooth down my black dress. I wish Mum had warned me about this. I haven't got anything prepared to say and my mind has suddenly gone blank. I should never have had that smoke.

'I'd like it if we could have a few words,' says Mum. 'Tom, if you wouldn't mind?'

I gape as Tom smiles self-effacingly and holds up his hands against the ripple of applause, joining my mum at the centre of the throng.

'Fucking hell,' breathes Donna.

'Oh, Heather, it was nothing at all,' says Tom. 'I don't just think of you as Gayle's mother. You've been good enough to welcome me into your family. And as I lost my own parents a long time ago ...' He smiles sadly. 'Well, I hope you don't mind if I say you're like a mum to me, too.'

There's a chorus of *Awwwws*. I feel Donna tense at the side of me. 'Gayle ...' she murmurs.

But I'm a step behind her, even when Tom says, 'And maybe it's time this family had a bit of good news, for once. Something to celebrate.'

'He's not ...' says Donna. 'Surely not here ...'

I really shouldn't have had that joint. I feel all disconnected and fuzzy. I've still no idea what's going on. Until Tom holds out his hand to me, and smiles, and says, 'Gayle Reiss ...?'

255

36

Gayle

New Year's Eve

We have a party at Tom's house – our house – for New
Year's Eve, with all his usual crew, and my mum, and even
Donna. It starts early. Too early for me. By five in the afternoon I've had too much gin and I'm starting to feel a little
odd and weepy. A lot of that is about Dad, of course. These
first big milestones hurt like hell. Christmas was hard, despite Tom's best efforts. Mum barely touched the dinner
he'd cooked, and couldn't even bring herself to compliment
the horseradish he'd made for the buffet on Boxing Day.
Now she sits at the table, a faraway look in her eye, nodding
in what I know she is hoping are all the right places as one
of Tom's friend's wives holds court. I catch her eye and give
her a tight smile. She gives me one back, and the look in her
eyes makes me tear up.

Why did Dad have to go and die like that? What was
he thinking of? I look around the kitchen, at the knots of
people drinking Tom's wine and spirits, picking at the snacks
he's spent all morning making. *Why aren't you dead instead?*
I glare at some fat, grey man laughing with a mouth full of
blinis. A woman shrieks as she knocks over a glass on the
worktop, then laughs like a braying donkey. *Why couldn't*

it have been you instead of my dad? I know these thoughts are uncharitable, I know they make no sense. I know you can't trade one person off against another. Nobody can choose who lives or dies. But why did it have to be my dad? Why so soon? There was so much I still had to do with him, so many things I still had to talk about.

Like Tom's proposal at his funeral. Which I still haven't said yes to. Or no, come to that. When he asked, making that stupid announcement, I could have fallen through the floor at the inappropriateness of it all. It was my dad's funeral. But then I saw Mum, the hope and longing in her eyes, her desperation for some kind of good news to ease the pain of what was happening, something to distract from the chasm that had opened up inside her.

So the champagne popped and everyone cheered and I smiled but I didn't say yes. Instead I took Tom outside, held his hands, and looked into his eyes, and said, 'That was a lovely, wonderful thing you just did. But I want to wait a little before we make this real. I need to grieve for my dad. Do you understand?'

A cloud passed over his face and his expression told me that no, he didn't understand at all. But he kissed my forehead and said, 'Of course, Gayle. Take as much time as you need.'

'We'll start making plans,' I'd said. 'Let's give it ... six months?'

His frown deepened, but this was something Tom could understand. A deadline. A timescale. This was how he worked. He brightened up. 'OK, yes. Let's say ...' he glanced at his watch, at the date. 'End of January, then?'

I nodded and kissed him, and then we went back into the wake, hand in hand. Everyone congratulated us. It didn't matter that they hadn't heard me say yes. Everyone just assumed I had, because why wouldn't I? But it mattered to me that I hadn't. It mattered to me that when I did, I would do it on my terms.

And standing there, in the kitchen, alone in a bustling crowd, I realise that it is not just because I am grieving for my dad that I want to put things off. There is another reason entirely. And I have just not known what to do about that until now.

With her unerring ability to read my mind, Donna zeroes in on me, weaving unsteadily through the crowd, holding a bottle of champagne and a flute. I nod at it and say, 'That was supposed to be for midnight.'

'Ah, you've got about forty bottles of this stuff,' she says, filling up her glass. 'And I do like bubbles. You should have some, Gayle. Remind yourself this is a party and not a second wake.'

Donna is the only person in the entire world who can get away with talking to me like this. I say, 'Who have you been upsetting, anyway?'

She puts a hand on her chest, a picture of innocence. 'Not a soul. I have merely been listening to Tom telling everyone about the plans for your wedding. Manchester Cathedral, hey? Very swish.'

I say nothing and she squints at me. 'You have actually said yes, I presume?' I shrug. Donna fills my glass and says in a low murmur, 'You know what I think about Tom, Gayle. You also know what I think about you. I love you like a sister. More than a sister.' She frowns. 'God, I can't stand my actual sister. Anyway. I want you to do the right thing. For you. I want you to do what makes you happy. And I do not want you to do anything that makes you unhappy, or that you're not sure of. Do you understand me?'

258

I do understand her. And suddenly, I understand myself as well.

'Donna. Can you cover for me for ten minutes?'

She looks around, at where Tom is holding court, animatedly waving his arms, and shrugs. 'Sure. Are you going to do something stupid?'

'Quite possibly.'

'That's my girl.'

Outside in the dark garden, the cold air hits me hard, not sobering me up but making me feel even more drunk. I go behind the summerhouse and light the cigarette I cadged from Donna. At least if Tom does come out here, I can claim the lesser of two evils and say he's caught me having a drunken smoke. Then I take out my phone.

It takes me five minutes to find the number. There's no guarantee anyone will be there at this time, gone five on New Year's Eve, but if I don't do this now, emboldened by booze and Donna's tacit approval, even though she has no idea what I'm up to, then I never will.

My thumb hovers over the green button then I take a deep breath and put the phone to my ear. It rings and rings and I'm just about to sigh and kill the call when it's picked up and a gruff voice says, 'Gwyn Jones's General Store.'

I start to babble immediately, the words tumbling out of me. 'Gwyn. It's Gayle. Gayle Reiss. From the school visits. Martin's friend. I need you to get a message to Martin for me. Can you do that? I have no other way of contacting him, and it's vital I get this to him. You might want to write this down. Are you ready?

'Tell him that Tom has asked me to marry him. I haven't said yes yet, but I might as well have done. It's all booked. Manchester Cathedral on the eighteenth of July. But I haven't said yes yet. That's the important thing. I told Tom it's because my dad died and I need to come to terms with it, and that's partly true, but only partly.'

Gwyn Jones grunts so I continue.

'I haven't said yes yet because of you. Not you, Gwyn. Martin. Can you tell him that? Please? Because of what's happened between us since we met up again. Because of the feeling inside me, that came flooding back as soon as I saw him. I love Tom, Gwyn. I really, really do. He's kind and generous and he loves me. But when I saw Martin ... it was like a piece of me that I hadn't realised was missing suddenly slotted back into place. And I don't have any other word for that than love. And I realise I can't love Martin and Tom at the same time, not in the same way. And I don't even know if Martin feels the same way, not really, not even after everything that's happened.

'But I want to be sure. So this is why I'm calling. Tell Martin that if he feels exactly the same way, and he cannot feel any less than that, he cannot feel anything other than what I'm feeling, then he must get in touch with me. And I have no idea what will happen then, I have no idea how it would work, but at least we can talk about it. I love him, Gwyn. I love Martin. But if I don't hear from him by the end of January, I'll assume that he doesn't feel exactly the same way, and I'll just get on with my life. I'll marry Tom, and I'll be happy, and I'll have nothing but fond memories of Martin, I promise. There won't be any drama. I'll understand.'

I stop, breathless, spent. I say, 'Gwyn? Did you get all that?'

There's a pause and I think maybe I've lost the connection, then he says, 'July 18th. Got it.'

I'm about to say more when I hear my name called from

the house. It's Tom. I quickly kill the call and shove my phone in my pocket as he walks across the frosty grass.

'Gayle! What on earth are you doing out here?'

I look guiltily down at the cigarette stub on the ground, and he follows my eyes, then tuts. 'Gayle Reiss. I'm very disappointed in you.' His eyes are smiling, though. 'Come on, it's New Year's Eve. Let's enjoy ourselves. God knows, after this year, we deserve it. You deserve it.'

I let Tom fold his arm around my shoulder and steer me back towards the house, my insides turning to water. What have I just done? When we get back into the kitchen, Donna directs a pointed stare in my direction, and I give her a smile.

'It's all OK,' I mouth towards her. And one way or another, it will be.

Year Eight

37

Martin

The ring glints in the summer sunlight, reminding me I really should get outside and clean the glass. I'm due an exterior paint touch up as well, so I should probably get all that done together.

It's my mother's ring. The one she gave me all those years ago, to give to Gayle. The one I had in my pocket that day in Affleck's Palace.

It's been a year since I saw her. A year since I heard from her. I'm not sure what that means. For one of the handful of times over the past seven years, I curse the fact that there's no internet or signal here. It seems such a strange and wonderful thing now, the idea of just picking up a phone and sending a message. Scrolling through someone's feeds to see what they've been up to. Looking for the little tell-tale green dot. All those things I took for granted in my old life, that sense of immediate, intimate connection, twenty-four hours a day, seven days a week. It's only when you don't have it that you realise it is both a blessing and a curse. I've never felt as free as I have since I came to Ynys Dwynwen, never felt so unassailed by anxiety, never so untroubled by what people think of me. The flipside of that, of course, is that in the dark hours of the dead of night, when you wake up and feel alone, the phone is just a blank screen, not a window or a lifeline.

Obviously, I could take the dinghy over to the mainland, walk a little way down the peninsula, and have full service on my phone. But somehow that feels like cheating. It feels like not fulfilling my promise to the island. To live here, to be the keeper ... it seems to demand complete and total submission to the job.

To be the keeper of Ynys Dwynwen is to withdraw from the world, and sit on the nexus of the land and the sea, dark and light, the world of the living and what lies beyond.

On Ynys Dwynwen, it feels like you're closer to the horizon than anywhere else on earth.

So yes, I could have gone to the peninsula, I could have contacted Gayle. But I did not feel it was my place. Not after seeing her fall into Tom's arms. I don't even know what happened. Whether her father lived or died.

The sun goes behind a cloud and the ring seems to dull in my fingers. A year to the day since I last saw Gayle. Britannia Brook will be coming in a few hours. What will she say to me? What will she think? Will she wonder why I never tried to get in touch? Will she thank me for stepping back?

Life – and possibly death – will have moved quickly for Gayle. Here, time moves at a more stately pace, like the fleets of white clouds drifting across the sky. I measure my life by the turn of the seasons, by the hatching of puffin eggs, by the maturing of the seal cubs on Bethan's Reef, by the lengthening and shortening of the days. And by the tick-tock-ticking of my thoughts. There's a lot of time to think on Ynys Dwynwen, a lot of time to plan.

A lot of time to come to decisions.

And here is mine.

I will go to meet the *Angharad* with my mother's ring in my pocket. And the second my eyes meet Gayle's, I will know. I will know what I have to do. I will know whether what I want to do is utter madness, or if it is what the magic of Ynys Dwynwen has wrought, by bringing her back to me.

Enough time has elapsed. Enough thinking has been done. When Gayle comes to my island, I will ask her to finish the last words she spoke to me, complete the sentence that has hung in the air through the long summer, through windswept autumn, through dark winter, through budding spring.

Martin.

I love you.

I've always loved you.

But we're not teenagers anymore.

I'm with Tom.

And what we've done is wrong.

But I can't escape the fact that—'

For a long year, those words have taken root, and I have nurtured them, and watered them. All I want now is for them to bear fruit.

If the flower that blooms on the branches of those words is *all I know is ... I love you and want to be with you*, then I will take the ring from my pocket and give her that choice. I'll say that I know she's happy with Tom, and with her life, and I don't want to step between any of that. But there's obviously something between us, and we have a chance to make it right, do what we should have done years ago, if that's what we both want. And no, I don't know how it will work either, but I have to try.

And if what blossoms is *all I know is ... we can never be together*, then the ring will stay in my pocket and no more shall be said. I'll be happy that we at least had these brief moments together after I'd long thought Gayle lost to me.

I put the ring back in its box.

I stand on the grass just above the jetty, watching the *Angharad* approach. I've been watching it for half an hour, seeing it slowly come into view, the mass of children on the deck. The ring weighs heavily in my pocket. Is this a wise move? Obviously not. It's like pinning down a butterfly. It's never as beautiful as when it's flying free. But there's something in me that demands some kind of focus, some kind of decision. Since Gayle came back into my life I have had a deep and abiding yearning for ... permanence. I think that is what Ynys Dwynwen has taught me. My life before was so transient, bouncing from one crisis to another. Ynys Dwynwen endures, through storm and sun, through wind and snow.

The *Angharad* is almost here. I stand up straight and scan the faces. Gwyn at the helm. The teachers, Mrs Gaskell and Mr Jensen. The bright, expectant faces of the children.

Gayle is not there.

'Keeper,' nods Gwyn, limping up the jetty once the *Angharad* has been securely moored.

'How's the leg, Gwyn?' I say, looking over his shoulder at the assembly from Britannia Brook, sure I must have missed Gayle. Perhaps she was below decks. At Christmas, Gwyn broke his leg. I'm not quite sure how; the details seem hazy, not least to him. It involved climbing a tree on Christmas Eve, and something to do with a cow. The result was that he was laid up for most of January, and I had to take the dinghy over to the peninsula, when weather allowed, to pick up my supplies.

'On the mend,' he says, rubbing his thigh. 'Still gives me

gyp when it's cold.' He catches me peering over his shoulder and says, 'She's not here, Martin Burney.'

'What?'

'Gayle. She's not here.' Gwyn puts a hand on my arm. 'Martin. I'm an old fool but I'm not a blind one. I'm sorry.'

'Sorry? Gwyn? What—'

Mrs Gaskell bustles up while Mr Jensen organises the children into unruly ranks. 'Ah, Keeper! So glad to see you again!'

I plaster a smile on my face. 'And you, Mrs Gaskell. However ... your numbers are depleted?'

'Ah, yes, Miss Reiss,' says Mrs Gaskell. 'So sad.'

My breath catches in my throat. 'What's happened?'

'She's gone, I'm afraid,' says Mrs Gaskell. 'So very unfortunate.'

I feel myself go pale. 'She's ... dead?'

Mrs Gaskell stares at me, then laughs uproariously. 'Dead, Mr Burney? Oh good heavens, no! She's left us. Left her post at Britannia Brook. Such a waste. She was a marvellous teacher. Had a real aptitude for it. And the children loved her.'

'She left the school,' I say, numbly.

'She's getting married,' says Mrs Gaskell. 'To her rich property developer. We should all be so lucky, eh? Anyway, I think Mr Jensen has finally marshalled the troops. Shall we get on?'

When the children have departed the island, I watch them go and then walk over to the far side of the island, opposite Bethan's Reef. I stand there for a long time, until the sun starts to dip towards the sea.

She's getting married.

I reach into my pocket, and pull out the box containing my mother's ring. I don't open it. It was a stupid idea, the

269

most stupid idea in the history of stupid ideas. I pull my arm back, then throw it, in a long, curving arc, over the sea, until it plops into the water, midway between the island and the reef.

Let my father find it, if he's down there. It's his, by rights, now Mum's gone. Not mine. Not Gayle's.

I stand there until the sun goes down, and then turn to watch the light burst forth from the tower, sending its message of hope and safety across the glittering sea.

The light never goes out. But the one inside me is tamped down, and extinguished.

Two weeks later, I have just finished my early morning run when I spot Gwyn's boat powering towards the island. I frown. That's curious. He was only here three days ago with supplies, and a letter from Mrs Carruthers which I decided not to give him because I wasn't entirely sure that the claims she made about a night with Roger Moore and Sean Connery in 1978 weren't actually defamatory. I'm not due a visit. He moors the boat on the jetty and jumps out, limping up the hill, waving frantically at me.

'Oh, Keeper!' he calls, his face twisted in anguish as I run over to him. 'Martin Burney! Disaster!'

'What on earth has happened, Gwyn?'

'*Disaster*, Martin Burney! Oh I'm a fool. But not as much of a fool as that absolute idiot Wyn Jones.'

I take hold of Gwyn's shoulders and shake him gently. 'Gwyn. Please just tell me what's happening.'

'Well,' says Gwyn. 'It was New Year's Eve, wasn't it? About five o'clock. I'd not been intending to keep the shop open that late but Blodwyn was having a New Year's Eve party and she's very particular about her whisky so I was waiting on a late delivery from the distillery in Ceredigion.

Their van had broken down, hadn't it? And with my leg being all gammy, I needed a bit of help, so Wyn Jones had come over on the promise of twenty quid and a bottle of the whisky.

'So it was about five, like I said, just after maybe. And the phone rings. And I'm trying to get some stock from the back so I ask Wyn to take a message. I guess it'll probably be Blodwyn, spitting feathers and wondering where her whisky is. So he's on the phone and I hear him humming and ahhhing and then he puts the phone down and that's it I don't give it a second thought.

'Oh, Keeper! If only I'd taken more care! If only I'd asked that idiot Wyn Jones who was on the line! Yes, yes, I'm getting to that. So this morning, Wyn Jones comes into the shop, hanging around as usual, making the place look untidy, and suddenly pipes up, oh it's that wedding today.

'"What wedding?" I say to Wyn Jones, not having the slightest clue what he's on about.

'That woman who phoned on New Year's Eve, says Wyn Jones. I think she wanted you to cater a wedding or something? I put it on the calendar.

'Well, I run over to the calendar on the wall and sure enough, there it is on today's date. Wedding. Manchester Cathedral. Bloody idiot, is Wyn Jones. That calendar is from 1995. I don't use it as an actual calendar, I just like the steam trains. Funny thing about Wyn Jones is, Martin Burney, he's an idiot but he never forgets a date. He's like an elephant. One of those photographic memories, I dare say. So he scrunches up his face and says, now I think on it, it wasn't to do with *catering*!

'Disaster, Martin Burney! It was Gayle! Gayle Reiss from the school! And she thought she was talking to me! She wanted me to pass a message to you, saying that she was going to get married but if you said not to, then she wouldn't get married to this Tom at all! But she was only going to wait until the end of January for you to respond, and if she didn't hear from you, then she would assume that you didn't love her!'

I stand there, hardly breathing, as Gwyn relays the story. Then I ask him to tell me again. I say quietly, 'And this was New Year's Eve. And she wanted me to get back to her by the end of January. And now ...'

'And now, she's getting married! She's getting married *today*!' wails Gwyn, tearing at his hair. 'Come on, Keeper! We don't have any time to lose!'

38

Gayle

18 July

It's my wedding day. Donna comes into the room and strikes a pose. 'What do you think?'

She's wearing a slim-fitting three-piece man's suit in a dusky pink, with black leather Chelsea boots. She looks great. I tell her so, and say, 'Aren't you supposed to ask me that?'

She casts a look over my dress. Off-white silk, lace-trimmed décolletage. Hideously expensive. Wildly beautiful.

'You look gorgeous, Gayle. Haven't I told you umpteen times?'

'You can never tell a bride she looks beautiful too many times on her wedding day,' I say.

Donna sits on the bed and watches me at the dressing table, finishing my eyes. Tom wanted to get me some Instagram-famous make-up artist, but I just want to do this one thing for myself. He's chosen the church and the venue and the honeymoon and the cars and my dress. This little thing, doing my own make-up … it makes me feel at least like I'm contributing to my big day.

'Cheer up, love, it might never happen.'

I look at her in the mirror. 'Do I look sad?'

'Well, you don't look like a woman who's about to get married to the man of her dreams at Manchester Cathedral, have a reception at the Lowry, then jet off to Mauritius for three weeks, no, to be quite honest.'

'I'm happy,' I say, smiling at her.

'Well, tell your fucking face, Gayle.' She gets off the bed and comes and crouches beside me, our eyes meeting in the reflection.

'That'll be enough of that language, thank you.' Mum stands in the doorway, and when she sees me she starts to tear up. 'Oh, God, Gayle. You look beautiful.'

Donna stands up and gives her a handkerchief. 'Bloody hell, Heather, don't wreck your make-up again. You've done it three times already.'

'I can't help it,' says Mum, dabbing at the corners of her eyes. 'My little girl ... getting married. I wish your dad was here to give you away.'

I blink away my own tears. I don't want to be doing this make-up again, either. I say, 'You're giving me away, Mum. That's more than enough for me.'

'It's not traditional though, is it?' Mum looks at Donna. 'Nothing about this wedding is traditional. A best woman? Why can't you just be maid of honour, Donna, love?'

'Because I wasn't wearing that dress you picked,' says Donna. 'I'd have looked like that crocheted doll my nan used to cover her bog rolls with.' She gives a little twirl. 'Don't you think I look smart, Heather? I hope there's some hot lesbians at the reception. What do you think the chances are?'

Mum shakes her head. 'Donna? Can you just give me a minute with Gayle?'

'Course,' says Donna. 'I'll go for a ciggie in the garden.'

'Not one of those funny ones, I hope.'

'I only take drugs to funerals, Heather. I'm not a monster.'

I swivel round and Mum perches on the end of the bed. She takes my hands in hers. 'I really do wish your dad was here to see this.'

'So do I, Mum. You know that.'

'He'd have been made up. And I know you were a bit on the back foot when Tom proposed at the funeral. But I'm glad you came to the right decision in the end. I mean, it was never in any doubt, was it? You love Tom. He looks after you.'

'I don't need looking after, Mum,' I say softly. 'I've done all right since I left university.'

'Of course you have. And I'm proud of you. Me and your dad have always been proud of you.' She puts her head on one side. 'You didn't really want to leave the school, did you?'

No, I really didn't want to leave Britannia Brook. But that was one of Tom's *conditions*, though he'd never have couched it in those terms. He'd made it quite clear that becoming his wife wasn't just a case of being his live-in lover with a ring on my finger. He wanted to involve me in the business, wanted me to ostensibly take on a role as his PA, which would mainly involve doing a lot of lunches with clients and prospective business partners, both with him and on my own. There would be an expectation that I'd devote as much time to him and his business as I had to my job at the school.

'Those kids … I worry about them,' I say. 'I worry about what'll happen to them when I'm not there.'

'The school managed before you, love. They'll manage after you. Besides … Tom was saying that maybe this doctor friend of his … it's not necessarily that you've no chance …'

Yes. Tom's doctor friend. With whom Tom has been discussing my ovaries and womb as though they're just part of another property deal he's striking.

'Mum, I'm thirty-seven. And after what happened ... I wouldn't hold out any hope of being a granny. And nobody's actually ever asked me if I want to have children. I'm sorry.'

'Well,' says Mum. 'That's a conversation for another day. This is your wedding day.'

'Mum,' I say suddenly. 'Do you remember Martin?'

She frowns. 'Which one was he?'

'I was with him through university. And just after. You met him. Several times. You remember.'

'Oh. Him. What about him?'

'He's a lighthouse keeper.'

She waits for me to go on, and then shrugs when I don't. 'Ah. Lovely.'

'Yes,' I say. 'He lives on an island off the coast of Wales, the one I went to with the school. It's a different pace of life, Mum. Simpler. Less complicated. Less ...'

'Less comfortable, I reckon,' chuckles Mum. 'I bet he doesn't have an American fridge-freezer and a tap that gives you water hot enough to make a cup of tea.'

'No,' I say. 'He doesn't.'

'Well, then,' says Mum, as though that's sorted, though neither of us really know what exactly is sorted.

There's a knock at the bedroom door and we both turn to face Donna. 'Are you done with the mother-daughter bonding? Because a big vintage car just pulled up outside.'

'It's a Daimler,' I say. 'Tom booked it.'

I stand up. Mum takes my left arm and Donna comes in and hooks her arm through my right. We look at ourselves in the dressing table mirror.

'I think we'll do,' says Donna.

'Right,' I say. 'Let's go get married, shall we?'

39

Martin

'Don't be ridiculous, Gwyn,' I say. 'I can't go to Gayle's wedding.'

'Of course you can, Martin Burney!' says Gwyn, dragging me towards the tower. 'I have to make this right! She would not even be getting wed if I'd got this message to you in time. Come on! Get into your proper clothes! Eddie Jones is waiting. He's going to get you to Manchester!'

'And then what?' I say, as Gwyn propels me into the lighthouse.

'I don't bloody know, do I? Do something! Stop the wedding! Be like *The Graduate*, won't it?'

I can't really do this, can I? I can't go and crash Gayle's wedding? Declare my love for her?

Before I know it, I'm dragging off my running gear and climbing into my trousers and shirt, while Gwyn spits on my boots and polishes them with my tea towel.

'Quickly, Martin Burney!' He thrusts the boots at me. 'We have no time to lose!'

'All aboard the love bus!' bellows Eddie Jones as Gwyn pushes me on to the rickety coach after the crossing from Ynys Dwynwen. 'Manchester Cathedral, is it? Just need to stop at Gareth Jones's farm to get some red diesel then we're on our way.'

'No dilly-dallying, Eddie Jones!' scolds Gwyn, wagging his finger at him through the open doors. He takes off his Greek fisherman's hat and slaps it on my head. 'For luck, Martin Burney!'

'Don't you worry, Gwyn Jones,' says Eddie. 'I'll get our boy to Manchester in time to stop this bloody wedding!'

I sit down but jump up again as Eddie crunches the gears on the coach. 'Gwyn! The lighthouse!'

'I'll go over and keep an eye on her!' shouts Gwyn as the coach jerks and pulls away on to the coast road. 'You get your girl! I'll make sure the light doesn't go out!'

After stopping to fill up with diesel at Gareth Jones's farm, where Eddie also takes surreptitious delivery of several bags of lamb, pork and chicken, which he stashes in a cool box in the boot, we rattle on north and east, through Caernarfon and Bangor and Llandudno.

'About two and a half hours, depending on traffic,' booms Eddie over his shoulder. 'Haven't been to Manchester for a good while, have I? Last time was when we had to stage an intervention with Wyn Jones. Silly bugger. Got himself high as a bloody kite and dressed up as Superman and tried to climb up the Arndale Centre to protest about not having access to his kids, didn't he?'

'Did it make any difference?' I say. 'Did he get to see his kids?'

'Doesn't even bloody have any!' roars Eddie. 'On the shrooms, he was. Invented himself a whole life where he was a recently divorced insurance clerk with three children, and not some bloody meth-drinking waster who sleeps on the benches at Pwllheli.'

Eddie hugs the coast, majestic Snowdon rising up to our

279

right. 'Yr Wyddfa, we call it,' says Eddie. I roll the name around my tongue. *Er With-va*. 'Means *grave*, so it does. Rhita Gawr the giant is buried up there, after King Arthur did for him. Epic scrap that was, so they say.'

I watch the names flash by on the signs. Abergwyngregyn. Llanfairfechan. Abergele. St Asaph. Eddie puts on a tape of house music, nodding his head to the beat.

'Bloody loved a good rave in my day,' he says. 'We used to have them in Gareth Jones's top field, when the farm was owned by his old man. Deaf as a post, was old Jones. Bloody hundreds of us up there, gurning like guppies, those poor cows. Wyn Jones always had a baggie or two. Happy days, Martin Burney.'

And then we're on the M56, into England, passing Chester and Runcorn and Warrington, and the signs for Manchester appear, and my stomach starts to flip. Crossing the border from Wales, where magic always seems to ripple on the horizon, back into England, where the skies have clouded and mundanity clings to the verges along the motorway. I wonder what the hell I'm doing. Is it too late to tell Eddie to turn around, and forget this whole ridiculous enterprise?

But we're on the outskirts of Manchester, the familiar buildings rising up around us. Eddie swears and beeps his horn then slams a fresh tape in the stereo. He begins to sing 'Love Will Tear Us Apart' at the top of his voice, just as the square clocktower of Manchester Cathedral hoves into view.

My breath catches in my throat as Eddie squeals the coach to a stop. There, ahead of us, is a long, white vintage car adorned with purple ribbons. And climbing out of it is Gayle.

She looks absolutely, heart-stoppingly stunning. There's

a figure in a pink suit beside her, which I suddenly realise is Donna. I haven't seen Donna for years. They talk for a moment, and Gayle's mother joins them, taking Gayle's arm.

Then they begin to walk towards the arched entrance of the imposing stone cathedral, as a melodious pealing of the bells begins.

Eddie turns in his seat. 'So, Martin Burney, what's the plan?'

I don't have one. I have absolutely no idea what I'm going to do.

'Maybe you should catch her before she goes in the church?'

I take a deep breath, then stand, and Eddie lets me off the bus. I start to walk towards the cathedral, then break into a run. Gayle is almost inside. All I have to do is shout. Call her name. Make her turn round. Make her stop this.

Donna glances over her shoulder as I approach, and her eyes widen to the size of saucers as she recognises me.

'*What. The. Fuck?*' she mouths at me.

Gayle turns to her, giving her a quizzical look, and seems just about to look behind her as I slow to a halt, but Donna takes her arm and rushes her inside the cathedral, casting one last glance behind her and shooting daggers at me.

Then they're inside, and I hear the wedding march strike up on the organ. I glance back at the bus, where Eddie is having an arm-waving argument with a traffic warden. Then I look ahead, take another deep breath, and head inside the cathedral.

A couple of people on the back rows glance at me, but most eyes are on Gayle as she proceeds along the aisle to the altar, where Tom, in a navy blue suit, is turning to greet her, his eyes full of love. I sit down on an empty seat at the end of the back row, beside people I don't recognise. They ooze wealth and privilege, and a man my age looks me up and down, his eyes dancing with mirth, and says in a stage whisper to the woman beside him, 'Who invited Captain Birdseye?'

I feel small and insignificant beneath the vaulted ceiling and gothic arches of the grandiose building, the vast, golden pipes of the organ rising up behind the altar. Small, insignificant and suddenly on the wrong side of history. I should not be here, I think, as the congregation shuffles to its feet and sings the first of the hymns. I should let myself out, quietly, right now and disappear.

But I have to see this through. Because I do not know what I am going to do, yet, and this is my last possible chance.

The dean begins the ceremony, and it seems to gallop along, time spooling between my fingers, my window of opportunity contracting to almost nothing. Very traditional service. Classy, I imagine. Just the sort of thing this Tom would go for.

And then it comes.

'I require and charge you both, as ye will answer at the dreadful day of judgement, when the secrets of all hearts shall be disclosed ...' reads the dean.

The secrets of all hearts shall be disclosed. Even mine? Even the secret that burns there? Do I have the right?

' ... that if either of you know any impediment, why ye may not be lawfully joined together in matrimony ...'

I stare down the aisle, past the sea of well-wishers and friends and family, at Gayle, standing looking up at Tom. And here I am, the impediment himself. Sitting at the back of the cathedral, smelling faintly of fish.

' ... ye do now confess it. For be ye well assured, that so many as are coupled together otherwise than God's Word doth allow are not joined together by God; neither is their matrimony lawful.'

And I stand up, and I slam my fists down on the back of the pew in front of me, and everyone gasps and turns to look at me, as I shout, 'No!'

Except, of course, I don't. I don't shout or slam my fists. Nobody turns to glare at me. I simply look at my boots, and after a moment there's a ripple of slightly relieved, amused laughter as the dean makes some quip and carries on with the service. And I just want to run as far as possible from this place, but I know I can't leave without making a fuss. So I listen to the readings and sing the hymns and shrink as small as I possibly can in my pew as Tom and Gayle pass me on their way out of the cathedral. But I needn't have worried. They only have eyes for each other.

Donna, on the other hand, bends low as she passes and hisses in my ear, 'You. Outside. Now.'

I lurk a little way from the cathedral as the wedding photographs are taken, and Donna extricates herself as soon as she is able and stalks over to me.

'Martin,' she says. 'Good to see you after all this time. But what the actual fuck are you doing here?'

'I ... I don't know,' I say helplessly.

She runs a hand through her hair. 'Jesus, Martin. You could have ruined the whole day.'

'That was kind of the idea.'

Donna gapes at me. 'Seriously? You came here to stop the wedding?'

I shrug. She shakes her head. 'I should deck you. Look, you tit, this is her wedding day. Do I like her new husband? Would I rather see her walking down the aisle with you, who obviously makes her so happy? It doesn't matter, Martin. This is what Gayle wants. And I love her. So you do not—'

'Martin.'

Neither of us have noticed Gayle approach us. She stands there, puzzlement crinkling her smooth brow, holding her bouquet loosely in her hands. She looks utterly beautiful, like a piece of heaven made flesh.

'Gayle.'

'Martin was in Manchester on a training course,' says Donna. 'Thought he'd come and see you on the happiest day of your life.' She enunciates the last five words with slight kicks to my ankle. 'But now he's got to go. That lighthouse won't light itself, will it?'

'Actually,' I say, 'it's almost fully automa—' But then fall silent at Donna's glare.

'Martin,' says Gayle again.

'I got your message,' I say.

Donna glares at me, and then Gayle, narrow-eyed. '*What* message?'

She nods. 'You didn't get back. So ...' She looks back and waves at the wedding party milling around in the cathedral grounds.

'What message?' says Donna again.

What I don't say is, *but I only got your message today*.

What I don't say is, *if I'd got it in January I would have told you not to marry Tom*.

What I don't say is, *I love you, Gayle. I've always loved you. And despite all this, I always will love you*.

What I do say is, 'It was a lovely service. You look beautiful. I really hope you and Tom will be very happy together.' Then I turn and walk to Eddie's coach without looking back.

Year Nine

40

Gayle

August

The first time, I think it's an accident. He drops his napkin under the table and reaches down for it, and the back of his hand brushes my bare calf.

The second time, when he momentarily rests his hand on my knee as he reaches over the table for the bottle of wine, I dismiss it as absent-mindedness.

The third time, when he asks me to pass the salt and I lift up a little out of my chair to lean over, and I feel his hand brush my backside, I have to stop making excuses for him.

His name is Roger and he's about sixty, with a florid, booze-tanned face, a paunch that hangs over the trousers of his expensive suit, and a gaze that grabs yours and holds on to it, as though he's trying to fuck you with his eyes.

I detest Roger. But he's a potential investor in some project Tom is cooking up, and as I am now part of Tom's property development operation, though I don't seem to have an actual title or a defined role, nor an actual salary other than the money Tom puts into my account whenever I need anything, I am expected to spend time with these people.

Which is why Tom, Roger and I are around a table in an exclusive little bistro in the Northern Quarter, and I am

287

wearing a short, figure-hugging dress. I plaster a smile on my face as Roger adjusts the noticeable bulge in his trousers and I try to ignore it.

Tom is talking about returns and yields and Roger is listening and nodding, and stuffing slices of rare steak into his mouth. I feel his knee suddenly touch mine, and he holds it there.

'It's a solid gold investment, Roger,' says Tom. 'It's an unmissable opportunity.'

Roger washes his mouthful of food down with wine and says, 'You know me, Tom. Never like to miss an opportunity.'

Then his hand falls beneath the table, and comes to rest on my thigh.

I stand up sharply, and Tom looks at me in surprise. 'I just need the loo,' I say, trying to keep the shaking out of my voice. I glare at Tom, nodding my head imperceptibly towards the toilets.

'I, uh, think I might go and see what dessert wine they've got in,' says Tom, wiping his mouth with his napkin and standing up. 'You'll excuse me for a moment, Roger?'

Roger waves his hand dismissively, his eyes roving all over my body. 'Take your time, dear boy. I'm sure Gayle can look after me properly when she comes back.'

Outside the toilets I grab Tom's arm and hiss, 'He's not stopped groping me all night!'

Tom actually chuckles. 'He's renowned for his wandering hands, is old Roger.'

I stare at him. 'Aren't you going to say something?'

He frowns. 'He's harmless. And rich. Stinking rich. I need him on board for this project, Gayle. Just be nice to him.' Tom looks at me, critically, his head on one side. 'Did you make an appointment at the clinic yet?'

Ah, the clinic. My first anniversary wedding present from Tom, presented to me with a flourish along with a pot of coffee, a glass of champagne, and smashed avocado on sourdough toast as I lay in bed, the day before we flew out to Capri.

I opened the envelope to find a voucher, for an eye-watering amount of money, to be spent at a cosmetic surgery clinic in the Cheshire countryside. 'You can spend it on what you want, of course,' Tom had said. 'I might suggest ...' he cups imaginary boobs on his chest. It makes me feel sick.

'I've not had a chance to call the clinic yet,' I say frostily, heading into the toilet.

When I get back to the table, Tom is showing Roger photos of our Capri holiday on his phone. Roger is more red-faced than usual, and as I sit down I see that he's lingering over pictures of me in my bikini round the pool.

'Oh, very nice,' he says, as though he's sizing up a cut of beef. 'Very, very nice indeed.'

Tom sits down and as the waiter clears our main course plates away he says, 'So, Roger, have you given any thought to the proposals ...?'

'Oh, can we wait until after coffee?' says Roger. 'Talking business on a full stomach gives me indigestion. And we're having such a lovely time, aren't we?'

Then he takes my hand and rests it on his napkin, spread over his bulging crotch.

'So what you're basically saying is that you're now a whore,' says Donna.

'Donna!' I hiss, wide-eyed, as we sit in the sunshine at a pavement cafe in Alderley Edge.

'Well, how would you describe it?'

'I'm a senior account executive,' I say primly, having pinned Tom down to giving me an actual title for my role. I suspect he just plucked three random words out of the air, but at least I've got some nice business cards out of it.

'With special responsibilities for old perverts' stiffies,' says Donna, sipping her coffee. She looks at me. 'Gayle, I feel I can say this because I love you. You were a brilliant lawyer doing some brilliant work for important environmental causes. You were a brilliant primary school teacher doing brilliant work for disadvantaged children.'

'And now?' I say, meeting Donna's gaze. 'I'm just a whore, is that it?'

She shrugs. 'You know I didn't mean that, not really. Look, you've got a wonderful life and everything you could ever want and yes, I am a bit envious of the fact you don't have to worry about how to make the rent or pay the gas bill or have to decide between a package holiday in the Canary Islands or getting the car through its MOT.'

'I'm not rich,' I say. 'Tom is. I'm not.'

She looks at me for a long time. 'Remember back in university? You were always going to save the world.'

I look away, at the busy street with its boutiques and cafes and expensive cars. 'That was a long time ago. And one person can't save the world.'

She finishes her coffee and stands up. 'No, but one person can make a difference. Even a small one. Look, I've got to go. Thanks for lunch. Let me know when you have your tits done and we'll go out and wet the puppies' heads.'

Every couple of weeks I go into Tom's offices in central Manchester. He has a PA called Veronica, who is constantly buzzing around, organising his diary and getting his lunch and fussing over him. There's an architect, Theresa, who comes in a couple of times a week, a frostily stylish woman in her fifties who has an amazing figure. There's a young woman in her twenties called Lois, who answers phones and arranges appointments, directed by Veronica. And there seems to be a constant stream of interns, daughters of Tom's friends and contacts who generally sit at desks and gaze all starry-eyed at Tom whenever he breezes through the office.

And then there's me. The wife. The wife with the job title senior account executive which means nothing at all. I am treated with the appropriate deference for my status, but I always feel as though my presence is an imposition on the rest of the office, that all these women would be having a far more relaxed time if I wasn't there.

Tom is rarely there when I am in the office, either in his own little sanctuary tucked away, or out meeting people. I tend to tap away at a computer, mainly just shopping online or playing games. Very occasionally, I will get something to do. Like today.

Veronica approaches me, her false smile plastered to her face. 'Gayle. Tom's double-booked this afternoon and wants you to take one of his appointments for him.'

'Great,' I say, closing down the website where I was just about to buy four hideously expensive scatter cushions that I neither need nor particularly want.

'It's at Brown's, at two. Roger Claybourn.'

My heart sinks.

I make my own way home after the meeting as Tom is on a run of appointments, and by the time he gets home I've done in the best part of a bottle of wine.

'How was the old goat?' he says.

'Fucking awful,' I say, as Tom pours himself a glass of wine and sits at the kitchen island. 'Please don't send me to meet him again. He literally propositioned me, Tom. He said he could get a hotel room and we could basically go there and he would, in his own words, give me the sort of pleasure I had never thought possible.'

Tom laughs heartily. 'Oh, he's a terrible old flirt.'

I glare at him. 'He wasn't flirting. He was propositioning me. He was rubbing my thigh with his horrible podgy little hand while he said it. He had a bloody erection, Tom.'

'He's harmless,' insists Tom.

'Really? Because he was telling me about a girl who used to work for him. Said she was feisty, like me. Played hard to get, like me. Said he took her away once to a conference and reminded her that he was her boss and that she ought to know, in his words, which side her bread was buttered on. And that once he got her to his room, she wasn't particularly willing at first, but he rather liked that. Showed spirit, he said. But in the end, he had his way. Because Roger Claybourn always has his way. Doesn't take no for an answer, see. And he gave her the sort of pleasure she never thought possible. So I should bear that in mind.'

Tom's smile falters a little. 'I'm sure he was just exaggerating a bit. You know what men are like.'

'I know what men like that are like,' I say, going to get a fresh bottle of wine. 'Entitled, over-privileged pricks who are used to getting what they want.' And I look at Tom, and I wonder, *are you a man like that?*

'Well,' says Tom cheerfully. 'Whatever you said or did, it seems to have done the trick. Roger called me before I left the office. He's in. My major investor. Which means my project can finally go ahead.'

'What even is this development?' I say.

'Oh, it's a biggie. Going to give us some very good returns indeed.' He goes to his leather briefcase and gets out a manila envelope. 'Gayle, I don't suppose you'll remember, because I'm away a lot, but just before your dad died I went on a research trip for a few days.'

I do remember. I stare guiltily into my glass. That was when Martin came over and we spent the night at Mrs Carruthers' flat. The last time we slept together. Just before the last time I went to Ynys Dwynwen. I say, 'Oh, yes, I think I remember.'

He smiles and sits down across from me. 'Well, it's been a bloody long time coming, and there are still a lot of planning hoops to jump through, but with Roger on board I can finally go through with this.'

He pushes the envelope towards me. I pull out a glossy brochure. On the cover is an artist's illustration of a contemporary house, with a swimming pool in front of it, and a glittering seascape.

'This is very high-end,' he says. 'It's going to cost a fortune, but it'll be worth it. Holiday rental.'

Wait. Behind these houses, on the artist's impression ...

'But very, very elite. Millionaires. Film stars. Oligarchs. I mean, it's remote, but that's why we're pushing for a helipad.'

It's a lighthouse.

Tom nods enthusiastically. 'And the best thing is, we can go whenever we want! I went to your island, Gayle! When I went away. After I'd seen your photos from the school visit, I knew it was perfect.'

'Ynys Dwynwen,' I say numbly.

'Yes!' says Tom triumphantly. 'I've only gone and bought it, haven't I?'

41

Martin

'You're selling Ynys Dwynwen?' I say, uncomprehending.

'It isn't quite as simple as that,' says Heledd Davies, sitting across a wide, mahogany desk opposite Gwyn and me in her house on the Llyn Peninsula.

I should have known something was wrong when Britannia Brook didn't come for their visit a few weeks ago. I was standing there, waiting on the jetty, nursing a vain hope that Gayle would somehow have taken her old job back and would be on the *Angharad*.

But the *Angharad* did not come. Britannia Brook did not come. Only Gwyn, in his little boat, with a few supplies, and some news.

'Only heard myself this morning. The school visit is off.'

I'd presumed some funding or staffing crisis, until Gwyn got in touch this morning to say, 'Keeper, we've been summoned. By the duchess. To her place.'

Her place is a large, rambling, Welsh slate house nestled in the valley a little further around the peninsula, where Heledd lives with her brother Hywel. The house is in a state of disrepair, and Ms Davies looks old, and frail, and a little defeated, since the last time I saw her at St Dwynwen's Day.

'What would Edward Davies say?' Gwyn says, shaking his head and rubbing his chin. 'Selling the island?'

'As I said, it's a little more complicated than that,' says Ms Davies. 'We have been in negotiations for some time about potentially developing the old cottages on the island. The land itself will stay in the family's hands. But there will be something of a handover of a large portion of the territory. And we had to stop the school visits. For good. It's a shame but it's a matter of ownership, now.'

She pushes a brochure across the desk at us. I flick through it then give it to Gwyn. 'A swimming pool? A helicopter landing pad?'

'It is envisaged that this will be something of a bolthole for the rich and possibly the famous,' says Ms Davies. 'A private little island with the novel advantage of its own lighthouse.'

'So I'm out of a job, then?'

Ms Davies shakes her head. 'Not at all. In fact, quite the reverse. You are something of a draw, Mr Burney. An attraction. The rustic lighthouse keeper tending his tower right on the doorstep of this elite holiday home. I'm told those who will be spending eye-watering amounts of money to stay here will find that quite entertaining.'

'You're turning Ynys Dwynwen into bloody Disneyland!' says Gwyn angrily.

Ms Davies fixes him with her level stare. 'I'll thank you not to raise your voice in my home, Gwyn Jones.'

As Gwyn mumbles an apology, I say, 'But why? When I arrived here, you told me how ... sacred Ynys Dwynwen is. How important. To your great-grandfather. To your family.'

'That was almost a decade ago, Mr Burney. Things have changed. And not for the better.' Ms Davies stands, with some difficulty, and walks with the aid of her stick to the tall window that looks out into the grounds. 'We are in need of money. Lots of money. We have made some bad investments. There are wolves at the door. My brother, Hywel, is not in the best of health.'

'Maybe you should sell this rambling old pile and downsize,' I say.

She turns and glares at me. 'It is the family home.'

'Ynys Dwynwen is the family island.'

There's a long silence. Ms Davies turns back to the window. Beyond the overgrown gardens is the glittering sea, and on the horizon, the island.

Eventually, she says, 'This is not a matter for debate, gentlemen. I merely thought it prudent to keep you abreast of the latest developments. There is much to do in terms of planning regulations and appropriate permissions. I do not envisage anything happening inside of a year. Mr Burney, I suggest you return to Ynys Dwynwen, continue your duties. Tonight, as every other night, the light must never go out.'

'I think, in a little way, it already has, Ms Davies,' I say, and Gwyn and I take our leave.

We spend a largely silent hour motoring back to Ynys Dwynwen over the choppy water, brooding on what this means. Gwyn is as invested in the island as I am; it has been a part of his life for as long as he can remember.

'On the plus side, you'll be able to charge a fortune for Viennettas,' I say, trying to lighten the mood.

Gwyn sighs as he steers the boat to the jetty. 'It's a bloody disgrace, is what it is, Keeper.'

Despite my attempt at levity, I have to agree. It's an utter disaster. Gwyn says, 'What will you do?'

'I don't know,' I say, looking at the tower, framed against the pale blue sky. I mean, I could leave. But where to go?

What to do? Ms Davies said it will be at least a year until anything happens. A lot could happen in that time.

'I came to Ynys Dwynwen to escape the world,' I say. 'It seems the world is not that keen on letting me go.'

'I'm sorry things didn't turn out right for you with Gayle,' says Gwyn. 'She was a lovely lass, that one. You were good together.'

'We were,' I say with a tight smile. 'Or at least, we could have been. But what could I offer her, Gwyn? The lonely, unsophisticated life of a lighthouse keeper's wife? I don't think that would have done for her. She's happy, now, I'm sure of it. And in some way, that makes me happy too.'

'What a load of old ram's bollocks,' says Gwyn. 'Of course you're not bloody happy, Keeper. Not without Gayle. Not with the duchess selling the island from under you, turning you into some kind of zoo animal for rich kids to poke with a stick. It's all a bloody disgrace.'

'Yeah,' I concede. 'Not the way I was hoping this would turn out. But I suppose nobody *deserves* a happy ending, not really.'

Gwyn climbs back into his boat. 'You're a writer, aren't you, Martin Burney? Then write your own bloody happy ending. That, at least, you can do.'

At dusk, I take a bottle of wine out and sit on the grass in front of the cottages. Right where the swimming pool will be, according to those drawings. I sit very quietly and watch the tumbledown buildings, until my eyes acclimatise to the gloom. I like this brief moment between the sun sinking and the light bursting forth. It doesn't last for long, but it feels as though this is the most special time. Nature's light extinguished, man's not yet lit. This is the time when you could make wishes, and expect them to come true. This is the

297

time you could believe in magic. This is the time when you could be sitting in the cool grass and it could be this world, or the next, folding into each other, in the gathering dark.

I wait for the telltale movements in the empty windows and doorways. The Dwynwen Voles. I ponder what they must think of me. The tales passed down through the generations, the giant in the tower. They must think of the lighthouse as a god, and me as its high priest. And in the course of the next year, they will be gone. Their home, the cottages, bulldozed. Swimming pools and helicopters and brash, rich, people. The Dwynwen Voles will be wiped out and their passing will be barely noticed.

And what of the puffins? What of the Manx Shearwaters? What of the seals? What of Bruce?

What of Bethan? She'll never find her way home now, never be reunited with Edward.

And then the light bursts forth from the tower, shining out in four directions, painting the land and the sea with its cold, white beam. It doesn't feel like a comfort, now. Doesn't feel like a beacon of safety, guiding those out there on the dark sea to safety. It seems more like it is declaring its existence to the world, it is calling those here who do not belong. It is an advertisement of the secret, magic territory of Ynys Dwynwen, a betrayal of the island. *Come*, sings the lighthouse. *Come here and take it. You've taken everything else. You may as well have this, too.*

The next morning, after my run, I fish on the shingle beach. Bruce swims over and I toss him something from my catch. How to tell him? How will he understand?

'I think I might have found your dad,' says Bruce as I cast the line out into the deep water.

★

This ship (says Bruce), was built in a place called the Netherlands. Fifty-odd years ago. Owned by a company working out of Grimsby. Registered in the Cook Islands. Complicated business, this shipping. Anyway, the *Cygnet*, they called her. She was taking a load of limestone from Colony Bay down to the Isle of Wight, when she got into trouble ten miles off the Llyn Peninsula. Five miles from here, Martin Burney.

Big storm blew in. Force eight. Big wave crashed down on the *Cygnet*. And for some reason, they'd put all this stone right in the middle of the deck. Basically broke the back of the ship, it did. Straight to the bottom she went, eighty metres down.

Twelve men there were aboard. Six made it off the ship. Six did not. This chap, he didn't make it. And he says he's sorry, Martin. He's sorry he never came home.

'Describe him,' I say, hardly daring to breathe.

'Big man. Kind face. Beard. Hair.'

'Bruce. I think it might be him.'

Bruce nods. 'I thought so, too. Said he had a son. Except he was only four last time he saw him. I told him about you. He seemed very proud.'

'What else did he say?'

Bruce screws up his face, remembering. 'He said ... he said that things are worth fighting for. Even when it seems like everything is hopeless. He said even in the darkest night, there is always a light. Always hope. Even when your ship smashes in two, even when you feel yourself dragged down into the dark depths, even when you feel the air leaving your lungs and being replaced by cold, salty water, even then you never give up hope.'

'But he's wrong,' I say. 'Because sometimes, there is no

hope. Sometimes the person you love more than anything else in the world marries someone else. Sometimes the place you love more than any other place in the world can be sold and ruined in the name of money. Sometimes the planet you live on can be choked by plastic and rubbish.' I look out to sea, beyond Bethan's Reef. 'And sometimes, when you're a little boy, and you're waiting for your daddy to come home from the sea, he doesn't come. And that's when you realise hope is a fragile, silly thing.'

'Oh, he sent you something as well,' says Bruce, and then he begins to cough and gag, and spits something on the shingle beach. 'Sorry. No pockets. Or hands, come to that. On account of being a seal.'

It's a small box. Faded and bloated by the sea, its edges ragged. I bend down to pick it up, and open it.

My mother's ring shines in the morning sun.

'He said, don't give up hope.'

'Thank you,' I say. 'For finding my father.'

'Knew we'd get there in the end, Keeper. Now toss me another of those mullets and I'll be off.'

42

Gayle

September

I'm in the bathroom, studying my face in the back-lit mirror, when the doorbell rings. I ignore it. It'll probably be the postman or a delivery driver, with some parcel of things I don't really want but which made me happy for the few moments it took to buy them online.

I inspect my brow, my jawline, my cheeks. I'm thinking about finally cashing in my voucher.

I don't feel old. I look like a thirty-eight-year-old woman. Do I really want to try to look like a twenty-year-old? I'm happy with who I am, what I look like. Tom, evidently, is not. At least I won't look out of place among all the slim, smooth, toned women he surrounds himself with if I get some work done.

The doorbell goes again. 'All right,' I mutter, taking one last look at my face – with a sudden sadness, as though I'm saying farewell to it – before switching off the bathroom light.

'Do I need to sign?' I say to the kid on the doorstep, looking around for the parcel.

'Sign, miss?'

He doesn't have a parcel. I frown and say, 'Sorry, I thought you ... who are you, anyway? What do you want?'

He smiles and something flickers in my head. He's about sixteen or seventeen. Tall. Slim. Pale and blond. He says, 'It's George, miss. George Bentley.'

My eyes widen. George! George Betley! George entley who fell off a cliff on Ynys Dwynwen! 'I didn't recognise you! You've grown up so much! Come in!'

I make George a coffee in the kitchen while he looks around, awestruck. 'Wow, miss, you live in a massive house.'

I remember George, and his desperate mum and string of abusive stepdads, and feel a pang of guilt. But he looks so grown up now, so different. So happy. I say, 'Are you still at school?'

'Just started sixth form, miss. I'm doing my A levels.'

'Oh, George, that's wonderful! What are you hoping to do afterwards?'

'University, miss, if I get my grades. I'd like to go and study something involving the environment.' He smiles shyly and looks down. 'That's all thanks to you, miss. You believed in me. Believed in all of us.'

I turn away so I can wipe the tears from my eyes. God. I'd forgotten. Forgotten how good it felt, teaching those kids.

I put the coffee in front of him. 'How did you find me?'

He pulls a face. 'I went into Britannia Brook. To talk to you. They told me you'd left. I asked for your address. I hope nobody will get in trouble for giving it to me.'

'You went to find me? Why?'

'For my Geography A level project,' says George, sipping his coffee. 'I wanted to do something on Ynys Dwynwen. And the voles. You remember them, miss? Only place in the world you find them. I wanted to use some photos of the school visit in my project.'

'I probably have them on my laptop if you want them. And some from other years.'

'They didn't go this year,' says George abruptly. 'They're never going again.'

I stare at him. 'What?'

'Somebody's bought the island, miss. They're going to build something on it. For rich people to go on holiday.' He looks at me. 'The voles will die, miss. They'll be wiped out.'

I look away. I can't meet George's stare. He says, 'So that's what my project is going to be about now. The destruction of Ynys Dwynwen's unique ecosystem. The puffins will probably stop nesting there. The seals on the reef will probably find new feeding and mating grounds.' He sips some more coffee, and looks around the kitchen again. 'So I looked for the plans online. It's your husband that's doing it, isn't it, miss?'

'George,' I say, my eyes full of tears. 'Why did you come here?'

'I was hoping you might speak to your husband, miss. Ask him not to go ahead with the development.'

I sigh raggedly. 'I can ask. But he won't listen.'

'I suppose not,' says George, looking pointedly around the kitchen. 'People with money just want more money, don't they, miss?'

I say, 'And you don't have to call me miss, George. I'm not your teacher anymore.'

'No,' he says with a sad, pale smile. 'No, you're not.' He takes a piece of paper out of his pocket. 'This is my email address. If your husband wants to send me something about why he's doing this for my Geography project, I can use it.'

I take the paper and the doorbell goes again. George drinks the rest of his coffee and stands up. 'I'll go now.'

As I open the door to let George out a delivery man brings

out a teetering pile of cardboard boxes from the back of his van. George watches him place them on the step, almost up to his waist, and says, 'I'm glad you're happy, miss. Bye.'

Later, I'm on my laptop, waiting for Tom to come home, when a notification pops up. *See your photo memories from 20 years ago today!*

I click on it and a flurry of pictures load, from when I'd just started second year. I smile wryly at the images, me in big boots and stripy tights, hair scraped back, hardly a spot of make-up on. Donna's in the pictures too, hair vibrant pink, piercings in her nose, ears and lips. And Martin. I smile again, fondly, my fingertips tracing his outline on the screen.

There are a set of pictures from a protest. We are all carrying placards, marching through the streets of Manchester, faces frozen mid-chant. It's a climate change protest, and I can vividly remember painting that placard, the slogan *No Planet B.*

I look furious, animated, on fire with righteousness. Donna is beside me, caught in the act of eyeing up some girl beside her. Martin tags on behind, waving his own placard in a slightly desultory fashion. Poor Martin. I always used to drag him along to these things. He was never really that interested. But he did it for me. I suddenly remember what Donna said to me, the last time we had lunch. *You were always going to save the world.* I suppose I did, for a while, or at least tried to, when I worked for EnviroMonitor. I feel proud of my successes there, even if they were only little wins, small battles in the bigger war. And later, at Britannia Brook ... I think about what George said. *That's all thanks to you, miss. You believed in me. Believed in all of us.* Again, not saving the world. But maybe making someone's world just a little better, for a while.

Funny how things have changed. Martin is on his island, ferociously protective of the environment of Ynys Dwynwen. And here I am, complicit.

I am about to close the laptop when Tom comes in, with a couple of bottles of wine and a takeaway. 'Chinese,' he says, holding up the bag. 'I chose for you. Hope that's all right.'

He puts the bags on the work surface and says, 'Oh, while you're on that. Can you show me the photos from the school visits to the island?'

I shrug and call them up, and he leans over me and scrolls through them. My breath catches in my throat as he opens up one of Martin, standing proudly in front of the light-house, surrounded by the children.

'That's him,' he says.

'That's who?' I say, as neutrally as I can.

He gives me a quizzical smile. 'The lighthouse keeper, of course. Take a look at these.'

He delves into his briefcase and pulls out a sheaf of papers. They are sketches, fashion designs. Variations on a theme; a nautical outfit, blue and white, some with a peaked cap, some a roll-neck sweater. Tom says, 'I had these drawn up. What do you think?'

'What are they?'

Tom looks at me as though I'm a particularly slow child. 'Uniform ideas. For the lighthouse keeper. I haven't met him in person, but from these pictures he looks a bit … shabby. I thought we could get him done up in some kind of livery. Maybe with the company name embroidered on it. Tastefully, of course.'

'Uniform? He's a lighthouse keeper, Tom, not an amusement park character.'

'Oh, I know, but, given the sort of people who'll be renting

305

out this development, it would be nice if he looked the part. Was a bit tidier. All adds to the experience, doesn't it?'

'He'll hate it,' I murmur.

Tom opens a bottle of wine and starts to take the lids off the foil boxes. The smell of Chinese food permeates the kitchen. 'Well, that's not really a consideration, to be honest. He's fixtures and fittings, isn't he? He's got to fit in.'

'Tom,' I say. 'Those old cottages you're going to pull down ... there are voles living there. The Dwynwen Voles. They're very rare.'

'Yeah, so I heard,' says Tom. 'Do you think I should get a pest exterminator in first? I was thinking the construction would probably just see them off anyway. I mean, they're not like rats, are they? They're not going to be dangerous. Or are they? I'll look into that.'

I take a deep breath. 'Tom, would you at all consider not doing this? Not doing the Ynys Dwynwen development? If I asked you to?'

He barks a laugh. 'And why would you do that? Gayle, I've been working on this for two years. I'm not about to throw all that time and money away.' He puts the dishes on the island. 'Get this down you before it goes cold. And then have a look over those uniform designs, let me know which you like best.' He checks the cork on his bottle of wine and I hear it glug into glasses. 'And just think, we can take holidays any time we want on ...' He pauses. 'What's the bloody name of the island again? It won't stick in my head.'

'Ynys Dwynwen.'

'Ynys Dwynwen.' He rolls the name around his mouth. 'Hmm. You know, it's a bit of a mouthful, that. A bit un-memorable. A bit ugly, all those Ys and Ws. I might think about a re-branding exercise, actually. I'll get a couple of people on it.'

'You can't change the name of the island!' I say, shocked. 'St Dwynwen is the Welsh patron saint of love. There's history there. Tradition.'

'History is written by the victors. And those who have the most money. And tradition is just stuff that happens more than once. We can make our own traditions.' He pauses and says, 'Hey, what do you think of *The Isle of Love?*'

'I hate it,' I say in a tiny voice.

He comes behind me, sliding his hands around my waist, and kissing my neck. 'Speaking of love ... I think we are very overdue an early night, don't you?'

I turn my head and let him kiss me on the mouth, closing my eyes to blink away the sudden tears.

43
Martin

30 November

The milestones that used to mark the year have gradually become meaningless. I know it's Christmas because Gwyn comes over, weather permitting, every Boxing Day with the leftovers of his big meal at Blodwyn's, and we enjoy turkey and sprouts and roast potatoes warmed up in the microwave. I dimly suppose that among the explosion of spring on the island, Easter must lurk, though it is of no importance. July I know is when Britannia Brook visits, or used to. So I am surprised to note, purely by glancing at the old calendar on the wall, that it is the last day of November, and not only my birthday, but my fortieth.

It seems no more relevant a number than thirty-nine or forty-one, here on Ynys Dwynwen. Age is all relative. The Dwynwen Voles live for eighteen months. The Manx Shearwaters, fifteen years. Puffins, perhaps twenty. Atlantic Grey seals, up to thirty-five. Out in the depths, the bow-head whale, a rare but not unknown sight in British waters, can live for two centuries. I am an immortal to the voles, a brief, passing fad to the whales.

I spend my birthday as I would any other day. A run, six circuits of the island, in driving, cold rain. Some routine maintenance of the generator and lamp. Checking the oil store, cleaning the living areas. Some reading. Some thinking. Looking out at the lowering light, the day fading swiftly on the trudge towards midwinter. I take some fish from the freezer for my evening meal, then wrap up in my oilskin and boots and walk around the island.

Ynys Dwynwen shrinks into itself in winter, battening down the hatches, waiting for spring. It is a dead, cold time, but beautiful, too in its own way, the stage on which violent storms are played out, and snow fights an ongoing battle against the salty air. I have had snow once while I have been here, waking up to see the island blanked out, as though set adrift in the night, towards the Arctic.

When Gwyn came to see me a week ago he seemed a little shocked by my appearance. 'Keeper!' he'd said. 'Overdue a beard trim and a haircut, I think. I've brought my scissors.'

I declined, though I realised I'd changed in the preceding months. Let myself go, people out there would say. My hair is shaggy and long, my beard unkempt. I am going longer between clothes washes, and my tidying of the living quarters is desultory at best. My summer tan has faded to a winter pallor, and my face is lined, my eyes hollow. There seems little point in anything.

Gayle is gone and Ynys Dwynwen is going to fall under the boot heel of progress. I feel the magic draining away. This place, this wonderful, secret, island ... this time next year, it will just be like anywhere else. And there's nothing I can do about it.

I walk over to the shingle beach, an icy wind whipping off the Irish Sea. Wouldn't surprise me if I get snow again. I see the seals huddled on Bethan's Reef, and what can only be the bulk of Bruce swimming towards me.

He's taking his time. I stand on the beach, my hands

309

thrust into my pockets, watching his lazy progress. Not so much swimming, as drifting in the tide.

He rolls in the surf as he nears me, displaying the scars on the left side of his body, his badge of honour from the encounter with the shark.

There's something not right.

'Bruce?' I call.

He rolls again, righting himself, his head still underwater. Drifting towards me. Not moving.

And then I'm splashing into the shallows, ignoring the icy shock of the water, wading forward to where Bruce drifts, unmoving save for the pull and push of the tide.

I reach out and take him in my arms, roll him over. His eyes are black and glassy, staring sightlessly up at me.

'No.'

I turn and drag Bruce against the flowing water, pulling him on to the beach, the waves crashing on us.

'No.'

He is hard and heavy and quite, quite dead.

Poking out of his mouth is a corner of something blue. I prise open his jaws, and pull it out. A plastic carrier bag, emblazoned with the logo of a supermarket from a country far, far away. Stuck deep in his gullet. The piece of plastic that has choked him.

I turn my face to the gathering clouds and let loose a primal, formless roar.

All through the afternoon I work, sawing and nailing together planks of old wood, boiling up the tar used to weatherproof the apron around the base of the lighthouse. I work silently and quickly, creating a long, narrow structure with raised sides and a flat base, which I turn over and paint with the tar, sealing up the cracks in the wood. When it is dry I take it down the shingle beach with a bag of candles, a wooden bowl, and a can of oil.

Bruce's words come back to me from so long ago.

'They do these big fancy funerals, that lot, don't they? Burning boats.'

'Vikings? Yeah, I think they did.' I frown. 'How do you know that?'

Bruce shrugs. 'I pick up all sorts, Keeper. Quite fancy that myself, when I go. Burning boat.'

And that is what he shall have. A funeral fit for a warrior. The Atlantic Grey seal who saw off a blue shark, and became my only friend, and brought me, after a fashion, my father.

I sit the makeshift boat in the shallows and heave Bruce's lifeless body into it. I place the small tea lights around the rim of the boat and light them, then fill the wooden bowl with oil and place it at the stern, below Bruce's flippers. Then I touch the lighter to it and flames skitter across its surface.

Dusk has fallen early and heavily. I stand for a moment, the water up to my ankles. I feel as if I should say something, but perhaps all has been said between Bruce and me. So I just bend forward and push the boat as hard as I can.

It moves with the ebbing tide, strong and sure, cutting a path towards Bethan's Reef and the open sea beyond. The oil in the bowl is blazing, the candles form a ring around Bruce's body. On the reef, the other seals seem to sit up, and watch the passage of Bruce, past them and out to sea.

Then the oil burns through the wooden bowl, and flames lick high into the cold air as the wooden planks of the boat start to catch as well.

The tide is taking Bruce swiftly now, out into the dark, the boat blazing as it moves.

'Goodbye, Bruce,' I say.

And then the light, my light, bursts forth, the tower sending its cold beams out into the early November night. The light plays over the freezing sea, guiding not the ships of men through safe passage, but rather the soul of my sainted, beloved warrior-friend Bruce to whatever Valhalla awaits.

When I get back to the tower I open a bottle of rum. I sit down at my typewriter and scroll a piece of paper into it. Then I begin to write. I write with fury and righteousness, I write with love and desire and hate and anger and every emotion I can summon. I write a better world, a fairer and more equitable world. A world where I can shape the course of events, a world where I am not at the whim of others like a piece of plastic floating on the tides. I write through the dark nights of December and the howling storms of January. I write into February, and the first, distant hints of spring. I write until I have finished, I write the story of Ynys Dwynwen, and Gayle, and Bruce and the lighthouse and most of all I write the story of me, because it is just as Gwyn said. The world is on fire and I can do nothing about it except write myself a happy ending. That is exactly what I do.

On the first day of March, Gwyn comes to me with news. The developers have achieved all the necessary permissions to begin construction on the island. They are due here in June. There will be two boats bringing excavators and bulldozers and cranes and men. The rape of Ynys Dwynwen shall begin.

'What's this?' says Gwyn, picking up the top sheet of five hundred pieces of typed paper that sit by the Underwood. '*There Is a Light That Never Goes Out.* You have been writing again, Martin Burney?'

I glance over from where I am brooding over coffee at the kitchen table. 'What? Oh. That. Yes, I was writing again. But I've come to a realisation, Gwyn.'

'And what's that, Keeper?'

'Writing won't save Ynys Dwynwen.'

'Nothing will save Ynys Dwynwen,' says Gwyn absently, reading the first page of the novel. 'I know I'm not much of a reader, Martin Burney, but this seems pretty good to me.'

'It's trash, Gwyn,' I say. 'Pointless rubbish. Take it away for me, will you? Put it in the recycling.'

'Of course,' he says, bundling it up into a paper bag.

'I think you might be wrong, Gwyn,' I say slowly.

'About the book? Like I said, I'm not a great reader.'

'No. About there being nothing that can save Ynys Dwynwen.'

He looks at me curiously. 'What do you mean?'

'There was a seal,' I say haltingly. 'I called him Bruce. Big one, with the scars on his side.'

'I know him,' chuckles Gwyn. 'Quite a character.'

'He died. In November. Choked by a plastic bag.'

Gwyn shakes his head. 'Absolute disgrace, the state of these seas. Shocking, it is.'

'It doesn't have to be this way, Gwyn.' I say. 'Humanity has as much of a right to live in this world as everything else. But we're just doing it wrong.' I stand up and walk to the small window, overlooking the island. 'Except here. Here on Ynys Dwynwen. Here it is done right.'

'How do you mean, Keeper?'

'I mean ... this lighthouse.' I smack my fist against the curved stone wall. 'This is how you do it. It's part of the island. It works. It works alongside the natural world. It's like ... a dovetail joint. It fits snugly. It is made by man, but it's *right*.'

313

I turn to face Gwyn. 'This whole island is a masterclass in how to do it right. It isn't owned by the Davies family. They're custodians. Curators. And old Edward Davies was right. Ynys Dwynwen is at the crossroads between worlds. Between one life and another. Maybe not this life and the afterlife, though. Maybe the world that humanity built, and the natural world they built it on.'

I turn back to the window. 'Ynys Dwynwen is where the stories of men and the stories of nature collide. I understand that now. I thought I was just wasting my time writing over the past three months, but perhaps I wasn't. I was adding to the stories of Ynys Dwynwen.

'It's all stories, Gwyn. Everything is stories. The blooming of the flowers, the growing of the grasses. The hatching of the eggs. The Manx Shearwaters cry their stories into the night. Stories never end. And the story of Ynys Dwynwen, the one place, maybe the last place on earth, where we got everything right, that story isn't going to end in June when they come with their bulldozers and cranes. I didn't give Bruce a warrior's funeral so I could give up now.'

'But what are you going to do, Martin Burney?' cries Gwyn.

'I'm going to stop them,' I say. 'I'm going to save Ynys Dwynwen.'

'In that case,' says Gwyn, 'you're going to need a bloody haircut.'

Year Ten

44

Gayle

June

A week before my thirty-ninth birthday, Donna calls. 'Where's Tom?' she asks.

'London,' I say. 'I think.'

'OK, good. I'm coming over.'

I have coffee brewing when she arrives. She hands me a bottle of wine instead. 'You'll need this.'

'What's going on?'

Donna sits down at the kitchen island and takes her laptop out of her bag. I say, 'Donna, what's going on?'

'I've been to London, too. I've been doing a bit of training. Front of camera stuff. Not that I'm ever planning to do it. Happy enough editing.'

'Brilliant,' I say, though a little mystified.

'I got back last night. I was in Mayfair yesterday afternoon.' She pulls up her photos on the laptop, and looks at me. 'I saw Tom.'

'Oh, fab. Did you speak to him?'

She looks at me. 'Gayle. I thought long and hard about this. But you're my best friend in the entire world. So when I say I thought long and hard, I mean exactly thirty seconds.'

She turns the laptop towards me. On the screen is a photo

317

of Tom, wearing a black suit, walking into what looks like a hotel bar. There's a woman with him. I frown for a moment and then laugh. 'That's Veronica. His PA.' My face crinkles up. 'Donna, why did you take a picture of Tom?'

'Because I'm a journalist and I can smell shenanigans a mile off,' she says. 'Look at the next picture.'

It's taken in the interior of the bar. Tom and Veronica are sitting in a booth, ordering drinks from a waitress.

'You followed them inside? How did Tom not see you?'

Donna sighs. 'If you must know, there was a guy outside selling sunglasses and hats from a little stall. Next picture.'

It's a selfie, in the wine bar, of Donna wearing cheap, red plastic-framed sunglasses and what appears to be a cowboy hat. I laugh. 'I wouldn't be waiting for MI5 to call.'

'Gayle,' says Donna, turning her forefinger in a circle in front of her face. 'Look at me. Do I ever miss the opportunity to make a joke or take the piss? This is my serious face. Next photo.'

I sigh. 'It's just Tom with Veronica. He's always away on business. Sometimes she goes. It's no big deal.'

'Next photo, Gayle.'

So I click on. And then I click on. And on, and on, and on. There are perhaps a dozen photos in all. Tom and Veronica getting their drinks. Tom and Veronica chatting. Veronica laughing. Veronica putting her hand on Tom's shoulder. Tom with his hand on Veronica's face. Tom and Veronica kissing. Tom and Veronica kissing. Tom and Veronica kissing. The last picture shows the backs of Tom and Veronica, holding hands, climbing a staircase beside a sign that says ROOMS THIS WAY.

'I sat in that bar for three hours, until I had to go for my train,' says Donna. 'They didn't come down.'

I say nothing for a long time, just staring at the laptop,

clicking back and forth through the photos, trying to convince myself I'm misconstruing what I'm seeing, trying to deny the evidence before my own eyes. Even though I know it's incontrovertible. Even though I know Tom has form here, form I've chosen to ignore.

I can't ignore it any longer.

Donna is biting her lip and looking at me. 'Do you hate me?'

I can't help thinking I wish she hadn't told me. I wish I didn't know. Because that's the easiest thing, isn't it? To not know. Even if you suspect. Even if, really, you do know. Because knowing means having to make a decision. Having to do something. Even if doing something means doing nothing, and carrying on as before, but with the burden of knowing.

'Of course I don't hate you.'

'So, what are you going to do?'

'What do you think I should do?'

Donna sighs. 'You know what I think about Tom. I've always been of the opinion that he's a bit of a shit. But he always seemed to make you happy. And if you were happy, then I was happy. But I couldn't let this go, Gayle.'

I nod. 'But what do you think I should do?'

'I can't answer that. It's for you to decide. When's he back?'

'Tomorrow night.'

'Do you want me to stay over?'

I shake my head. 'Just send me those pictures. I need to be alone tonight. I'll call you tomorrow.'

Donna gives me a big hug, and when she's gone I download the photos to my laptop and ask myself the question Donna asked, over and over again. *What are you going to do?*

★

When Tom walks in I am sitting in the kitchen, with a glass of wine and my laptop. 'Babes,' he says, throwing his briefcase in the corner. 'Pour me one. Hectic few days.'

I don't move. I just say, 'The first thing I need you to know is that I'm not angry.'

He gives me that quizzical raised eyebrow look that I always found so endearing. 'Angry about what, Gayle?'

'About you fucking Veronica.' I turn the laptop to face him, displaying one of the pictures of him kissing her passionately.

He looks at it as though it's something from an alien world, or a scrap of papyrus with indecipherable hieroglyphics. Then he laughs hollowly. 'Oh, ha ha, that isn't what it looks like.'

'Tom,' I sigh. 'Shall we just skip this part?'

I see lies forming on his tongue, like tiny white crested waves far out to sea that will eventually crash thunderously on the rocks as they gather force and power. Then he stops, and shrugs.

'It doesn't mean anything. It's just sex.'

'So you don't love her?'

This time his laugh is genuine, as though it's the most ridiculous thing he's ever heard. 'It means nothing to me and nothing to her.'

'How many more have there been?'

And something in Tom changes, then. If he was ever going to be contrite, or apologetic, that's passed. He's going on the offensive. He intends to hurt.

'You mean since we've been married, or while we've been together?'

'Why?' I ask. 'Didn't you get enough sex from me?'

He shrugs. 'Well, you know. After you lost the baby ... it took a while, didn't it? For us to be intimate again. And after your dad died ...'

'Fucking hell,' I breathe. 'And you couldn't *wait*?'

'It's just how I am, Gayle.' He takes a deep breath, and pinches the bridge of his nose between his fingers. 'OK. Look. I know I've got a problem. I should thank you, actually, for confronting me like this. It's making me face up to it. Gayle, I think I'm a sex addict.'

Now it's my turn to laugh. He puts a hand on my arm. 'I'm serious. I think I need help. Counselling. You can come with me. We can work this through together. I mean, these pictures, they're a bit of a wake-up call.' He frowns. 'How *did* you get these photos?'

'Donna happened to run into you in London.'

'That fucking bitch,' he mutters. 'She's never liked me. You see that, don't you, Gayle? She's trying to come between us. Trying to cause trouble.'

I have been through this conversation a hundred times in my head the last twenty-four hours, played out every possible permutation of what Tom might say. I was ready for this. I was ready for all of it. Because he's just so bloody predictable.

'Tom, did you ever love me?'

'Gayle! Of course I love you!' He crouches down beside me, taking hold of my hands. 'I'll do whatever it takes. I'll fire Veronica tomorrow. There won't be any more. Ever. I promise, baby.'

I pull my hands away from his and reach for my phone, where Donna's number is already on the screen, waiting for me just to press the button. She answers immediately and I say, 'You can come now.'

'Gayle?' says Tom. 'Baby?'

I stand up and walk out of the kitchen and into the living room, where there are three cases waiting for me. He stares at them and says, 'Gayle?'

'I've only packed what I bought with my own money,' I say. 'Clothes, make-up, toiletries, a few bits. Nothing that you bought for me. Nothing that you chose for me, Tom, whether I liked it or not. I've left the wedding dress upstairs.' I tug at my engagement and wedding rings and place them on the coffee table. 'I'm going, Tom.'

He looks from the cases to me. 'OK, go spend a couple of nights at Donna's. Then we'll talk.'

'No, Tom. This is it. I'm leaving. We're over.'

And then he laughs, a horrible, sneering thing. 'Don't be ridiculous. You're going to give all this up? The house and the car and the holidays? We're going to Rome next week for your birthday. What about the parties, and the dinners, and the shopping trips? You're throwing all that back in my face? You're really that ungrateful, Gayle?'

'You know what, Tom?' I say calmly. 'I think I'm just another project to you. Another development. And when you'd designed me to your satisfaction, when you'd chosen my clothes and given me fucking vouchers for cosmetic surgery, you got bored. You flipped me like you flip your houses. And you know what, Tom? I really, really don't like what I let you turn me into.'

The doorbell buzzes and I push past Tom to the hall. He follows me, angrily shouting, 'You'll regret this, Gayle. As soon as you walk out of that door, you'll regret this. And I'll be here. Waiting. Ready to talk.'

I open the door and Donna marches in, glaring at Tom. He glares back at her. 'This is your fault. Spying on me. You bitch.'

'No,' she says. 'It's your fault. Because you couldn't keep your tripe in your trousers, Tom. And if you hadn't been so intent on trying to get your hand into that slag's knickers in that bar you might have seen me dressed like Secret fucking

Squirrel.' She turns to me. 'Where's your stuff, Gayle?'

I lead her into the living room and we wheel the cases out. As we do, another figure appears at the door. Mum.

'Thank God, Heather,' says Tom. 'Have you come to talk some sense into her?'

'No,' says Mum, stalking in and grabbing one of my cases. 'I've come to get my daughter away from your clutches, you philandering, coercive, narcissistic shag-bandit.'

'Mum!' I say, shocked but delighted.

'She got that off me, I'm afraid,' says Donna.

'And,' says Mum, pointing an angry finger at Tom. 'I always thought your horseradish sauce was shit.' She turns to me. 'Come on, Gayle. I'm taking you home.'

45

Martin

July

It's a warm, clear day when the boats are due to come. I get up early, do my run, and stop at the shingle beach, waving at the seals on Bethan's Reef. They ignore me. I wonder about Bruce, and whether he got to Valhalla. I shake my head. Living alone ... it can do funny things to a person's mind.

I have a hearty breakfast and shower, then get into my clothes. The boats bringing the machinery and heavy plant are due at around three o'clock. That gives me plenty of time.

I stand at the jetty and watch Gwyn approach, his little boat laden with planks of timber. 'There'll be hell to pay for this, Keeper,' he says as he helps me unload them.

'I imagine so, Gwyn. I want you to go back, now. I don't want you implicated in all this.'

He nods and sets off back to the mainland. I heave the timber down to the south-west corner of Ynys Dwynwen. That's where the boats are planning to come in. The land behind the jetty is too steep for them to unload on. Down at the south-west, beyond the storm-bent trees, the water is shallower and the island a little flatter.

All morning I work, screwing the timber together and fashioning six-pronged crosses out of them. I make half a dozen then gaffer-tape big rocks to the bottom staves, and position them in the shallows off the water. The rocks keep them in place. They won't ultimately stop the boats landing, but they'll slow them down. Someone will have to get off and shift them out of the way. It'll buy me a little time.

Then I go back to the lighthouse, and set up the pulley and harness used for maintaining the exterior of the tower. Lowering myself down in stages, I begin to paint big, blocky letters all down the side of the lighthouse that faces south-west. When I get to the bottom I stand back to inspect my handiwork.

N
O

S
U
R
R
E
N
D
E
R

I spent all yesterday digging up the biggest rocks I could find and rolling them down to the south-west corner, to form a makeshift barrier by where the boats will have to offload the bulldozers. Again, it won't take them long to shift, but it will slow them down. And on the biggest rock I used my masonry drill to attach two metal rings. I've already attached one end of the handcuffs to them. Gwyn brought my package over a few days ago, shaking his head and laughing. 'You should have seen Eddie Jones's face when I told him I wanted to go to a sex shop in bloody Llandudno. These are the strongest ones they had, Martin Burney. Sorry about the pink furry bits.'

So that is my plan. I will delay, and harry, and obstruct. I will chain myself to a rock and give the people who would ruin my island a headache. It will not stop the march of progress, but what else can I do? I'm only one man.

There are three hours to go. I take a walk around Ynys Dwynwen, drinking in every sight, scent and sound. The eerie cries of the Manx Shearwaters riding the thermals high above. The Dwynwen Voles scurrying around the stones of the cottages, with no idea what is about to happen to their only home. I sit for a long time and watch the puffins. A white, lightly speckled egg tinged with lilac shakes and shudders, and then cracks. A baby puffin edges out, beak first, all white and black fluff, blinking at the world as its parents fuss over it. Out on Bethan's Reef the seals sport in the warming waters, diving deep for fish, surfacing with triumphant barks.

Life on Ynys Dwynwen continues at its own pace. It is a groove I have settled into, matching my rhythms to those of the natural world. This is the start of what will be my tenth year on the island. I can barely remember my life before; it feels like a movie I once watched, and didn't particularly enjoy. I have been here exactly as long as I lived out there after university. After Gayle. I wonder what will come next.

Because something must come next. This feels like an ending. Even if my attempts to halt the development go unpunished, I do not feel I can continue my life on Ynys Dwynwen, not with what I've planned. I look back at the tower, now defaced, and the cottages, and try to imagine what it will be like. A helicopter landing and spewing out people, with their brash noise and wasteful lives, trampling over the island, shouting and playing music and gradually claiming Ynys Dwynwen for the outside world, colonising it, homogenising it.

The puffins will go. The voles will die. The seals will flee. And the magic will be chased away.

I walk over to Edward Davies's grave, and tidy up the grasses growing up the headstone. I wonder if the magic went awry, and instead of bringing Bethan to Edward, it brought Gayle to me. Or maybe that's the nature of the magic after all. Maybe it brings people together, even for a very brief time. I'm grateful that we got to meet again, even if it awakened in my heart something I'd long thought dead, even if it softly blew on the embers burning inside me that I'd long thought extinguished. Would it be better to have not met Gayle again? In a way, I suppose it would. Ignorance can be bliss. But I would not give up those moments, however bittersweet and brief, for anything. I am a changed man due to my time on Ynys Dwynwen, and Gayle's part in that cannot be overstated.

It's almost time. The two big boats are coming from Bristol. They will be rounding the headland in an hour. I will go and watch for them from the balcony at the top of the lighthouse. My lighthouse.

For an hour, I stand there, leaning on the balustrade, nursing a cup of coffee. My stomach is churning. My head feels light and fuzzy. I put my cup down and pick up my binoculars, scanning the horizon.

And there they are. Two long, flat loaders, chugging around the peninsula. I look at my watch. Right on schedule.

It will take them another hour, I suppose, to land. I'll watch them for a while longer, then go and handcuff myself to the rock. Like that old story from Greek myth. Prometheus. Gave fire to mortals and was punished by Zeus, chained to a huge rock where an eagle would come and tear his liver out each day, and it would grow again overnight so his punishment could be repeated for ever and ever.

I have no fear of such punishment. My heart has already been torn out. What could be worse than that?

Then there is a sound, a hooting horn. I swivel my head, and frown. There, motoring over from the mainland, is the *Angharad*. What on earth is Gwyn up to? Why bring out the big boat?

I train my binoculars on it, and gasp. Gwyn is not alone. The *Angharad's* deck is full of people. Hands shaking, I try to focus the binoculars. And then I see her, standing at the prow, the warm wind blowing her hair behind her.

Gayle.

46

Gayle

Tom tries to get me back, of course. He still considers me his property, a work in progress. He never leaves a project unfinished. He calls, he messages, he even sends me a long, rambling letter about how he's a changed man and he'll do anything to win me round.

I ignore it all. If Ynys Dwynwen had its own particular magic, Tom's house was its dark antithesis. Once free of it, and him, the scales fall from my eyes. I see the person he'd tried to mould me into. I see how I'd been seduced by the comfort and riches. I see, now, that I do not love him, and perhaps never did.

In late June, Donna and I are sitting around Mum's kitchen table while she serves us up a full English breakfast, our recovery after a heavy night before. Donna has been my absolute rock. She's been there for me, giving me strength, taking me out, gradually reintroducing me to the real world. And so has Mum. They listen with open mouths as I tell them the things Tom has done, which I'd ignored or pushed to one side, wondering how I'd ever fallen for it all.

As Donna tucks into her breakfast she says, 'I've been keeping an eye on the planning application for that island.'

'Ynys Dwynwen?'

She nods. 'They're starting work in about three weeks.'

'Poor Martin must be beside himself,' I say.

'It's a shame something can't be done,' says Mum.

I laugh mirthlessly. 'Nobody ever stops Tom from getting what he wants.'

'You did,' says Mum mildly.

'I looked something else up as well,' says Donna. 'Apparently there's some rare rodent on that island.'

'The Dwynwen Vole. The kids used to love watching them play around those old cottages.'

'Unique to the place,' says Donna. 'See, that's a story, that is.'

'How do you mean?'

'Development wipes out rare cute furry thing. People love that sort of story. Only thing is, it needs someone to protest for it to be a news item. Needs a visual hook.'

'You were always protesting when you were younger,' chuckles Mum. 'That reminds me. I found something in the loft when I was clearing out some of your dad's things. One tick.'

I put my hand on Donna's arm. 'Wait, are you saying you could do a story on this? For the BBC?'

'Like I said, only if there's a protest. Give it the human angle. I mean, that school you used to work at, they've been going there for years, haven't they?'

'Here it is,' says Mum, coming back into the kitchen. 'Can't believe I kept it so long. Must be twenty years.'

She holds up a placard, dusty and faded but all in one piece. A painting of the earth and the slogan NO PLANET B.

I turn wide-eyed to Donna. 'Remember you said I was always going to save the world?'

She nods. I stand up and take the placard from Mum. 'Well, how about I start with Ynys Dwynwen?'

The first thing I do is email George Bentley, and tell him what I'm planning. I ask him to go and speak to Mrs Gaskell at Britannia Brook, and see if she'll give me a call. The following week I meet with her at the school, and outline my plan.

'We'll have to get the parents' and guardians' permissions, of course,' she says. 'And tell them exactly what we're doing and why. But I think that this is exactly the sort of thing Britannia Brook should be doing.'

Then I go to visit Beryl Carruthers and Harry. She thinks it's a wonderful idea. 'You can count on us!' she says. 'My, this will take me back. I remember taking part in a protest against the Vietnam War. Jane Fonda was there. Hanoi Jane, they called her at the time. We ended up having the most Sapphic encounter in the back of a Volkswagen Beetle parked in an alley off The Old Kent Road.'

And then I find the number for Gwyn Jones.

'Gayle Reiss!' he says. 'Martin told me he came to stop your wedding but he was too late. Terrible business. All my fault. If I'd only given him that message in time ...'

'Wait, what?' I say. 'He came to stop me marrying Tom? When did he get the message?'

'That bloody day! Oh, it's all my fault. I am such an idiot. Wasn't me you spoke to, it was that cretin Wyn Jones. If Martin had got it in time ... well. No use crying over spilled milk now, is there? I hope you're very happy in your marriage.'

My mind is whirling. Martin didn't get the message in January. He hadn't ignored me. He came to stop me ...

'Gwyn, I'll tell you all about that later. But listen. I've got a plan. To save Ynys Dwynwen.'

'But the bulldozers are going to come tomorrow, Gayle Reiss!'

'I know. Which is why we have to act fast.'

Which is why, on a warm, sunny afternoon in July, myself, thirty children from Britannia Brook, Mrs Gaskell and Mr Jensen, George Bentley, Beryl Carruthers and Harry, and Donna, and a film crew from the BBC are packed on to the *Angharad* and half an hour away from Ynys Dwynwen. Even my mum comes along. 'I haven't had a day out for ages,' she says. 'And I'd love a chance to stick it to that narcissistic twat.'

Her language really has gone down the sewer since she started spending time with Donna.

'Oh, bloody hell, he's only gone and vandalised the tower,' says Gwyn, from the prow of the boat.

'Get that in the background,' says Donna. 'Are we close enough to the island to film now?'

The cameraman nods and looks around. 'Where's Steven?'

'You mean your reporter chap?' says Gwyn. 'Last time I saw him he was at the back throwing his guts up over the side. White as a sheet. No sea legs, that boy.'

'You're going to have to do it,' says the cameraman to Donna.

'What?'

He shrugs. 'Somebody's going to have to do it. If Steven's out of commission, it'll have to be you.'

I stand behind the cameraman as Donna stands at the starboard side of the *Angharad*, the island framed behind her. She takes a deep breath, then nods.

'And we're just approaching Ynys Dwynwen, the remote little island off the coast of the Llyn peninsula in North Wales, which has become a battleground between developers and environmentalists,' says Donna. I grin and give her the thumbs up. She's brilliant. The cameraman pans round to the kids who all cheer and wave their placards. *HANDS OFF YNYS DWYNWEN* and *SAVE THE DWYNWEN VOLE* and *GO HOME RICH PEOPLE*. Then he pans back to Donna who says, 'A tiny vole, unique to this island, has become the flashpoint in the fight to stop a development that would see their habitat destroyed and replaced with a holiday complex.

'Children from Britannia Brook, an inner-city school in Manchester, have decided to take the fight to the developers, after their annual visits to the island were cancelled because of the proposed plans.'

Then I'm being pushed into the shot as Donna says, 'And it's all down to former Britannia Brook teacher Gayle Reiss, who organised this protest with the help of a former pupil, George Bentley. Gayle, can you tell us why you're doing this?'

I look straight at the camera, straight through it, straight into Tom's eyes, because I know he'll be watching this, shaking in impotent fury. And I say, to him more than to anyone else watching, 'Because people like the man behind this development have to be shown that they can't just take what they want. There are things more important than money and power. And we're going to prove it.'

The cameraman gives Donna the thumbs up and she relaxes.

When the segment airs Donna's phone starts pinging. 'Bloody hell, that's gone crazy. All over social media.' She looks up at me. 'The hashtag #SaveYnysDwynwen is trending already. God knows how anyone can spell it.'

'Look lively!' calls Gwyn. 'Land ahoy! And it looks like we've got a welcoming committee, Gayle Reiss!'

I turn as Gwyn angles the *Angharad* towards the jetty, the children all cheering wildly, where a figure stands, ramrod straight, hands clasped behind his back. And a huge grin on his face.

Martin.

47

Martin

She runs up the jetty to me, and we embrace. I say, 'Gayle, what have you done?'

'The right thing, at last,' she says. She holds me at arm's length, looking at me seriously. 'Martin. It's Tom who's behind the development.'

'Your husband?'

She nods. 'Though not for much longer. We ... Martin, I left him.'

A teenage boy appears behind Gayle and coughs. She turns and smiles. 'Really, it's all down to George. He's the one who told me something had to be done. You remember George?'

I frown and then my eyes widen. 'The little boy who fell off a cliff! Look at you! How did that happen? You're all grown up.'

Then Donna is elbowing in. She brandishes what looks like a walkie-talkie at me. 'Sorry to interrupt. It's the studio. On the satellite phone. They want us live in five minutes. This story's going bonkers, apparently.' She nods towards the south-west. 'And it looks like we have company.'

The two big boats are just minutes away now, the yellow bulldozers and generators visible on their wide, flat decks. The teachers usher the children down to the beach, as

Mrs Carruthers suddenly appears and gives me a huge hug.

'Darling! Harry and I wouldn't have missed this for the world! What a thrilling adventure!'

Harry shakes my hand. 'Bloody good work, son. Your dad would be proud.'

'Yes, I think he is,' I say.

Donna holds up two fingers at me. 'Two minutes, Martin. I want you live down there with the boats behind you.'

Gwyn grabs my arm as I start to follow. 'Best not mention you've been talking to the seals, Martin Burney. Don't want them to think you're doolally tap.'

I stare at him. 'How do you know I've been talking to the seals?'

He winks. 'One of the puffins told me. Terrible gossips, they are. Now come on! You're going to be on the telly, aren't you?'

We get down to the shore as Donna is about to be filmed, the children chanting '*Save Ynys Dwynwen!*' and waving their placards behind her. Just before the cameraman gives Donna the thumbs up, she calls to Gayle's Mum, 'Heather, love, do you mind getting out of shot? We can't have you standing behind the kiddies waving a placard that says *TOM IS A WANKER.*'

Then she turns to the camera, clears her throat, and begins.

'Coming to you live from Ynys Dwynwen, a tiny island off the north Welsh coast, where boats carrying the construction workers who are about to start work on a controversial development are minutes away from docking. And with me I've got Martin Burney, the lighthouse keeper of Ynys Dwynwen, who was staging a one-man protest against the plans until former Britannia Brook teacher Gayle Reiss turned up unexpectedly with a group of children to try to help stop this hugely contentious proposal. Martin Burney, why should this island be saved? Aren't you just standing in the way of progress?'

I look into the camera, my mouth suddenly dry. For nearly ten years I've barely spoken to a soul. And now I'm about to address millions of people. I glance at Gayle and she gives me a winning smile that makes my heart swell.

'Because this is one of the last places on earth where man and nature can truly exist in harmony,' I say haltingly. 'Because Ynys Dwynwen is wild and untamed, and yet the site of one of humanity's greatest achievements.' I turn and point at the tower. 'The lighthouse. A feat of engineering, a perfect example of what people can build. And not just for personal gain or hubris, but as a force of good. As something to help, to guide, to save lives. It's in perfect harmony with nature. This is progress. This lighthouse. Progress with humanity. That ...' I point at the boats, stalled in the water just off the island. 'That *progress* helps nobody. Except the rich, who will just get richer.'

There's a round of applause and cheering from the kids and the adults, and suddenly I feel exhausted. Donna winks at me and the cameraman turns to her.

'And after that heartfelt plea from Martin Burney, the keeper of Ynys Dwynwen, we are now waiting for the developers to arrive. We'll be bringing you the very latest on this developing story as it happens. Now, back to the studio.'

When the cameraman gives the signal that they're off air, Gayle runs to me and throws her arms around my neck. 'That was wonderful,' she says.

'Not sure if it'll do much good,' I mutter, looking over her shoulder at the boats.

She kisses me on the cheek. 'You tried, Martin. You tried your best. That's all anyone can ask, isn't it?'

337

'Well,' says Donna. 'I suppose we could ask a *little* more. Are you going to chain yourself to these barriers, or what? It's good TV, Martin.'

'Hey,' calls the cameraman. 'We've got company.'

We all turn to see a small powerboat slicing through the waves between the big boats, heading for the island. 'Advance party,' I say. 'I suppose somebody better tie me up.'

'Now's not the time to get kinky, Martin,' says Donna, and Gayle punches her arm.

'Wait,' says Gwyn from one side, shielding his eyes with his hand. 'That's the duchess.'

Ms Davies leans heavily on her stick as she stands and surveys the desecration of the tower, and then looks at the construction company's boats. 'Well, Mr Burney,' she says. 'Quite the day's work.'

I start to speak but she holds up her hand. 'Walk with me.' She looks Gayle up and down. 'You, too. And Gwyn, you may as well come.'

She leads us silently across the island to Edward Davies's grave, and we stand there together, waiting for her to speak.

'Needless to say, Mr Burney, you are fired.'

Gayle says angrily, 'You can't do that! He's trying to save your island!'

Ms Davies stays silent for a long time, considering Edward Davies's headstone. She says, 'You have taken care to tend his grave, Mr Burney. I thank you for that.' She looks out to Bethan's Reef, where the seals sport in the surf. I get a sudden pang as I think of Bruce. She says, 'But you have acted directly against the family's express wishes.'

Gayle starts to speak again, but I put a hand on her arm. 'It's OK. I knew this was going to happen. It would have to happen.' I look at Ms Davies. 'But I couldn't not try. I hope you understand that.'

She sighs heavily, and with the end of her stick traces the name on the headstone. 'I think Edward Davies would be very proud of you.' She meets my eyes. 'But times have changed, and Edward Davies is long gone.'

'Except he isn't,' I say fiercely. 'He's in every rock on this island, in every blade of grass. He looks out from the eyes of the Dwynwen Voles, the Manx Shearwaters call his name at dusk.' I look back and wave my arm across the panorama of Ynys Dwynwen. 'His heart beats in the machinery of the tower. And that light, that light that never goes out ... that's his, Ms Davies. His work. His soul is in those lamps, lighting the way for those at sea. For those lost at sea.' My voice drops to an almost inaudible whisper. 'For those like me. I don't know if Edward ever brought Bethan back to him, God knows I think he did, sometimes, when the wind blows around the tower and the storm rages outside, as strong as love should be. But I do know it brought Gayle to me. Ynys Dwynwen saved me, Ms Davies.'

Ms Davies is looking at me with an expression I cannot read. Then she looks at Gayle, and finally at Gwyn. 'It appears that Ynys Dwynwen has worked her magic again, Gwyn Jones.'

He chuckles. 'I think you're right, Ms Davies.'

'I remember telling you the story of Edward and Bethan. And how he built the lighthouse to guide her spirit back to him. Whether they were ever reunited we shall never know. Not in this life. But Ynys Dwynwen has a habit of bringing lost souls to her. Lost souls like you, Martin Burney. And fixing what is broken in them.' She looks at Gayle. 'And finding their missing parts. It isn't the first time. It won't be the last.'

'It was a good one, this,' says Gwyn. 'Very satisfactory.'

'But it will be the last time,' says Gayle. She points to the ships. 'Because those bulldozers are about to land and flatten this place, and turn Ynys Dwynwen into some kind of … of theme park for rich people. You believe in magic, Ms Davies? You think the magic will work then?'

'The lighthouse will still do its job, Miss Reiss,' says Ms Davies, her mouth a thin, bloodless line. 'There will still be a keeper. Nothing will have changed.'

'Except everything will have changed,' I say quietly. 'Oh, I know it's over for me. But …' I look at Gwyn. 'Ynys Dwynwen saves lives. It heals hearts. It remakes souls. You said this places fixes broken people, Ms Davies. It's like that Japanese thing … with the smashed pots.'

I glance at Gayle. She says, 'Kintsugi.'

'Kintsugi,' I nod. 'They break pottery and fix it up with glue made from powdered gold, or silver. And what comes out of it is stronger and more beautiful than before, and it bears its scars proudly. And Ynys Dwynwen has done that to so many people, Ms Davies. It's done that to me. And it would be a tragedy if I was the last person that Ynys Dwynwen fixed.'

I'm done. I'm empty. I've said my piece and I can't say any more. Gayle takes my hand in hers and squeezes it. She knows, too. I've done all I can.

There's a commotion from far behind us and we turn, to see a small boat heading towards the island. This time it is from the construction boats, carrying three people. I see Gayle squint at it, then gasp.

'Oh,' she says. 'It's Tom.'

'Well,' says Ms Davies decisively. 'I thank you for your words, Mr Burney. They were heartfelt and powerful and have not gone unheard. But now it is time for me to go and talk business.'

48

Gayle

I stand on the shingle beach, facing Tom. He's wearing chinos and a crisp white shirt, top two buttons undone. He looks handsome and tanned and healthy and perfect. And like the glittering sea behind him, he's all surface. Inviting and warm, yet you get down a little way and it's cold and dark in there.

Everything around us seems to blur and fade, the sound of the waves and the engines of the boats and the chatter of the children just slowly mutes. I hear Donna tell the cameraman to stop filming, and his protestations that *this is great TV*, and her final, sweary insistence, and then she's gone too. There is only Tom, and me, facing each other.

'I couldn't believe it when I saw you on the TV,' says Tom. 'And then … it all fell into place. The lighthouse keeper.' I'm expecting him to sneer, or pull a face, or say something horrible. But he doesn't. He just looks a little … lost. 'How long has it been going on?'

I take a deep breath. 'If I'm honest, about twenty years. We knew each other at university. I know now that I never stopped loving him.'

'Even while you were married to me.' It's a statement, not a question. He follows it up with, 'Did you ever love me, Gayle? Truly?'

Tears prick my eyes. Because I did love him. He was kind and generous and thoughtful and loving and handsome and caring and all those things. And they were good and vital things, things a relationship needs, but they were always tempered by something else.

'Of course I loved you, Tom,' I say. 'But I could never compete.'

His face crinkles. He grabs my arms and I don't push him away, or flinch. He says fiercely, 'You never had to compete? You mean Veronica? That meant nothing. I told you. I was weak, I slipped, I fell. I'm sorry. She's gone, moved on, I'll never see her again. I never loved her, Gayle. Not like I loved you. Not like I *love* you.'

'I don't mean compete with Veronica, Tom. Or any of the others. And I know there have been others. I mean compete with you. Because nobody could ever love you as much as you love yourself.'

He opens his mouth to speak, then closes it again. He lets go of my arms and takes a step back. 'It's not true,' he says eventually. 'I tried to get you back. I phoned and messaged and even wrote letters. I can't bear losing you, Gayle. I don't want the divorce to go through. I want us to try again.'

I look over his shoulder at his boats, ready to land on the beach, and laugh. 'Tom. If you really, really loved me, you wouldn't be doing this.'

'I'm doing it for you!' he insists. 'It was always for you. For us. For our future. Everything is for us.'

I shake my head. 'Do you even know me, Tom? Really?'

Then he's looking over my shoulder, and I know who at. 'You've slept with him, of course. While you've been married to me.'

'Tom, you can hardly—'

'We're as bad as each other, Gayle. We've both been

342

unfaithful. I mean, if you really want this divorce to go ahead ...'

I know what he means, what he's saying. He'll fight me to the bitter end. If he has to let me go, he'll not give me a penny. He'll not let me have any claim on his empire, his home, his life. He really, really does not know me at all.

'I'll not be asking for anything, Tom,' I say quietly. 'Don't worry yourself about that.'

He looks at me for a long time. 'Can I ask you a question?'

I shrug. He says, 'Why did you stay with me for so long, if I'm such a terrible person? You could have left at any time. I'd have fought for you, and tried to persuade you, and showed you how much I loved you, but you could have walked at any point. You weren't a prisoner.'

And it is only then that it properly hits me, and I think it is because I am on Ynys Dwynwen, and perhaps Ms Davies and Gwyn and Martin are right, there is some kind of magic here. The magic of clarity and freedom and peace and nature. The light never goes out on Ynys Dwynwen, but I let my light go out a long time ago. I let a stronger, brighter light show me the way, and followed that instead. I forgot that, and I followed Tom's light, and it led me to a gilded cage, one I built myself.

'I gave you everything you needed, Gayle,' Tom says, sullenly.

I shake my head in frustration. 'And that's what you'll never understand, Tom. When I first met you ... I wouldn't have cared if you lived in a bedsit. In a tent. It was you I loved, not your wealth or your success or your house. And I saw something in you, something I thought would grow and flourish. Kindness. Generosity. A loving, caring nature. But you thought that meant giving me *things*, and money, and

343

deciding what was best for me. And I didn't want another relationship to fail, Tom, because I knew you were a good person. But I didn't realise that being with you ... it was making my own light dim. And you never noticed either.'

'I thought you were happy,' he says in a small voice.

'So did I,' I say.

He pauses, and squints inland again. 'And you'll be happy with the lighthouse keeper?'

I feel tears running down my cheeks. Because, despite everything, I have had happy times with Tom. And even leaving him, even ignoring his calls, never felt as final as this. For either of us. And all I have to do is say the words, and it will be well and truly over.

So I do.

'Yes, Tom. I know I'll be happy with Martin. He lets my light shine as brightly as his own.'

Tom nods, and his jaw tightens. 'Well. I suppose we'll put everything in the hands of my solicitors. Bearing in mind everything I've said.'

'I don't want anything from you, Tom. I just ... I just want you to be happy. If you can be.'

He smiles thinly. 'I'll be happy. As soon as I've started on this development. Nothing is going to stop that, Gayle.'

And suddenly the rest of the world twangs back into focus, the ships behind Tom, the noise of the children and the cries of the gulls, and the sudden voice of Heledd Davies at my arm.

'Oh, I'm not sure that's precisely true, Mr Cassidy.'

Tom raises an eyebrow at Ms Davies. 'I think the deal we have signed suggests it is.'

Ms Davies takes a deep breath. She turns and looks at Martin, then at the defaced lighthouse tower beyond. Then she turns back to Tom. 'I have changed my mind.'

I realise I've been holding my breath and let it out in a ragged sigh. The gathering behind us falls silent then starts to murmur. From the corner of my eye I see Donna frantically waving at the cameraman to start filming.

Tom pinches the bridge of his nose. 'What? You can't change your mind. Not at this stage.' He waves a hand towards the boats. 'Do you realise how much this has cost just to get to this point?'

'I do, and I apologise. But I have come to realise, in no small part thanks to Miss Reiss and Mr Burney, and these children behind us, that the cost to Ynys Dwynwen far outweighs the financial outlay any of us have made so far.'

Tom takes a deep, ragged breath. 'You just ... cannot do this, Ms Davies.'

'I am doing this, Mr Cassidy.'

He fixes her with his steely gaze. 'Then I shall sue you. For breach of contract. You won't get away with this.'

I turn to Ms Davies and clear my throat. 'Then you are going to need a good lawyer, Ms Davies. One well versed in environmental actions. I'd like to offer my services.'

Tom gapes at me. '*What?*'

'Had you forgotten, Tom? What I used to be? What I used to do? Before, with what I expect you believe were the very best intentions, you took it away from me? I was a lawyer, Tom. And a bloody good one.'

He just stares wordlessly at me. I say, 'Some lights really do never go out, Tom. I've not just found Martin. I've found myself again.'

Then he turns on his heel, starts to climb back in his powerboat, and curses as a wave splashes over his Italian leather shoes. As the engine roars and the boat executes a turn, a huge cheer goes up behind me.

Martin hugs me for a long, long time, as though he's

trying to make up for twenty lost years. When he finally lets me go, he says, 'You were absolutely brilliant.'

We both turn to Ms Davies and Gwyn. Martin says, 'Thank you.'

She inclines her head. 'Thank *you*. For taking a stand, and for making such a bold and eloquent case.' She looks at me. 'Both of you.' Then she says mildly, 'You're still fired, Mr Burney.'

Martin nods. I don't say anything this time. I think we both know that Ynys Dwynwen is over, that we need to look forward. Martin says, 'What will you do for money?'

She shrugs. 'We are not completely on our uppers. And as you suggested previously, the family home is worth quite a considerable amount. It is too big for me and Hywel.'

Ms Davies looks out to sea, at Tom's departing boats. Ms Davies says, 'I shall expect you to stay until the end of the month, until I can organise for a relief keeper. And you can use the time to re-paint the lighthouse, and put all those rocks back.' She smiles at Martin. 'Ynys Dwynwen thanks you for your tenure here, Mr Burney. As do I. But now it is time for you to rejoin the world. And, perhaps, take the lessons you have learned here and try to teach them to others. Who knows? Perhaps the two of you will make a better world after all.'

49

Martin

Hand in hand, Gayle and I watch Donna making a live broadcast, the receding dots of Tom's boats behind her. She says, 'And after those amazing scenes here on Ynys Dwynwen, it appears that the proposed development, that would have seen this idyllic Welsh island become a high-end luxury holiday bolthole has been abandoned. Whether there will be a legal challenge remains to be seen, but for now, Ynys Dwynwen is safe.'

The cameraman pans to the Britannia Brook children, who are all jumping up and down and waving their placards. Donna furiously waves at Gayle's mother to get out of shot. As soon as the cameraman gives Donna the thumbs up to say he's finished, Donna puffs her cheeks out and blows a sigh. 'Bloody hell, what a day.'

A figure weaves uncertainly towards her, a shockingly pale young man in a dishevelled suit. Donna turns to him, hands on hips. 'Steven. Our intrepid reporter. You decided to join us at last.'

He shakes his head. 'Oh my god, I've been sick as a dog. I've slept for hours, I think. I don't know if it's seasickness, or something I ate ... Are we ready to film?' He looks around, frowning. 'Did I miss anything?'

I turn to Gayle, who is staring at me, tears in her eyes.

347

'Martin. You did it.'

'We did it, Gayle. *We* did it.'

Then I take her in my arms and kiss her.

Ms Davies says she must take leave of us, and takes Gayle's number. 'I've a feeling I shall need you.'

Gayle shrugs. 'I don't know, Ms Davies. Tom doesn't usually admit defeat, but on this occasion ... I don't know. We'll see.'

Gwyn has thoughtfully prepared a packed lunch for the kids, which they eat in front of the tumbledown cottages. The cameraman gets some more shots of the Dwynwen Voles scampering about as if they know they've been saved. I walk with Gwyn and Gayle across the island.

'So,' I say. 'What happens now?'

'Between us?' says Gayle.

I nod. 'Between us.'

She stops and stands in front of me, taking hold of my hands. 'Gwyn told me about New Year's Eve. About the message. How you didn't get it in time.'

'Bloody fool, I am,' says Gwyn. 'Or rather bloody fool is Wyn Jones.'

'Would you have not married Tom, really, if I'd asked you not to?'

She nods. 'I should never have married him.' She bites her lip. 'Martin. I have no idea how it would work between us, but ... do you think we should try?'

I sigh, and look across at the graffitied tower. 'I'm not sure what sort of life I can offer you, Gayle. I certainly can't give you the one you've had.'

'It's not about you giving me a life,' she says fiercely. 'I'm done with people trying to give me a life. I want to make my own life. And I think I want to make it with you. However

348

that might work. I have things I can do. I can practise law. I can teach. And maybe you can write your book …'

'Oh bloody hell!' shouts Gwyn, slapping his forehead. 'Book! Oh, Martin Burney, you're going to hate me all over again!'

He pulls an envelope from his pocket. It's already been opened. It's addressed to him. 'What now, Gwyn?'

'Read it, Martin Burney! Read it!'

I take out the single sheet of paper and my eyes widen. I pass it to Gayle. 'Gwyn, what have you done?'

'Well, remember you wrote that book, and you said it was a pile of old rubbish and I should throw it in the recycling?' says Gwyn. 'Well, I didn't. I read it. I thought it was very good. So I dug out that letter you got last time. From that chap. In London. The literary agent.'

'Gwyn …'

'And I sent it to him!' declares Gwyn. 'And this came this morning and with all the excitement I forgot about it all!'

Gayle begins to read the letter slowly. 'Dear Mr Jones. I must say, I have never had quite as unorthodox a submission as this. It is most unusual for someone to submit a completed novel without the author's knowledge or permission. That said, curiosity got the better of me and I read *There Is a Light That Never Goes Out* by Martin Burney. And I am very glad I did. Mr Jones, I would like you to arrange a meeting between Mr Burney and myself at the earliest opportunity. Not only would I be honoured if he would accept my offer of representation, but I have been somewhat unorthodox myself. I have shown this to several editors in London and there is great interest, and something of a bidding war is about to take place, with Mr Burney's permission, of course. I look forward to hearing from you.'

She looks at me. 'Martin. You're going to get a publishing deal.'

When Ms Davies has gone, and Donna has filmed her last report, and Gwyn has loaded up the children and passengers on to the *Angharad* and taken them back to the mainland, there is only Gayle and I left on Ynys Dwynwen.

As dusk creeps over the island, we stand on the observation balcony, sipping from glasses of wine. We have my binoculars trained on the tumbledown cottages, and suddenly Gayle calls, 'There! I see one!'

The Dwynwen Voles are at play as daylight fails. She says, 'Do you think they have any idea how close they came to being wiped out?'

'Does anyone?' I say. 'Who knows how many brushes with death we have every single day, and are blissfully unaware.' In my pocket is my mother's ring in its swollen box. 'That's why we should seize the day. Waste no more time.'

I leave the ring there. For when it's the right time. Which, now, I'm certain will come soon.

Gayle says, 'Tell me about your book. I can't wait to read it.'

I shrug. 'It's the story of Ynys Dwynwen,' I say. 'But most of all, it's the story of us.' I gaze out at the darkening sea. 'Once, when I was at my lowest, and thought things would never get any better, Gwyn said to me that I should write my own happy ending. So I did.'

'And what happens at the end of your story, Martin?'

'Do you really want spoilers, Gayle?'

She nods.

'This,' I say, taking her in my arms and kissing her, just as the lamps fizz and pop and burst forth their blinding white beams, illuminating the wild world around us and silhouetting us against the light that never, ever goes out.

50

Gwyn

Hello! Is this thing on? Tap-tap. That's what you do, isn't it? Ha ha. Only joking. Gwyn, here. Gwyn Jones. Run the store. Boatman. Hairdresser. Do all sorts. But you probably already know that.

I suppose you want to know what happened next. Well, it was all rather exciting, wasn't it? Bloody big boats and protests and everything. And everybody was talking about it. About Ynys Dwynwen. All over your social medias. Some people came over to the island and they slapped a dirty big preservation order on the voles, and banned any idea of anybody building on there ever again.

So Martin Burney stayed until the end of the month, and Gayle Reiss stayed with him. I was sorry to see them go. Lovely couple, they make. You hear folk saying that people are meant to be together, but I never really believed it until I saw those two. Made for each other, they are.

Martin went off to London to meet this literary agent chap. And that's all very exciting too. He sold his book to a big publisher and it's coming out soon. Everybody is going crazy for it. There's talk it might be a film or one of those binge telly series. It's the sort of story everybody wants right now, you see. Talks about the world and how we live in it, and it's a thumping good love story. Not a dry eye in the house at the end, I bet.

Gayle, she has options. Maybe get back into teaching again. Maybe at Britannia Brook, maybe somewhere else. But with poor kids. She inspires them, you see. She believes in them. Doesn't hold with all this about them not being as good as anybody else, just because of where they're born and the fact that they're skint. Sees the good in everyone, that girl. Thinks anybody should be able to do anything. Then again, she's a good lawyer. The plan to sue Ms Davies for breach of contract was quietly dropped, and I think that was her doing when she started to build the case. And God knows, the world needs saving. It needs people like Gayle Reiss championing it.

Wherever they end up, I think they're going to be all right, that pair.

See, the duchess is right. Ms Davies, that is. When she talks about Ynys Dwynwen and magic. That light, it brings people here. People who need Ynys Dwynwen. And when they leave, they're never the same person. They're better.

Martin Burney said a funny thing to me a few months ago. When we were talking about his book. He said it's all stories, everything. Even what the animals and fish do. Even if they don't even understand what a story is. Everything is a story. Everything. We are all made of stories, and we add them to this great big book that the entire planet is writing, the stories of everyone and everything on it. It's not money that makes the world go round, it's stories. Everybody has one. And I think maybe here, on Ynys Dwynwen, is where the earth listens to those stories.

Ms Davies advertised for a new keeper, and gave someone the job a couple of weeks ago. In fact, here she comes now. Fresh off Eddie Jones's bus, walking down to my shop.

I'd better go and talk to her. Take her over to the island. To Ynys Dwynwen.

She has a sad look on her face. She thinks maybe her story is over, which is why she's come here, taken this job. She's wrong. Whatever's happened to her, whatever has broken her heart, she's the keeper of Ynys Dwynwen now.

And her story is only just beginning.

Acknowledgements

In the summer of 2021, following the publication of my previous novel *The Handover*, a brainstorming session was arranged on Zoom with Zoe Yang, then an editor at Orion, and now moved on to pastures new.

I wanted to talk through ideas, because I was keen to write something that recaptured the magic of my first novel for Orion, *Calling Major Tom*, in 2017. *Calling Major Tom* was a combination of the inherent comedy in real life, even the tragic moments, and a quirky central concept – the main character was on his way to Mars, having turned his back on the world, and too late rediscovered his connection to humanity through accidental contact with a working class family in Wigan.

My subsequent novels majored heavily on the working class life aspects of *Calling Major Tom*, and while they had somewhat unusual backdrops – a nursing home on the Lancashire coast in *The Growing Pains of Jennifer Ebert* (also known as *The Lonely Hearts Cinema Club* for reasons too complicated to go into here) a cemetery in the 1990s for *Things Can Only Get Better*, and a museum of social history in *The Handover* – well, once you've written about going to Mars, everything else seems a little prosaic.

For my next novel for Orion, I wanted to latch on to that sense of loneliness and withdrawal from the world as a vehicle for the main character, or at least one of them, to remove himself from life in order to reconnect with it.

What, Zoe and I wondered aloud, could be the perfect setting for that? If we were playing *Blankety Blank* on TV, we would have simultaneously held up pieces of card with lighthouse written on them.

Thus was born the germ of the idea for what became *There Is a Light That Never Goes Out*, and in it a salutary lesson for any writer. In this novel (and I hope you read it before you read these acknowledgements) Martin Burney answers a job advertisement for the position of lighthouse keeper on a remote Welsh island. He thinks life is so awful that he doesn't need anyone else. And he's proved wrong.

Similarly, while we writers might think we are, metaphorically at least, ensconced in our remote lighthouses creating art in splendid isolation, we are also wrong. Because a book like this isn't created by one person, despite the fact there's only one name on the cover.

It's a team effort, and that began with Zoe Yang in 2021. It continued with the efforts of a huge number of people, both inside and outside of Orion, some of whom whose names I don't even know. Sam Eades, of course, my editor at Orion. Laura Williams, my bulldog (in the nicest possible way) of an agent. Rachael Lancaster, who designed the absolutely fabulous cover on this book. Flora McMichael and the rights team at Orion who have been spreading the word about this book across the globe. Fellow northerner and writer pal T.G. Hambleton who read the first draft and offered cheerleading and sage advice. Sahil Javed, who has met every broken promise of me hitting edit deadlines on time with nothing but cheerfulness. And my family, Claire, Charlie and Alice, who have always kept me grounded. Special mention must go to my children who have got almost through the entire British education system without ever bragging – nor, to be honest, even mentioning – what I do for a living. To anybody. Ever. Anyway...

And finally, to anyone who has ever picked up one of my books and not hated it, *There Is a Light That Never Goes Out* is for you. May you all find your own light in life, and may there always be a Bruce out there for you somewhere.

David M. Barnett, the North of England, December 2022

Credits

David M. Barnett and Orion Fiction would like to thank everyone at Orion who worked on the publication of *There Is a Light That Never Goes Out* in the UK.

Editorial
Sam Eades
Sahil Javed

Copyeditor
Laura Gerrard

Proofreader
Laetitia Grant

Audio
Paul Stark
Jake Alderson

Contracts
Anne Goddard
Humayra Ahmed
Ellie Bowker

Design
Rachael Lancaster
Joanna Ridley
Nick May

Editorial Management
Charlie Panayiotou
Jane Hughes
Bartley Shaw
Tamara Morriss

Finance
Jasdip Nandra
Sue Baker

Marketing
Yadira Da Trindade

Production
Ruth Sharvell

Publicity
Alex Layt

Sales
Jen Wilson
Esther Waters
Victoria Laws
Rachael Hum

Anna Egelstaff
Frances Doyle
Georgina Cutler

Operations
Jo Jacobs
Sharon Willis